LAURA NAVARRE

GEMINI KINGS

I summon the dragon.
I claim my throne.
The warlocks of Icarus Academy claim me.

I start my night with a heist in a Catwoman costume at a Vegas casino… and end up shifting into my dragon form for the first time ever in mid-plummet from the roof.

Except I can't actually fly. Oops.

Turns out being the first dragon shifter queen to rule the witching world (while I'm simultaneously a student at the Icarus Academy) isn't, like, a party. Especially when I go into heat. Because now I have… needs… that no warlock at the Academy can satisfy. Plus the only full-blooded male dragon shifter on the planet intends to kill all my warlocks and make me choose just him for my king.

As.

If.

Sweet Jesus, this Maxim guy's causing a world of trouble. Vasili and Ronin are fighting over whether to kill him or kiss him. My wolf shifter headmaster Lucius has his paws full trying to keep us all from getting expelled. And my sweet bookworm Neo needs something new we're all afraid to give him.

When a rival rises to threaten my throne, it'll take major trust between me and *all* my warlocks—including that vicious dragon I've sworn I'll never claim—to save us all from an assassination attack we'll need a miracle to survive.

Gemini Kings is a spicy New Adult dark witch academy why-choose paranormal romance and the sequel to *Gemini Queen*. This deadly duet delivers a seductive and lethal warlock court, teacher-student forbidden love, possessive alphas, enemies-to-lovers (and enemies with benefits!), first-time MM, bi awakening, explicit and extended group encounters, a satisfying climax (no cliffhanger), and enough fast-burn heat to set your Academy uniform on fire!

For content notes, please visit the author's website at
www.LauraNavarreSciFi.com.

Chapter One
Zara

You haven't fucking lived till you've secretly crashed a casino czar's X-rated bash at the Double Gemini in Vegas, dressed in a latex Catwoman costume and mask, with your hair dyed green.

Like, for real. You haven't.

This is actually one adventure I could've lived without—and not just because my dad's literally gonna kill me if he catches me hiding under this catsuit. Since he did take out that seven figure hit on my head.

A hit he apparently never bothered to cancel.

You might be thinking the concept of a psycho fuck like Mick Gemini gunning for my runaway ass would give me a cold chill or something. And it's not like the situation makes me happy.

But if I'm gonna be honest?

Dear old dad's been trying to erase me forever. Ever since I took off years ago and (the way he sees it) humiliated him in front of the whole witching world.

What.

Ever.

These days, that whole bounty on my head just pisses me off.

But the ex-lover I've been hunting since he betrayed me for a goddamn paycheck came here to my dad's casino for a reason. And he's the reason *I'm* here.

I'm here for Xiao.

I'm here because it's payback time.

I hang back and play it all casual while I track my lying backstabbing shit of an ex-lover through the poker den. The red-carpeted floor vibrates under my platform boots. A chorus of ear-piercing screams spirals over the noisy clatter and ping of the slots.

Xiao lingers for a sec to watch the action, so I park my ass next to the panorama window. There I pretend to appreciate the neon blur of the Gemini's double corkscrew coaster streaking past the eye-popping flash and sparkle of the Vegas night.

But I'm pretty much the only rat in the joint who even bothers to look.

This costume party's for the tourists, and a lot of the players here at the Double Gem are regulars. The high rollers stay huddled in total absorption around the poker tables. The identical twin cocktail girls—one of my dad's signature gimmicks—keep giggling and wiggling their drink trays and their push-up *bustiers* through the handsy joes placing bets on the horse racing.

The rotating bar three floors up? That's a tourist draw, packed with Gemini showgirls in carnival masks and feathers and not much more, tossing a glittering hail of Mardi Gras beads down to the looky-loos on the casino floor.

Even Xiao strolls over to scope out that scene.

I stroll after him.

Still keeping my distance. But not for long.

I'm itching to take him down.

My ex is dressed for clubbing in a clingy black shirt that shows off his narrow waist and the bulging biceps under that silky skin I used to love marking with my teeth. His dark head keeps swiveling to scan his six, which tells me he's wary as hell despite his casual clothes.

And under those leather pants he's rocking, he has an ass that stops traffic and a cock that won't quit.

Sure, he was always a decent fuck. But he's dead to me now. He sold me out. He sold me out to my fucking father and almost got me killed by Gemini hitmen in Singapore.

Besides, he's not the guy I wanna wake up next to.

Not anymore.

Right on cue, Xiao prowls past the craps pit. And there's practically an orgy going down in the mob scene jostling around the center table. That's where the hottest guy in the whole damn joint's getting eye-fucked by all the chicks and half the guys in the house.

God.

Damn.

Even in a casino full of costumes, Ronin Pendragon draws every eye without half trying. Tonight his powerful frame is mouthwatering as he looms over the hottest action on the floor, all broody and smoldering in the black tunic and cowl of his Kylo Ren getup. He's propped his black-and-gold pharaoh mask next to his stack of chips. So I can fully appreciate the perfection of his feral face and tawny skin.

With his smoking looks and bad-boy pout and that mane of black hair pouring halfway down his back, Ronin's a dead ringer for Adam Driver even without the costume.

That's part of what drew me—all that dark intensity and don't-fuck-with-me attitude—like a heat-seeking missile the night we met.

That's the night Ronin and Lucius kidnapped me, right out from under those Gemini hitmen, and dragged my rebel ass (furious and scheming) into royal captivity at the Icarus Academy.

We've been through a lot of shit together, me and Ronin and all my guys, since that crazy night in Singapore. At first, I didn't want anything to do with the Academy, my pain-in-the-royal-ass title, or that lethal Gemini witchcraft I can still barely control.

And I definitely didn't want a mate.

Much less four of them.

Sweet Jesus.

But right this moment, I'm not quite as opposed as usual to the concept of being the polyamorous queen-in-waiting of the whole witching world. Yeah, this queen gig's a cage I've been chafing to break free from—even if only for one night. But I fucking love that Ronin Pendragon has a starring role in my harem and my bed.

And I'm sure as shit not gonna let him get spaced, the way it goes down in the movies, saving his girl.

I save my own ass.

Xiao's still on the move, and I need to stay in his six because, despite my Catwoman camouflage, he could actually recognize me. Still, I put an extra sway in my hips when I sashay past the craps pit, just for Ronin's benefit.

And despite the beehive of activity seething around the table where the chips rattle and the dice roll and the stickman narrates the action in his lightning-quick patter, Ronin slides a slow hot look over my latex-sheathed curves with those tiger eyes of his.

It's a look that just about melts my pussy.

I give him a smirk and swish the mane of green curls swaying halfway to my ass as I swank past.

Like what you're looking at, Adam? I whisper in his head.

And because he's a warlock and almost pure Valyrian, not to mention one of my mates, he volleys right back at me in that intimate telepathic growl that gooses my snatch every damn time he does it.

I'll fancy it even more later, when Vasili and I peel you out of that bloody costume with our teeth.

Except for those scrumptious boots. Those we'll let you keep. Vasili's silky whisper purrs through the bond we all share—a mating bond that's getting stronger and more potent by the day. My harem's dominant alpha (a.k.a. the Goblin King) is parked somewhere up there at the rotating bar, with all that sexy he wields like a weapon tucked away behind a carnival mask.

That's one visual of Ronin and Vasili I can definitely get behind. Because the two of them individually are hella hot.

But the two of them together?

Fuck.

Me.

Sideways.

Fuck me *all* the ways, actually.

Heat floods my skin under my Catwoman mask and makes me sweat despite the arctic chill of the Double Gem's A/C. Under my panties, my cunt gets slick. In a heartbeat, the gusset is damp and clinging to my girly parts.

Oh yeah, my reaction to the guys tonight is even more intense than usual. Because that fat disc of moon floating above the corkscrew coaster is waxing toward full.

Which means, thanks to those mating bites I'm sporting from the shifters and quasi-shifters in my harem, I'm going into heat.

Major heat.

Again.

But, fuck, please, *not* till I'm off the clock.

This heist is way too important to let myself get distracted, even by the sledgehammer wallop of my looming heat and that scorching visual of getting stripped and double-dicked by Kylo and the Goblin King.

Not to mention Lucius and Neo. I miss the shit out of those two—my broody wolf shifter professor and my sweet blushing bookworm. But there's no way Lucius and Neo, who are both so responsible, would ever have understood my need for breathing room.

As in, *literally* no way.

When he isn't railing one of us with his thick cock till we beg for mercy in my big medieval bed, or running wild on all fours through the forest by moonlight, Lucius is the respectable headmaster of our residential college.

And Neo? He's First Boy on the Dean's List. In other words, a model citizen.

So the three of us villains just, uh, ghosted those two. We left the good guys back home.

Which officially makes the three of us here in Vegas… the bad guys.

Cheese on toast. The literal minute we turn back up on Academy grounds, Lucius will probably clap all three of us in detention in his office crypt till I'm forty—

Xiao slips out his phone and glances at the screen. His shoulders square with a ripple of tension. Then he prowls, purposeful as hell, for the discreet locked door of my dad's private lair.

That's gonna take him right off the casino floor.

Which means his ass is officially mine.

Adrenaline spikes my pulse and makes the hair I've dyed green (because my trademark teal is way too well-known) float around my shoulders in a crackle of psychic charge. That's what happens when my Gemini witchcraft slips the leash.

I tamp that shit down and keep back in Xiao's six near the roulette tables. For a few secs I idle with the tourists watching the action, heeding that prickle of hunch that tells me someone's watching *me*—after all, there are security cams everywhere, and I'm kinda hard to miss—and pretending to eyeball the little ball whizzing around the game wheel like it matters.

While the target of my actual interest taps out a quick message on his phone and slides a goddamn keycard from his pocket.

Which tells me Xiao's *still* in cahoots with my goddamn dad. I swear to Christ my ex is gonna regret the way he fucked me over.

For real.

Okay, boys, it's showtime, I fire at my warlocks. Suddenly I'm tingling with nerves and aggression. I bare my teeth in a bloodthirsty grin. *Time to do your thing, Adam.*

I'm expecting a provocative reply, so the uncharacteristic hesitation that ripples through our bond knocks me off my game.

You sure about this? Ronin sounds grim as the effing reaper, even though I'm only hearing him in my head. *Sure you fancy going in alone with that wanker? Even knowing he's in deep with your dad?*

I know Ronin's on my side, they both are, they couldn't *be* any more on my side. They just fucking hijacked the Academy's private jet to get us off the island without permission, for Christ's sake. I was hellbent on going alone till the guys sussed out my secret (because Ronin's a telepath, Vasili's a snake, and there's no hiding shit from them). Now it bugs me like hell that Vasili's probably gonna lose his newfound faculty privileges over this stunt.

Until he graduates this spring, Vasili's only provisionally on the faculty (and only because there's, like, a major shortage of powerful warlocks in the witching world).

If he loses his spiffy new gig, it's pretty much gonna be my fault. Even though I ordered both of them not to come.

But Vasili never gives a shit about any kind of censure.

Now it's Ronin dredging this painful thing back up, after we already fucking settled it, that sets my teeth on edge. And *not* just because that prickle of nerves and that sense of hidden eyes is making my skin tingle and my scalp itch. It's because my mate's resurrecting the closest thing to a fight—a bad one—the three of us have had since they joined my harem.

They don't want me doing this.

But I'm determined as fuck to do it.

I don't buy into that whole bullshit narrative that I need to be all sheltered and protected twenty-four/seven because I'm the queen-in-waiting—a role I'm still fighting to accept. I've always been on the wind, here today, gone tomorrow. Free spirit. I refuse to let this queen gig turn into a ball-and-chain.

Besides, my shitty ex-lover did more in Singapore than betray me and abandon me for dead.

He underestimated me.

And tonight's the night I prove that.

I'm a bad enemy to have. Xiao and Cleo almost got me killed. My gal pal's gone deep, where I can't find her, but Xiao's not as cautious. Or maybe he's just more cocky.

That kind of betrayal isn't the kind of shit you just get over. And I'm not the type to forgive.

Too bad for him my dad's wet boys couldn't finish the job.

We're not having this convo again, I tell my mates in my queen voice, glaring at Xiao's back as he fiddles with the keycard. I angle my wrist to scowl at the racing digits on the dive watch strapped to my wrist. *We honestly don't have the time. Odds are my dad's on his way here to pay off this lying sack of shit right now.*

Hmmm, Vasili muses.

Which means my snake is thinking.

That's when he's at his most dangerous.

The roulette ball drops in a pocket, somebody hits it big, and a round of cheers and whistles breaks out right next to me. Which makes me way too conspicuous.

I mosey out of Xiao's line of sight behind a bank of slots and wait to hear if my snake's gonna weigh in too. Getting Vasili not to crush every bone in Xiao's deceitful body, with one whack of his telekinetic witchcraft, the tick we saw Xiao stroll into the Double Gem (thus confirming every single suspicion I've been harboring about my goddamn ex) has been the hardest part of this whole job.

Matter of fact, it's pretty fucking crystal that neither one of my mates is happy with me—like, *at all*—for trying to do this without them. Or for leaving them off the VIP list for the impending Xiao-Zara throwdown. Ronin and Vasili wanted ringside seats. Instead they're in the nosebleed section.

And pissed about it as fuck-all.

When Vasili stays silent and doesn't argue, that fist of tension in my gut unclenches. Ronin won't buck the plan now, at the eleventh hour, if Vasili and I both back it.

Although, in Vasili's case, he's probably only silent because he's smart enough to know I'm going in anyway.

Don't fucking toy with him then, Ronin grumbles at last. *Bastard's already betrayed you once. Get what you bloody came for, then get the hell out. And no trying to leave us behind this time.*

I won't. I promise. A rush of elation shoots to my head, laced with a relief so strong it's a revelation. Because I really *don't* want to do this heist… or any heist, actually… without them.

Which makes me wonder if maybe I'm getting a little *too* dependent on my spiffy new harem? I'm not used to depending on anyone, much less trusting anyone. Look what literally just happened with Xiao and Cleo, right?

It's one thing palling around with my new guys at the Academy behind magical wards that conceal the whole island from these unsuspecting mortals who have zero clue the witching world even exists. Nothing gets past those wards without the Dean's say-so (except us, apparently). But now we're back in the real world.

Still. This whole harem thing's built around the concept of trusting my guys to have my back.

So that's what I'm gonna do.

Trust.

I can do this.

I tamp down my nerves, get my head back in the game, and roll my shoulders to loosen up. *Ready to do your thing, guys?*

Oh, we'll do our thing. Dark with promise, Ronin's voice strokes every nerve in my body like a hand sliding down my spine. *Long as we can do your thing later.*

Now behave, darlings, do. Vasili breaks his silence at last. *Daddy Gemini just strolled through the south entrance with a devil's dozen of his armed baboons. They're definitely headed your way, little queen.*

My heart gives a hard kick against my sternum. Fight-or-flight instinct shoots through every synapse and makes my fingertips crackle. I haven't been under the same roof as dear old Dad since I took off.

Right before he put out that hit on my head.

I have to remind myself I won't be under the same roof now for very long. I rub my fingertips together to dispel the electric charge of my power.

A power that's way too dangerous to unleash in a casino full of people.

Once was more than enough for that shit.

I swallow hard against the burn of old grief that swells my throat. Grimly, I watch Xiao flash the keycard over the lock and let himself into my dad's lair. The door clicks shut between us.

Okay, I whisper to Ronin. *Light the place up.*

Behind me at the craps tables, a blinding flash of light goes off, followed by the sudden crackle of flame and a blistering pulse of heat. I don't need to look, because that's Ronin's psi fire.

He's the Leo scion, one of the twelve great witching world families. Which officially makes Ronin Pendragon a human flamethrower.

Almost before he lights the fuse, an electric surge of anticipation has me bolting for the ventilation grate next to my dad's office door.

So I'm already on the move when the screaming starts.

Right on schedule.

Chapter Two

Ronin

The second Zara gives me the green light, I sweep an arm across the felt-topped craps table and spray the thing down with enough liquid fire to light it up.

Fuck, yeah.

That niggling itch of nerves I've been fighting all night scatters like ash in a strong wind under the head rush of wielding my witchcraft.

Joy burns through me and fire pours from my fingers like flaming kerosene. Players scatter screaming to the four winds like the table's an anthill and I just fucking kicked it.

They're not the blokes I'm gunning for, I'm not actually gunning for anyone except Zara's bloody wanker of an ex. But a little terror never hurt anyone, did it? Exhilaration slams through me like a freight train and makes every cell in my body sizzle.

Bloody hell. Nights like these are what I'm made for.

Literally what I was bred for.

Because you don't wind up with witchcraft as strong as mine by accident. I'm the scion of my clan for a reason. I'm destined to rule the whole clan and lord it over the witching world once Zara ascends (assuming we survive that long, with all the enemies we've got). Plus I've honed my genetic bag of tricks at the Academy till I'm lethal. But students are almost never allowed past the wards.

Which makes tonight a rare chance to let the full force of that magical punch I'm packing out to play. The chance to give my queen what she needs.

And I'll give Zara fucking Gemini anyfuckingthing she needs.

Actually, I know exactly what she needs.

Because I know a fair bit about rebellion. And I know more than a bit about revenge.

Through a sheet of flame, I catch a flash of moss-green hair and a gleam of liquid latex. That's my queen in action. She snatches the Phillips from her utility belt and pops the grate on the ventilation shaft in literal seconds. That's because my girl's a *bona fide* cat burglar as well as the queen-in-waiting, and she really is that blooming good.

Even without calling on that powerful Gemini witchcraft she's still wary as fuck about using.

The eye in the sky's watching, since Daddy's got this whole place kitted out with security cams. That's why my girl needs this diversion. What with the fire and the screaming and the panic, all that Gemini muscle's suddenly got way bigger problems than Catwoman breaking into Daddy's digs.

Which means I've got a solid five secs to withstand the wall of heat roasting my front and the sting of smoke filling my lungs, while Zara scrambles into the ventilation shaft like a slinky jaguar, to appreciate the pornographic visual of my queen's luscious arse.

Bollocks. I wish to gods I was crawling into that shaft with her. But clearly my queen fancies the notion of taking out her own trash.

And I don't like it one bloody bit.

Later, when we're back on board the private jet and headed home to Icarus, I swear to fuck I'm going to pound into that sweet arse from behind while she goes down on Vasili's—

Pay attention, he snaps through our bond. *This wretched place is crawling with casino cops. And Mick Gemini's storming toward you in an absolute rage. Tend your campfire while I deal with Daddy.*

I rather fancy the notion of dealing with Zara's homicidal parent myself. Truth is, though, my trick fire's spreading fast. Way faster than I planned across all that flammable felt, and already lighting the carpet like it's drenched in petrol.

Long story short?

This blaze is raging well beyond what I can tamp out with my gift.

And we don't actually intend to burn the place down—even though I'd fucking love to do it—given the magnitude of the collateral damage we'd cause. This casino's crawling with tourists, and Zara's determined not to hurt a single one.

I've never been one to fret over collateral damage. But what does propel me into damage control mode is the fact that, if I lose control of this bonfire, I'll put Zara in danger.

Even more danger than she's put herself in already.

So instead of carving my way with my knives through this scrum of two-bit players, all clawing and scrambling and fighting for the nearest exit, I slip between two hysterical Gemini showgirls, bat one of their big peacock feathers out of my fucking face, and yank the fire alarm.

The whoop of the siren adds to the bedlam and just about splits my head open. I bark out a curse and wrestle the fire extinguisher out of its cradle. I'm bringing the nozzle into play when, in my pocket, my blooming mobile vibrates.

"Bloody hell, Red. Not now," I mutter under the siren's wail.

Neo's been lighting up my phone all night long from the landline back at Icarus. In fact, he's been lighting it up for days. Probably since the tick he got back from his Honors Science of Witchcraft class and tumbled to the fact we ghosted him.

Neo Mercury's just about the sweetest male fuck I've ever had, an honest-to-gods virgin till Zara and I popped his cherry. He's a genuine sweetheart who still blushes every time I talk to him, and I feel guilty as hell about kissing off the bloke.

Well, I'll make it up to him later.

On my knees.

I'll unzip those prep school chinos he fancies and suck him off till he forgets every academic fact lodged in that encyclopedic brain of his and unloads down my throat.

Even now, the prospect of Neo Mercury coming undone under my hands and mouth gives me an instant boner. Too bad both the bloke and my boner are going to have to wait.

I finally get the nozzle sorted and aim my extinguisher at the blaze—

The rapid *chut-chut-chut* of gunfire punches through the sirens and chews into the wall behind me. A stinging slice sears my shoulder. Heat spills down my arm.

Fuck. That's a blasted bullet just grazed me.

I dive and roll for cover behind the burning table, clutching the extinguisher like an infant to my chest. "Who the fuck's shooting? There's bloody tourists everywhere."

I've got nothing in the mate bond, which tells me Vasili's got his pretty hands full running interference with Daddy Gemini and his hired muscle. And I haven't felt a thing from Zara in the bond since she scrambled into that shaft.

Fuck.

My chest gives a ping, because I'm a wicked strong telepath and I definitely ought to be hearing her. Scowling, I finish my drop-and-dive and roll to my feet—

Right in time to find a security goon built like a rugby player looming over me and jabbing a flaming craps stick at my face.

I barely dodge the fiery stick and swing my extinguisher like a club. The cylinder slams into the bloke's head and down he goes. Could be dead for all

I care. Snarling at the rat-faced fuck for trying to take my eye out, I spin and spray a torrent of foam over the burning table.

A flicker in my nine o'clock's all the warning I get before some kind of copper's coming at me, one of the boys in blue, probably the guy with the sidearm that just winged me. I spray down his face with a creamy sputter of extinguishing foam. The copper swipes at his foamy face and squeezes off a blind round that ricochets wide and just about drops a fleeing woman.

Arsehole.

I could take the trigger-happy bastard out with a spurt of fire, but there's rather enough fire about the place to contend with, even for a badass fire sign like me. Instead I sling my extinguisher into his chest like a bowling ball at ninepins.

The guy goes down with an agonized groan and hopefully a splintered rib or two, pistol flying from his grip. I kick it out of reach.

I don't need a firearm when I kill.

Between the gunshots and the barbeque, it's pandemonium in the Double Gem, with panicky players still clawing through the doors and showgirls stumbling and tumbling in their platform heels down the spiral stair from the rotating bar. The smoke's burning, my eyes are watering, my throat's on fire.

And my blooming mobile's still buzzing.

Shit.

Neo's nine time zones off, safely tucked away behind the wards (and thank fuck for it, because gods know Red's never been much good in a fight, unless it's a spelling bee or something). But his obvious desperation over Zara's safety—and probably mine, damn it, because he's sweet like that— it's eating me alive.

Where are you, love? Still feeling guilty, I grope about for Zara. But there's nothing, bloody nothing in the link.

My chest gives another ping that feels a bit too much like panic.

I scramble over my fallen foes and skirt the flaming table to get a proper look at the shaft where she vanished. *Vasili, I've lost track of—*

Not now. Vasili sounds petulant, but I'm so bloody grateful to hear him that I take zero offense. *Daddy Gemini's really a bit pissy, and couldn't we have managed without* quite *so much smoke? I can't cast where I can't see. And I'll never get this wretched stench out of my hair.*

Sorry, love. I'm instantly contrite, because he knows just how to punch my buttons.

Hmmmm. I'll make you pay for it later. Then he's gone. Before I can ask about Zara, blast it.

And I'm alone again inside my own damn skull.

Yeah, I might've done it a bit thick with the psi fire. I'd really rather fancy the fire suppression system kicking in—

"Hold it right there, mother fucker!"

That command swings me round in a rush to find one, two, three casino goons big as American linebackers barreling down on me through the smoke. I bare my teeth in a grin.

Bring it.

I snatch the flaming craps stick and brandish it like a fiery sword. That keeps the uglies off me long enough to launch a proper attack. Because I'm not the Academy's top-ranked fighter for nothing, am I?

I crouch and sweep my leg round in a scything stroke that connects with bruising force and takes out the first bloke at the knees. He drops like I've just clubbed him with a battering ram and lands on his coccyx with a yell.

Good.

I hope I broke his fucking tailbone.

I uncoil to my feet, cock my arm, and launch my stick like a burning javelin at the next guy, which makes him curse and veer. That maneuver buys me the tick I need to slide the long knives from my boots and spin into ninja mode.

These knuckleheads are armed with police batons and yeah, they're big and pissed and snarly. But they haven't been training in hand-to-hand combat since they were in nappies, which I have. I whirl into the fray like a proper Jedi, hair and cloak flying wide. A few slices from my blades carve through clothes and flesh. Then my hammering sidekick throws one guy into a bank of slots and knocks him out cold.

The last bloke standing legs it out of there, dripping blood all over Mick Gemini's carpet.

Too right.

This is the kind of action I relish. I'd actually be enjoying myself if not for the gnawing worry in my gut for my girl.

I take advantage of the breathing room I've earned with my blades and my rage and my badassery to stride through the smoke to the ventilation shaft that's swallowed my fucking queen. The fire suppression system switches on with a sputter—*finally*—and lukewarm water hisses down from the spigots to spray my skin. We've still got too many tourists stumbling about to suit me, some of them scooping up fallen chips by the bucket, despite the firefighters pouring through the north entrance and bellowing orders to the civvies to clear out.

But I'm going nofuckingwhere without my mates.

Both of them.

And if that means I need to belly through that shaft after Zara like a blooming garden snake, then that's what I'm going to do. And if she doesn't fancy company, that's too fucking bad. I sheathe my knives and scramble for the shaft. My nostrils sting with a sudden whiff of sulfur and brimstone—

Right before something hard and heavy slams into the back of my head like Thor's mythic hammer.

White light explodes in my skull and the room tips sideways. I stagger and grab for the wall to catch myself. But my depth perception's gone to shit. Oh fuck, I'm… falling…

The floor rushes up to meet me.

Somehow I get my hands underneath me to catch myself. But the casino's all blurry and wavering.

"Sorry for that, Pendragon," a voice growls in my ear. A voice that sounds like Vasili's Russian accent on steroids. "I cannot have you in the harm's way, yes?"

Bollocks. Who the fuck is this now?

I'm swaying on hands and knees, struggling to swing round on whoever's just sucker-punched me so I can bring my fire into play, when another blow connects with the back of my ringing head.

And my whole damn world goes black.

Chapter Three
Zara

I slither through the chute like an electric eel, with nothing to light my way except the witchy purple light that's leaking from my eyes. That's my power rising in anticipation.

Which, if you're just tuning in to the Zara show, is worrying news.

Because I definitely don't plan to use it.

My Gemini witchcraft is still way too unpredictable and way too dangerous for casual use, especially without Lucius here to ground me. Every time my palms make contact with the metal chute, sparks crackle and snap from my fingers.

And that shit *stings*. I hunker down flat and wiggle through the chute on my elbows, just so I don't electrocute myself by mistake.

Or warn Xiao that I'm coming.

The muffled whoop of the fire alarm makes me smirk with satisfaction. Yeah, I don't think my lying shit of an ex will be seeing my lizard king dad anytime soon. Maybe Xiao isn't even gonna get paid the last installment of that blood money.

Especially since, you know, I'm still breathing.

Dead ahead, lamplight leaks through a grate.

Almost through, I send to my guys, feeling all floaty with expectation, but also kinda apologetic over our big blowup (now that I've gotten my way, but at what cost?) *I appreciate the two of you.*

But the bond between us is, like, empty. Which is weird.

And unsettling as fuck.

I've had the guys at my fingertips… mentally and physically, in *all* the ways… since we first hooked up. Now I give that bond between us a good mental tug, because I promised the guys I'd stay in contact.

No joy.

Well, I'm already smelling smoke, so maybe Ronin's got his hands full. And Vasili's a Mogadon and not a strong natural telepath like Ronin and (it turns out) me, so maybe we're just too far apart right now for the mumbo-jumbo?

I fish out my burner phone, which I made sure to charge before we left. I've got the guys on speed dial, but turns out it doesn't matter. The freaking phone's dead as a rock.

Peachy.

Apparently I've accidentally shorted the gizmo. You know, with my Gemini witchcraft. (That whole unpredictable power thing, right? Now you see how it works.)

With a grimace, I tuck my useless phone away. This development makes me even more cautious as I wiggle the last few feet down the chute and peek through the grate.

My dad's offices all have a certain look. All gleaming wood he pays someone else to polish and vintage artwork he never pauses to appreciate and shelves loaded with classic literature he never bothers to read.

It's all meant to impress whoever he brings in here.

He's a warlock too, of course, because witchcraft is genetic in the arcane races. The basic traits are inherited, and we hone them (or not) at the Academy. But Gemini witchcraft is sex-linked to the Y chromosome, so Gemini women have all the power, like the lightning voice. The men just pass it down to their offspring. That same power killed my mom—a night I'll never unsee and a guilt trip I'll drag behind me like an anchor till someday, maybe, that power kills me too.

Maybe it's not totally a bad thing that I'm the last purebred Gemini (that we know of). Not to mention the last purebred female in all four arcane races, period.

Yeah, that's right. We're all slowly going extinct.

Darwinism.

It sucks.

Anyway, I'm the next queen in the witching world conga line (what little remains of it) and, like it or not, it's my job to do something to stop that whole extinction event. I mean, it's my job whenever the current Aquarius queen (who's now childless) kicks the bucket.

But Dad? Despite all that fancy Gemini DNA, he's a weak witch. A sperm donor. In our world, he's pretty much nothing.

Dad compensates for all that inadequacy by being filthy rich. You know, like casino king rich.

And, uh, he's not subtle.

Too bad the effort's totally wasted on Xiao.

My ex is a gamer and a grifter and a goddamn genius with tech, but he's never admired a painting or cracked a book (that I know of). Now he's prowling the open space between my dad's supersized desk and the private elevator with his mobile pressed to his ear. In fact, he's pacing like a caged tiger.

Good.

"Come on, Gemini," he mutters under the alarm's muffled whoop and wail. "Pick the fuck up."

Yeah, no. My dad won't be answering, butthead. Because by now, I guarantee you, Vasili's got his complete fucking focus.

I've been wondering how I'll feel seeing Xiao again. You know, after he betrayed me? Since I sussed the truth out of Lucius, I've been pretty much livid.

Well, I guess this is how.

Xiao's still slim and sleek with his inky hair and his chiseled looks. And he used to be able to flip my switch with one look from those hungry eyes.

But I'm pretty well fucked these days (in all the best ways) and I'm relieved to realize Xiao just doesn't light my fire.

Like, *at all*.

I'm over him.

What does light me up is that Spanish doubloon he's wearing on a heavy gold chain around his neck. He always wears it, picked it up illegally diving a wreck in South America before we ever met, said once he felt drawn to it for more reasons than what it's obviously worth. He's, like, obsessively attached to it. Never takes it off, not even to swim or shower, even though I never much liked the thing hitting me in the face when we fucked (which gave me a great excuse to straddle him, something he never seemed to mind).

But I digress.

The point is, he's still got it. He's still obsessed with it. It's still his most treasured possession. Well, *my* most treasured possession is my fucking freedom, you asshole. Which you were apparently one hundred percent okay with that kill squad taking from me.

Permanently.

So guess what I'm gonna take from *you*?

Suddenly I'm all done with caution. Even though the smoke's getting thick enough to sting my eyes and I still can't feel my warlocks in the link.

While Xiao paces and mutters into his mobile, I slither around in the chute till I'm situated feet first, wedge myself with my arms to get leverage, coil up tight, then shoot my platform boots at the grate with the full force of my black belt body behind the blow.

The impact slams through me. The grate flies free with a clang like it's got wings. I swing out of the chute right after and land on my feet.

Right in front of my shitty ex.

"Ciao, bello," I croon with a vicious grin. Cleo was Italian, and vocal when she got sexed up, so that's what our whole *ménage* always spoke when we fucked. "Did you miss me, baby?"

"Zara?" Xiao freezes in his tracks like a cornered rat. Dismay flickers in his bad boy face, for literally like an eyeblink. Then that confident grin spreads over his handsome puss. "Fuck, *bambina*. For a sec, you scared the piss out of me."

"Oh, I bet," I say sweetly. "Thought you saw a ghost?"

"Yeah, pretty much. You fucking disappeared in Singapore. Where the hell have you been all these weeks?" His words come easy, they always have, but unease lurks in his tone as he takes in my Catwoman getup. He's checking to see how I'm armed, if I'm carrying my stiletto. (I'm not, don't need it, never need a knife these days to cause carnage.)

His gaze flickers to the chute behind me, which is him checking to see if I've got backup.

Yeah. I fucking do.

But he can't see that.

"Wondering if I'm alone?" I ignore his question and shimmy a slow step forward, which makes him ooze a slow step back, angling so he doesn't get trapped between me and the bookcase. "Alone like I was in Singapore?"

His brows pinch together and he pushes out a breath. "You're thinking I set you up. Of course you are. Baby, that was *Cleo*. She set us both up."

Oh, I wouldn't doubt it. There's a reason my former bestie's on the wind and not answering any of the pings I've sent through our usual channels to feel her out.

But just because she's probably guilty does *not* mean Xiao's probably innocent.

"Nice try, *bello*." I slink toward him. He tries to sidle around me, but I keep between him and the door. "Yeah, it coulda been the two of you together on the take. But, see, here *you* are all alone, with your hand in my dad's cookie jar. You're either about to get paid off or bumped off."

"For fuck's sake, you think I'd be here if I had any other choice? Here where you could find me like you just did?" Xiao slicks a hand over his trendy hair, lamplight flashing on his dive watch. "I'm telling you, it was Cleo who fucked us both over."

"Why would she do that?" I ask. Because I honestly need to know, and I just can't figure it out. "You know she doesn't need the money. For her, it was never about the money."

"The fuck if I know." His smooth con man voice turns sharp enough to draw blood. "She's into some weird shit, deep into it, sometimes I'm not even sure she's fucking human, all right?"

Desperation gives him a dangerous edge, and I know he's packing heat and can't be trusted. But something in his voice gives me pause. He's not a warlock or anything, he's solidly part of the 99.9 percent of the human race that doesn't even know there are arcane races rubbing shoulders with the mortals. Xiao doesn't even know the witching world's a thing.

My own witchcraft's so unreliable and, until recently, so untrained I could never read his mind.

And it's frustrating as fuck to realize I still can't.

Come *on*, Gemini superpowers. I mean, I hope they give me *something* tonight besides a fried phone.

But Cleo's always been weird, Xiao's telling the truth about that much. And one thing I learned from Cleo while the three of us shared a *ménage* is you can fuck someone for months and think maybe you even love them, yet never really feel close to them.

Shit.

It still effing hurts that they *both* betrayed me.

But Lucius was pretty clear that he paid them both.

Yeah, you got that right. Xiao betrayed me twice. He took money from Lucius to disappear and leave me high and dry the night my warlocks kidnapped me, *and* money from my dad to tell the Gemini wet boys where to find me.

A muffled shout seeps through the door behind me and gets my head back in the game. That's the voice of authority back there, like the cops or the fire crew. My dad won't be far behind, unless Vasili's stopped listening to his elusive better angels (which are always the underdogs, given my snake's vicious streak) and solved our Mick Gemini problem his own way.

Like, you know, permanently.

Which means I need to finish up fast with Fuck Boy here and get the hell out.

So I put our past behind me and make my voice hard as bedrock. "Too bad for you Cleo's not here to take the fall. Which means I'm gonna have to take it out on your ass. Sorry not sorry, you feel me?"

I close on him in a rush.

Alarm fires in his face.

He dives straight for the little 2.7-millimeter Hummingbird he carries strapped to his ankle under his pants.

Even in mid-attack, hurt and fury flood through me and make my skin crackle. So much for being innocent. I'm a temporary inconvenience my supposedly innocent ex is about to eliminate permanently.

I scream with rage—a scream edged in the deep bronze echo of the lightning voice.

Fuck.

That right there's my power rising.

The desk lamp sparks and the bulb bursts. Xiao's panicked gaze veers toward it. So I seize my moment, twist sideways, and launch into the air, my dominant foot shooting out in a flying sidekick.

Since he's bending for his gun, my kick catches him square in the chest.

He flies back with an *oof!* and slides on his ass across my dad's massive desk, knocking the broken lamp to the floor with a crash.

Xiao's still scrambling to unholster his heat when I shove between his sprawled legs, knock aside his left hook, push him flat on his back across the desk, and grab a fistful of his balls.

Wisely, he freezes, all sprawled across the desk, hair falling in his eyes and chest heaving. Our gazes lock, me looming over him between his spread thighs, forearm planted on his chest to hold him down, his entire sexual future cupped in the palm of my hand.

"Shit," he whispers.

His lids drop and his eyes smolder.

Under my touch, his heartbeat quickens. A fraught silence stretches between us, heavy with all the things we're not saying.

Then he flexes his hips, ever so slightly, and pushes into my grip.

Because, yeah, Xiao does have a major submissive streak. And guess who just flipped his switch?

He's mine right now if I want him.

But I don't.

Halleluia. I really am over him.

"Don't even think about it, *bello*," I snarl. "And don't fucking tempt me, or I'll rip your balls off."

"Okay." His eyes roam over my catsuit and linger on my scowling lips. "So what comes next, *bambina*?" His voice drops and thickens. "You or me?"

Yeah, no. Not happening.

Not even a little bit.

I square my stance in my platform boots and pretend not to notice how hard he's getting under my hand. "Take off the medallion."

"What?" He blinks, and some of the heat cools in his eyes. "Why?"

"Cuz I wanna hold it." I smile sweetly and tighten my grip until he hisses. "Give it to me."

In a tick, his face goes hard and wary. "No."

A trickle of fear runs through him like an electric current. Under my grip, he practically vibrates. That shit feels genuine, which is surprising.

But also gratifying. Because I'm not exactly listening to my own better angels tonight either.

Who knew revenge would feel so satisfying?

"Oh, you think I'm *asking*?" I tilt my head and give my ex a wicked grin. "Let me put it this way. Give it to me or I'll take it. Your choice."

Desperation surfaces in his face, and I lap that shit up like a cat laps cream. "Look, Zara, I know it's a payback thing, I get it, okay? I get that you're pissed—"

Right when he's getting going with the begging part of tonight's performance, the blip of the door unlocking interrupts this beautiful moment. I'm already mainlining adrenaline like it's oxygen and I need that shit to breathe. Now my pulse shoots through the roof and the hair lifts off my shoulders in the psychic voltage that lights me up.

If that's my dad, this little showdown is about to get *way* more interesting.

Still pinning Xiao to the desk, I twist to get a gander behind me. Which is how I see one, two, three—sweet Jesus, more guys that I can count, all wearing carnival masks and Mardi Gras krewe costumes, they're the guys who were throwing beads from the rotating bar, which makes zero fucking sense—pouring into the room, silent as spilled ink.

Okay, so it's *not* my dad, because his ego's way too big to fit behind any kind of mask.

And he's never silent. His mouth's always running with his smooth casino schtick.

But whoever these guys are, they can't be anything good.

A conclusion that's totally validated when the lead guy bellows, *"ZARINA SELENE GEMINI."*

That mouthful's my full name, and it's what warlocks use for Compulsion spells, which are common magics just about any trained witch can cast.

But you need a bond with the caster for that shit to work. This guy's probably counting on the fact that I'm a Gemini in a Gemini casino and he's tied somehow to my dad.

Maybe that woulda been enough in the old days.

But not since I've come into my power.

Right now, I just feel like someone goosed me a little with a shot of voltage. Hell, that's barely unpleasant enough to piss me off. Still, the insult makes a hum gather in my throat—the dangerous hum of the lightning voice. My hair floats around my head in a crackle of psychic charge.

While carnival goons pour into the room and I'm all distracted, Xiao twists under me and snags the Hummingbird from his ankle holster.

Which is a *really* shit idea.

I roar out a curse in the lighting voice and swing around to face him.

My arm sweeps up to connect with his wrist before he can bring his heat into play and fire his goddamn pistol in my face.

And I'm so amped up that when we make contact, a jolt of electricity arcs between us.

That's the little lightning, not the major bolt I can summon when I mean it. (That's when I do the full-on electrical equivalent of Hulking out. You wouldn't like me when I'm angry.) But the jolt that arcs from my body to Xiao's, that fuckery a lightning witch summons with her voice, lights up the room with a flash of ultraviolet that makes my world go white.

The big halogen light in the corner explodes in a shower of sparks and jagged metal. Guys shout and dive clear of the shrapnel. The air floods with the industrial scent of ozone and burning metal.

When my vision clears, it's dark as fuck except for the ruddy emergency light flashing through the open door and the violet glow spilling from my eyes.

On the desk beneath me, Xiao's knocked out cold.

Maybe he's dead—which, God, isn't what I meant to happen—but I don't even have time to check. My little Thor son of Odin moment knocked the lead guys over, but the uglies in the back are still coming.

"Do you have a death wish?" I snarl to the room at large.

That's a theme I'm almost pissed off enough to pursue, but the last thing I want—as in, the *very* last—is a repeat performance of what happened the last time I lost my electrical shit in a Gemini casino.

The time a casino full of innocent tourists and looky-loos lost their lives, just because I lost my cool.

Which means it's time to go.

As in, *now*.

I shove upright and pivot to check out my options.

"Stay where you're at, sweetheart," one of the goons croons at me through his mask. "We only wanna talk. No one needs to get hurt."

"Yeah, *right*," I snort under my breath.

What kinda idiot do these guys think I am?

I snag the medallion from around Xiao's neck, and he gives a heavy groan. I puff out a breath of relief. Despite every fucking thing between us, I never meant to kill him in cold blood, because I'm not (quite) that coldblooded.

And he's lucky as fuck I wasn't still twisting his balls when my lightning went off, or Xiao would've been singing soprano for the rest of his natural life.

A rough hand grips my shoulder from behind. In reflex, my leg snaps back in a donkey kick that connects with someone's kneecap.

You know, the hard way.

Bone crunches, the guy howls, and that invasive hand on my shoulder falls away.

I vault over the desk and Xiao's stirring form, barely evade some other guy's fist that's grabbing for my hair and still manages to rip out a few strands—ouch, dammit, that stings like a bitch!—and land behind the desk in a crouch.

The door's out of reach right now, and the ventilation chute's a rat trap I don't wanna get caught in. But the elevator's right in front of me. I punch the button and loop Xiao's medallion around my neck.

At last something goes my way (finally!) because the elevator's down here waiting and not idling at the helipad up top. The doors shoot right open—

Just as someone's arm locks around my neck from behind.

"He doesn't wanna hurt you," the guy rasps in my ear. Probably the same asshole who just ripped out a chunk of my damn hair. "He only wants to talk."

"Sweet Jesus," I mutter. "When are you guys gonna get the message? I'm. Not. *Interested.*"

I punctuate that newsflash with an instep stomp that loosens that arm around my neck PDQ. Then I jab a reinforced elbow into the guy's torso. Mr. Handsy gives a good *oof!* and I duck free, my foot shooting back to hammer him right in the nuts.

He wheezes and doubles over in extreme pain.

As he fucking *should.*

I don't get to use my combat skills much while I'm queening it these days—which is one more reason I don't like the gig. I'm not cut out to be some shrinking violet. But I work pretty hard not to get rusty, I train with Ronin so I won't, and it feels straight up exhilarating to let loose.

When I dart inside the elevator and punch the button, I might actually be grinning.

There aren't many options to choose from, because my dad's express elevator only exists to cart his self-important ass between his helipad and his private office.

You know, because he's too important to take the regular lift with the average joes?

I catch one last glimpse in the horror-show half-light of Xiao struggling to sit and gaping at my amped-up lightning witch persona, with my hair floating and my eyes glowing. Yeah, that'll be a problem if we ever hook back up, but right now I'm not fucking planning on it. Behind and around him, faceless dudes in carnival masks are swarming over those guys I took out and bolting toward me.

The last thing I hear before the doors slam shut is some guy barking into his phone, "Tell the Russian she's headed for the roof."

Then I'm shooting up at warp speed (because my dad doesn't like to wait) as the elevator powers for the roof.

Who in the freaking hell's *the Russian*?

My unholy exuberance eases off and a little trepidation creeps in. But I'm still high on adrenaline and pheromones, which makes it really hard to think. The only Russian I know, um, intimately is Vasili. And it's not like the Goblin King isn't eminently capable of betrayal.

But that scenario literally makes zero sense.

If Vasili wanted to take me out, the way he used to—because he and I met cute, back in the day—he could've made his move a million times at the Academy. And he would have left Ronin (who he's, like, obsessively in love with, and totally protective over) clear of this mess.

Nope. Vasili's on my side. That Russian on the roof is someone else.

Which reminds me…

Hey, Goblin King, I send to Vasili through our bond. *Uh, any chance you can get my ass down from the roof?*

Which isn't as far-fetched as it sounds, because he's not only the new professor of Mogadon Magics at the Academy. He's also pretty much the biggest badass in the whole Mogadon race. Most Mogadon have one gift tops. Vasili's got, like, multiples. And with his particular skill set and the tools in his arcane toolbox?

Let's just say altitude isn't gonna be an issue.

Unfortunately, what is an issue is that I'm still getting nothing through our bond.

Zero. Zip. Nada.

Either from Vasili or from Ronin.

"Geez." I frown at my Catwoman reflection in the glass wall. "Where is everybody?"

Xiao's medallion gleams against my chest. So warm and heavy, the thing almost seems to pulse and hum in the dim light like a second heart. I wrap my fist around the ancient Spanish gold with a curl of satisfaction.

Xiao's gonna regret what he did to me every time he looks in the goddamn mirror and doesn't see King Ferdinand of Aragon looking back.

Outside the glass, the casino falls away as the lift shoots up. Now I've got a primo view of the Las Vegas Strip spread out before me, all neon billboards and flashing lights and laser shows pulsing against the night. The shadowy skeleton of the Gemini coaster's big hill flashes past.

With my guys incommunicado, I guess I better get ready for the goddamn Russian.

Whoever that is.

A hum builds in my throat, but my mouth is dry and my tongue sticks to the roof of my mouth. Suddenly my heart is hammering.

Lucius has been teaching me to control the lightning. And yeah, I might be the Gemini clan's only functioning lightning witch, but I *really* don't want to try summoning that shit without Lucius.

Because last time I summoned lightning in a Gemini casino, even though it was unplanned and involuntary and purely in self-defense, eighty-seven people ended up dead.

Including my psycho mom.

My chest tightens with old grief and my gut twists in a knot of guilt. That's not gonna happen again.

Not ever.

Sure, I'll use the little lightning if I have to, like I just did with Xiao. But I definitely *won't* summon the little guy's big brother.

Because I'm not, like, homicidal.

That's one more reason I'm lukewarm at best about this whole queen gig. Once I ascend, I'll be expected, required, practically forced to use my witchcraft.

The same witchcraft that's always terrified me.

The problem with using it tonight is, my newly honed witchcraft's never really been tested like this, in actual combat, not without Lucius. I ache with a violent longing for my broody headmaster, the guy who makes me feel safe when I summon, the guy who even makes me feel safe when he's growling threats and vibrating with violence and his wolf's rising and his monster cock's reaming me in our medieval bed.

The elevator floods with the sudden scent of roses and vanilla. That's my mating scent, that truckload of pheromones and come-fuck-me biochemicals. Which is pretty much the only Mogadon trait I manifest.

I scent when I get horny.

I scent to mark what's mine.

My reflection floats against the Sin City night, hair drifting around my shoulders like seaweed in a current, light pouring from my turquoise eyes, which is a pretty witchy effect that's heightened by the big dark ovals of my Catwoman mask. My bubblegum pink lipstick and drama queen mascara have somehow survived the fray without a smudge.

When I snap my fingers, lavender sparks and crackles.

That light in my eyes is psi fire. That's a Valyrian trait, and it's a trait Ronin shares, he's almost pure Valyrian. The lightning's a weather gift, which is Kryll like my fated mate Neo. The shifter genes from my splash of Protean DNA are all recessives, not generally good for much, though I've got a pretty strong hunch that, since both Lucius (full shifter) and Vasili (part shifter) have given me mating bites, that's maybe gonna change?

Someday.

Sure, these days I'm feeling kinda shifty, but I haven't exactly sprouted wings. Suffice it to say, despite having a cocktail of genes from all four arcane races in my Gemini DNA, I got nothing in the witchcraft department that's really gonna help me on that roof…

Except the lightning I'm terrified to use.

Yep.

Queen or no queen, right now it sucks to be me.

The elevator gives a cheerful *ding!* The doors slide open. I'm already on the move, because I'm not gonna die trapped like a rat in a cage.

I dive through the opening doors with a hum gathering in my throat and electricity crackling around my fingers.

No one tries to stop me, and for a sec I'm alone up here in the night on my dad's empty helipad, floating one hundred stories above the Vegas Strip, with a dry hot wind whistling in my ears and lifting the hair from my shoulders.

Then the *thokka-thokka-thokka* of churning rotors drowns out the wind's whistle.

And the chopper rises into view.

With its side door open, goons in carnival masks hanging out, and the swoopy double pillar Gemini sign painted on the side.

I've got a sec while I'm pelting across the roof away from the chopper to make the connections in my head. That it's my dad gunning for me (again) and he obviously knew I was coming. That Xiao's the bait he used to lure me out. That the emergency stairwell's the only escape route I've still got. And that I better dive into it before that chopper cuts me off.

But I'm only halfway there, even at my speed, when the stairwell door opens and more goons pour out to cut me off.

Sweet Jesus, can't a girl ever catch a break?

I could summon the lightning and be free in a flash (literally). I can't hear the rumble of thunder over the chopper's roar, but heat lightning dances in the crisp winter sky, already drawn by the hum in my throat. That lightning's so close all I'd need to do is raise my arm and yell to hurl it.

But damn it, I'm not taking the roof off another casino.

I'm not psycho like my mom.

I'm not a killer. I'm *not*.

Except when I have to be.

I push away the unsettling memory of Bjorn the polar bear shifter, his furry bulk all smoking and scorched and lifeless in the courtyard of our *domus* back home. A death that's still under active investigation by the AIB. That shifter would've killed Lucius if I hadn't done my thing.

I'm in control now when I kill.

I am.

I veer away from the fire escape and head for the edge of the roof, not even knowing why, because there's nothing close enough for me to jump to (though I've been known to try stunts like that before).

The chopper veers to cut me off, hovering twelve feet above the helipad. Then tendrils of rope spool out and guys in carnival masks start dropping like spiders through the door.

Now it's time for these fuckers to show me some respect.

I growl low in my throat—the brassy rumble of the lightning voice— and stomp my foot. Lucius and I have been working on this. I'm channeling the little lightning.

An ultraviolet sheet of electricity spreads from my boot, rolling and crackling across the helipad. It's strong enough to give a nasty jolt to everyone standing on it.

Except me, because I *am* the fucking lightning.

I'm the Gemini queen.

My jolt knocks every joe on the helipad on their asses like they've just been tasered.

Savage joy surges through me and lifts the hair off my shoulders. I pivot toward the elevator, figure maybe I'll try this trick with the boys downstairs…

Just in time to see the elevator doors slide open. And wouldn't you know it?

There's my fucking father.

Yep. Mick Gemini's pretty impossible to mistake. Even though he's looking kinda disheveled from whatever Vasili did downstairs to delay him, with his tie all crooked and his jacket torn. But Mickie boy still has that broad-shouldered frame in his trendy suit that draws the girls and the commanding lift to his Irish mob boss head that intimidates the boys.

Or maybe, you know, that's just his money talking.

God knows he's got plenty of that.

"Aw, shite, Zara." My dad checks out the mess of stunned and twitching men I've left scattered all over the helipad and shakes his head. "Jaysus, why d'ye always have to make such a fecking mess?"

I boil over with hurt and rage. It's the contempt and dislike he all too clearly feels for me—the same contempt and dislike he felt for my mom— that cuts the worst and always has. That right there's the real reason I ran away.

Cheese on toast, it's like I never even left.

"Guess that's why you tried to kill me, huh?" I shout above the chopper's whirring blades as the bird hovers behind me. "I'm not here to see you. Get out of my way. Or I'll show you a fecking mess."

"Will I now?" My dad jams his hands in his pockets and cocks his head. I can almost see the canny gleam in his baby blues as he takes my measure. "Ye've been out having the craic long enough. Ye've had yer fun, girl, and for donkey's years. Now ye're queen and all, and that's just grand. But it's time to come home."

So, before you ask. Yeah, the guy really talks like that. It's ridiculous. Especially when he's pissed. Like it gives him an extra shot of Irish.

"I don't think so, boyo." I keep my voice hard and confident. His goons are still filling the stairwell (though now they're afraid to come out), and his chopper's still hovering, and Mick Gemini's not dumb enough to vacate the lift with me hurling lightning out here.

But I'm not going back under his roof or his thumb ever again.

I mean it.

The edge of the roof's still tugging at me. Slowly I pivot to eye it. I'm a cat burglar, so I'm not afraid of heights, and I've gotten downright comfy in the air with Vasili. That swollen moon hovers overhead, so close to full, almost close enough to touch. I've been really well bitten by both my shifters (though Vasili has too much Mogadon in his DNA to actually shift). But I haven't been able to shift myself.

Still.

I know what I'm turning into, don't I?

Yeah, we haven't been sure. It's pretty fucking rare, even in the witching world, that thing I'm becoming.

But no time like the present to find out.

Every cell in my body starts tingling. That's my power rising. The rush is so heady it almost lifts my feet from the tarmac. Arms loose at my sides, sparks leaking from my fingers, I drift toward the edge.

"Awww, c'mon, ye're off your head, girl," my dad calls after me. "There's no bleedin' place to go!"

"Watch me." I shift into a lope.

"That's it then," Dad barks to his boys, all that Irish charm discarded like a cheap suit. "Take her out. Take her the feck out!"

Shit.

Or, as Dad would say, shite.

When the first shot rings out, I'm already running. These guys have been pulling their punches all night, because supposedly Dad "only wants to talk," but now the gloves are off.

The helipad ends. There's a low metal barricade and then empty air and the Strip one hundred stories down.

A bullet whines past, so close it grazes my ear in a slice. And I've got just enough precognition, thanks to my Valyrian DNA, to have a pretty strong hunch that the next bullet's gonna bury itself in my brain.

Call me crazy (because it's been said before).

But every bone in my body is humming with certainty.

I am the lightning. I'm the bridge between earth and heaven. I'm the fucking Gemini queen.

I got this.

Thumping against my chest, Xiao's medallion throbs and burns. I dredge up an extra spurt of speed, then hurtle over the barricade and leap from the roof.

For a few electrifying seconds I keep moving forward through the air, like I really can fly. My heart singing, my limbs churning, the wind stinging, my hair floating.

And then, of course, I fall.

Chapter Four
Maxim

I am braced in the open door of Mick Gemini's chopper above three hundred meters of gloriously empty air in a wind that is screaming my name when I see Zarina Gemini falling.

For a breath, I can scarcely believe my sovereign has actually jumped.

One moment, there she stands, all sleek strength and movie star curves, encased in that alluring catsuit with hair green as venom coiling like Medusa snakes around her shoulders. There she stands, summoning lightning like some flamboyant Avenger in a Hollywood film and knocking every one of Mick Gemini's *bratva* on their brainless behinds.

Christ, that girl has so much raw power coursing through her circuits, she has nearly crashed this chopper.

Now here she is hurtling through the air like the queen of the sky—which I swear to you she damned well *is*—and she is validating every single shifter instinct that has dragged me here to this crass American city from the wretched depths of the Siberian tundra to witness for myself this miracle of the witching world's awaited savior.

I am still transfixed by her desperate trajectory, limbs pistoning as she churns through the air, as though she will run for kilometers on nothing but empty sky and courage—every cell in my body tingling, my whole heart wedged in my throat—when my queen loses her forward momentum and plummets toward the ground.

I am out of this death trap in an eyeblink, evading the startled hands that clutch at me, ignoring the desperate voices that shout at me, plummeting after my sovereign through the dry desert night.

The wind slashes my skin and untwists my hair from the long braid I wear for combat to lash around my face.

The downdraft peels the leather jacket from my shoulders to flutter behind me in free fall.

Thirty meters below, my queen is tumbling and clawing through the air and fighting for purchase. But her edges are blurring. Around her, the air shimmers. The blaze of witchcraft builds to a flash of blinding light.

Her scream unravels through a shrill human cry to a deep brassy bellow.

When my vision clears, Zarina Gemini is transformed. From a flightless witch tumbling through the night, she has become…

Her dragon.

She is slim and sinuous, long and lean as the locomotive of a Red Star bullet train barreling through the Russian night, glittering with teal-and-diamond scales, tail lashing and legs scrambling and wings beating as she fights to master her shift.

But learning to fly is not done in a day.

I, of all creatures, should know.

Zarina Mikhailovna—daughter of Michael—as she will be known among my people when she takes her throne, might be the dragon shifter queen of the witching world.

But she is still falling.

Ours! My beast roars to life in my head to thunder his demands. *Maxim, she is ours. Claim our mate!*

In free fall myself, I fling back my head and trumpet to the heavens in triumph. The hot tingling rush of the shift sweeps through me, obliterating my mortal limits and scalding my skin.

My world goes white with glorious witchcraft.

I beat my wings in a powerful downdraft that arrests my descent. I angle my long neck to arrow through the wind after my mate. The breeze caresses my night-black scales and wraps around my mighty frame. Bones groaning, sinews straining, scales stretching, I settle into my shift.

A few mighty strokes of my massive wings funnel me through my mate's slipstream.

The skeletal hill of the twin coaster looms below me, metal grinding as two trains packed with plump Las Vegas tourists chug up the big ascent. Barely ten meters shy of the track, I pluck my mate out of free fall with my forelegs and latch my teeth into the vulnerable crest of her neck. My vast wings beat hard to slow our plummet.

My mate's coiled body writhes against me in shock and rage. This is the dragon's savage fighting instinct, taking her over, even though I am trying to spare her life.

I lock my rear legs around her to subdue her and I twist in midair to avoid colliding with the climbing coasters.

Sparing all those miniscule mortal lives by less than a wingspan.

Furious to be restrained, my mate opens her fanged jaws and bellows defiance. A fork of lightning jags from her mouth to slam into the casino's gaudy neon sign. The contraption explodes in a shower of sparks and goes black.

Saints of the northern steppes, my mate is a lightning dragon. The first of her kind the witching world has seen in centuries.

I release my hold on the scruff of her neck to roar my satisfaction.

Mine is a triumph too powerful to be blunted, even when the double coaster clatters over the hill and the flash of myriad cell phone cameras lights the thing up. Tiny shouts of astonishment and shock flutter like confetti in the Vegas night.

A ticker tape vision of tomorrow's tabloid headlines scrolls through my dragonish brain. *Twin Dragons Sighted Over Downtown Las Vegas! Mythical Creatures Exist!*

Christ.

God willing, Mick Gemini can claim it is a publicity stunt. Some sort of Hollywood special effect.

Because if he cannot manage to pull that off, if I have just destroyed the fragile shield of secrecy that barely protects the witching world from mortal discovery and mortal persecution, my Lady Mother will have my head.

It is bad enough that I am here at all.

For I came in direct defiance of her formidable command. For this defiance, when I return, she will make me suffer.

And for this debacle in the mortal skies, truly, she will flay me.

My mate twists her neck to eye me. Her golden orbs, divided by slitted pupils, glow with intellect and suspicion. Human speech is impossible in dragon form and, as a purebred shifter, I am surely no telepath.

I suppose the sight of my monstrous head, steam leaking between my toothy jaws and fiery eyes flaming with wrath, does not do much to reassure.

I rumble at her, long and low, to calm her until I can bear us off the Strip and safely to the ground.

Somewhere.

My sovereign's eyes narrow as though she suspects I am seeking to play her. She snaps at my face in warning.

Clearly, she wants down now.

Then those brilliant eyes of hers telescope wide. She bugles in alarm.

I register the rapid *thwap* of chopper blades a heartbeat before gunfire spatters the air. Hot embers of pain pepper my outspread wings and ricochet from my scales.

Those unconscionable pricks in the chopper—they are, what is it, shooting at me?

No, it is worse than that. They are shooting at *her*.

My.

Fucking.

Mate.

A crimson rage erupts in my chest like a fiery volcano.

I curl my mighty frame around my sovereign to protect her—she is so slender, this royal mate of mine, she is barely more than a juvenile, while I have achieved my full growth, I am a mature dragon at the peak of my strength. I spiral in midair to confront this insectile machine that is mortally offending me by threatening my mate.

Deep in my belly, a scalding heat blooms and builds. I stoke it like a giant bellows.

This Gemini aircraft is no combat chopper. No, this assault is merely those stupid fucks with handguns hanging through the open doors and shooting like idiots, the way their posturing Irish Gemini *otyets* (the father) told them to do. Unfortunately for them, my beast and my mating instincts are fully in my command. We obey no one's *otyets*.

And I am in no mood for mercy.

The drive to protect my mate and kill my enemies is paramount.

Snarling, I part my massive jaws and rumble. A column of fire rolls up my throat and pours from my mouth to engulf the chopper like kerosene from a firehose.

Because I myself am a firedrake. Classic dragon, yes? I am the Russian equivalent of the Black Dread from the American epic *Game of Thrones*. I am a modern-day Balerion.

But no man commands me.

I complete my spiral and turn my back to the inferno. I plant the bulwark of my body between my precious sovereign and any hint of danger. Even though she is now thrashing and screaming in rebellion of my summary handling of her royal body—and perhaps my summary execution of those hapless men.

She is tender-hearted, this mate of mine. I saw that much on the roof when she spared those men her wrath.

Well, no matter. I am killer enough for us both.

By the time the chopper explodes, I am winging hard away. Hard enough that I barely feel the flush of heat from the conflagration warming my flanks and back. Beating my wings steadily to gain speed and altitude, I head for the open desert, lashing my tail and trumpeting a deafening warning to the night.

My limbs are wrapped tight around my mate.

Blessed Saint Sergius be my witness, I would like nothing better than to take wing with her now for Siberia. I will not rest until I have my priceless queen safely tucked away in my remote Arctic lair. Until I have vanquished every one of my rivals who wallow in sin and scandal in her warlock harem. Until I have bitten her and mounted her and bred her in the pale glow of the white nights, flooding her fertile womb again and again with my potent dragon seed.

Until she is spent and sated and mated and her beautiful belly is round and full with my clutch.

But my queen does not yet seem to share my mating instinct.

She is agitated and writhing in my grip, growling in the back of her throat, her ominous vocalizations laced with the rumble of thunder. And even my beast (who is far from discerning, God knows, especially this close to rut) realizes my mate is not exactly in the mood for a mating flight just yet. In truth, she is far from it.

My mate wants *down*.

And she wants it now.

Well, in this, surely, I can oblige her.

And when my rivals for her bed track her to ground, they will yield their place to me, their superior.

Or I will slaughter them all without mercy.

Chapter Five
Zara

The second this flying Godzilla lands his big ass in the desert night, well beyond Vegas or any sign of civilization, and blessedly lowers me to the ground, the shift sweeps over me.

My edges blur, my tummy twists, and a wicked surge of disorientation wrenches my balance out of whack and drops me to my hands and knees—because I have those again. Actual hands, I mean. My entire body tingles like I just shoved a fork in a socket. My mouth is hangover-dry like I've just come off a three-day bender (not that I'd ever be so irresponsible, etc.) and my heart is sledgehammering.

But, fuck, I'm exhilarated.

I just freaking *shifted*. I shifted into a freaking *dragon*. A dragon that breathes *lightning* (though that specific part is kinda scary, given my mixed feelings about my witchcraft). How freaking cool is that? Even if I still can't fly, I can figure out that whole flying aspect of my dragon superpowers later.

Right now, the first thing I have to figure out is clothes.

Because, of course, I'm naked.

"Another catsuit ruined," I mutter, getting used to the concept of human speech again. Grateful as fuck for it, actually. It was frustrating as hell not being able to communicate with that big galoot behind me—except through squirms and growls and a few pointed nips to get his attention—while we were in the air.

I lift my head and shake back the teal chaos of my hair, so I can see. That green dye was temporary, a one-wash wonder, looks like it vanished when I shifted. I'm actually intrigued (and relieved) to see that my silver nipple rings survived the shift.

And I'm really intrigued to get a proper eyeful of that dragon.

He's still looming behind me. I can hear the thing's deep rumbly breaths. He oughta be huffing and puffing, but he isn't. How is he not even winded, for Chrissake, after flying his big ass and mine like twenty miles or something into the Nevada desert?

With me complaining and fidgeting the whole way.

Because I appreciate being saved, but I don't much like being carried.

Whoever he is, wherever he came from—since given the high-handed way he acts, I don't doubt for a sec that he's got a dick rather than a vag back there, something about this dragon just *screams* testosterone—anyway, he's set us down next to the shuttered shell of a decrepit gas station near an old asphalt road that's definitely seen better days.

And he pretty much validates that whole conclusion about being an entitled male when he leans in to nose my bare back with his hot silky muzzle.

Without asking.

Then he drags that forked tongue of his down my spine and snakes it right between my fucking legs.

At the first intimate flicker, a pulse of heat goes off like a bomb in my clit. He just about sets my skin on fire.

"Cheese on toast!" I yelp, scrambling to my feet and putting plenty of distance between me, that marauding muzzle, and that oddly tantalizing tongue, before I spin around to face him.

And he's… a lot to take in.

Mother.

Fucker.

He's a monster, literally, an actual dragon, all sleek and coiled and powerful, towering higher than the gas station roof. Even when he's resting on his hind legs with that thick forked tail curled around his feet. He's glistening black, with glints of indigo and venom glittering in the joints of those plate-sized scales in the streetlight. Under curving black horns, his eyes are gold, they're narrow slits right now while he takes my measure, with oblong pupils like a goat or a demon. (Not that demons are a thing, as far as I know, but I read paranormal romance, the smuttier the better. So I'm telling you, this guy has eyes like a demon.)

As I was saying.

His jaws are filled with dagger-sharp teeth. His sinister head, hovering over my naked self like a serpent poised to strike, is pretty much the size of my whole body.

And then some.

With the smell of me thick in his muzzle and the taste of me lurking on his tongue, I'm pretty sure that lidded gaze and toothy grin are what a dragon looks like when he's smiling.

Especially when he lowers his head to pull in another long whiff. Yeah, that fat wedge of moon is swelling toward full. I'm betting this guy can smell it on me.

My impending heat.

Just the thought of my heat makes me slick and wet between my legs. Because my last heat was a real doozy.

It took all four of my warlocks to fuck me through it.

I try not to think about the fact that I'm naked (*and* wet) as I plant my hands on my hips to square off with Puff the Magic Dragon. Because it's time to establish some boundaries.

For real.

Sweet Jesus, I can still feel the slick of that wicked tongue between my legs.

"Okay, here's Thing One. Hands off the merchandise, big guy." My gaze shifts to his big scary-looking tyrannosaur forepaws. "I mean, paws off. And, like, tongue off. No licking." (Especially not there!) "That's Thing Two. And assuming you can actually shift to human form? Now would be the time."

He settles his bulk on the asphalt and huffs out a rumbling snort that sounds like a chuckle. Tendrils of steam leak through his nostrils. That's when I notice he's got something snagged on one of those curving front claws.

Something gold and shiny.

My nerves tighten and my skin sings. Suddenly I'm tingling with a rush of exhilaration. That's because I've got a pretty good inkling of what that thing is. It's not lost after all. And I want it.

It's mine.

But first things first.

"You heard me." I cock my naked hip and tap my bare foot. "Shift. I wanna talk to you."

And the whole time I'm checking him out, I'm definitely *not* checking out his junk. Even though that tool nestled between his back legs is, like, massive. *And* barbed.

He has… a unique peen.

I wrench my gaze away.

Nope.

Not looking.

Not even when he obligingly shifts his big dragon body and unfurls his wings to give me a better view of his badass self. Yeah, he's definitely showing off. This guy's got plenty of ego to match his size.

Then again, so do I.

Maybe it's a dragon thing.

His head snakes closer, fiery eyes sweeping over me, from the wild mane of hair tumbling around my tits and halfway to my ass to my nipple rings and the nonexistent landing strip down below that I don't bother to cultivate. (Being a Brazilian girl, hygiene-wise, there's nothing there to cultivate.)

So, yeah, it's pretty much the Zara show down there. Well, nothing I can do about all that right now.

"My eyes are up here, big guy," I tell him. "And you better keep that tongue of yours to yourself. I mean it."

He puffs out twin jets of steam that warm my cold skin. Because, yeah, a Nevada night in February isn't, like, tropical. Once I calm down some from all this excitement, I'm gonna start shivering.

But the guy does swing his head up to meet my eyes. His pupils dilate to take me in. I tilt my head and hold his dragonish stare without flinching. Somehow.

When you're dealing with a predator, the key thing to remember is never show fear.

Only confidence.

Even when you don't exactly feel it.

The big lug ripples and wavers in my vision like a mirage. Then his edges get all blurry. He goes bright with a hot white light. So bright I have to close my eyes.

When I open them, there's a guy standing there.

It's definitely a relief not to be dealing anymore with the dragon. That thing coulda sneezed and blown me across the state line.

He's still taller than me, but that's a given. When you're only five foot two, everyone's taller than you. In his human form, he's got golden hair sweeping straight back from his forehead and falling halfway down his back and a cold cruel face that's all raking lines and angles and, holy fuck, fierce eyes like molten gold with those same slitted pupils as his dragon. This guy's gonna need to wear sunglasses or some kinda custom contacts or maybe weave some glamor magic to pass for normal.

Which has to be, you know, lonely.

His shoulders and arms are rangy with muscle and ropy with sinew, sun-bronzed skin stretched tight over all that sexy like he doesn't get enough to eat. Pale scars lick over his shoulders and biceps from behind like someone scourged the shit out of him with a cat o' nine tails or something a long time ago.

And he's naked.

Of course, he's naked.

Even though I virtuously keep my gaze *above* the waist.

"You wished for me to shift, yes?" His speech is low and guttural, like Vasili's Russian accent on steroids. "Tell me. Do I please my sovereign?"

He's careful with his words. Clearly this isn't his mother tongue (but I'm carefully not thinking about tongues, especially his, right now).

"Uh, depends." I clear my throat and sneak a peek at his hands, loosely balled at his sides. A glitter of gold leaks from one fist. He's still holding Xiao's medallion.

Which is now *my* medallion.

He clearly doesn't like my prevaricating about whether or not he pleases me. His eyes narrow to slices of molten fire and his brows bunch together. Which makes this guy look even more intense. His shoulders hunch and he looms over me.

"On what does my sovereign's pleasure depend?" he says, low and fierce.

He rolls his R's and hisses his S's like Lucius, but he's not Hungarian like my wolf shifter. Nope, this is the so-called Russian.

Which means he's somehow in cahoots with my so-called father.

I pull in a sharp breath. Under the old stink of spilled gas and sunbaked asphalt, the reek of musk and leather floods my Mogadon senses, spiked with the acrid bite of brimstone.

Fuck. That's his mating scent.

It's involuntary, so it's not like I can blame him for it, but that shit's pouring off his skin in waves.

Which makes me wonder if he can still smell my heat.

I take a step back to give us both some breathing space. That placement also lines him up nicely for my roundhouse kick.

Just in case I have to fight him.

"You wanna please me? You got something that belongs to me," I tell him, keeping my voice nice and level. "Hand it over. Then we'll talk."

Yeah, big guy. We'll talk about you being in cahoots with my dad. Same dad who just fucking tried to kill me, BTW.

"I belong to you in my entirety, my sovereign," he says gruffly, eyes burning into mine. "But I sense you are speaking of the artifact, yes?"

Whoa. I'm not like a fairytale queen, I don't demand fealty from my subjects, I barely even grasp yet what it means to be queen or have subjects. I've just barely accepted this whole queen-in-waiting concept at all after the last one—my brother's bitch fiancée Cybelle Aquarius—was murdered by the queen killer. Along with my asshole brother (which was no great loss, believe me).

Better just focus on the here and now.

"I'm talking about that medallion in your fucking fist. It's mine. Hand it over." I open my palm and hold it up between us.

He tilts his head like a raptor to study my outstretched hand. One corner of his mouth curls in a predatory grin. Because now he knows I want it, he has power over me.

But only until I take back what's mine.

Then I'll have the power.

"A powerful artifact, this," he muses softly, lifting the medallion to dangle on its chain between us. "I captured it when I captured you. I sensed its power from the roof."

I frown and shake my head. Because no one fucking *captured* me. Besides, Xiao's no warlock, and there's no way he's been wearing a magical artifact around his mortal neck all this time.

"It's just a necklace." I force a shrug. "Sentimental value."

His voice goes deep and rumbly. "Oh, it is far more than that. Trust me to know. I collect such treasures for my lair."

I'm tempted to make a grab for it, because he's dangling it between us like he's daring me to try, and I've never met a bet I won't take. But if I tip my hand like that and miss, he'll hold even more power in our little exchange. Besides, the concept of him having an actual lair packed with booty like Smaug in *Lord of the Rings* makes me curious.

About him.

Clearly he knows who I am. Because he's been calling me his sovereign in that quaint formal way of his. So that's another advantage he holds over me.

Time to tip the scales my way.

Eyes holding his, I saunter a slow step forward. A subtle ripple of tension rolls through the sinews under that sleek bronze skin, but that hint of a grin widens. He knows I'm up to something.

And I bet I just triggered his hunting instinct.

Idly he swings the medallion between us. The profile of Ferdinand of Aragon glimmers and winks in the streetlight like the old Spanish king is calling me.

Sovereign to sovereign.

But I wasn't born yesterday. I don't grab for it. What I do instead is draw in a slow breath of musk and leather and finally let my eyes wander over all that naked real estate on my shifter.

I mean, not my shifter. *The* shifter.

He's not streamlined like Vasili or tattooed like Ronin or gym rat buffed like Neo. This guy looks like he fought for his meals growing up and maybe still does. He's really young, not any older than I am for sure, which would make him twenty, tops. He's all suntanned skin stretched over wiry strength, the parallel slash of old claw marks raking his ribs (I can count every bone) and scoring the taut column of his abs.

And, whoa, his cock is… unique. In human *and* dragon form. Kinda barbed at the tip, I mean. It's forked like a devil's tail.

And he's definitely, um, endowed. His whole junk's thick and curving and jutting straight out.

Looks like he's really glad to see me.

The sight of that barbed cock lights up a pulse of heat between my legs that makes my pussy slick. It's the heavy throb of my mating heat, just days away, but there's a hot tight clutch of need in my uterus that's new.

And extra intense.

Like an ache that's dying to be filled.

Which is fucked up. The only passenger that hitches a ride in this uterus is my IUD, believe me. Because, sure, I'll eventually need to pop out a few witchlets to propagate the royal line. Maybe even more than a few, because all four arcane races are endangered.

For the shifters in particular—the Protean race—there are only a few of them… I mean *us*… left in existence.

But propagating the royal line's *way* in the future for me.

My gaze skates up the new guy's chest in a hurry, trips on the silver barbells piercing both nipples (did I mention I'm a sucker for pierced nipples?), and lands on his sexy smirk (because he totally caught me looking).

I'm in trouble with this guy.

I really am.

Or I would be, if I wasn't about to electrocute his dragon ass for taking what's mine and taunting me with it.

I swipe my tongue over my lips and watch his eyes ignite. My voice comes out low and husky. "What do I call you, big guy?"

"I am Maxim." He says it the Russian way, *Maxeem,* leaning hard into the second syllable, every guttural vowel rolling over his tongue. His shoulders straighten and his head lifts with pride. "Maxim Grigorievich Rasputin. I am the Sagittarius prince."

"Prince, huh?" The rest of the witching world calls it a scion, the heir to each of the original twelve witching families. The scion can be any gender (I'm the Gemini one), but they're typically the strongest witch with the purest genetics in each of the twelve clans. Anyway, I know from Vasili that these old Russian houses, with their Old World imperial blood, they do their own thing.

So I guess that makes this dude a prince.

Whatever.

"Well." I clear my throat. "Sounds like you know who I am."

I wanna hear him say it. And he doesn't disappoint.

He lowers that princely head so his hair spills forward around his face. "You are Zarina Mikhailovna Selene Gemini. You are the last of your kind, as I am the last of mine. You are my queen, as I am meant to be your king."

"Whoa." Despite wanting that medallion with a need that makes my palms itch, I take a big step back and fold my arms across my chest. Which also has the advantage of covering up my tits and the way my nipples are suddenly tight and tingling with heat.

It's unsettling, the way I'm reacting to him.

Definitely not something I want to advertise.

"Well, you're half right," I mutter, sounding sulky even to myself. "I'm your queen all right, at least I'm the queen-in-waiting, but I don't have a king right now. And no offense, but if I did? You'd have to stand in line."

Because I might be mated the old witching world way, the common law way, to all four of the warlocks who share my bed—we're all mated to each other, actually, we're a polycule, even though some of my guys are still navigating their way through that whole enemies-to-lovers dynamic and they haven't all fucked each other (yet).

But there's a whole lot more to this thing than me shacking up with four hot bi warlocks.

According to witching world law, I can legally marry all of them, because our queens are polyamorous. That's a special law they made just for us. The ruling royals. The more we all fuck, and the more we all like it, the better it's supposed to be for the whole witching world.

When our queens are weak, when they're celibate, when they're infertile, the witching world suffers. Which is a lot of responsibility riding on one vagina—currently the vagina of Messalina Aquarius, Cybelle's mom, the ruling queen—but it's one explanation for that whole extinction scenario.

Anyway, long story short, I haven't officially married anyone. Or made any sort of formal betrothal announcement.

And I won't, not for a good long while.

Because I'd kinda like to graduate first, you know? And I started late, so I'm only a freshman at the Icarus Academy.

Not that this guy needs to hear any of that right now.

"Give me that medallion, Maxim," I say flatly. "Then we'll talk."

His head lifts and his eyes fire. Somehow, I know it's because he likes hearing me say his name. Which gives me another little pulse of heat down below.

I tamp that shit right down, because me getting all sexed up for this dragon is a distraction I definitely don't need.

Then I watch with mounting anger while he loops *my* fucking medallion around his own fucking neck.

"I will gift it to you," he says, in his careful way, "after our mating flight. When your belly grows round and full with our clutch."

My mouth falls open with honest indignation. "What are you, brain dead? I already have a whole harem, big guy. My bed's pretty damn full. There's not, like, a vacancy."

His hard face turns sharp and cruel and stubborn. "Those puny men cannot break a dragon queen's heat. Only I, a male dragon, the last of my kind, can satisfy your need." He stalks closer. "This need I can smell even now, yes? You are perfuming this desert wind."

Well, shit, *that's* awkward.

My face heats up to scorching.

But I'm not about to get sidetracked. "Not looking for another mate right now. And I'm definitely not looking for a baby daddy."

He plants his hands on his hips and sneers.

This bastard fucking *sneers*.

"These lesser men you have taken to your bed will give way to me, their superior," he states, with a degree of certainty that's infuriating. "They will defer to me as the dominant male in your harem. In exchange for their deference, I will permit them to serve you… even to… service you… as is your sovereign right. But it is I who will rule at your side and fill your womb with my dragonets."

Is this guy for real? I honestly wonder if he's been smoking something.

"One," I announce, unfolding a finger that glitters with the opal polish I've been wearing all week in blatant defiance of the Academy's bullshit dress code. "I'm not looking for another mate, and neither are they. Two." I unfold another finger. "Even if we were? You and your my-way-or-the-highway ultimatums aren't exactly our type. Three." I add a third finger. "There's no one fucking *servicing* me, because we're all fucking equals. We're not really a harem in that traditional way. And four, I'm not about to start popping out babies—of *any* kind, much less freaking *dragonets*—while I'm still in school and simultaneously queening it and trying to figure out my shit. I'm literally twenty years old."

His brows rush together in a scowl.

Still, I can see he's fighting to sound reasonable (for him) and not lose his temper and go apeshit on the asphalt.

"You are young, yes," he says softly. "As I am young. Yet you have taken these others. These men who are lesser, who can never take wing beside you and mate with you among the clouds. Once you have experienced what only I can give you… the sublime pleasure of dragon mating dragon, the world cowering beneath you as you own the skies… I will be first among your mates. Then these others will know their place."

"Know their place, huh?" I snort out a grim chuckle. "You haven't met Vasili yet, have you?"

Vasili's more than the dominant alpha among my guys, he's even gotten our headmaster Lucius to accept his mating bite. (And, yeah, the two of them together are hot. As. Fuck.)

Actually, I'm kinda expecting Vasili and Ronin, who's clairsentient and so can sense my whereabouts with his Valyrian gifts (it's kind of a geolocation thing), to turn up right about now.

Even though I'm still feeling nothing in our bond.

Which is deeply disturbing.

Maxim's nostrils flare with disdain. "I know well of Vasili Romanov and his untraditional ways and his sinful passions. What witch or warlock does not? The queer son, exiled in disgrace, who is the scandal and the shame of his noble clan."

My mouth drops open in total fucking outrage.

"Hey." Now I get right up in his face, rising on tiptoe so I can glare at him properly. "Vasili's the biggest badass in the whole Mogadon race. He's the strongest warlock at Icarus. He's the Scorpio scion and he doesn't give a shit about his family and he's worth twenty of you, lizard brain. He's *everything*."

Color darkens the jut of this dragon's Russian cheekbones and his pupils slit with rage. His upper lip curls back to bare his teeth in a snarl. He doesn't seem to have permanent fangs like Vasili.

Of course, in dragon form, this guy's fangs are *way* bigger. In dragon form, he looks like he tears out throats with those saber-tooth tiger fangs of his.

"You fancy yourself to be in love with him, yes?" he growls.

"It's not some freaking fancy." I plant my hands on my hips, but he's still not listening.

"He is unworthy of you," he says, soft and savage. "Vasili Nikolaievich Romanov is my inferior. As are they all, to the last man. If these mates of yours will not accept this, if they will not know their place, then I will kill them. Just as I killed those men in the chopper who gave me offense."

I swear to fuck, if he doesn't stop threatening to kill my warlocks, I'm gonna do real damage.

Which reminds me of something else I've been meaning to raise.

"Yeah, about that." I poke a hard finger into his unyielding chest. "Those men back there. The ones you flambéed with your Godzilla breath? They were just dudes doing a gig. Some of them probably had kids and stuff."

"Meaning?" Looking curious, he cocks his head.

Sweet Jesus, the balls on this guy. It's all I can manage not to roll my eyes.

"*Meaning* you can't just go around killing people, Maxim."

His golden eyes go lidded. "I reserve for myself the right to go around killing these people who are trying to kill my mate, Zarina."

Clearly, we're not getting anywhere.

"It's Zara," I grit through my teeth. "And I'm running outta ways to say this. But let me try once more. I. Am *not*. Your mate. I'm *their* mate."

I figure the point bears repeating. Because he just doesn't seem to be getting it.

"Then I will kill them," he growls, low and guttural. That seems to be the point *he* thinks bears repeating. "All your so-called mates. Indeed, that way is most efficient. Losing your mates will bring on your superheat."

"My *superheat*?" I don't even know what the Sam Hell this guy's talking about. What is this, some dragon thing? Like the African savanna? Are we a pride of lions, with the new guy killing the competition so the female goes into heat? "Okay, listen up. You lay a single scaly claw on any of my mates, you big iguana, and I'm gonna electrocute your ass like you wouldn't believe. Am I your broodmare or your fucking queen?"

He looms over me like a force of nature and smolders, intense as fuck, while he stares into my eyes. "You are my universe and I am yours. There is no one on all this earth for me but you. We are the last of our kind. And I will prove this to you, my Zara. I will prove this here and now, my body with yours, to your utter satisfaction."

He reaches for me. Adrenaline shoots through every synapse in my already hyped-up body and a flood of my Mogadon pheromones spikes the air. And, just in case you're wondering, that's *not* my mating scent.

At least, not totally.

It's more like aggression.

He isn't asking. He's taking. And I'm not in the mood to tolerate that shit.

My fists sweep up by instinct, body twisting into a vicious sidekick that never lands.

Because a force of nature that's way more terrifying than this big lizard in a rage has just arrived.

That would be the force of nature called Vasili Romanov.

Not to mention the full force of Vasili's telekinesis, fueled by a thousand years of Mogadon genetics, going full Avenger on Maxim's ass.

With a flick of his hand, Vasili's witchcraft hurls Maxim Rasputin fifty feet backward through the air like a scrap of paper and crushes him flat against the gas station wall.

Where the shifter writhes, pinned against the wall a good five feet in the air. Somehow still breathing after an impact that could easily have killed him.

"Little Maximka," Vasili purrs, absolutely silken with menace. "*Privyet, malchik.* How long has it been, darling? Four years since our cozy seaside summer? And yet somehow not a thing in the world has changed. You still covet what's *mine*."

Maxim snarls at him like he's already in dragon form (which seems like a real possibility now that my alpha's on the scene and attacking him). Every ropy sinew in the shifter's naked body strains against that telekinetic hold Vasili's got clamped around him like a fist of iron.

But I've been on the receiving end of Vasili's telekinesis when he's Hulking out myself, and it's not exactly a situation you wiggle out of.

Let's just say this new guy's going nofuckingwhere.

"Romanov," Maxim growls, rolling his R's ferociously, eyes flaming, his dragon lurking in his voice. "Still you are a filthy skulking sneak who refuses to fight me fairly? Just as your ancestors slaughtered mine in shameful ambush. Release me and face me like a Russian."

Okay, I gotta give this guy some credit for moxie.

Vasili showed up out of nowhere and hurled Maxim all the way across the parking lot without laying a finger on the dude. My alpha's levitating fifteen feet off the ground for intimidation effect. And even dressed in his David Bowie Goblin King attire, long legs encased in heeled boots and breeches, sparkly coat draped over the corset laced around his lean body to such lethal effect, hair blowing in the wind and face chiseled out of ice and eyes absolutely wicked with intent… Vasili looks pretty fucking terrifying.

Half rock star, half pit viper.

That's my warlock.

If it was me pinned five feet off the ground against the gas station wall while this hooded snake reared over me with his fangs dripping venom, I'd be pissing myself.

"Hmmmm," Vasili murmurs, sublimely unimpressed by all this dragonish bluster. "Last time, as I recall, I turned the other cheek and overlooked your little temper tantrum so I wouldn't spoil my manicure. This time, *malchik*, I do believe I'll punish you."

Chapter Six
Vasili

Karma can be a vicious bitch.

Oh, you can trust me to know. I've always supposed I haven't seen the last of him. I'm talking about this so-called prince, this perfect paragon, this spoiled prick whose swaggering ego and tattling tongue cost me so dearly.

Four years ago, this wretched little worm cost me everything.

And I've been lurking and watching long enough just now from the darkness to ferret out precisely what new mischief he fancies he's brewing. This Rasputin cunt imagines he's going to swoop in and claim Zara like she's some sort of medieval virgin, exterminate the rest of us like cockroaches, then fuck my queen through her inconsolable grief.

Enter, stage left, that vicious bitch called karma.

Let's just say Maxim Rasputin owes me a *substantial* karmic debt.

Well, darling, it's payback time.

I'll confess it's simply delightful to be holding this bastard prince pinned to the grimy wall above the dumpster with the merest fraction of my telekinetic strength. Purely for effect, I'm levitating high enough to intimidate any fool with eyes (because you don't get a second chance to make a first impression).

I hadn't come into my power that summer our grotesque families spent together at sea, with little Maximka and his odious clutch of brothers terrorizing the crew and kissing my father's aristocratic ass and polluting our gaudy superyacht with the sulfurous reek of dragon.

Let's just say Vasili 2.0 should come as *quite* the nasty shock to this rotten little imp of a Rasputin who tried his piddling best to ruin me.

He glares at me now from where I've got him pinned, naked as the day he was hatched (I suppose, not having been there, you know) like he's going to breathe fire and set me alight the way he did those hapless Gemini buffoons in the chopper. And because I too have eyes, I can hardly avoid noticing, as he writhes and strains quite futilely against my witchcraft, that my boyhood nemesis has grown into *quite* the specimen of manhood. He's all smoldering intensity and scowling menace and ropy muscle bunching and flexing under that Black Sea suntan.

Then there's that absolutely intriguing forked dragon cock whose angles and length I'd normally be dying to explore with my tongue—

"Fight me like a man, Romanov," he snarls in his gutter English, presumably for Zara's benefit, since he and I obviously grew up speaking Russian.

This bit of bluster on his part effectively shatters my fantasy, which is really just as well. Our harem might be polyamorous, yes, but the five of us are entirely exclusive. We're only with each other.

And Maxim Rasputin is definitely *not* invited to the prom.

Apparently the lizard king doesn't care for my eye roll, since he bares his teeth at me in a dragonish grimace and tediously repeats himself. "Fight me fairly, coward, I dare you! Fight me for the right to rule her bed."

"Oh, dear God," I murmur.

Zara's eloquent snort makes me smirk. She's sauntering across the parking lot to say hello, also naked and owning it in that ballsy way of hers I absolutely adore.

"*Do* join the twenty-first century if you can, Maximka," I drawl. "Zara rules her own bed. I merely fuck her, and everyone else, in it."

Oh, very well, perhaps I'm fibbing just a bit. I haven't *actually* fucked Neo Mercury (yet), either in our bed or out of it, although not for lack of trying, I assure you. We two were deadly rivals until Zara came along and claimed us both. Not to mention Mercury was an actual virgin until first Zara and then Ronin quite thoroughly deflowered him.

For some reason (admittedly a rather good one given our shared history), my former enemy still doesn't seem to trust me.

It's as though he suspects I have a vicious streak, darling.

Can you imagine?

"You?" Dripping contempt, the dragon's flaming eyes rake over me, looking entirely unimpressed with my scrumptious couture. "Permit me to say, I have my doubts. Do you forget I have seen firsthand that you prefer a man to a woman in your bed?"

I give him an extra squeeze for that impertinence.

In fact, it's all I can manage not to grind his bones.

Four years ago, it was little Maximka, spying on me going down on the Italian stallion captain of the family yacht, then tattling to my homophobic father about my naughty exploits, that got the poor captain fired and me shipped off to the Academy in disgrace.

Fuck you very much for that, *malchik*.

"Haven't you heard? I'm bisexual." I take a violent satisfaction in divulging this tidbit, even though the label still feels a bit odd.

Until Zara came along, I was quite happily convinced I was gay.

She's still the only woman I've ever wanted. The only woman I ever will want, I strongly suspect—but I'm hers *completely*. I'm her alpha. I'm her snake. I'm the dismay and the terror of all her enemies. I call the shots in our harem (mostly) when she isn't doing it herself, which makes me a sort of unofficial king in the witching world, even if our queen and I haven't actually married.

If I'm being honest (a phenomenon you should enjoy while it lasts), I'm more than obsessed with Zara.

I'm dangerously in love with her.

But that's a secret so dangerous I only share it within the group.

Hearing now that I've lost my gay boy gold card due to my recent foray into bisexuality, the dragon blinks. His brow furrows in surprise.

Well, join the club on that one, Rasputin.

"This is not convenient," he mutters after a bit. His cold Slavic features shift from cruelty to disgruntlement.

"I'm terribly sorry to inconvenience you," I sniff, giving him another good telekinetic squeeze to amuse myself.

"Still," he grunts, panting a bit from the atmospheric pressure I'm inflicting, "I am beyond thankful you never wedded my sister."

I'm gratified to hear I've winded the brute with my fit of pique. Although I'm definitely squeezing, I'm careful not to close his airway (even if I do enjoy a bit of breath play from time to time). If he feels truly threatened, the wretch will surely shift, and I'm not at all certain I can hold him and all that reptilian mass and fury if he does.

"That makes two of us." I suppress a delicate shudder at the thought of his bitch sister (who's still single, incidentally, for a reason). *That* was supposed to be the unappealing climax to our lovely summer at sea. A fairytale wedding to unite the witching world's two Russian clans, the Scorpio and the Sagittarius, which of course I utterly spoiled by being gay.

Or so I earnestly believed at the time.

Until Zara.

The dragon scowls at my little jab just beautifully. He's amusing to torment, this one. In fact, tormenting Maxim Rasputin may just become my new favorite hobby.

By now, Zara's prowling past, and his head swivels to follow her like she's got the poor boy's nose tied to a string.

This terror of the skies is an apex predator.

Yet he's positively riveted on the force of nature that's our queen.

It's a preoccupation I can surely understand, because Zara's delectable at all times, but especially when she's naked. She's tiny and curvy with absolutely gorgeous breasts, all pert and pouty and crying out to be suckled, the most delicious pink nipples pierced by silver rings it drives her utterly mad to have tormented, the prettiest cunt you've ever seen, and she hasn't entirely lost the string bikini tan lines she picked up reef-diving the Red Sea coast in Egypt over the winter before the Academy sank its claws into her.

While the dragon's so nicely distracted by our succulent morsel of a queen, I also seize the opportunity to appreciate *his* nudity.

Admittedly, that dragon's put on plenty of muscle since the last time I saw him when he was a scrawny, scowling, skinny scrap of a brat three years my junior, absolutely *green* with envy because I have a father and he doesn't. The dragon carries most of that new muscle in his shoulders and biceps, with a bit left over for those sinewy thighs. I'll confess (secretly) that the lean column of abdominal muscle and that deep pelvic V he's exposing look positively lickable.

And, oh, have I mentioned? I'm more than a bit intrigued by that barbed dragon cock.

Still, I find myself frowning.

He's half-starved (don't they feed him?), and it looks as though his brothers have been at him with those razor claws and teeth of theirs, judging by the scoring of old scars that lick across his hide. They're only wyverns, his brothers, not proper dragons at all. Rather like venomous worms with stunted wings that can barely lift the wretched creatures aloft. Oh, they flutter about and spray lethal poison like an absolute menace, but proper flight is beyond them.

My own levitation skills are far superior.

Amid the general decline of the arcane races, the dragon shifters are among the most endangered. They're poised on the very edge of extinction. Their bloodline is so diluted with earthbound mortal DNA that most so-called dragons can only shift to wyverns. It's rather sad, really, that this once-mighty line has been reduced to *that*.

Still, the Rasputin brood were always vicious little pricks, and they always hunted in a swarm. Maxim was the runt of the litter, they bullied him relentlessly, and I might actually have felt sorry for him that summer if he weren't such an insufferable shit.

I suppose the first time he shifted and revealed his dragon, the worm turned with a vengeance.

Because it's he and not his big brothers who was ultimately named the prince.

That makes him the ruling heir of the Sagittarius clan.

Of course, I saw him filling the skies tonight above the Double Gemini. You could hardly have missed him (which, given all these mortals lurking about with their digital devices, is going to be a real PR problem for those spin doctors in the Arcane Senate).

No matter how you spin it, in dragon form, he's a monster.

I find I'm still watching him, in fact I can scarcely seem to look away… for some reason. As for him, *he* can scarcely seem to look away from the saucy sway of Zara's spankable ass as she saunters over to greet me properly.

He's still staring when the deep-throated roar of a Harley shatters the desert night.

My gaze veers from the dragon to the motorcycle peeling into the parking lot in a spray of gravel. My glower gives way to a predatory grin. When the rider pulls up, cuts the engine, and wrenches off his helmet to glare at me, I can't help purring with appreciation.

My, my, look who's in a temper.

My boyfriend is absolutely smoldering. Ronin's silky long hair is disheveled, color darkens his cheekbones, his talented but mutinous mouth is scowling, and his amber eyes are burning like flambeaux.

If he's still in this incendiary mood when I rail him later, he's going to set our sheets on fire.

"You couldn't bloody wait two ticks while I got the blooming bike?" he snarls at me, toeing down the kickstand and slinging a leg over the seat so he's standing to confront me. He's still wearing his Kylo Ren tunic and breeches, and suddenly all I can think about is how hot he's going to make our little queen playing Kylo when he fucks her.

"Sorry, darling," I murmur, unrepentant. "There's not much point having levitation skills if one can't keep up properly with the flying worm who's gone winging off into the night with one's queen, is there? Besides, I knew you'd track me with your clairsentience, clever boy."

For the moment, he utterly ignores my sweet compliment and my faux apology (an impertinence I'd rarely tolerate, but I'll overlook it this once because he's striding straight to Zara). Neither one of us much liked it when we lost her in our link.

His long legs devour the distance between them while he peels the tunic over his head. He drops the garment over her lightning-blue hair.

She flashes him an appreciative grin and tugs the tunic over her curves, the hem kissing her thighs. Then she rises on tiptoe to wind her arms around his neck. His hands lock around her hips to drag her close.

He bends to claim her mouth in a brutal kiss.

Beneath my breeches, my naughty cock sits straight up and pants like a dog in heat.

My queen's sexy as fuck, her heat's looming, *and* she's hot for my boyfriend. I can actually smell her slick under the creamy roses and vanilla of her Mogadon mating scent. And now Ronin's naked too from the waist up, all tawny skin and flexing muscle and that mane spilling down his corded back.

I float gently to the ground so I can appreciate the two of them properly.

And I'm not the only one who's looking.

Well, well.

Little Maximka's about to combust with wrathful jealousy. In fact, it's just barely possible that he's eye-fucking *both* of them. I've always wondered (when I bother to consider him at all) if the real reason he was so mortally offended to find me fellating the Italian stallion, way back when, was because little Maximka was itching to mount… oh, whatever his name was… the same Roman stud I was riding all summer.

Looks like I might have been right on the money.

Not that either of our Russian Orthodox families would ever have tolerated that sort of thing. Mine haven't even spoken to me since the day they learned I was gay and thus *defective* and packed me off hastily in disgrace on the next plane to the Academy.

It's not that I minded being rejected and abandoned and shipped off like that by my mortified parents. Just whisked half a world away in a mad scramble, an embarrassing secret best tucked out of sight. If I weren't an only child with promising genetics and every indication of powerful witchcraft, no doubt they'd have disinherited me entirely.

I've always told myself good riddance.

Fortunately, tonight I have far more enjoyable matters than my cold and loveless parents to command my full attention.

Particularly when Zara surfaces from having Ronin's wrathful tongue shoved halfway down her throat. He's still pissy with her, ever since she foolishly tried sneaking off the island without us (as if!) to confront her odious ex alone.

Now she sashays over to me.

I'm profoundly aware of the dragon's burning stare shifting to me. I wrap a possessive arm around my girl's waist and tuck her up tight against my side. She rises on her sparkly toes (I painted hers when she painted mine, it's one of our little rituals) and nuzzles my cold cheek with her hot mouth.

I'd really like to lean in for a proper kiss, but I've still got this dragon to manage, and I can't risk getting distracted. Truly, the heat rising from her soft skin and Hollywood curves as she snuggles up against me is enough of a distraction. She and Lucius are both getting ready to go into heat again—which is apparently to be a monthly occurrence, thanks to those mating bites I inflicted on both of them.

It's a lot for me to manage as well. Yes, I'm part shifter (hence the mating bites), but that's a part of our family legacy the Romanovs have always fiercely shunned. I'm still learning my limits and the rules.

So that I can thoroughly shatter them, of course.

In any event, I'm Zara's alpha. Tonight I can barely manage to keep my hands off her.

Ronin's watching this performance, so I beckon him over with a curled finger and a sultry smirk. I fully expect him to balk, but Zara's taken the edge off his vile temper. He's used to indulging my spiteful whims, and he prowls over with the hint of a grin lurking on his luscious lips. Of course, he too knows the dragon is watching. In fact, Maxim's still darting glances at my boyfriend's sculpted physique (which *is*, admittedly, impressive). I particularly love that dragon tattoo spewing black flames across Ronin's chest.

Because we have an audience and I'm a bitch, it gives me even more pleasure than usual to snake an arm around Ronin's feral heat and drag my tongue down his throat.

He growls under my touch and wraps a hand around my cock.

I arch into his wicked touch, those knowing fingers sliding up and down my shaft at exactly the right pace and pressure to steal my soul one stroke at a time. Beside me, Zara's heat rises and her breath quickens. Her arms coil around my waist.

"Going to fuck both of you so bloody hard tonight," Ronin groans in my ear. "You're ready for me right now, aren't you, love?"

The dragon snarls with jealousy and my cock pulses with heat. My hips twitch with the drive to rock into Ronin's grip and fuck his fist exactly as he's inviting. My balls are already drawn up tight and swollen. I'm simply aching to feel the hot lick of Zara's tongue.

Christ, I'd love nothing better than to fuck both of them to a screaming climax right here in this parking lot and make Maxim Rasputin watch.

But my casting hand, which I have curled in a fist against Ronin's back, is starting to tingle. That means the dragon's fighting me, he wants out, and even for a warlock as powerful as I am, I can't hold him immobilized forever.

"First things first." Although it nearly kills me to do it, I shift away from this captivating hand job Ronin is delivering and try not to breathe in quite so much of that intoxicating hit of pheromones my queen's kicking out. "What shall we do with our scaly friend?"

Zara's head swivels toward the creature and her face turns thoughtful. "Lower him down. And, um, Vasili? *Not* in the dumpster."

"Spoilsport." I pout. (She knows me so well.)

But I oblige her with a sigh.

A subtle gesture with my casting hand lowers the surly dragon to the asphalt. Still, I keep a good telekinetic hold on him as Zara slips out of my grasp and strolls over. The brute watches her close in, his face feral and disreputable as a damn alley rat, gaze narrowed and nostrils flared.

My, that lovely cock of his is absolutely rigid. If he were literally anyone else, I'd definitely saunter over there myself and steal a taste. There's something about the notion of tying Maxim Rasputin spreadeagled to my bedposts and sucking him off until he bucks into my mouth and cries out my name and begs me hoarsely to finish him that makes me positively savage.

Ronin moans and twines his sinewy frame around me, because of course he's reading my mind. His thick cock is pulsing against my thigh. He's practically dry-humping me, because he too is very nearly in heat.

Of course, it's Lucius who bit him, allegedly by mistake. (If you say so, darling.)

As for myself, I don't need to bite Ronin to make him wild with wanting me.

Yes, he's my boyfriend. But he's an insatiable manwhore, I like to indulge his appetites, and we all quite happily fuck him.

Hurry up and finish with that dragon, I send to my queen through our mating bond. *I intend to see Ronin ride your naughty mouth tonight until you choke.*

Ronin growls and bites my earlobe with those sharp teeth of his, breath rough and eager in my ear. Of course he's sharing this pornographic fantasy, and he's already fully on board.

Alas, the effect is totally wasted on Zara, who's out of the link again.

And suddenly I grasp the significance of that trinket around the dragon's neck. It's a nullifying object—a null, according to the Magical Objects textbook in our senior seminar. And the strain of witchcraft this particular object nullifies is obviously telepathy.

It's the only plausible explanation for why Zara drops out of the link every time she's near it.

Don't ask me how Zara's unmagical mortal got his grabby little hands on such a thing, or why he's been wearing it so compulsively around his mortal neck.

Zara stops before the dragon's taut and trembling frame. Clearly he's burning to touch her, or for her to touch him. Good God, after the show we just gave him, if she laid a finger on him, she'd get him off in approximately two pumps.

If it even took that long.

Deftly she rises on tiptoe to lift the medallion from the dragon's neck. Being Zara, she looks straight into his face while she does it. Since I'm standing behind her, I can't see much, but I can clearly visualize her expression.

She's giving that dragon her *don't fuck with me* look.

He smolders back at her like he's going to light her on fire with his eyes. If ever a man looked like he wanted to fuck a girl blind, that's the look Maxim Rasputin is wearing right now. He's positively straining to reach her.

Straining hard enough that my casting hand is burning with the effort to hold him.

And it's hard to imagine my queen is unaffected. Christ, when he looks like that, I'm half tempted to fuck him myself.

She drops his bauble over her own wild mermaid head. The accursed thing settles between her breasts like those Spanish conquistadors made it just for her. She clasps her hands behind her back (possibly so she won't be tempted to touch anything else that belongs to the dragon) and studies him with her teal head tilted. "How you doing, big guy?"

Well. The spigot opens and the words simply pour out.

"This night is not the end between us, my Zara. This night is our beginning. And I swear, when we meet again, I will slaughter him," he growls like an absolute philistine. "I will slaughter Vasili Romanov for daring to touch what is *mine*."

"Tut, tut," I sigh. "How tedious."

"And what about Ronin?" My queen's voice is deceptively sweet, but I know her, and she's ruthless. "Are you going to slaughter him too?"

The dragon's gaze knifes to Ronin, and the flash of raw hunger in his cruel face betrays him.

Damn if that smoking look isn't so potent it gives me an instant boner.

"It is your right as sovereign to have many mates." Maxim's tongue swipes over his lower lip. Which, admittedly, gives me a bit of a frisson. Despite all the history between us, there's simply no denying it.

The man's grown up sexy as fuck.

"I will… I will take that one also," he mutters at last, his slitted eyes on fire for *my* fucking boyfriend. "To share our bed."

And there it fucking is. Certain proof, not merely suspicion, that this spoiled prick who did his level best to replace me in my father's nonexistent affections and then destroy me is more than a bastard.

He's also a coward and a hypocrite.

His sneaking slyness and his tattling tongue got me shunned and all but excommunicated by my wretched parents for the very same thing he wants himself.

Fuck.

Even if he isn't entirely aware of his own desires (which seems all too likely), and even if he would be mortally offended if I ever let him in on the secret, it appears our little Maximka likes the D.

My blood sizzles with an unexpected spurt of wrath. I bare my teeth to expose the unpleasant shifter fangs I never asked for and can't retract in an intimidation display I can't suppress. Then I clench the fist of my casting hand until the scaly bastard grunts and glares.

Speechless (for once) with fury, I glare right back.

Ensconced by my side, precisely where he belongs, Ronin voices a scornful snort and says loud enough for dragonish ears to hear, "Good luck with that, mate. Before you climb into my bed for a proper shagging, dragon, you can start with an apology for that cosh on the noggin. My blooming head's still pounding."

Zara pivots from her own stare-down with the brute to gaze at Ronin, her bubblegum pink lips falling open with indignation. It's a reaction I'm viciously delighted to see, because it's a highly effective counterweight to all that sexy the dragon's cranking out.

"Oh. My. God. You fucking *hit* him? What, from behind?" To my considerable pleasure, my queen gets right in the dragon's grille and jabs him in the chest with an outraged finger. "What is *wrong* with you?"

"He is rumored to be the best of all the fighters at Icarus. When I came to you, my sovereign, I needed him to be not present." Maxim smolders down at her, all fierce intensity and imperial Russian ego (trust me to know). "Be thankful I did not kill him."

Ronin chuffs out a grim chuckle, because he knows perfectly well just how our Zara's going to react to a statement like that.

Even my own aggravation ratchets back a notch. It certainly doesn't take a rocket scientist to discern that Maxim's come to Vegas a-courting. But he's going about the entire affair so ineptly that, truly, he's dooming his own cause with our little queen with no particular persuasion required on my part.

What.

So.

Ever.

"Okay, big guy." Pointedly she glances at her wrist, despite the fact that she lost her favorite dive watch, along with every stitch of clothing she was wearing, when she shifted. "You have two minutes to make me like you. Two minutes *tops*. Then I'm outta here."

"And let's keep our performance G-rated, shall we?" I murmur, dripping with spite.

God knows this derelict gas station's seen more than enough X-rated activity for one night, thanks to this priapic dragon with his furious erection.

For the first time all night, Maxim Rasputin actually looks uncertain.

He lowers his savage head (as much as I'll allow) and looks up at her from under his brows. "Saving your life when you fell from the roof… this was not sufficient?"

"Yeah, I appreciate it, but I woulda figured out that whole flying thing myself," she says, with that absolute confidence I so adore in my mate. Truly, who knew this little queen would turn out to be such a badass? "The way I see it, breaking my fall doesn't even start to make up for the fact you're in cahoots with my freaking dad, you asshole. And don't even think about denying it. His goons mentioned you—the Russian. They saw you as an ally."

"You wanted your revenge on the… Oriental, yes?" he says, with no apparent awareness that the term in English gives hideous offense. Of course, he barely speaks the language and is blissfully ignorant of nuance, so it's likely he meant no harm and one should make allowances, *et cetera*.

But naturally this dash of inadvertent bigotry does nothing to aid his cause.

"We don't use that word around here," Zara informs him in a tone that brooks no nonsense. "Xiao's Asian."

"The Asian, yes." He frowns and ducks his head, looking for an eyeblink like he's actually embarrassed by his caveman English. That moment of self-awareness passes quickly, of course. "Mick Gemini summoned the… Asian… because he wanted to lure you out and take his revenge on you, this daughter who defies him. And I myself have wanted nothing more from the very moment I learned of your existence, my sovereign, but to claim you as my mate. If I made this, how do you say, devil's bargain to win you and pleasure you and protect you from all your enemies on this earth, for this I make no apology."

He's so earnest and so intense about all this that even I'm reluctantly impressed (despite myself).

Zara plants her hands on her hips and peers up at him, her painted toes tapping.

"Let me make sure I get this straight," she says slowly.

Dear God, she's going to utterly eviscerate him. My own toes are already curling inside my ravishing boots in anticipatory delight.

"First my dad set me up by dangling Xiao as bait." She pauses barely long enough to let the dragon nod. "No offense, but I kinda figured that part out on my own. So you hooked up with my dad to get in on the action and, what, protect me from him?"

The unsuspecting idiot nods again.

Now my queen's voice acquires a wicked edge that's utterly delicious.

"But you planned from the start to stab my dad in the back." Her hip cocks and her head tilts. "Was that whole betrayal scenario gonna go down before or after you killed my warlocks?"

"Ah, well…" Far too late, the buffoon senses danger, but Zara has the bit seized between her sharp little teeth, and now there's no stopping her.

Truly, I could almost feel sorry for this dragonish fool of a Rasputin, if not for our unfortunate history.

Striding back and forth before him, Zara lets her voice rise. "Then, once you buried that knife in my dad's back and gave it a good twist, you were gonna toss me over your scaly shoulder and fly me off to Siberia to start making babies? Which would also get me expelled from the Academy and deprive me of my magical education, possibly dooming the entire witching world to extinction. Because, you know, I'm supposed to save it and all and I'm still not sure how, but apparently none of that matters in dragon land." She stops and spins to face him. "What part of all that's supposed to make me like you?"

The dragon strains against his bonds until the cords stand out in his neck. He bares his teeth to push out the words in a tone like shredded silk dragged over gravel.

"When your heat rises and your body burns for what only I can give you, when you take wing in your first mating flight and I hunt you among the clouds and bury my dragon cock deep inside you until you scream with pleasure, when I lavish you with every treasure your dragon heart can possibly desire and allow these lesser mates of yours to breathe and share our bed to please you, when we restore glory to our failing race and fill the skies with our magnificent offspring…" His voice plunges to a raspy whisper that scrapes against my senses. "Then you will like me well enough, my Zara."

Well, *fuck*. Admittedly, even I'm feeling frisky after that declaration. This dragon may be a prick, but damn if he isn't a sexy one.

Fortunately, Zara *really* doesn't seem to like him.

"Yeah, no, not doing that," she snorts, completely unimpressed with him. "Like I said before, there isn't a vacancy in my harem. And right now? It's fucking freezing out here and we got a plane to catch. So it's been funsies, but going now." Unexpectedly, she pivots to face me. "Do your thing, Goblin King."

By which the little queen means I'm allowed to choke him unconscious so we can finally be free of him.

A lick of malice lashes through me. I bare my pearly whites in a vicious grin.

But, as I've already observed, this flying iguana will shift in a flash if he feels threatened. Thus, with regret, I leave his precious airway unmolested.

Instead, I trot out a new trick I've been practicing on the sly. A tiny gesture with the index finger of my casting hand closes his carotid artery, just for a blink.

The dragon slumps senseless in my telekinetic grip. I'd like to drop him, but from deference to Zara's tender sensibilities, I lower his unconscious frame gently (for me) to the asphalt. Still, she bends to check his pulse, which causes the hem of Ronin's tunic to play peekaboo with the lush curves of her derrière.

When she twists around to shoot me an appreciative glance, she totally catches us both staring.

"Not bad, Goblin King." Gently she smooths a swath of hair out of the dragon's eyes, then tugs Ronin's tunic over her ass with a knowing smirk. "Not bad at all. What exactly did you just do to him?"

"It's like the Vulcan death grip without hands, darling." I preen under her admiring gaze. "I trust you're suitably impressed. Of course, that dragon will pop up any minute cursing my name and breathing fire and vowing some tedious but bloody vengeance, so I do advise we not linger."

Right on cue, a cell phone buzzes in the desert night. It's not mine, Zara's hasn't been working all night, and the dragon is still naked, so obviously it's not his.

Ronin slides the phone from his pocket and checks his voicemail with a frown.

"Best get our arses back to the plane right smartly," he says at last, tucking the thing away and addressing both of us, since Zara's finally stopped fussing over that damn dragon and abandoned him on the asphalt to rejoin us, her proper mates. "Neo's been ringing me up all night, and he's definitely not feeling very charitable toward any of us just now. But that last message? That one was from Lucius."

Despite my general badassery, my gut tightens with a feeling that's uncomfortably akin to guilt. If pressed, I can't deny feeling a bit of a qualm.

To tell the truth, this entire situation is rather... delicate.

I may be Lucius' alpha since I persuaded/seduced/forced him to take my mating bite in a fit of uncontrollable lust for my wolf shifter headmaster that was suppressed and denied by both of us for far too long. But our relationship is considerably more complex than mere lust. In the privacy of our bed, Lucius Aries might beg for my cock and take it in all the ways like a champion. (I fucking adore that about him, and I positively dote on him when he does it.)

But in the cold light of day where I'm simultaneously a graduating senior and a probationary assistant professor at the Icarus Academy, Lucius is my teacher and my superior.

And judging by the tightness of Ronin's face and that muscle ticking in his jaw, Lucius really isn't very happy with any of us.

I lace my fingers through Ronin's and lift his hand to my lips to kiss each of his knuckles one by one. Just as I'm Lucius' alpha, Lucius is Ronin's. (Yes, I know it's all very complicated, but do try to keep up.)

This simply means it's unsettling for Ronin when Lucius is angry.

"Shit," Zara sighs, brows drawing together in a worried pucker. She wraps a comforting arm around Ronin's waist and cuddles up against him. Lucius is also one of her alphas, of course, so she knows exactly how he's feeling. "Lucius is pissed as fuck, isn't he?"

"You don't know the fucking half of it," Ronin says grimly, tucking her up against his side for mutual comfort. "Yeah, he's ticked at you, Zara, for risking your royal behind for a childish prank—his words, not mine—and he's ticked at me for running off halfway round the world without telling him, especially when I'm about to go into this blooming heat."

His gaze slices sideways to pin me. "But he's particularly ticked at you, love. Says if you're not standing on the carpet in his office in the crypt submitting your professorial arse for discipline within the next twelve hours, we needn't bother coming back at all, because the Dean's going to give your probationary hide the boot and expel all three of us for violating the fucking Academy Codex. And if for some reason the Dean doesn't promptly initiate the process, Lucius will bloody well do it himself, because you're faculty now and he counted on you to know better."

That flutter in my tummy isn't getting any better, especially since I haven't quite swallowed the bitter aftertaste of that cocktail of family memories, spiked with rejection and rage.

"Oh, dear." I make light of the affair, but I know I'm not fooling anyone, least of all myself. "Seems the poor thing *is* rather vexed. I suppose we'll have to kiss off our front-row Cirque de Soleil tickets and penthouse suite at the Bellagio and have the pilot fuel up the plane, darlings."

"Guess so," Zara says with a sigh. "I really hope Lucius isn't too pissed. I already know Neo's upset. He takes this fated mate stuff so seriously, you know? I'll definitely tell them both it was all my idea and I tried to go without you, so you were basically forced to come along to protect me. If they're gonna be pissed at anyone, it might as well be with me." She fiddles with the coin around her neck. "Anyway, we got what we came for."

"Sweet revenge?" I purr.

And I'm not referring to her revenge against Xiao.

I'm referring to mine against my boyhood nemesis. It's a comeuppance that dragon richly deserves.

"And then some," Ronin mutters, with a glance at the sleeping Maxim. "A bloody dragon shifter. Fuck."

With any luck, we'll be wheels up and well on our way back to Icarus by the time that dragon wakes in a foaming rage.

Because when he does, he'll be hunting for my blood.

Chapter Seven
Ronin

This Kylo costume's a right proper pain. The long black coat belted round my waist flares dramatically with every step. And the gold-and-black pharaoh mask that looked so intimidating in the bathroom glass wreaks bloody havoc on my peripheral vision when I'm actually moving.

I feel ridiculous stalking the corridors of the Academy's private jet like this. I can barely imagine fucking with this blasted thing on.

But fuck if I won't do it to get my girl off.

She's been calling me Adam (for the blooming actor, I finally realized) since the literal night she and I met and hate-fucked in that penthouse loo in Singapore.

Well, she can call me Kylo tonight. Fact is, she can call me anyfuckingthing. With the way my heat's looming, I'm going to rail her so hard she won't be able to walk afterward.

I'm going to ruin her.

Anticipation licks through me and quickens my breath. I'm sporting a boner shoved up against my trousers well before I pitch up outside the in-flight library where my girl's been holed up since we took off for Icarus.

I ease my head round the lintel to scope out the scene, because I fully intend to make a proper entrance.

In the warm glow of a single lamp, Zara's curled up barefoot on the oxblood leather couch in yoga pants and a vintage rock tee shirt, with her mermaid hair in pigtails. She's got one of the antique witching tomes from the bookcase spread open across her lap and a dozen others scattered round her on the sofa.

Well, no worries. I'll respect her studies. At least, I'll not disturb those books she's mucking about with.

Instead, I'll bend her over and fuck her to a noisy climax across the expansive surface of Lucius' leatherbound desk.

She can hardly avoid hearing the thought either, since I just bloody lob it at her like a sex grenade.

Zara lifts her head from her book and gives my getup a good long look. Her gaze slides slowly down my body and lingers on my eager cock. A sultry grin curls her lips and her eyes heat to a turquoise simmer.

"Hold that thought, Adam," she says, all low and husky. "I just wanna finish this chapter first."

"You don't know the power of the Dark Side," I tell her, sliding all the way into view to give her the full effect. "But I bloody well intend to show you. Face down over Lucius' desk. Right bloody now."

Color flares in her cheeks under her California tan and her teeth sink into the plump bow of her lower lip. Bollocks, I'm ready to bite it for her. She's so blooming gorgeous, even in yoga pants and pigtails, just looking at her makes my chest tight.

But she still hasn't put aside that blasted book.

Her lashes sweep down and her gaze drops to the grimoire spread across her lap. "I'm boning up on dragon shifters. Figured I should get a little smarter, seeing as how dragons exist outside the confines of Middle Earth—like, seriously, who knew?—and how I am one now. One of the very few, apparently."

Now she sounds pensive, and she's certainly entitled given what all went down tonight. At least she's tucked that blasted medallion away, like Vasili told her, in the lead-lined box in Lucius' desk that nullifies magical objects.

Which means all three of us are linked again. Which, for me, is a comfort. I'm Valyrian and the strongest telepath of the lot. I'm missing the fuck out of Lucius and Neo, but Vasili and I are linked so tightly he's always in my head.

And now I've got my bond back with Zara.

Truth is, my noggin's still aching from being sucker-punched by that fucking dragon, though there's a potion on board that's nixed the worst of it. I pull off my mask with a sigh of relief, since clearly my girl's not ready to be rogered into a sex coma by Kylo Ren just yet, and roll my head on my shoulders to loosen up a bit.

"We'll help you sort through this clusterfuck tomorrow, we all will," I tell her with as much confidence as I can muster. "When we're back home right and tight with Neo and Lucius."

Of course, that's assuming Neo and Lucius are inclined to forgive us taking off like this without them. Assuming they're inclined to forgive Zara for putting herself and the entire witching world at such phenomenal risk for the sake of what she fancies to be revenge, though it was actually more like rebellion against that royal cage she's trapped in. Assuming we're not all expelled for slipping past the wards without permission, lying to that earnest young pilot and the unsuspecting Academy flight crew, abusing the fuck out of Vasili's spiffy new faculty bennies, and basically stealing the Academy jet.

And assuming we don't get called to account for that unfortunate incident in the sky over downtown Vegas, which the Arcane Senate and the fucking AIB must surely be scrambling even now to cover up. That lot might even call in the queen—I'm talking the sitting queen, that Grade A bitch Messalina Aquarius, not Zara who's the queen-in-waiting—for damage control.

That PR disaster over the Double Gemini was rightly the blooming dragon's fault.

Still…

I've got to admit our chances of being forgiven by our infuriated mates for the part we played in all that mayhem don't sound all that promising, based on that icy message Lucius left on my mobile. We haven't got working internet at the Academy, because the island wards fuck with electronics, but there's an ancient rotary phone in our *domus*. That's how Lucius rang me up.

It's not a good sign, actually, that Lucius hasn't rung up Vasili.

Maybe the Dean will fire Vasili from the faculty, but still let him finish out the semester and graduate as a student. Not that it'll help much, because then he'll still have to leave. Only students and faculty are allowed past the wards onto Academy grounds. Zara's still a freshman, I'm just a sophomore, Lucius is the headmaster of our residential college and deeply committed to his job, Neo has more than a year yet to go, and having to choose between his fated mate and his precious education would bloody destroy that sweet lad.

But none of us can survive without Vasili.

Not anymore.

We're a polycule. That means we belong together.

But he'll have to leave once he graduates if he's fired.

If he's also expelled, he'll have to leave immediately.

Well, nothing much I can do about that looming crisis just now, is there? It's not easy, but I push all that angst to one side, cock my head, and rivet my queen with a smoking look.

"Think you should put that book aside and come to bed, love," I growl. "Assuming you don't fancy being fucked on the desk."

"I will in just a bit. I promise." The vixen shoots me a look under those long lashes that's brimming with heat and mischief. "Don't worry. I know you have a galaxy to terrorize. I won't keep you waiting long."

Gods, I'm horny as fuck. I don't want to wait a single bloody tick to peel off her pants and drag her legs over my shoulders and tongue that sweet cunt of hers until her clit swells and her pussy weeps and she's fucking my face.

Before I can decide how far to press my luck, a frown turns down my girl's Hollywood pucker.

"Go find Vasili," she says softly. "He needs you. He's hurting. Something's been bugging him since we met Maxim. He won't tell me what it is."

My pornographic fantasy recedes a bit.

Now a fist of concern ties my guts in knots.

Vasili and I have been together a long time, and there isn't much my boyfriend and I haven't shared, including his whole fucked-up family history, so I've got a pretty fair notion what's troubling him. I know who Maxim is and I know what he did. Yeah, Vasili puts on a proper show and claims he's over being rejected by his whole fucking family just for being who he is.

But, ever since, he's been alone.

Of course, being Vasili, when Zara asked about all that history between him and Maxim, the bloke just shrugged it off with one of his deft evasions.

But yeah, he's hurting.

"I'll go find him," I agree with a sigh. Not that I think it'll help much. You don't just get over being tossed out like rubbish by your own flesh and blood. No matter what Vasili likes to pretend, or how well he pretends it. "Come join us when you can. Whatever happens with that fucking dragon, and you fucking shifting, and whatever the fuck's waiting for us at Icarus, we'll deal with it together."

The pucker between her brows smooths out and her worried mouth softens.

I love that about you, Adam, she whispers in my head. Which is pretty much the closest she's come to saying out loud that she loves me. *I mean, I love that you feel that way.*

We're all still getting used to this. Getting used to being all together. I'm still getting used to the concept of commitment after a lifetime of one-and-dones, with Vasili the only constant of all my come-and-go partners. She's still getting used to the concept of queening it and having her own harem.

So even though my ticker swells up in my chest till I can barely breathe, I just quip back, *I love that you love it,* prop my Kylo mask on the desk to keep her thinking about me, and saunter off to find Vasili.

I don't have far to look. I'm clairsentient and we're bonded, so I know he's in the loo. He's left the door cracked for me, so I don't bother knocking.

I'm still horny as fuck and I'm prepared to make shagging me worth his while, so I expect he'll be glad to see me.

But I don't expect to find him crying.

The sight gives me a proper turn.

In part because normally Vasili's hard as nails. In part because he's standing naked in the glass-walled shower, water beating down on his defenseless head and shoulders, eyeliner streaking his cheeks to mingle with his tears so it looks like he's weeping ink.

Shit.

My gaze skates down his slender build. He's taller than me, slimmer, he's sleek and sinuous and lethal as a rattlesnake. We're sparring partners as well as lovers, so I've learnt a healthy respect for his speed and strength.

And there's no part of him I don't love.

Vasili's a runway model when he's all dolled up (and, being Vasili, he's always dolled up). But he's a bloody work of art when he's naked.

Somehow, he's even perfect when he's crying.

Maybe I feel that way because that vulnerable side of him, that lonely queer boy his whole world rejected, is a side of him he so rarely lets anyone see.

He's pretty as a girl, even with makeup rimming his eyes in charcoal circles and running in ribbons over his cheekbones and dripping from his blade-sharp jaw. His hair's slicked back against his elegant head and that lip gloss he fancies has washed away.

Still, he tries to make light of the mess, one corner of his cruel mouth curling in a mocking grin. "Don't look, darling. I'm afraid I'm a perfect fright. Wouldn't you know, I left my cold cream behind at the Bellagio?"

He puts on a right good show, but I know him. Under the hiss of water on gunmetal granite, his voice is all raspy.

You know, the voice you get when you're crying.

"Fuck the cold cream. You're bloody gorgeous and you know it." I peel out of my Kylo clothes with indecent haste and leave everything tossed willy-nilly on the tiles.

He watches me strip down to my skin with less of that predatory menace that always makes me feel so deliciously hunted and more of that naked need he never lets anyone see. I shove open the glass door and crowd into the shower with him, gasping when the spray from the rainshower head scalds my skin. I'm a fire sign and I like it toasty, but I curse and give the knob a hard twist to cool the water down before he scalds himself.

"Sorry," he rasps, with another wobbly smile. "Somehow I can't seem to get warm."

"I'll take care of that. Come here." I gather him into my arms with way more care than we're used to. Normally he likes it brutal when we fuck. And normally *I* like whatever gets him off.

But tonight isn't normal.

We're kilometers away from anything that's normal.

Even for us.

Despite the scalding spray, he's shaking like blazes. I wrap myself round him, pulling his face down to my shoulder and pushing my face into his neck. His Mogadon mating scent wallops into me, all caramel and sandalwood, potent enough to make me drunk, because in his need he's kicking out a truckload.

Zara, I send to her. *Whenever you can, I think he needs both of us.*

The instant spike of her concern bounces back through our bond. I know beyond a doubt she'll back-burner her boning up on dragon shifters to give our mate what he needs. Which means she'll be here with us in a jiffy.

Because that's the kind of queen my girl is.

Vasili's arms slide round my waist—but he's clumsy, hesitant, almost shy, which for him is unheard of. And, so help me gods, his shyness makes me savage. My hands slick down the long sweep of his back, grab a double fistful of my boyfriend's tight ass, and drag his pelvis hard to mine.

Against my neck, his breath rushes out in a grunt of surprise.

I'm not normally this aggressive, not with him, he's got me firmly under his stylish boot and loving every tick, though Zara and Neo are a different story and I dom the shit out of both of them in the sack.

But Vasili's hurting, that bastard dragon and his own bastard parents hurt my love, they made him feel unwanted, unloved, unlovable.

Well, I won't blooming stand for it.

My fingers dig into his ass hard enough to leave bruises on that pale silky skin and I spread him wide for me, which is the exact opposite of the way things usually unfold between us. His nails sink into my back hard enough to sting.

"Darling…" he murmurs into my neck. The seed of a protest blooms in our bond.

"Something you want to say to me, love?" I let go just long enough to pump a lavish squirt of raspberry-scented bath gel from the wall unit into my palm, then spread him wide again and slick my hand down the crevasse between his ass cheeks.

Right over his tight pucker.

A low moan rolls out of him. It sounds like a moan of protest, but we both bloody know better. Because he's hard as tungsten against my belly, gods, he's hot for it. Hot for me. He's still shivering in my arms, but he's not cold anymore, he's burning up.

He's shuddering with pleasure.

Heat rushes into my dick as I share the full sentiment in full fucking measure. Stiff and aching, I rock my pelvis into his. My rigid cock shoves between his thighs. My middle finger teases his hole, all slick and slippery. A deeper moan—raw and hungry—claws out of him.

"Like this, don't you?" I growl, hardly recognizing my own voice.

"Not normally," he gasps around a chuckle. But I'll take that any day of the week over his tears. Though it's true, we're doing this backwards.

I like it all the ways, especially when it's with him.

But Vasili always, always tops. With everyone.

Well, first time for everything, and all that rubbish.

I rim his entrance and probe him just a bit. His breath gives a sharp hitch, but he doesn't tell me to stop. So I push one finger inside him slowly, so slowly, a centimeter at a time, just to the first knuckle. He's already so hot and tight I nearly lose my goddamn mind. He snarls into my skin, his baby fangs scraping my neck like a damn vampire, and rakes his nails down my spine to make me hiss. Of course he's bloody marking me, I'll be wearing his marks for days.

But, gods, he'll be feeling *me* for days too, if I get my way tonight.

"Vasili." I'm so husky I have to clear my throat. "You ever done it like this?"

He's silent for so long I don't think he's going to answer. At all. I rock my cock between his thighs and pump him with my finger, still slow and easy, working past the tight clutch of resistance until his passage softens and gives and lets me in deeper.

Gods, he feels like absolute heaven. I'd give everything I own to feel all that tight heat strangling my cock.

"No," he gasps on an indrawn breath, finally answering the bloody question, after I've practically forgotten what I even asked.

Then he's feeling that stretch and burn of his back door being opened for the very first time, that intimate invasion you simultaneously yearn for and fight like hell to resist, and I utterly adore that it's me who's giving that to him.

"I… I don't…" He trails off with another wee hitch of breath as I push deeper, then he moans softly through his teeth. Now he doesn't seem able to finish, and I don't give him a proper chance to try. I wiggle a second digit into his hole and scissor my fingers to open him wider.

A sharp cry rips out of him to echo from the dripping walls.

"That's it, love, breathe out and open for me," I coax him. His breath shudders out of him and he pushes into my fingers just a bit, sending an instant jolt of heat through my junk.

"Oh God," he whispers on a scrap of breath.

"Vasili," I groan, working deeper, crooking a finger to peg his prostate.

"Fuck fuck fuck," he hisses, grinding his face into the side of my neck. *"Ah!"*

"I've got you. I've got you," I find myself panting in his ear. "I've got you and I swear to fuck I'm never letting you go."

Water pours over us in a hiss of steam, slicking my hair down my back and in my face, there's water in my eyes, but I don't give a single flaming shit. My mouth clamps around the sensitive spot where his neck curves into his shoulder and I suck hard enough to mark him. He thrusts back into my fingers, pushing me in deeper, all the way to the last knuckle.

Then he fumbles to grab my cock and his in a rough fist and strokes us both together.

My dick is jerking in his frenzied grip like I'm hooked up to an electric current, balls clamped tight against my body, and he's rutting against my shaft and fucking himself on my fingers like I'm nothing but a goddamn sex toy for him to use till he gets himself off, which isn't going to take very long given the determined way he's going about all this.

I grip a fistful of his hair and drag his head up to claim his breathless mouth in a soul-sucking kiss.

His tongue plunges deep inside to claim me right back, his mouth crisp with the juniper sting of vodka. He's normally careful—way more careful than I want—with those baby shifter fangs of his. Because he's still self-conscious as fuck about them.

Tonight, he's like kissing a cobra, and I absolutely can't get enough of him.

"Ronin," he moans into my mouth, rocking his cock against mine, leaving an eager slick of precum all over both of us, his hole spasming and clenching round my fingers. "Oh God, oh God."

"Don't you dare come," I growl into his mouth. "I want Zara to watch when you take my cock in that perfect peach of an ass for the very first time. Now turn around for me."

He doesn't like hearing that, he wants to come now, he's still not completely sure he wants a cock inside him at all, and he's used to calling all the shots. But that's not how we're going to roll tonight. He was fucking crying when I found him, and now he's not, and I'm going to keep doing whatever it takes to get him out of that fiendishly clever head of his and make him lose his goddamn mind.

I slip my fingers out of the hot clutch of his hole, break free of his fist before he can finish both of us off, and spin him round hard so his back's to me. One rough nudge with my knee shoves his thighs apart. His hands rise to splay against the glass and his head falls forward. He's panting so hard and fast he's almost hyperventilating with need. I can actually hear him over the spray.

But I'm not one to hold that against him, since I'm huffing and puffing like a locomotive myself.

My hands slick down his perfect little ass, all tight and perky and pink with heat. My dick juts between us, jerking and all but purple with craving, the heavy ring of my Prince Albert gleaming in the wet, a rope of precum drooling from my slit. We haven't used a condom once since we all hooked up, because we're all clean and we're all exclusive. But he's brand new to being on this particular end of things.

The receiving end.

He's turned on as fuck-all. But I can sense that dissonant note of uncertainty still ringing through our bond.

For the sake of common decency, I've got to at least consider the possibility that maybe Vasili really isn't ready for me to empty my load inside him.

I span his narrow waist with my hands and lean forward to whisper in his ear, my voice rough with hunger. "Here's your one and only chance to tell me to bugger off and make me finish in my fist. Or I'm going to wreck your pretty hole. And I'm not going to bloody stop till you feel my spunk dripping out of that sweet ass and running down your legs."

His head snakes round to pin me, eyes burning with gaslight heat, mouth seizing mine in a violent kiss. His ass shoves back against my boner with an insistence that makes me huff out a surprised breath. There's something so raw and needy about him tonight, he's making me an absolute beast.

But if he isn't absolutely certain he wants this, then I won't… I *won't*…

His mouth gentles mine, easing back till I can just feel the brush of his breath against my lips.

His whisper slips out soft and naked. "Do you still love me, Ronin?"

My heart gives a ping so hard it feels ready to shatter. Like it's made of glass and he's just dropped it.

He's heard me say it, heard me think it, he bloody well knows I feel it, but clearly he needs all that again tonight. How could he possibly ever doubt me?

How could he ever doubt *us*?

Just one more grudge for me to hold against that bloody dragon.

"Good gods, d'you really have to ask?" I tuck up against the back of him, my aching cock nestled between his ass cheeks but trying to be polite about it. He's craning round to look at me, searching my face for reassurance, and the angle is awkward as blazes, but I press my forehead against his and stare deep into his desperate eyes. "I've loved you since the day I met you, even though you were and are and always will be an absolute brat. I'm blooming mad for you, love. We all are. And, fuck, you don't need to let me do this just because—"

His mouth crashes against mine to stop my speech in a desperate kiss.

"Then I want you to fuck me," he moans against my lips, every syllable scraped raw with anguish. "I want you to fuck me so hard I scream. Fuck me so hard I can't walk. Fuck me so hard I forget.

"Fuck me so I know I'm still yours." He finishes in a whisper so soft I can barely hear him, except in the secret nooks and crannies of our bond. "God, Ronin. Fuck me so I know you won't leave me."

Chapter Eight
Zara

Finding the two of them together like this, hearing that minefield of buried grief in Vasili's voice and feeling all that loneliness, rooted way down deep in his soul, just about breaks my heart.

For real.

Because he's *mine*. He's my snake. He's my love. And *no one* is fucking leaving him.

Not ever again.

And it's only when his head jerks up to find me through the glass that I realize I've been thinking all that kinda loudly. But maybe that's what he needs from me right now.

That—and what Ronin's clearly about to give him.

This isn't the way they normally do this, like, *at all*, with Vasili bent over and Ronin lining up behind. But my Goblin King's face is streaked with eyeliner and fractured with need, lips parted and panting so those wicked fangs of his are showing. And Ronin's absolutely ruthless, hair streaming over miles of black ink and golden skin, eyes flaming as he slicks a fistful of bath gel over his thick shaft, then grips Vasili's narrow hips hard enough to bruise and starts working his way in.

"Vasili, love," Ronin grits between his teeth. "I swear to every god that ever was. I'll *never* leave you. Never." With every tiny nudge, Ronin grunts the word again. "Never."

And Vasili's face is a wonder to watch, every sinew taut with focus, eyes closed and brows pinched together in mingled pain and pleasure. In fact, he's so fucking beautiful like this that I skirt Ronin's abandoned clothes, walk right up to the glass, plant my palms on the pane opposite Vasili's, and lean my brow against his through the glass.

Now Ronin must have breached him, because Vasili's eyes fly open, pupils blown wide, and stare straight into mine.

"Little queen," he gasps, all high and strangled. "Need both of you so much. I need to be… inside you."

Oh hell to the yeah.

I love watching all my guys together, and sometimes I really do just wanna watch. Especially since they're all starting to learn the things they do to each other that get me and them off the hardest.

But here, now, tonight, I need to be much closer.

Ronin's watching what he's doing, which right now is pumping himself into Vasili in slow shallow strokes that let both of them adjust to this whole new thing for them. But he swings his head up to meet my stare and growls, "He means *now*, love. And you'd best be bloody ready to take us both before we're through tonight."

I'm pretty sure I've never been happier to peel my shirt over my head and push my pants down my legs and shimmy my panties down my hips in my life. Especially with both of them staring at me through the steamy glass like they're going to incinerate me with their eyes.

I honestly feel like my skin's about to ignite.

I leave everything on the floor wherever and slip into the shower's steamy heat. Warm spray sluices over my skin and soaks my pigtails in seconds, but I can't look away from the two of them, muscle bunching and flexing under Ronin's skin, his cock thrusting into Vasili's pert little ass, all rosy with heat and passion. Vasili's curving shaft juts straight before him, bobbing with every thrust as Ronin works deeper and really starts to fuck him, the wet slap of skin hitting skin and breaths rising to grunts in a building rhythm.

My nipples are tingling and my clit is pulsing. And I gotta admit the slick heat that saturates my pussy doesn't have much to do with the actual shower. That butterscotch incense of Vasili's mating scent mingles beautifully with the flowery sweetness of mine. I'm not telekinetic or anything, not like the Goblin King (there's no one like him), but I've got enough Mogadon in my DNA to scent.

Anyway, who needs telekinesis when you can fucking summon lightning?

I hum low in my throat. An electric buzz crackles over my skin. Normally that kinda shit would alarm me, but tonight it actually makes me smile.

For once in my goddamn life, the lightning voice makes me feel powerful instead of freakish.

"Something strike you funny then?" Ronin scrapes out between grunts, because he's *really* getting into the way Vasili's taking his cock. "Hope you're not waiting for me to—put that fucking—mask on?"

Now I can't help giggling. "I don't think the Goblin King wants you to stop what you're doing. And honestly speaking? Neither do I."

Vasili's got the prettiest cock and the longest of any of my guys, just like Lucius has the thickest (I'm talking soda can, he's freaking brutal with it), Neo has the overall biggest (monster cock for my sweet bookworm, who blushes every time I even look at it), and Ronin has that Prince Albert and knows exactly how to use it.

Right now, my mouth is watering for a taste.

I want both of them.

But Vasili needs me more.

So I slide a hand over both their locked and straining bodies, purely for the pleasure of feeling all that slick skin and straining muscle. Ronin's the essence of everything masculine, while Vasili with his silky skin and graceful slimness is more androgynous. I actually love that he leans into his feminine side, because I'm bi myself, I go for the glamazon type, but I'm the only girl in our relationship.

Vasili purrs at my touch, but Ronin snarls at me, because he's kind of a big bully until you get to know him, "On your knees for him. And no backtalk."

"Are you reading my mind?" I joke, because of course he totally *is*. But that's the only way Vasili's getting inside me right now, with the three of us standing in this slick-ass shower with nothing to brace against, Vasili a good foot taller than me, and Ronin still fucking him.

So I'm already sliding between Vasili and the glass and folding to my knees.

Vasili's rigid arms are still spread against the glass, barely anchoring him in place against Ronin's increasingly brutal thrusts. That gorgeous Goblin cock is bobbing roughly 2.5 inches from my face. Now, as I stare up at him from my knees, his gilded head snaps down to trap my gaze.

"Something you want?" I tilt my head back with a wicked grin.

Even in the middle of losing his anal virginity to Ronin's ruthless cock, my snake arches a wicked brow.

"Suck my cock for me, darling," he says, deep and throaty. "All the way down. When I spill down your throat, I want to feel you absolutely gagging on it."

"Promises, promises," I tease.

Right before I wrap one hand around his base, all slick and hot from the shower, then slide the other between his legs and past his balls so I can feel Ronin's cock pistoning into him.

Without a condom, of course, which gets me even hotter.

My touch makes both of them moan.

I lean in to tease the swollen crown of Vasili's cock with my tongue, swiping over his tip to taste the liquid seeping from his slit while he moans and tries to seat himself in my mouth. Still teasing, I back off, then trace a slow circle around him with my tongue.

"Suck me," Vasili hisses on an indrawn breath like the deadly reptile he is. "Make me come. And I swear you'll swallow every drop if you know what's good for you."

My cunt clenches hard with hunger. "Will I get fucked if I do?"

"Six fucking ways to Sunday," Ronin pants. "By both of us. Gods, Vasili! You're *so* blooming tight."

"Enjoy it while you can," Vasili gasps. I guess he's saying this is a one-time thing.

But his last word unravels in a long sex-drenched moan as I open my mouth and swallow him slowly to the hilt.

He tastes like salt and musk and Vasili, he tastes like my snake, he tastes like effing heaven. His tensile length slides over my tongue and hits the back of my throat. I master my gag reflex and swallow him down like a champion, then back off his cock slowly and do it all over again.

And it gives me such intense pleasure to feel him come apart as my throat muscles ripple and milk him, his velvety cock weeping spurts on my tongue, his hands desperate as they grip my head and pull my hair, his hips twitching at first and then bucking outright into my mouth, hard enough to bruise my lips.

That's right, I lash out through our bond. *I've got what you need. So take it. Harder.*

"Oh fuck yeah," Ronin groans, clearly eating it up as my head bobs up and down the Goblin King's dick, all three of us linked tight. "Love the way you take his pretty cock."

I'm not really expecting it—although I really *should* be, given how raw and desperate Vasili is tonight, given the way I just dared him—when the Goblin King wraps my wet pigtails around his fists and starts fucking my mouth for real, every thrust hard and brutal, trapping me in place by the hair and pulling hard enough to sting while he uses my mouth for his own crude pleasure like a glory hole.

And I fucking love it.

I love giving him what he needs.

I love moving in tandem with Ronin to work him over while Vasili comes apart between us. His cries rise sharp and urgent above the slap of flesh and the wet sucking sounds of me taking his gorgeous cock. Saliva runs down my chin and tears burn in my eyes and my hand sneaks down to circle the hot pulse of my clit.

"Christ, yes, *Zara*." The Goblin King's voice unravels and his rhythm stutters and gets erratic. "Ronin… oh darlings… oh God…"

"Ask me for it, love." Ronin slams into him. "Tell me what you fancy."

"What I fancy is you coming in my ass while she fucks her sweet cunt with her fingers and I unload down her throat," Vasili rears up and hisses, vicious as a viper. "I want to feel the burn of your rod deep inside me and I want to drip with your spunk for a week."

Ronin snarls deep in his throat and slams hard and fast into Vasili, which makes Vasili slam hard and fast into me. I wrap one arm around Vasili to brace both of us against Ronin's punishing thrusts and buck into my fingers.

But he's still holding back somehow, Vasili, he's afraid of letting go and trusting us to catch him.

Come for me, bad boy, I fire through our bond. *Come for me and Ronin. We're never gonna leave you, Vasili. We love you. We* love *you.*

That's what finally makes my snake arch his back and shout to high heaven and unload down my throat in jerky desperate spurts. That's what makes Ronin clamp one arm across Vasili's chest and grip my shoulder to hold us all steady while he pumps deep into our mate and fills him with his essence with a hoarse groan, staring deep into my eyes while his face convulses with pleasure. And that's what makes me writhe against my fingers and thrust one digit deep inside to clench around when I squirt all over my hand and moan around the Goblin King's still pulsing cock, filling my mouth and throat and almost choking me, while my own ferocious climax claws through me.

In fact, it feels like my words are still echoing in the ether between us when Ronin fumbles to turn off the shower.

Gently, he and Vasili between them coax me to my feet. Vasili lifts my hand to his lips and wraps his mouth around the finger I just had deep inside me, purring with pleasure at the taste of my cunt while he sucks me absolutely clean.

"My darling little queen," he murmurs, far more tenderly than he typically says anything. "Did you mean it?"

"You know I did. We both did. We love you." I lean into him with a sigh and he bends his tall frame to kiss me, one of his nicest kisses with soft sucks to soothe my swollen lips. Then he gives me plenty of tongue, humming with satisfaction to find his own taste still coating my mouth.

Ronin nudges him softly aside to lift me completely into his arms and cradles me against his chest and sort of herds Vasili before us into the adjoining cabin, with Vasili scooping up armfuls of thick plushy towels as we go and mumbling something fretful about conditioning rinse that we both pretty much ignore.

Not long after, I'm snuggled up between my warlocks in the dim cabin under thick covers in this soft bed, all of us naked and drowsy and more or less dry. Ronin props himself on one elbow to frown down at me, damp hair spilling over one shoulder.

"Didn't mean for you to finish yourself off, love," he groans. "Selfish bastards, the both of us, really. Tonight was supposed to be all about you." He pauses. "Still not too late, of course."

"Vasili needed us more tonight," I mumble sleepily, snuggling up tighter against the Goblin King, who's already sleeping so deeply he's producing cute little snores with every exhale (which would completely horrify him if he knew). "I picked up bits and pieces about why, you know, through the bond and hearing the two of you talk. Tomorrow, I'm hoping I'll hear the rest."

"It's his tale to tell, and it may take a bit of coaxing, but I'm thinking he'll spill the beans for you. You told him just what he needs to feel safe doing it." Ronin draws the thick duvet slowly down my body until he bares my tits. His amber gaze crawls over me.

And even though I literally just fucking came, my nipples pucker right up under that heated stare.

Especially when he flicks one of my rings, then gives it a cruel twist that makes me gasp. He knows I like it rough with the nipple play, and I'm already getting slick for him.

"Ronin," I moan, half in protest, because I figure Vasili really needs his sleep.

And there's no way he'll sleep through anything that goes down with me in this bed without waking up and joining in and probably running the whole show.

"Zara." Ronin mimics my tone perfectly, the beast. Even as he leans in, diabolical with intent, to lick a purposeful circle around my nipple.

A little whimper spills out of me and I arch into his touch.

Which is all the encouragement he needs to close his mouth around my tingling nipple with a hard sucking pull that wrings out a louder whimper.

Vasili stirs heavily against me. His breath unravels in mid-snore into a sigh. He slithers onto his side to face us, sleepy but interested.

"Hmmm, what have we here?" He leans in to nuzzle my other nipple, pricking me with his sexy fangs just hard enough to draw blood. Playing at the actual mating bite he sank into my tit a few weeks ago that left twin scars he and Lucius both love to tongue. They tend each other's mating bites, Lucius and Vasili, which is just sweet as fuck.

I gasp out a breathless curse.

Vasili laps at the tiny new wound and gauges my reaction slyly under his lids.

"Tell me," Ronin whispers, teeth scraping my nipple and tugging on my ring to make me writhe. Sweet Jesus, now they're both nibbling on me! "How d'you fancy me putting that Kylo mask and costume back on for you, love? You'll be my fiery Jedi captive, determined to resist my terrible power. And let's see how Vasili does as that poncy General Hux."

Chapter Nine
Lucius

That rampaging goat in my third period Common Magics class has all but destroyed my classroom.

It's an all-too-damning testimony, of course, to my students' general lack of aptitude at the Compulsion spell they're supposed to have mastered by midterms, which are fast approaching. Before I allow them to tinker with their classmates' fragile minds by unleashing the exercises in the textbook on each other, they're supposed to practice on the goat.

The infernal creature's done its damage and been dragged off in disgrace, but its indignant bleating still echoes above the chatter of lunch hour foot traffic down the corridor of this old Gothic church where classes have been held for centuries at the Icarus Academy.

In point of fact, that cloven-hooved devil might as well be blowing a victory trumpet. None of my underclassmen so much as fazed the wretch.

Good Lord, even my reliable juniors barely managed to slow its depredations.

In the end, if Racetrack hadn't managed to teleport the troublesome beast into the corridor, it would still be overturning desks and trampling chairs to kindling and wreaking general havoc in here.

Truly, it's one more indication I don't need of the failing magic that weakens the witching world as the arcane races drift toward extinction. Centuries ago, the deconsecrated church hidden behind enchanted wards on this abandoned island in the Med would have echoed with prolific hundreds of young witches and warlocks wielding powerful magic.

Today, we have fewer than thirty students at the Icarus Academy, most of them rather weak, and barely enough faculty to run two tracks of coursework. This circumstance is entirely the reason the Dean continues to tolerate my own presence—the scandalous headmaster who fornicates with his barely legal charges.

Dutifully I straighten a toppled chair and rescue someone's trampled spell book, left behind when the church bell sounded and my terrorized students went skulking gratefully off to the commons for lunch. In the gray light leaking through the row of arched windows, I breathe in the dusty scent of chalk and parchment and swallow a worried sigh.

I seem to do rather a lot of that these days.

Of the four warlocks in our queen's new harem, I'm the one who worries.

As befits the headmaster of Villa Augustus, the elite residential college of witches and warlocks I've hand-picked for our *domus* from the dwindling student body, I'm the responsible one.

God in Heaven knows, someone in this harem needs to be.

For once, my outraged bitterness at being left behind—uninvited, unconsulted, and unmissed—while Zara and half her harem wreaked holy hell in America is blessedly short-lived. I'm righting an overturned desk when my shifter senses detect the thud of familiar footfalls rushing toward me down the now quiet corridor, coupled with the clean dry whiff of sage.

My wolf growls in happy anticipation and claws at my skin. He wants out of this prison of skin and tweed and professorial propriety. Out to play with Neo.

Actually, playing with Neo is what we'd both like.

Even that secret admission feels like a sin. All the blood in my body rushes straight to my groin. I'm scant days away from going into heat—yet another reason I curse Vasili daily for leaving. What damnable sort of alpha leaves his mate in this wretched predicament, hot for him as Dante's inferno and cursing his alpha's very existence?

But my looming heat is not the reason I'm currently hard.

Carefully I contain the impulse to stride to the classroom door, drag my visitor inside, bend him over my lectern, shred his uniform trousers to ribbons with my claws, and rut savagely into my prize pupil until we're both mindless and howling with pleasure.

Instead I clear my throat, sternly will the unruly erection swelling behind the zipper of my houndstooth trousers into subsidence, and turn with suitable composure toward the door.

"Master Aries?" Neo Mercury, perennial First Boy on the Dean's List, model citizen, respectable scion of the Capricorn clan, and Zara's fated mate, skids into my classroom at a dead run, his loafers squeaking on the age-scarred Venetian marble floor. "It's Zara and Ronin and Vasili. They're back!"

His broad chest heaves under the moss-green jacket of the Thursday uniform with the Academy crest embroidered on the breast. His stylish dark-rimmed spectacles are sliding down his nose and his magenta curls are tumbled around his face in permanent disarray. Even though he's sworn to me earnestly that he's furious with all of them for leaving, precisely as I am myself, he looks so sweetly flushed and excited by their return that it's all I can manage not to pin him to the chalkboard and kiss my star pupil senseless.

"The three of them are in a great deal of trouble," I remind him sternly, clasping my hands behind my back and fighting the urge to slide my fingers through his tousled hair to tidy him. "And we're terribly angry with them, are we not, Mr. Mercury?"

I'm diligently working not to recall all those times he's cradled my face gently between his big hands and kissed me so tenderly, like a ministering angel, while we've all made love in our queen's curtained bed.

During those times, I always call him Neo.

"I know. We are. I am." He rakes an earnest hand through the curls that graze his shoulders, to no discernible effect, and blinks at me owlishly through his spectacles. "I'm giving them their space like you said while they get settled back in at the *domus*. I'm letting Vasili come to you first like you said, so you can tell him how much trouble they're in. They got in hours ago, but I didn't know because I was up at the Dean's Tower finishing my Honors Alchemy experiment, so I haven't even said hi to her… I mean *them*… yet."

I grope about at random for some sort of professorial utterance. "And how did your alchemy experiment turn out?"

"Copper into bronze." He rushes impatiently past this remarkable achievement that no other student at Icarus has managed in at least a decade and reverts at once to his true topic of interest. "But… still… is it okay that I'm glad they're back?"

"Sweet boy," I whisper, the words slipping out past my guard despite my best effort. "Nothing you could ever do would be wrong."

His chiseled face softens beautifully all over, the blush rising to warm his skin all the way to his hairline. He's been hovering uncertainly in my doorway, filling the space and his uniform with that impressive physique he hones for hours in our *domus* gymnasium. Now he inches fully inside, a shy smile curving his lips.

He does that a great deal with me lately. Blushes, I mean to say.

Ronin claims my star pupil is crushing on me. In fact, Ronin has taken to urging me rather impatiently to bugger my fine sensibilities and bloody get on with it.

Nonetheless, I continue doggedly to resist his ruination.

Neo Mercury has been First Boy on the Dean's List and my pride and joy in the classroom since his freshman year.

Not to mention the unmentionable: he's a full nine years my junior.

True, Ronin is younger still but, Christ, Ronin is no sweet innocent. Ronin was born to sin. Born to drag others cheerfully beside him (and inside him, oh God) straight down the road to damnation. Heaven knows, Ronin pursued me relentlessly for years before I finally succumbed to his irresistible enticements and claimed him with the savage mating bite he demanded.

Now he's our new mate, and my wolf and I have been deliriously happy and utterly tireless and shockingly shameless in our carnal attentions to him ever since.

At least, we *were* doing all of that until Ronin absconded with the jet.

Now, we'll all be exceedingly lucky if he isn't expelled.

"I, um, like what you're doing with your hair now," Neo blurts out suddenly. Awkward, adorable, and still rosy with blushing.

"My hair?" I echo, one hand rising absently to pat at my head.

He waves his own hand and looks flustered. "It's, um, getting longer."

"Oh, I see. Well, hair grows quite quickly for shifters," I explain, barely resisting the habit to deliver an instructive lecture on the topic. "Normally, I'd keep it trimmed, but Zara seems to like it longer."

"I do too," he says quickly. He's a natural redhead under all that magenta, and there's nothing like a fair-skinned redhead for blushing. Now I watch with an admiration that is surely unseemly as that blush deepens. "I mean, we all do, Master Aries. And now you're pulling it into that man-bun thing, like that vampire in *Morbius*, who's so hot." Looking deliciously self-conscious, Neo shrugs his big shoulders. "It just, um, it works for you?"

"Sweet boy." Dear God, it's no use at all resisting when he's this delectable. Surely, just this once, I can—

"And, for your information, I'm not a boy. I just turned twenty-one, remember?" he flares with a sudden flash of stubbornness. "So you're allowed to… want things with me, you know, Lucius."

He says this with utter sincerity, just as though the sight of him smiling shyly and blowing out the candles on the big birthday cake Dez baked for him hasn't made me fantasize feverishly about painting his buff naked body with a generous layer of buttercream frosting and then licking it all off him and tonguing that sweet cock he's so shy about until he loses that brilliant bookworm mind of his and whimpers and writhes and begs me breathlessly please never to stop.

"Wanting things with you isn't the problem, believe me." I fiddle with my cuff links.

"You're allowed to *do* things with me too," he persists, brows rushing together above his eyes. "I mean, if you ever wanted to."

"Do things?" There's snow falling from the pewter skies beyond the leaded glass windows, but suddenly it feels a trifle hot in my classroom. I clear my throat and straighten my tie.

"Yes. You know. *Things.*" Indignant at my obtuseness, he scowls at me. "I mean, you don't have to rush out of bed two hours before the bell every single morning before I wake up just so you don't have to see me or… or touch me…"

"Merciful Christ, is that what you've been thinking?" I'm appalled at my own clumsiness, far too appalled to conceal.

The actual reason I've taken to rushing out of our bed before dawn every morning since the three of them absconded with the jet is because Neo spoons in his sleep and, when it's just the two of us in Zara's big medieval bed, *I'm* what he ends up spooning.

He's bigger than I am, but somehow with me he's always the little spoon.

I've been far too embarrassed to wake up every damned morning with my arm wrapped tight around my trusting student's waist so he can't get away, my face buried in his hair so I can smell him while we sleep, his luscious rump tucked up snug against my groin and his back pressed to my chest so I can feel his every breath, and my obscenely rigid shaft nestled between his bitable buttocks.

Even though Neo sleeps shyly in his boxer briefs, and even though I've taken to wearing linen pajamas to bed to guard his virtue and mine while we're the only two occupying that bed, I'm far too disconcerted by the thought of him waking to find me like that, furiously erect and lusting over my innocent student, with my shaft in my hand while he slumbers.

Thus, I've been slipping out each morning and taking matters privately in hand (as it were) in the Roman baths under the *domus* before anyone else awakens.

I can't be certain how much of this he's picking up. Neo is a Kryll and an absolute non-telepath—except with Zara, his fated mate. Ronin links with him and everyone else because Ronin's Valyrian and a wickedly strong telepath himself. But Neo and I have no such bond, and we won't unless I bite him—which, needless to say, I have utterly no intention of doing. The fact that I've bitten Zara and Ronin (both of them students under my charge) is more than enough indiscretion.

My precious career has barely survived the backlash.

"It—I—" Atypically, I find myself at an utter loss for words. "Neo, that is very far indeed from the truth."

Yet he's a clever boy. His big green eyes lock onto mine as though perhaps he's intuiting a great deal of what I'm carefully not saying.

"Well, you don't have to," he repeats, blushing and pushing his spectacles (which tend to slide down when he's excited) farther up the bridge of his nose. "Because I… I *want* you to do those things to me, Lucius. I want that. And I'm the only person in our bed you won't fuck."

Despite all my resolve, the wounded look on his face and the buried hurt in his voice are my undoing.

Not to mention the use of my Christian name and the word *fuck* on his nearly virginal tongue.

"Sweet boy," I groan for the third time, and I swear it's as though he's bespelled me.

Why do we delay? my wolf growls in my head. *He craves us. He is ours. We should claim him.*

As my wolf fights to surface, I bound across the entire width of my classroom in three swift strides, lunge past Neo to close the door and slip the lock, then push his startled body flat against the door and seal my mouth to his.

His breath whooshes out in surprise against my face and his soft mouth parts willingly. He yields to me so gently, even when I've clearly caught him off guard by pouncing on him in this uncouth way. He smells like sage-and-lavender soap, and he tastes like spearmint, and the fact that he self-consciously ingested a breath mint before coming to see me is very likely another indication that he is indeed… crushing on me.

Under the scent of all that innocence lurks the gamy reek of wolf, which means I've been vigorously scenting him (despite all my virtuous intentions) while we spoon.

His chest is warm and solid under my urgent hands, so different from Ronin's lean twisting savagery or Vasili's sleek and vicious grace. His hands come to rest on my waist to steady both of us—again, with that gentle patience that's so unlike anyone else in our harem—but he's eager too.

Mother of God, he's so eager.

He's breathing fast, all but panting under my commanding grip, and he voices a soft desperate sound while I absolutely ravage his mouth, nipping at his full lower lip, sucking on his tongue, my own tongue plunging deep into all that cool minty sweetness. Again and again, his tongue collides with mine in a ravenous hunger that makes my soul ache and my shaft throb with all that need for him I've been suppressing and denying for what feels like a slow eternity.

When his innocent tongue probes the roof of my mouth where my fangs reside when they're retracted, my palate tingles. It's all I can manage to keep those wicked canines of mine from descending.

Dear God. Surely my eyes are flaming red, which happens before I shift.

Helpless to suppress my carnal instincts any longer, I crowd him hard against the door the way my wolf pins his prey, then knee his thighs roughly apart so I can wedge my pelvis against his and frot him through our layers. Under his uniform trousers, his manhood is absolutely rigid.

A growl rips out of me.

My heat blooms without warning.

Now this entire kiss threatens to career off the rails entirely and become everything I so desperately want with him, but flatly forbid myself to take.

"Lucius," he pants into my mouth. "Oh Lucius. Are you really hard like this all for me… or… is it just your heat?"

He's a wise boy, sharing our harem with three shifters or part-shifters.

Zara, Ronin, and I were all bitten within a very short span of time, so Neo knows we'll all be in uncontrollable heat and insatiable for days once the moon is full. When his hand dips between us to wrap around my throbbing length, with only my trousers between us, another growl claws from my throat. My hips shove forward into his grip.

"This is all for you," I snarl, thick and guttural as my wolf lunges and snaps at my skin, simply desperate to rise. My hand drops to his belt and tears open his buckle. "Is all this for me?"

"It is, it really is, but… Lucius," he gasps between my increasingly frenzied kisses. "If it *is* just… your heat… and not me, I mean, it's okay, I get it. I can still… be with you. I'd even…" He hesitates, then the words rush out. "I'd even let you bite me."

My wolf howls with primal triumph and my fangs punch through the roof of my mouth.

But I am not my wolf.

Not entirely.

Viewed through the lens of my moral human scruples, this infernal offer dashes over me like a bucket of icy water.

I freeze in mid-rut, in the midst of feverishly unbuttoning Neo's trousers as though I truly do intend to take him here and now before my fourth period History of Witchcraft class comes trooping up with their books and satchels and starts rattling the locked door to stop their professor and the First Boy madly fornicating against the wall.

"No, I would," he insists, as though I've only stopped so he can reaffirm his sincerity. He ducks his head and fiddles with my tie. But he keeps stealing shy little peeks at my now fully distended fangs. "I'd totally let you bite me. I'd, um, uh, I'd actually like that."

"Blood of Christ." Somehow, I manage to pry my hand off his fly before I can get him unbuttoned and my fingers inside, while my wolf howls in protest.

Exerting a truly Herculean effort, I even manage to stop myself from rutting into his intoxicating grip, which is still kneading my shaft through my trousers.

I fight like the dickens to retract my fangs and silence my wolf, who's pacing and snarling inside my skin, more than ready to take innocent Neo up on this scandalous offer before my student returns to his senses and revokes it.

"My dear boy." Resolutely I buckle his belt and straighten his tie and try my damnedest to ignore both my raging erection and his, although none of this is easy. "You have absolutely no idea what you're offering—"

"I do, though. I really do." Even as I'm tightening his tie, he's loosening mine, blushing as he works out the knot. "You all think I'm so innocent, but I've been watching all the rest of you. Every single one of you has either given a mating bite or gotten one or both. Everyone… except me."

With a sudden rush of insight, I realize there's a tender bruise on this gentle creature's heart that none of us has ever guessed.

He's hurt.

He's deeply hurt.

Because none of us has bitten him.

Here, now, today, he finally intends to do something about it.

By this point, he's gotten my tie unraveled and he's starting to work on the buttons of my shirt, head ducked, brow furrowed, curls tumbling over serious eyes. He appears determined to seduce me, as if that's what it will take for me to lose my infernal mind and bite him.

My wolf, of course, is no help at all. That lecherous beast is entirely on Neo's side.

"Neo," I say firmly for both their sakes, "stop trying to undress me for a moment and listen. The effects of a mating bite can be dangerously unpredictable, especially when the recipient has no Protean DNA and thus is not a shifter. Since you yourself are not a shifter—"

"Neither are *they*." He looks positively mutinous, but he's finally stopped unbuttoning me, at least temporarily, which I tell myself is a good thing. It is.

No, really.

"Both Zara and Vasili have shifter recessives," I remind us all patiently. "In Zara's case, there's actually enough shifter in her DNA that our mating bites have apparently now triggered her own latent ability to shift."

He nods, because he overheard the earful I received on the landline before breakfast from the outraged arcane senator who read me the absolute riot act over my wayward student's disastrous antics in America. Neo's a senator's son himself, so he understands how bad this is, and how desperately hard the entire ruling class must now labor to cover up Zara's indiscretions and protect the secrecy of the witching world that is so essential to our precarious survival.

Of course, Neo doesn't yet understand the full price Zara is about to pay for those indiscretions.

Very soon now, they'll both learn.

Then there will be literal hell to pay.

"But Ronin doesn't have any shifter. He's almost pure Valyrian." Neo's trusting gaze lifts to mine, and every thought of witching world politics slips from my mind.

Merciful Christ, I can see his hurt lurking deep within. I even fancy I can feel it like a dull ache in my chest. My wolf wants so badly to mate him that I'll have to be exceptionally careful not even to give this boy a love nip during foreplay.

This is yet another reason, if I needed one, why I shouldn't be getting involved with him like this.

"I never meant to give Ronin a mating bite. He's always been so rebellious, I meant to administer a disciplinary bite to make him heed me, but my wolf had other ideas. You know there's art as well as science in witchcraft. Mating bites aren't a precise craft." I pull in a long breath and clench my fists. "We're all exceptionally fortunate Ronin suffered nothing worse than a bad bout of mating fever—which could have killed him, had it been left untreated as he stubbornly intended—and some uncomfortably intense heats. I won't roll the dice and tempt fate like that a second time."

"But Lucius." Neo grips the lapels of my tweed coat in tender protest and stares imploringly into my eyes. "It's my body. Don't you think it should be my decision? Once you've explained the risks, shouldn't it be my chance to take?"

"You're still so very young," I sigh. "You're the scion of the Capricorn clan. A powerful warlock and an exceptionally gifted alchemist with nearly pure Kryll DNA. You're all but destined to be elected to your father's seat on the Arcane Senate. You're our queen's fated mate, the only one of those she's got, even though we're all in love with her. You're certain to be one of her kings when she ascends."

As I articulate his vast potential, my certainty swells and rings in my voice like a bell. "I won't risk the life of a future Gemini king of the witching world, while the arcane races hover on the brink of extinction, to salve anyone's wounded heart. Not even yours, my boy."

"So what you're saying is," he says slowly, his voice thick and uneven, "I'm sweet and all, I'm everyone's baby, but you still won't bite me and you still won't mate me. You won't even let it be my choice?"

His head is bowed and all that tousled hair has sort of flopped forward, and I wish desperately that I could see his face.

Just a short while ago, I might have lifted his chin to sweeten his disappointment with a soft slow rain of apologetic kisses.

But now I dare not waver.

"I'm sorry, Neo, but I simply won't."

"Okay then." Head still ducked, he twists abruptly to unlock the door. "Guess I've got my answer."

I can't help reaching for him, but he slips deftly out of my grasp, pivots away from my imploring face without ever once meeting my gaze, and jerks open the door to leave.

I'm staring at his rigid shoulders and averted back with my whole chest aching when he says briefly, without turning, "I was gonna mention I saw Vasili heading down from the *domus* toward your office in the crypt. Sneering of course, just typical Vasili, but looked like he was going where you told him in that note you left him. I guess you better go talk to him."

Then he simply leaves me to it.

This behavior is extremely unNeolike, because he's typically quite social, and we've always enjoyed each other's company even before we became… romantically involved, as I suppose I must now acknowledge that we are. But if the alternative that would satisfy him means risking his life and the fate of a future king by biting him and mating him, I'll take this stiff and heartsore option.

This unhappy and unmated but breathing option.

Still, that doesn't mean I have to like it.

Swallowing another worried sigh, I button my shirt and knot my tie and clear my mind as best I can for the coming ordeal before I follow him dutifully out of the classroom and descend grimly to the crypt.

Chapter Ten
Neo

I run all the way from the church to the *domus*.

Honestly, this isn't so easy when it's straight uphill, zigging and zagging through the narrow cobblestone streets, up and up and up all these endless flights of stairs. That's not even counting the fact that I'm wearing my winter boots and my big woolen coat (because even in the Med, the wards that conceal this island from the mortal world really mess with the weather).

Thanks to those wards, I'm wading through a foot of fallen snow that slips and slides under my feet.

The snow muffles the way my steps echo and crunch against the faded stucco walls. I'm surrounded by abandoned and crumbling Renaissance buildings. This island's pretty much uninhabited these days, we could house way more students than we actually have, because enrollment's way down, so I don't run into anyone on the way.

But all that treadmill time I put in every day to stay buff for Zara works out to my advantage.

It's a blessing the exercise helps distract me from the ache of all that jumbled-up hurt and disappointment I've been carrying around in my chest ever since that awful morning I woke up to realize Zara left me behind. Plus the cold wind cools the burn of embarrassment that's heating my face (because I'm fair-skinned and constantly blushing) due to this latest rejection from Lucius, who bit Ronin and bit Zara and even accepted a bite from Vasili (of all people!) That snake doesn't even shift, so I have no idea what's gotten into him or why he's going around now biting people.

Well, he's Vasili. He's always been impossible.

But Lucius is pure shifter. And Lucius refuses to bite me.

And only me.

If I stop to think about it, the hurt and humiliation of that flat-out rejection from my trusted favorite teacher—who's also the unattainable guy I'm crushing on—would cut up my heart like a lungful of shattered glass.

So I don't. Not right now.

I don't let myself think about it.

Still, this incline's pretty brutal. By the time I top the last ziggy flight of stairs with my book-filled backpack bouncing on my shoulders (because midterms are coming and I'm already cramming) and finally reach Villa Augustus, the residential college where our student cohort dens up and bunks down—most of us together these days, except for Dez and Racetrack who only bunk down with each other—I'm all flushed and breathless.

But it's more from excitement than exertion.

I know I should take a sec to catch my breath and mop the steam off my glasses and remember all the things Lucius and I agreed we will or won't say to our mates who left without telling us and put Zara at really horrible risk and jeopardized the secrecy and thus the survival of the entire witching world.

But she's my fated mate. I can't stay away. She hurt me so bad by leaving me behind, they all did, and I'm not just going to let that slide.

I'm really not. I can't. They hurt me.

Still, right now, I'm just so glad she's back.

Lucius can lecture them all later, just like he's doing with Vasili back at the church right now, about how irresponsible they've all been, how the whole witching world's in an uproar, how even the Dean's taking heat (because Lucius took that call from her on the landline in the kitchen and I have big ears) and how it's going to cost all three of them bigtime, both academically and in other ways. I actually have some things to say later to Vasili myself, because he's faculty now, even if it's only provisional until he graduates… *if* he graduates. And, honestly, he should've known better.

But Zara? She's my beloved. She's reckless and brash and badass. That's what makes her Zara.

It's gonna be hard staying mad at her for long.

I push my glasses up my nose, shake the snow out of my hair, and fish out my big antique key to unlock the front door of our *domus*. We never used to lock it, but now we have the next queen living under our roof, and two bad guys already got in once and tried to take her.

We killed them.

I swung the poker that finished off that creep Master Zerxes myself. I don't even regret it. Sure, the AIB is suspicious and definitely investigating. There's no way to avoid it. The Academy's last Mogadon Magics professor just died by violence (even if it was pure self-defense on our part) and there's no covering that up.

But this is one of those times having my dad be the Ted Kennedy of the witching world works out in my favor.

The investigation's been slow-rolled, with no charges filed. Dad's army of lawyers is working pretty hard to make sure it stays that way.

Anyway, now we always keep our door locked.

It's centuries old and it sticks sometimes (like now) but I put my back into it and shoulder it open. In the shadowy vestibule, Zara's black Academy peacoat and beret are tossed over their wall pegs next to Ronin's leather biker jacket.

Just seeing their stuff hanging back where it belongs gives me a giddy rush of butterflies in my tummy.

I've actually had major butterflies going crazy in there ever since Lucius kissed me in the classroom. Somehow, I've developed this embarrassing schoolboy crush on him, it's gotten way more intense since it's just been the two of us, and he's normally so reserved and so focused on his teaching that it's really hard to get his attention, so that kiss was just so wonderful!

You know, until he pushed me away.

Now I focus on keeping it together and not rushing through the *domus* like it's on fire and scaring people. Dez and Racetrack are down at the commons for lunch with the other students, and the great room where we all study and hang out at night is nice and quiet, with cold winter light pouring through the glass doors from the peristyle courtyard, coals banked and glowing in the central hearth, the big steel fridge humming in the kitchen, and the geriatric furnace chugging away doggedly like a beast in the basement.

I try to go slow, but it's no use. I climb the stairs two at a time and trot down the open hall that overlooks the great room, past Vasili's closed door and Ronin's open one (his duffel's thrown on the bed, but no one's in there) straight to Zara's bedroom… I mean, *our* bedroom.

Sure, I have one of my own down the hall where I store my clothes and books and stuff. But I really live in here with her.

My beloved.

Her room and her bed is where we all sleep. At least, it's where all of us guys sleep.

With Zara.

Lucius and I kept sleeping in here while she was gone, just to feel closer to her (in my case) and in order to smell her and his alpha and Ronin (for Lucius).

Yet now, for some reason, I feel like I need to knock. This might seem unreasonable since it is my own room and all. But everything's been all weird and off kilter since the other three left.

I mean, since the other three left *us*.

All of a sudden I feel awkward, standing there stranded in the drafty hall with my big hands and my big feet and my glasses sliding down my nose again, my breath too loud in the stillness.

Awkward… and unwanted.

Why did she leave me behind?

I'd expect it from Vasili, because we're still kind of frenemies (at best). But Ronin's always so nice to me these days, he holds my hand and kisses me and fucks me all the time like he can't get enough of me, he's the only guy I've ever been with that way, and I'm like secretly in love with him? So it hurt.

But what hurt the most was being left behind by Zara.

I clear my throat, push a hand through my curls which have to be all messy from the run and from making out like that with Lucius, tell myself firmly *not* to blush, whatever I do, and knock.

"Neo?" Sounding all sleepy and befuddled, Zara's voice seeps through the wood. Either because she knows my knock, or because she can sense me through our mating bond. "Why're you knocking? C'mon in here, baby."

Oh gosh, it's no use.

Pleasure rolls through me and warmth rushes into my face.

Her eagerness to see me hums through our bond. My heart floats up like a helium balloon. Despite everything, she's so happy, so happy to know I'm out here. I fling the door open and bound into my fated mate's boudoir like the big eager German Shepherd Vasili used to sneeringly call me (you know, before the ceasefire. Now he mostly just sneers.)

Zara's creamy stucco walls are glowing in the snowy light that's streaming through the glass doors at the foot of her bed. There's a fire crackling and dancing in the hearth to chase away the chill. My mate's hot pink suitcase, covered with punk rock decals and dive shop stickers, lies open on the mosaic floor with her wild club clothes and freshman schoolbooks already spilling out of it and flung willy-nilly across her desk and vanity like a clothes grenade's gone off in here.

The blue velvet curtains on her old-fashioned bed that are meant to stop the drafts are tied back, the way Lucius and I left them this morning. And right there, curled up under the duvet, Zara and Ronin are snuggled up together half asleep, with my fated mate's wonderful mermaid head tucked up against Ronin's shoulder.

Even half asleep, Ronin looks wary. He knows they messed up leaving me behind, he knows it, and he looks kinda guilty too for ghosting my calls.

Good.

He pushes a swath of hair out of his sexy eyes, levers his sexy body up on one elbow, and mumbles in his sexy British bedroom voice, "Morning, Red. Aren't you the sight for sore eyes then?"

Ronin always sleeps naked, except for that gorgeous dragon tattoo breathing flames across his chest. Under those blankets, he's naked right now.

And I, like, *really* missed him.

But I'm not going to get all distracted.

"It's afternoon, for your information," I tell them, closing the door behind me to keep the heat in. "And how can you possibly be sleeping? You guys are in *so* much trouble I can't even tell you. Not to mention you just missed like a week of class, and midterms are next week. Don't you care if you pass?"

What I really want to ask is how they could just come home and crawl straight into bed without looking for Lucius and me first.

Didn't they miss us at all? The way we missed them?

Zara rolls away from Ronin to face me. That soft sweet smile I just adore curves her lips and lights up her gorgeous pinup girl face.

"Oh Neo," she breathes in her husky sleep voice. "We're jet-lagged, baby. You were both in class. I know I screwed up and I know I hurt you. And I missed you both *so* much. Come right over here."

And that's all she needs to say, actually, for me to have a hard time remembering that I'm mad at her.

I drop my backpack to the floor and get across that room in five seconds tops. Even though I'm trying hard not to gallop, Vasili would still make fun of me for being so eager if he was here. Zara pushes back the blanket to make room for me. She's sleeping in her white schoolgirl panties and one of Lucius' Oxford shirts like she always prefers, which makes me slightly less mad at her.

I basically dive-bomb the bed and drag her into my arms and smother her with desperate kisses.

She gasps and giggles and moans all at once, her arms twining around my neck, her legs parting to wrap around me. The feel of her drives me so crazy, she always does, she's so warm and sleek and eager. The flowery sweetness of her mating scent fills my head and the cinnamon toothpaste taste of her mouth makes my lips tingle.

I groan and rut into her like an animal, hips burrowing and thrusting into her, one hand spearing through her hair to hold her, the other shoving up the crisp fabric of Lucius' shirt to find her smooth tummy and the lush swell of her breast. Her little ring nudges my palm and her nipple puckers, hard and eager, against my hand.

"Oh God, Neo," she breathes into my kiss on a long shaky sigh. "God, I missed you."

She's sweating and hot as a furnace pressed against me, because it's almost time for her heat. It's only her second one, and if she'd stayed away any longer, I might've totally missed it.

That thought makes me so crazy I'm having a hard time thinking.

I keep kneading her boob (because she's into that, and so am I) but I stop palming her hair and get my hand down between us to cup the cotton schoolgirl panties stretched over the hot slit of her pussy.

"Off," I grunt like a Neanderthal into the urgent suck of her mouth, trying to drag the fabric down her hips while I'm still rutting into her. My dick's already shoved up against the zipper of my chinos, it's hard enough to hurt, and precum is dampening the crotch of my boxer briefs.

"Neo," she moans, squirming under me to help, dragging my shirt free of my trousers and tearing at my belt. Her tongue shoves deep into my mouth and I lick at her sharp incisors.

Craving for her bite knifes through me, like I've just been stabbed with one of Vasili's cache of blades, which is totally a risk since he's still a snake, even if we're all sharing a bed these days.

This craving of mine for Zara's bite is totally stupid though, because she doesn't have fangs and she doesn't bite (except, you know, love nips).

Then my beloved wrestles my buckle open and drags my zipper down and wiggles her demanding fingers through the slit in my briefs to wrap around my dick.

That just makes me crave her worse.

God, she makes me so crazy. I shove into her grip with a deep groan and drag her panties down her legs.

"Easy, love," Ronin murmurs in my ear, his hard hand soothing as it slicks down my back and tugs at my blazer. "Let me help you out a bit, yeah?"

I growl and stiffen up all over, partly because Zara's started jacking me and I don't want to lose it and come in my pants.

But only partly for that reason.

"Not you." I twist my head to glare at him. "She never answers her phone and I figured it would just short out anyway. But you totally ghosted my calls for days. I'm mad at you."

Ronin stops tugging at my clothes and flops down on the pillow with a heartfelt groan.

"Told you," he says glumly to Zara. "I'm in the bloody doghouse. And for good reason. I'm absolute rubbish at relationships. Always have been. Never know what to say when I bollocks it up. And it's going to be ten times worse with Lucius."

He really has no idea, but I'm not talking about this now. I've finally managed to work Zara's panties down her silky showgirl legs and she's kicking out of them. I get my hand between her thighs to cup her soft, bare, wonderful pussy.

Oh Lord, she's already so slick and so wet and so ready for me.

"Babe," I moan, working one finger deep into her soaking channel. "Oh my God, you're so hot. Your heat's starting, isn't it?"

"Umph." Grunting, she clamps tight around me and rocks her hips into me with that eagerness that's part of what made me dive headlong into her and fall so deep in love I can't even find the surface of what used to be me anymore. "Um… day or two to go yet, I think."

It doesn't feel that way to me, it feels like she's ready now.

But it's her body, so she must know.

"Missed you so much." I slip another finger into her sucking depths and find the swollen bud of her clit with my thumb.

"God, Neo, fuck." She breaks free of my starving kiss to sink her teeth into my earlobe. Not hard enough to break the skin, but I'm so hot to be bitten right now that I just about come off the bed and spurt in her hand.

I cry out and writhe against her, my glasses steaming and slipping down my nose.

"She's starting early, I think. We both are. Dunno why." Sounding strained, Ronin slides off my glasses and rolls over to deposit them safely on the nightstand. Between pumps into Zara's hungry pussy, I rub the pearl of her clit and sneak a peek at Ronin's tight ass.

I guess I'm not mad at that part of him. If Lucius were here, I bet our headmaster would already be railing him.

Zara stops jacking me long enough to shove frantically at my pants, and I'm more than happy with where we're taking this. I barely let her skim the fabric down my ass before I'm easing my wet fingers out of her, which makes her whimper with disappointment.

But only until I envelop both fingers with my mouth to suck off her salty musk. A moan of delirious pleasure rolls up my throat. Her eyes meet mine, the eyes of my beloved, all heavy and pulsing with periwinkle fire. That's because she's a really strong witch, with loads of Valyrian DNA in her genetics, even if she doesn't know how to control it all yet.

That's why we're here. At Icarus, I mean. She needs to learn to control her power if she's going to ascend and become the strong queen we need on the throne to save the witching world.

"Fuck me, baby," she says, all low and throaty. "Fuck me with that monster cock."

Aaaaand that would be another reason we're here.

A fist of excitement tightens my chest and makes my dick jerk. She doesn't have to ask me twice, she never has. I'm already lining up my cock

(I'm so big right now it's embarrassing, but she absolutely does not seem to mind) even though my pants are still twisted around my thighs and I'm sweating through my tie and jacket and my hair's falling into my eyes.

Ronin smooths my hair behind my ear and leans close to mutter, "Gods, Red, I swear to fuck the two of you are so hot. Let me make it up to you, love. Need to be inside you so bad right now I'm mental."

His spicy scent of ambergris and bergamot steals through my senses. My balls clench up tight with need, because my dick's definitely on board with being fucked by Ronin while I'm fucking Zara. It's actually one of my favorite ways.

But he's not getting off the hook that easy.

"No. I'm mad at you." I know I sound petulant, and I'm still hurt and I still don't understand why they left me behind but I can't take it out on her, I just can't. Not by withholding sex anyway. She's my fated mate.

At the very least, Ronin's really going to have to grovel. For both of them.

He laughs, low and husky, because of course he's reading my mind.

"You fancy hearing me beg you for a shagging?" He stretches out on his back close beside me, shoves the blankets down to give me a good long look at all those lean muscles flexing under his skin, wraps his fist around his pierced dick, and starts to pump.

Which is *so* hot I almost swallow my own tongue.

"Oh fuck Red," he moans on a raspy exhale, arching into his own slow strokes. "This is for you. Both of you. Will you watch me?"

A whimper slips out of me.

"Behave yourself, Adam." Zara gives a breathless laugh and fits my dick against her soaking pussy. "And stop teasing him—"

She breaks off with a gasping cry. That's because I've just thrust deep inside her slick heat.

My eyes roll back in my head on a groan, because I've been literally on the edge of losing it since I saw her, and especially since she bit my ear. Right now it's taking every shred of my self-control not to shoot my load on the first pump. As I barely hold onto my looming climax by my fingertips, my teeth sink into my lower lip hard enough to sting.

"Oh baby," Zara whispers, low and shaking. "I'm sorry for hurting you."

Her hot hands snake around my bare ass and grip. Her touch discharges tiny sparks of staticky witchcraft that snap against my skin. Her pussy pulses around my dick, tight little flutters that tell me she's as close to losing it as I am.

I open my eyes and lock onto her stare. That gives me a start, because now her eyes are glowing amber, which is new. Her pupils are, like, elongating into slits. They're dragon eyes, and I'm guessing she has no idea, but now's definitely *not* the time to tell her. She's glittering with sweat, hair flung like seaweed across our pillow, breathless pants slipping between her parted lips. The ambrosia of her mating scent drenches the air with enough pheromones to make us all horny.

Right next door, Ronin's fisting himself and writhing in the sheets, which is definitely a major distraction.

"Bloody hell," he groans. "What the devil have the two of you been doing in this bed? These sheets reek with Lucius' mating scent."

The glow in Zara's eyes burns brighter.

"You and Lucius?" she whispers, with that throaty catch that tells me how much she likes the concept.

"Not… not yet." It's hard to pull my head together enough for actual speech right now. But I try for her sake. "He's, uh, resisting. But I… I definitely think I want to…"

And I still want him to bite me whenever he finally fucks me.

Both Zara *and* Ronin groan when they pick that up.

"Sweet Jesus." Her pussy clenches around my dick hard enough to make me groan too. Her legs wrap around mine and her hips shove into me. "That's gonna be *so* hot, baby."

Pleasure shoots down my spine and swells in my balls. My hips punch forward all on their own. Then it's like the dam breaks and I'm fucking her, my beloved, my cherished fated mate, like I'll literally die if I don't.

She can run away and leave me behind and not answer any of those voice mails I loaded into Ronin's inbox until the thing stopped working. She can hurt me by leaving me out of her crazy plans. She can take as many consorts as she wants to be her kings and share her throne with whomever she likes when she ascends.

But *I'm* the guy who's fucking her now.

I *won't* be left out or left behind anymore. I won't.

Not ever.

And right now I'm going to make her come so hard she summons her lightning and blows every circuit on this whole darn island.

I growl and hammer into her, setting a furious rhythm that makes the bed shake and the curtains sway and the headboard slam against the wall. Her eyes flutter shut and her brow furrows and her head tips back to bare her throat. She's still wearing Lucius' shirt, that gamy wolfish smell of him is everywhere in this bed—he's all around me, yet still so unattainable—and that makes me even crazier.

With a snarl, I clench my fists in that shirt and rip it open, buttons flying (sorry about that, Lucius) to bare Zara's perfect tits, just literally the most gorgeous breasts on the planet, full and crowned with those pink areolae and pert nipples I love so much to suckle, her rings bouncing gently with every thrust.

"Yeah, just like that," she moans through her bared teeth. "Love the way you give me your cock."

"Love the way you take it." I nuzzle my way down her sweating neck to tongue the little puncture scars on her boob that Vasili left when he bit her like the viper he is, because tonguing her bites is something I know she likes.

Even though this whole train of thought just gets me thinking all over again about why no one wants to bite *me*.

I shove that thought away and enclose one nipple with my mouth, sucking as much of her inside as I can, before I start worrying her tight nub with my tongue and tugging at her ring with my teeth.

Her hands clench around my bottom, nails digging hard enough to leave crescents. But it's the sparks flying from her fingertips that make me grunt and grip her wrists and pin her arms safely overhead.

Well, that, plus the fact that she actually likes being restrained when she's fucked.

Next to us, Ronin's on the edge of losing it, one fist clenched in the sheets, the other wrapped around his dick in hard punishing strokes made slick and audible by all that precum he's pumping out. He's grunting with every downstroke and his fiery eyes are riveted on Zara and me like he'll never look away.

I love that he's watching, that it's me with her now, that watching me fuck her is what's getting him off. Because, even though I'm mad at him, I'm also so deeply in love with him.

"Ah, shit, Red," he grunts, thrusting into his fist, his gaze locked on mine. "I'm sorry I ghosted, okay? Didn't know what to say to you. You're so blooming sweet you just wreck me."

Which isn't the same thing as saying he loves me back.

C'mon. You know how I feel about you, he whispers in my head. *You know.*

And, sure, I thought I knew.

Until they both left me.

"Never leave me again." My eyes veer from his to burn into Zara's. "I mean it. I need you to promise."

Her slitted pupils dilate wide. In our bond, guilt and worry surface through the hot haze of lust.

"Oh baby," she whispers. "I was trying to protect you. I was trying to protect all of you, but those two refused to be left behind. It was a combat situation. And you're not a fighter."

Infuriated, I pin her wrists with one hand (but not too hard, I could never hurt her, never) and hitch her thigh higher, shoving her knee up toward her ear to deepen the angle. That makes her moan and me shudder, goosebumps sheeting down my back and over my butt as our climax races toward us.

"Have you forgotten who swung that poker?" I grunt, hips snapping into her, punishing her with pleasure, which is the only way I can. "Vasili knifed Zerxes, but he couldn't take him out. Neither could Ronin. *I'm* the one who killed to protect you."

"Neo…" she pants, clawing at my hands, head tossing on the pillow. Sparks crackle and hiss from her fingers.

But I'm relentless, because I need her to hear me.

"I killed to protect you, babe. Just like Lucius would've killed that polar bear shifter to protect you. But you took—Ronin and Vasili with you—and you left—Lucius and me behind. You hurt us. Promise me you won't ever do that—again."

I've never angry-fucked before. It's not usually my thing at all. My emotions are all jumbled up and not easy to navigate and I don't really do complicated. I like things simple and straightforward. But this is definitely a whole new level of intense.

If she doesn't give in soon, I'm going to come so hard I sink this island into the sea.

And because we're bonded, her anger rises to match mine. She snarls at me like, well, a dragon, pretty lips peeling back to bare her sharp little teeth.

Suddenly I realize Lucius is no longer the only shifter in our polycule.

And if Lucius won't bite me, maybe Zara will.

"All right," she hisses, eyes burning like pinwheels. "I promise. Next time I won't leave you behind. You steal when I steal and you fight when I fight."

A rush of elation just about takes the top of my head off.

She *promised*.

Next time, she won't leave me behind. And she won't leave Lucius.

Totally overcome, my voice splinters and breaks. "Oh God, babe—"

She lunges up and nips my ear again with her sharp canines (Lord, I'm definitely going to come now!) and pants in my ear, "Now you and Ronin— kiss and make up. He needs to come and—you're driving him insane— staying mad at him. He said he's sorry, and he really is. Besides—it was all—my fault."

Blind and desperate as my climax rushes toward me like an avalanche, I twist to the side and slam my mouth down over Ronin's in a fierce open- mouthed kiss that's laced with desperation and triumph.

It's not absolution, because deep down I'm still angry.

But at least it's acknowledgment.

He fists my hair and arches into my touch, his whole body electric, his whole mind and soul blasting wide open to me at the touch. Our tongues collide and a cry claws up his throat. I kiss him to claim him while he pistons into his own grip and comes gallons all over his chest and abs and, crap, my uniform blazer which I still haven't gotten around to taking off.

Zara loses it too, because there's nothing she loves more than watching us guys lose our minds over each other. Purple fire spills from her eyes and static electricity races over the bed and the blankets and our skin. The bulb of the reading light on her desk explodes with a *pop!*

Then I'm so obliterated by my own orgasm I can't see or hear or think, only feel. My climax triggers my gift and the island rocks on its fault line while the tectonic plates under the ocean shift and groan.

That's my gift.

I summon earthquakes.

I kiss Ronin like I'm going to consume him and I pump my release into the indescribable heaven of Zara's writhing body like I'll never stop coming.

But even in the throes of my climax, my earlobe is still stinging from her love nip.

We don't even know if she's come into her full power. Sometimes, with gifts like hers, it takes a while. But her eyes are dragon eyes, she's going to be our dragon queen, and my chest aches and burns with a painful longing for my fated mate to bite me.

A longing for her to bite me for real.

Chapter Eleven
Lucius

Vasili waits like a coiled basilisk in my office in the crypt.

By rights, he ought to be on high alert since I've called him to the carpet with that peremptory summons I left in his faculty mailbox. Of course, being Vasili, he appears neither anxious nor apologetic.

Instead, he's sprawled languidly in my chair in his outlandish and flamboyant personal attire, entirely out of uniform, his booted legs propped on my desk. He's idly paging through my leather-bound grade book, his pretty face etched with a look of perfect boredom.

Just one look at the wretch makes my wolf whine with eagerness.

Our mate, my wolf growls in my head. *Our alpha. Go to him. We are his.*

This pernicious influence—the irrepressible sexual craving of a wolf for his alpha—I must absolutely deny. If Vasili will not submit now to my discipline (professionally speaking), there will be no saving him.

"Kindly remove your boots from my desk, Mr. Romanov," I say crisply, closing the door behind me and placing my briefcase on my desktop to reclaim my territory. "While you're at it, you may return that grade book to my locked drawer where it belongs. As you're well aware, student grades are confidential."

"Oh, you're no fun." Vasili pouts at me playfully, but he slips the grade book into my desk drawer and uncoils his sinuous body from my chair, which permits him to tower over me. "And hello to you as well. Have you forgotten I'm faculty, darling?"

"Then act like it." I glare at him over the width of my ancient desk, my patience already worn thin to the point of snapping. "Not like some sneering comic book villain."

"Dear pet." By the guttering light of the rack of candles he's lit (no doubt for dramatic effect, because I also possess a proper desk lamp, which he's ignored), Vasili presses an elegant hand to his chest and looks offended. "Do rest assured I've missed you dreadfully as well, but there's no need to get quite so personal."

Pet is what he calls me when he fucks me. Now that playful endearment has the same effect on me it always does. Just as the rogue intends.

My wolf wants nothing more than to bend for him.

That outcome would be disastrous.

Firmly I resist the impulse, although he certainly draws the eye with his silver hair artfully tousled to graze his jaw, his eyes rimmed in smoky liner, his cruel mouth slicked with gloss and smirking, not to mention those boots and breeches that showcase his slim hips and long legs to such lethal effect.

I barely manage not to leer. Instead, my gaze slides over his unorthodox attire in the frowning perusal that strikes fear in the heart of my students.

Oh, he definitely looks well tumbled, because by now I'm extremely familiar with the look. That well-fucked demeanor of his inevitably piques my interest and my wolf's. I have it from our mating bond in an eyeblink, because Vasili's bitten me, so we're linked telepathically. The damnable reprobate is inwardly preening over his sexual performance in some sort of steamy *Star Wars* role-play the three of them indulged in last night all over the stolen Academy jet.

To be precise, he's smugly congratulating himself for how relentlessly and repeatedly he and Ronin made our queen climax.

With her Gemini witchcraft and her precarious control, they're fortunate they didn't crash that plane.

"Merciful Christ," I mutter, tugging at my tie, because he's scenting heavily—the butterscotch and sandalwood of his mating scent—and suddenly this dank and drafty crypt is far too warm. "Kindly vacate my desk. And turn on that damned lamp. This isn't a vampire film."

"Hmmm," Vasili purrs, ignoring all my guidance in favor of leaning over my desk like an adder preparing to strike. He pulls in a slow inhale of my own wolfish scent. "Intriguing. You're pissy because you're going into heat. Rushing matters just a bit though, aren't we? The moon isn't full till Saturday."

My itchy agitation eases a notch.

At least this scoundrel hasn't been entirely unaware of my looming hormonal dilemma (and Zara's). He's been tracking my cycle like a proper alpha.

Shaking my head at his intransigence, I twist the knob myself to light my green-shaded desk lamp. A spill of golden light chases the shadows to the corners of the crypt and renders the entire encounter more businesslike and less dramatic. This sudden rush of light illuminates the actual sarcophagus looming in one corner, containing the rotted bones of some long-deceased Academy don under its stone lid, which I've always found to be rather atmospheric.

Now I stride straight past my looming alpha and erring student to the ancient relic and place one hand on the cold stone for fortitude.

Although, surely, no professor in the storied history of this Academy has been plagued with students as vexatious as mine.

"Mr. Romanov," I announce grimly to the room at large. "As your headmaster and your faculty mentor, I must advise that all three of you are in considerable disfavor with the Dean. Unfortunately, as Zara and Ronin are both students and still legally minors in the witching world, whereas you are a member of this faculty and presumably old enough to know better, the Dean has reserved her particular ire for you."

"That old witch." He slithers out from behind my desk at last and undulates back and forth across the narrow confines between my desk and the worn leather sofa where my wolf and I sometimes nap between classes. "I presume you're about to inflict some sort of tiresome punishment for my trivial violations of that antiquated Academy Codex."

"I'm afraid you've left me no choice. If I don't act now and with conviction, rest assured the Dean most certainly will."

Seizing my moment (since he's finally ceded my desk), I stride forward to reclaim my territory and lower myself into my chair. I spare a frown for the formerly locked drawer of my desk. Vasili's more than a wickedly powerful telekinetic. He pairs his astonishing power with exceptional control. Clearly, he's jimmied the lock.

He's so gifted, this student of mine.

Pity he's so damned unethical.

"I suppose you intend to suspend me." Still prowling before my desk, he utters a bratty huff that seizes me with the violent impulse to punish him with kisses. Of course, this is an impulse I forcibly suppress. "What do you fancy that will achieve? Unless you're planning to teach Mogadon Magics yourself—as a non-Mogadon—you'll simply have to face the music." He waves an airy hand. "There's no getting rid of me. I'm indispensable."

"You're certainly insufferable." Grimly I eye my wayward colleague, who merely smirks at my ire. "As you yourself have taken pains to note, you're more than merely a student at this Academy. But you're only provisionally a member of the faculty—a status which is easily revoked."

A hint of shock flickers in his perfect face before his mask of insolence slips back into place. "Are you actually threatening to fire me?"

If only I had that luxury.

I swallow a sigh.

Vasili Romanov is more than my student, my colleague, and now—greatly to my shock the night he bit me—my alpha. I'm also fighting tooth and claw the insidious suspicion that I'm falling in love with the brat.

That's one complication the volatile dynamic at this Academy, in our *domus*, and within our harem definitely doesn't require.

Well, our relationship has never been simple, his and mine. These days, it's damnably complex. What I'm feeling toward him now is far more than professional disappointment for his shortcomings. I'm suffering all the lovesick heartache and injured ego of a man whose lover doesn't trust him enough to take him into his confidence.

But what I'm required to say to him has nothing to do with emotion and everything to do with duty.

"No member of this faculty is indispensable, Mr. Romanov," I say sharply. "Yourself included. But you're new to this role. Fortunately, the faculty handbook contains a procedure for instructing unsatisfactory teachers."

He utters a scornful snort. "What do you imagine you'll do? Bite me the way you did Ronin? Ostensibly to enforce your discipline until, oh dear, the target of your formidable wrath goes into heat?"

He looks utterly appalled by the concept, as any proper alpha would be. He's never been bitten and, to my knowledge, he's also never been fucked. Not from, well, the receiving end. Vasili emphatically does the biting *and* the fucking in our bed. But I too am alpha—toward everyone in our harem *except* Vasili—and suddenly my wolf is slavering at the prospect of biting *him*.

God, to have him under me. To have him submit to *me* for once, gasping and mindless with pleasure.

I clear my throat and shift in my seat to ease the sudden hot swell of my shaft against my zipper. I can barely manage to meet my new colleague's wary gaze when I'm this hot to fornicate with him but, somehow, I manage it.

"I'm placing you on an improvement plan," I state briskly.

Naturally, he sneers.

I clasp my hands on my desk and give him my sternest look. This is the most delicate and difficult element of our confrontation, the moment I've been dreading. If he balks outright at the Dean's edict, there will be no salvaging either his academic career or his graduation prospects. To minimize the likelihood of his defiance, or perhaps merely to preserve the fragile and precious harmony of our polycule for just a little longer, I'm determined to tell him no more now than I must.

I drum my fingers on the desk and keep my voice level. "I'm endeavoring to put the fear of God into you. You claim to be the dominant alpha in this harem? Then, by Christ, it's time for you to act like it. Work with me like a responsible adult to protect our queen. Stop aiding and abetting her worst impulses. As you're all too well aware, she's criminally reckless."

"Well, of course she's reckless, darling." He rolls his pretty eyes. "She's Zara. Reckless is her middle name. She's like a tiger in a cage at this Academy, chafing and snarling at the bars. Besides, that wretched ex-lover of hers betrayed her—twice over, as it happens—and she wasn't about to let that stand. She would have claimed her vengeance, Lucius, either with or without us."

This, of course, is nothing less than the truth. Yet it maddens me to hear his defiance.

"Then you should have come to me!" I snap, smarting under the lash of his betrayal. "You should have allowed me to manage her."

"As if anyone could." His nostrils flare in derision.

This is another truth I don't care to acknowledge.

"Nonetheless," I forge on grimly, "I must know that I can rely upon you to temper our queen's rash and dangerous instincts, her rebellion against the strictures that are meant to keep her safe, both now at this Academy and later on the throne."

"Why rely upon me? She'll crown that imbecile Neo who was born and bred for it, then Ronin and perhaps you—but never me," he snarls, with a sudden flash of bitterness that startles me. "Believe me, no one wants a queer king on the witching world throne."

"For the love of God." I gaze at him in utter astonishment, because he's never been obtuse. Can he possibly believe this nonsense, or is he merely toying with me? "You're her alpha and the most powerful warlock in her harem. When she's ready to ascend, you'll be the first consort she crowns. What I need to know now—what the Dean needs to know—is that you possess the maturity and the discipline to behave responsibly when the time comes. To state it plainly, what's required now on your part is a demonstration of your obedience."

"Obedience! How precisely do you propose I demonstrate a quality I don't possess?" He's stopped pacing to loom scowling over my desk, arms folded across his chest in what could easily pass for hostility.

But he's my alpha, and underneath all that contempt he wields like a blade, he's… hurting. He's been hurting since he fired off that allegation that no one wants him ruling because he's queer.

I must proceed with care now, because I've no wish to hurt him worse.

"Well, don't keep me in suspense, darling," he drawls, one scornful eyebrow climbing over a venomous eye. "What tedious duties does this little improvement plan of yours entail?"

With difficulty, I tamp down this spike of concern for my student—because he is still that too, and I care desperately for his welfare and his state of mind, whether he wants me to care or not—and apply my concentration to the delicate maneuvering that is now required.

"I'm assigning you to tutor a student who urgently requires it," I say carefully.

"Oh God, not our resident Hufflepuff again." Vasili snorts. "I told you the last time we tried this nonsense. No amount of tutoring on my part is going to make Mallory McSnicker pass her midterms. She's a catastrophically weak witch. This entire endeavor is a complete waste of time. *My* time."

I proceed now with extreme care.

"The task may seem trivial, but I assure you, it is not. I'm well aware you're already teaching two classes and carrying a full course load yourself, with qualifying exams of your own to pass this spring."

"Qualifying exams?" Seemingly recovered from whatever was troubling him a moment ago, the villain bares his teeth in a contemptuous smirk. "Oh please. I could sit for those piddling tests today and pass every one with flying colors."

I'm well aware this fiendishly brilliant student of mine rarely studies. He scrapes through his courses on pure talent, buttressed with stubbornness and ego.

But I firmly refuse to be distracted by his hubris.

"Unfortunately, your mentee received none of the prep school coursework that's typically required for admittance, which imposes a considerable challenge." I unbuckle my briefcase and remove the weighty study plan I've written out by hand (because computers don't work behind the wards) in anticipation of this discussion. "I've designed a rigorous curriculum that contains all the necessary fundamentals. I'm relying upon you to administer daily lectures, assign and grade practical exercises as appropriate, and supply tutorials in Common Magics 101, Foundations of Witching World Law, Basic Science of Witchcraft, and Familiarization with Mogadon Magic. I'll take the newcomer in hand for History of Witchcraft, I'll ask Neo to provide tutoring in Alchemy, and Mistress Agrippina will make room for one more in her Genetics class—"

"And the student?" Vasili is eyeing me with open suspicion, because I've carefully closed my mind to him as my alpha, and of course he senses that. "We *are* talking about Mallory, aren't we?"

I place the improvement plan on the desk between us like the ultimatum it is and level him with my sternest look. "Will you undertake the task or not? Because if the answer is no, you might as well return to the *domus* right now and pack your bags for a one-way trip out on the next supply plane."

In the rhythmic hiss of his breath, my lupine senses pick up a startled hitch.

Utterly appalled, he gazes at me, and I wonder desperately if I've gotten through to him at all. Saints preserve me, it will kill Zara and Ronin if I have to send him away. It will utterly destroy this fragile family we've cobbled together. Indeed, if I'm compelled to repudiate my alpha, I'm not at all certain how I'll manage to survive these uncontrollable heats myself.

He plants his hands on my desk without touching the file I've left him and looms over me, all that porcelain prettiness of his honed sharp as a stiletto. "Tell me one thing more, Lucius, and I'll give you my answer."

Carefully I maintain my composure. "What is it, Mr. Romanov?"

His voice dwindles to a whisper even my wolfish senses must strain to hear. "If I have to leave, will you even miss me?"

My heart clenches hard in a fist.

"My God, Vasili," I breathe, staring up at him. "Is this another of your rotten, wretched, manipulative mind games? How can you possibly be so blind?"

He searches my face with his pale glittering gaze. For some reason, my heart is pounding and I can barely breathe. Within the shell of my skin, my wolf rolls to expose his belly and whines in desperate entreaty.

"Hmmm," Vasili says at last, lids falling over his searching gaze. "At least your wolf would miss me. In any event, he'd miss being fucked into a sex coma by his alpha, wouldn't he?"

"Oh, for the love of Heaven." Roughly I thrust to my feet and reach for him. "You have to know you're far more to both of us than just the man who fucks me—"

A curtain falls over that cruel beauty he wears. Deftly he evades my touch.

"Look in the drawer." His shuttered gaze flickers to the locked desk he's violated. "I brought you a souvenir from Sin City. A curious trinket to be filed and tucked away in the Academy vault. It's a nullifying object, quite a powerful one, which Zara claimed as tribute from that rotten little pinch-purse who betrayed her. I've locked it in a lead box."

In that moment, I hardly care what he's brought me. Without so much as glancing at the detailed instructions I've painstakingly transcribed for him, my impossible student pivots on his heel to saunter for the door.

Clearly he's preparing to leave, and he still hasn't given me the answer he's promised.

"Blood of Christ." Abandoning all restraint, I vault from behind the desk and rush after him. "Don't you dare leave this hanging. Do you intend to submit to my discipline or not?"

With one hand on the door, his arrogant head swivels toward me. Finally, the naked urgency that saturates my tone surfaces one of those cold malicious smiles for which he's so notorious.

"Let's just wait a bit and see, darling, shall we?" he murmurs. "Bring me your poor little student and take your chances."

Before I can stop him or voice any of the irritated objections to that plan that are bubbling to my lips, the infuriating wretch has vanished.

Chapter Twelve
Vasili

Hours have passed since Lucius issued his horrid ultimatum, night has fallen, and I've finally returned to the *domus* after fretfully paging through my long-neglected textbooks and a pile of student assignments in desperate need of grading, my labors interspersed with bouts of pacing the empty streets to work off my simmering agitation.

And I've barely gotten home when I have my inevitable run-in with that luscious little imbecile Mercury.

When I saunter into the great room, four of my housemates are already scattered about, studying for midterms in the blazing light and heat of the central hearth.

Racetrack's sitting cross-legged on the settee before the fire in faded jeans and a flannel shirt, her hard face stamped with her usual scowl. Deftly she scribbles in her journal (she writes appalling poetry with no meter, caps, or punctuation, and she fondly imagines none of us know) while she simultaneously toasts a marshmallow to a fiery crisp on a long stick.

Zara's curled up on the high-backed Renaissance sofa. There she nibbles on a pencil and frowns over her Common Magics grimoire. She's bundled her succulent body in one of Mercury's oversized Academy sweaters, with thick socks over her leggings. Ronin wraps around her from behind like a blanket while he studies over her shoulder from the same text, his long hair spilling forward to curtain her arm.

Looking well content with the entire arrangement, my boyfriend spares me a lazy grin.

Hmmm. It's obvious to me the two of them have been fucking again since I left. Probably with that overeager puppy Mercury.

I'm truly sorry I've missed it.

The peanuty spice of kung pao chicken and the sizzle of sesame oil emanate from the open kitchen, where Dez is handily whipping up one of her culinary masterpieces for collective consumption in the *domus*'s big wok. We all take turns on kitchen duty, but Lucius usually cooks on Thursdays, so that's something else our unscheduled absence has thrown off.

But Neo Mercury, notoriously my sworn enemy at this Academy until quite recently, commands the lion's share of my attention.

After the ordeal of this unauthorized separation from his fated mate, I fully expect to find him lying across Zara's legs like a lapdog, drooling and panting with contentment.

Instead, he's barricaded himself behind orderly piles of textbooks in his study nook in the corner, his broad shoulders and wide chest poured into another of those ubiquitous Academy sweaters as he bends diligently over a notebook lined with his copperplate script. A sloppy comma of magenta hair obscures his puppy-dog eyes.

Very briefly, I'm tempted to stroke it back for him.

Of course, his demeanor changes the moment he looks up to find me invading the room (where I have every right to be). His offensively gorgeous mouth hardens and his perfectly square jaw juts. Then he rakes back that ridiculous mop of purple curls, pushes his stylish glasses firmly up his nose, and shoves to his feet.

"Hi, bad boy," Zara murmurs to me from the couch without looking up, frowning as she underlines something in her textbook.

"Good evening, darlings," I purr to the room at large. "Did you miss me terribly?"

In fact, I'm not entirely certain of the welcome I'll receive, especially with Mercury circling his desk with that alarmingly purposeful expression and powering across the big room in my direction.

"Hiya, cobber," Dez calls cheerfully from the kitchen, her ponytailed head popping briefly into view. A mischievous smile animates her face. "Wouldn't insist on an honest answer to that one from this lot, yeah? Pop off those snowy boots, there's a love. We'll eat in a jiffy."

Racetrack spares my return an indifferent look and shoves her burning marshmallow deeper into the fire. "Dinner's gonna be late, obviously. Lucius is MIA. Didn't happen to run into him while you were out, did ya, Romanov?"

So much for being missed.

"Oh, hours ago at the church," I say vaguely, my gaze veering from Racetrack to Mercury bearing down on me.

We haven't attacked one another—not physically, at least—since Zara's added us both to her harem. But that could certainly change if little Neo's still as pissy about being left behind as all those voice mails he left on Ronin's mobile appear to imply.

"Careful," I murmur as he closes in. My fingers tingle with witchcraft, but Zara will be furious if I assault her precious poodle. "You're drooling, and this frock coat requires dry cleaning."

"You're such a jerk," he says roughly, which is certainly an understatement if ever I've heard one. "I mean it."

"Well, guilty as charged…" I simper.

"Shut up." His hard hands connect with my chest and shove me back into the nearest wall.

Then my nemesis at this Academy dives in, crushes his mouth over mine, and proceeds to kiss me absolutely speechless (an exceedingly rare occurrence, I assure you).

We've only kissed once since we joined our queen's harem, and that encounter was instigated by me, mainly at Zara's urging. So it's an entirely novel experience for him to initiate any sort of intimacy with despicable me. Now his big hands clutch my shoulders hard enough to bruise my tender skin.

But I've never been one to mind a bit of rough handling. Depending on who does the handling…

As a recent virgin, he's still supposed to be a novice at all this, but he shoves his minty tongue into my mouth and halfway down my throat like he truly means business. For a breath, it's like being kiss-raped by a determined mug of peppermint hot chocolate.

But he has the most luscious lips.

I've always secretly thought so, even when I hated him.

First kisses are invariably a bit awkward in my experience, given these horrific fangs I'm stuck with, which have to be worked around, since they're sharp enough to do real damage. (This is technically our second kiss, but still.)

All the same, our First Boy polishes my apple right from the start with the eager way he licks at my horrid incisors. It's as though he's all but daring me to bite him.

I hum with approval low in my throat and grip his corduroy-clad hips to ease him closer. His clean innocent scent of sage and hand-milled soap twines through my senses, spiked with a nice spritz of my own mating scent that makes us both shiver.

Hmmm, this is delicious.

He's delicious.

And we're both simply floating under the endorphin rush of all these pheromones I'm kicking out.

My tongue snakes around his to claim him and take control. I massage that slick organ of his until he sways and topples into me.

My, he's *blazingly* hard.

He's blazingly hard… for *me*.

This startling revelation sends a shock of heat searing straight down my shaft to clench my balls like a bolt of lightning.

My hands tighten around his hips until our cocks bump together through all our layers. That blaze of contact gives me another electrifying jolt that makes both of us moan.

He's notoriously shy, but he isn't acting like it tonight, and I'm seriously tempted to grip his scrumptious ass and grind up against that monster cock of his. This prospect is especially tempting since I sense Zara and Ronin watching, and I know just how much they'll enjoy this particular performance.

Before I can entirely make up my mind to press my luck, this delightful moment passes, to my regret.

With a breathless gasp, Neo wrenches free from my amorous clutches and lurches back to let us both up for air. He's blushing fiery red, and his glasses are all steamy.

"Jerk," he repeats for good measure, sounding positively winded (because I do tend to have that effect on a man).

He licks his well-kissed lips and pushes his glasses up his nose with an unsteady finger.

"Whatever I've done to piss you off, darling, remind me to do more of it," I murmur, unpeeling from the wall like a python to undulate after him. "Has anyone ever told you that you're adorable when you're all worked up like this? Rather like a furious puppy."

To be honest, I wouldn't mind another of his furious kisses, and I'm more than half-inclined to initiate the next one myself.

Clearly he recognizes the predatory gleam in my eye. He wisely backs away before I can shove him face-down over the settee, wrestle his prep-school chinos down around his ankles, storm the citadel of the First Boy's virtue, and rail him relentlessly until he wails his climax into the upholstery and I've finally put an end to this infuriating sexual impasse he's imposed between us.

My sole consolation is that the lone kiss I did manage to winkle out of him still has him blushing.

Not to mention the fringe benefit that our antics have thoroughly distracted both Zara and Ronin in the very best of ways. Heat is rising under Zara's suntanned cheeks, and Ronin's eyes are glowing with topaz fire.

Hmmm. They're both so delectably close to going into heat.

Perhaps Lucius wasn't entirely unjustified in his pique over the timing of our little exploit.

"Don't even pretend you don't know what you did," Neo mutters, by now in full retreat, adorably sulky and quite close indeed to pouting. In fact, if he sticks out that lower lip of his any further, I'm going to bite it, and I won't be held responsible for the consequences. "You're in major trouble, Vasili. And you of all people were supposed to know better."

"Yes, yes, don't be tedious. I've had all this already from Lucius." I wave an impatient hand, disappointed beyond words to see Neo retreat to his study nook.

I wonder if tonight, in our queen's bed, I'll finally have better luck with him.

Well, here's hoping.

To distract myself from that no doubt ill-advised temptation, not to mention this rather insistent boner he's given me that's so glaringly obvious to the entire room given the fashionably snug fit of my breeches, I shift my gaze to the unaesthetic (to me) sight of Racetrack's messy sprawl across the settee. I would've had to shove her aside to ream Neo across it. Of course, being Racetrack and notably gay, she's spectacularly unimpressed by this smoking guy-on-guy encounter she's just witnessed.

Wicked with all that frustrated lust Neo's stirred up in me, I scowl at Racetrack. Predictably, she flips me the bird and scowls back.

"Your marshmallow is a fiery coal, Abigail," I point out airily.

"That's just how I like 'em. And don't call me Abigail, you dick," she says without heat, rescuing her flaming treat from the fire at last. "No one here missed you, by the way."

"Oh, no doubt," I say silkily. I swank over to lounge beside Zara and Ronin on the sofa, then lean in to kiss both of them—at least *they* missed me, surely—before I toe out of my wet boots.

Hmmm, my girl gives me plenty of tongue, and her sweet mouth tastes like ripe strawberries. I hum with rising interest and return the favor. My queen sucks on my tongue like she's imagining it's my cock, which floods my shaft with a rush of tingling warmth and gives me all sorts of lovely ideas for later.

Dear me, she's flushed and sweating from far more than the fire. Her mating scent of roses and vanilla perfumes the air quite heavily. I wonder if her heat might not be starting this very night. If it does, we're all in for a wild ride, particularly if her heat sets Ronin's off.

Truly, it seems we've barely arrived back at Icarus in time. Perhaps, indeed, I ought to have insisted we not travel at all until—

This charming interlude is well and truly broken by Lucius' distinctive tread. Sadly, Zara sucks in a breath and ends our kiss, her worried gaze already darting to the vestibule.

Over the medley of Asian spices emanating from the kitchen and mingling with the revolting stench of burned marshmallow, I can't smell a whiff of our headmaster.

But I'd know the cadence of his footsteps blindfolded.

All that earlier agitation, from which I was so briefly but delightfully distracted by Neo's unexpected affections, comes rushing back. The prospect of prolonging my confrontation with Lucius, this time in front of the others, makes my skin itch. I've been doing my level best not to dwell on the fact that I'll most likely have to lower myself to kiss the Dean's ancient ass in order to avoid being both expelled and fired from the Icarus Academy with a single stroke of her vengeful pen.

Oh, I put on a convincing show at the crypt for Lucius. Convincing enough that I left the poor dear fuming at my horrible intransigence.

Still, despite my resistance, I suppose I'll have to eat crow and spend every spare moment from now to graduation slaving away to tutor Mallory McSnicker or whatever poor nitwit Lucius has dredged up to punish me.

The very notion makes me sulky.

And I'm an absolute bitch when I'm sulky.

By the time Lucius climbs the short flight of stairs and enters the great room, still wearing his tweed coat and gripping his briefcase, with his chestnut hair swept into a knot and his expression carefully composed, it's all I can manage not to say something cutting about his tardiness. Lucius is typically a stickler for being on time, and swiping at him would relieve the tension.

But he takes one look at Zara and Ronin bundled on the couch—his bonded mates, both of whom he's bitten, and whom he clearly hasn't seen since their return—and his predatory alpha instincts surge to the fore. He tosses his briefcase carelessly toward the hall table and leaps halfway across the great room to meet them in a single wolfish bound.

He's nearly upon us when he masters the impulse and pulls up short, his scholarly features under his goatee a study in restraint and barely contained fury.

Zara, bless her wild heart, suffers no such scruples. She scrambles to her feet to meet her alpha halfway and envelops him in a desperate embrace, with Ronin a breath behind.

Leaving me cruelly abandoned and pouting on the sofa.

Lucius is no match for the two of them, at least he's no match for them *now*, when they're both on the edge of going into heat. He drags them both hard against his rangy frame and rubs his face in their hair to scent them, eyes glowing red and fangs distended and face fractured with need.

"My dear ones," he says hoarsely, his wolf lurking in his voice. "You sweet wretched imps. Promise me you'll never do anything like this again."

Well, now I'm completely jealous.

He certainly didn't greet me that way at the crypt. I didn't even get a peck on the cheek. Instead, I received a tiresome lecture.

He still hasn't laid a finger on me since I returned.

"Don't blame Ronin," Zara mumbles into Lucius' neck as she cuddles against him, standing on tiptoe to wind her arms around him. "Or Vasili. Blame me. It was all my fault. It was my idea. I tried to go without them. They tried to stop me, but they couldn't."

"You think I don't know that?" Lucius growls through his fangs. "You think the prospect of you hurling yourself into a situation like that alone makes it any easier to bear?"

Neo utters a gruff noise from his corner that affirms this sentiment. Truly, I am beginning to wonder if we ought not to have consulted them, at least, before we went haring off. I'm even wondering whether our decision to indulge Zara's little rebellion might have done lasting damage to the fragile trust the five of us have only just begun to build.

And I'm wondering what it might take to repair that damage.

If it can be repaired at all.

"You going to suspend us, love?" Ronin mutters between desperate kisses that Lucius returns with a sort of savage fervor. "Because Zara can't afford to miss any more classes if you want her to pass her midterms. She's barely gotten settled—"

"Perhaps these are factors you should have considered, you scamp, before the three of you stole that jet." With a firm kiss for each of them, Lucius steadies them on their feet and disentangles gently from their clinging arms. "There now. We'll discuss all of this after dinner."

They're both still hovering, Zara and Ronin, both clearly craving their alpha's reassurance, but it's perfectly obvious (at least to me) that Lucius is feeling hurt and betrayed under all that professorial propriety. For him, our defection is not so easily forgiven. Still, he takes his responsibility as their alpha seriously. He isn't small-minded or manipulative, I'll certainly say that for him.

He spares each of them a brief distracted smile and a final reassuring squeeze. But it's all too clear there's a great deal weighing on his mind.

I definitely don't like the fact that his psychic barriers—against me, his own alpha—are still sky-high.

Reluctantly, the two of them give him the space he demands, tucking up against each other for comfort.

With a visible effort at restraint, Lucius' red-tinged eyes sweep over Racetrack making a complete mess of her disgusting charred marshmallow and Dez bustling about like a house elf in the kitchen and Neo watching closely from his study nook (blushing tomato-red again, for some reason, which wrings an affectionate smile out of Lucius even in his distracted state).

Finally, my headmaster's wary gaze settles on me.

I'd like to keep him in dreadful suspense as long as possible from sheer perversity, because I'm pea green with envy over those kisses and cuddles and smiles he's dispensing left and right for everyone in our relationship except me.

Of course, being me, I find myself uncoiling from the couch and gliding across the floor to torment him. Now he looks even more guarded, for which I can hardly blame him. I'm his most difficult student and, truth to tell, I'm a dreadful bully.

I'm terrifying, darling. I truly am.

Even in my stocking feet.

"I do believe you owe me a little something as well," I hiss.

"Behave yourself, Mr. Romanov." He levels me a look of warning. Of course, the menacing effect is rather spoiled by the way his hot eyes slide over me, all long-legged and yummy in my breeches. That red glow in his eyes deepens and his fangs descend further.

"Now where's the fun in that?" I slither into his personal space like the biblical serpent tempting Eve in the garden.

But I don't touch.

Not yet.

Instead I rear over him, my nostrils flaring wide to breathe in the musky scent of wet wolf rising from his skin and hair. His breath roughens. His pulse hammers in his corded neck above his starched shirt. Under all those layers of professorial propriety, his beast is prowling, rabid to be unleashed.

"Vasili," Lucius rumbles. Which is certainly an improvement from being addressed by my surname like an erring freshman.

"Pet." My voice drops to a whisper only he can hear. I bend to brush his ear with my lips. "Tonight I'm going to fuck you raw."

A shudder snakes through him and a groan wrenches from his throat. The sudden reek of predator floods the air. He's hard for me now and scenting. Hunger for him pounds hot and heavy in my groin.

"Not until you give me your answer." Strain threads his low voice and stretches each word to a sliver. "If you're leaving… there's no point…"

Christ, I love his resistance, even as I curse him for it. My cock in my breeches is an absolute rod.

"Hmmmm." My tongue traces his ear in a slow swipe. The dark taste of him—so familiar, yet so new after all these days apart—hones my senses rapier-sharp.

He trembles violently under my tongue, precisely the way he'll tremble later, when I rim him before I fuck him.

His voice splinters with need. "Damn it to hell, Vasili, I mean it."

"Dear pet." I trap his earlobe under one of my loathsome fangs and give him a nip that makes him gasp. "Don't fret. I'll tutor your rotten little hellion."

A surprised cry spills out of him. His face snaps toward me, transcendent with relief.

I smirk at him and dive in to steal a quick kiss before he can elude me.

He's not normally one for public displays of affection (to put it mildly), but he's so thankful I've agreed to his wretched improvement plan that he permits it, his delicious mouth all hot and yielding. Our lips fuse together, my tongue sliding into his mouth to unfurl over his palate and wrap around his fangs. His tongue spears against mine in a heated promise that he'll fight me like hell before he bends for me tonight.

This promising exchange is interrupted by the scornful snort that emanates from the shadowy depths of the vestibule, coupled with a hateful voice whose guttural cadence clenches my gut in a vise.

"Romanov, truly, you have not changed. Is there no man living who is safe from your unnatural lusts?"

A current of icy shock spills through me like a bolt of Zara's lightning. My head snaps up to glare over Lucius' shoulder at this intruder who's polluting my doorstep with his obnoxious and offensive presence.

Good God.

It's that fucking dragon.

My enemy.

My enemy has invaded my home.

Aggression floods through me and a growl surges up my throat. A filthy curse rips out of Ronin, who's thankfully standing with Zara behind me, well beyond the creature's grasp. Subtly I gesture to keep both of them safely where they are.

To be honest, I hardly expect Zara to heed me.

I glare straight across the room at the loathsome wretch. I burn to incinerate Maxim Rasputin with my eyes. Regrettably, that's an extinct gift (as far as we know), so the villain just keeps standing there in our home as though he has every right to be here.

At least this time he's wearing clothes. Even if he looks thoroughly disreputable lurking there, nearly as tall as I, lean and hungry-looking in a scuffed leather motorcycle jacket, ripped jeans that cling to his wiry hips, and battered shitkickers dripping snow all over our nice dry floor. His pale hair is raked back in a braid that bares every savage line and angle in his cold Slavic face. In those freakish eyes now locked on mine, his uncanny pupils slit narrow with menace.

"Truly," the fool persists, "is there no man living you will not despoil?"

I eye the prick with real dislike. "Well, *obviously*, Maximka. There's you."

At this point, I fully expect some sort of classic homophobic fusillade. Well, bring it on. I truly hope he will expose to Zara and all of them just what sort of creature this flying Godzilla with his narrow-minded Orthodox upbringing truly is.

However, to my disappointment, the dragon doesn't utter a single word.

For some reason, he actually looks a tad… distracted… by my little zinger.

"Damnation," Lucius sighs. "Mr. Rasputin, I asked you to wait quietly in the hall until I summoned you. Apparently, even that was too much to ask."

The dragon's shoulders square and his mouth hardens in a familiar stubborn line. "I have every right to be here in this house. The same right that this one does."

By *this one*, of course, he means me.

Rage courses through my blood. The rush of my Mogadon pheromones floods the air like a lethal gas. He's my enemy, he's inside *my* home, and he's here for Zara, I know he is.

What I simply cannot fathom is why on earth they've allowed this felon past the Academy wards.

Until he swings a battered backpack from his shoulder to the floor. A backpack which looks suspiciously loaded with… books.

Textbooks.

My soul erupts in an absolute volcano of rebellion.

"For fuck's sake, Lucius," I hiss, so livid I can barely speak. "He's, what, a student here now? Are you absolutely insane?"

I'd like to roll my eyes at the outrageous suspicions now racing through my brain, except I don't dare let that crocodile out of my sight.

Not even for an eyeroll.

Instead, I bare my horrid shifter fangs at the creature in an intimidation display that's pure instinct and entirely beyond my control.

Across the room, the dragon snarls back. I half-expect him to unroll a forked tongue and spray blinding venom in my face like his loathsome wyvern brothers.

"Now, gentlemen, stop growling. Both of you. And I'll ask you both to keep civil tongues in your heads." Firmly Lucius plants himself between us, exerting every ounce of his own alpha authority, as though he's fearful we'll tear each other to bloody ribbons. (Admittedly, the thought has crossed my mind, and I do have my knives.)

Lucius' stern warning look tells me he's picked up the thought.

But I'm so wrathful I scarcely care.

I don't dare even look for Zara, who's lurking so ominously silent behind me, her psychic barriers locked down tight—a degree of restraint that can't possibly last.

I do catch a glimpse of Racetrack gaping at this Shakespearean drama from the settee, her half-eaten marshmallow fallen to the upholstery in a gooey mess.

"I want that warlock's blood," Rasputin grinds through clenched teeth, glaring straight at me with his dragon eyes. I do hope he's not about to shift and bring the roof down. "He has dishonored me. He refused to fight me fairly and left me for dead—"

"If I wanted you dead, *malchik,* rest assured your odiferous corpse would be rotting in the Nevada desert—"

"Mr. Romanov is a member of this faculty and is to be treated as such." Lucius speaks over both of us (I know, how rude!) and sweeps his commanding stare over the room at large. "As for Mr. Rasputin, he is our newest student and resident of this *domus*. He merits the same courtesy as any other member of this cohort."

Well, *fuck*.

That hideous utterance confirms every horrid suspicion teeming through my brain.

"Oh dear God, then it's actually true," I groan in absolute disgust. "He's enrolled. He's moving in. And now you want me to tutor that fucking dragon."

Chapter Thirteen
Maxim

Of all the enemies who dwell in this place, where I am now trapped by my own choice deep in hostile territory behind wards I cannot escape, it is Vasili Romanov who poses the greatest danger. He would kill me if he could, just as I would surely kill him.

Yet it is she who consumes me.

My dragon queen.

Zara.

I have thought of nothing else since the night I plucked her from the sky. She of the lightning gift, she who knows no fear, she of the flaming eyes and the savage heart, she who commands gods to worship her.

For I am surely the closest creature to a god who walks this earth and rules these skies. And I do as she commands.

Beyond any question, I worship her.

Now this queen of mine lures my gaze away from Romanov (which is no small thing, for he is compelling in his own way, this deadly enemy of mine, with his hidden blades and his catastrophic beauty).

My sovereign draws me away from his terrible light to circle her irresistible flame.

She has claimed the space before the fiery hearth like the goddess she is. There she stands and eyes me, hip cocked, head tilted, stocking-clad toes tapping the floor. Her entire body simmers with impatience. Her aquamarine eyes are narrow with suspicion and her lush mouth is tight with anger.

Clearly she is angry with me for pursuing her, pursuing her to this island, pursuing her into the very sanctum of her home.

But I will pursue her anywhere.

I will pursue her to the ends of this earth.

There is nowhere I will not pursue her, wherever I must, to claim her.

She is wearing another man's clothing, which rouses all my protective instincts and makes me savage with jealousy, because it should be I who clothe her, I who comfort her, I who covet and protect and spoil her. My keen dragonish senses are swimming with the scent of these others who have mounted her and rutted with her and spilled their seed inside her.

Under the captivating perfume of her mating scent which fills this house like a compulsion no male can resist, she reeks of their passion.

To my eyes, her skin glows with heat. She may not wish it (because this much is becoming clear to me) but, all the same, her body is preparing her to breed. It is not even necessary to kill her mates (yet). My very presence—the presence of her dragon king—will be enough to trigger her superheat. Lightning crackles like static in her hair and her eyes swirl gold with dragonfire.

Truly, my dragon rumbles, his crafty hiss filling my head, *she is very close to rising. When she takes wing in her mating flight, we will claim her.*

Because she is so dangerously close to rising, my dragon is dangerously close to rut. He is vicious when we rut, even with those lesser wyverns that are the only females we have ever known—briefly and with so little satisfaction—until this queen of mine.

Already, our rut threatens to madden us. My cock swells and shoves against my zipper, my sensitive barb chafes against the fabric. My wings itch to burst forth from my back and spread. My breath turns rough and my chest feels tight.

Still, I will kill them all when I can, all these lesser mates who have had her, for daring to covet what is mine.

Except…

Briefly my gaze drifts past my angry queen to the one who looms behind her, the one with that silky hair spilling over his shoulders like ink poured from a pitcher and those eyes like Russian amber and that mouth that was surely crafted by the Devil for sin.

He is one of her mates, and one of Romanov's, he was all over them both in that crass American city in the most scandalous way. But after all, she is entitled to claim lesser consorts—after I have bred her. Very secretly, in this houseful of telepaths, I allow myself to admit that I will not mind if this one shares our bed.

Perhaps, if our queen wishes it, solely for her pleasure and in secret, he and I might even…

To my alarm, those amber eyes kindle with sudden wrath.

Yeah, keep telling yourself that, mate. A voice like bronze silk, edged with the crisp cadence of Britain, unspools through my very brain. *In case you haven't noticed, she really doesn't fancy you. And for what you did to Vasili, I could bloody well gut you myself.*

Sudden panic scrabbles through my brain. The panic I learned so well in childhood. The panic of knowing myself vulnerable, with no defense against my mother's endless punishments except to endure them. No defense against my brothers' hateful torments except my determination to survive them.

Now, again, I have no defense against this whisper in my head. No weapon against this intrusion into my guarded secrets.

Yeah, pretty much. That intimate voice licks through me. *Best get used to it. I'm full Valyrian and the strongest telepath at Icarus. You're shit at defense against a proper telepath.*

"I will learn," I mutter under my breath, because it is true, I do not have the ability to transmit my thoughts.

Afraid at the rate you're going, you won't be sticking round the place long enough to learn much of anything. No doubt I am imagining that his tone softens, because sympathy is a concept that is foreign to me, unless it is feigned.

"Enough," the wolf growls.

This is the headmaster, the wolf who brought me to this house. His command cuts through Romanov's venomous objections to my presence, which have persisted this entire time while I stand awkward and alone on their doorstep, making it clear (in case I harbor any doubt) how very much I am unwelcome.

Clearly Lucius Aries is the alpha beneath this roof, because they all turn toward him in the way of those who have formed the habit of obedience, from the fuming queen simmering over my presence to the boyish girl scowling on the settee.

Even Romanov recoils in vicious silence, like an adder poised to strike.

"Mr. Rasputin is now a student of this Academy and a member of this cohort. That decision is final and not subject to debate," the wolf announces to the room at large, in a tone that leaves no room for argument. His whiskey eyes lock with mine and his pupils swell. "He has sworn to follow the rules of this Academy and obey all faculty instructions. So long as he honors that promise, he stays."

My dragon snarls and paces under this alpha's challenge, but I withstand the wolf's menacing stare.

My queen voices a skeptical grunt.

"It is true," I say to her gruffly, my beast lurking in my voice. "I have promised, on my honor as a dragon."

That promise was the price of my admittance to this Academy. A dragon is careful with his words, and I promised nothing I cannot abide.

I would have promised far more for the honor to serve my sovereign.

In truth, I did not mind so much swearing my oath to this wolf. Authority figures are monsters in my experience, all of them, power is ruinous in a dragon. For that, my Lady Mother is the best possible example—

and the worst. I pray she does not soon learn where I am now hidden. Inevitably, once she does, this entire Academy will suffer her fury. But this wolf… this wolf is… different. He actually took my side and argued my case with the Dean, who was more than reluctant to admit me after my dragon's notorious appearance in that city of sin. The Arcane Investigative Bureau is still shutting down the video clips sprinkled across the mortals' social media, and the Arcane Senate is still lying to cover it up.

After this wolf spoke to the Dean in my defense—an experience which happens to me so rarely it is nearly unheard of—I thought myself prepared to give Lucius Aries my obedience.

Of course, that was before I realized my new headmaster is also one of my queen's mates, and therefore my sexual rival.

That revelation, gleaned while I lurked in the vestibule just now and spied on my new cohort, came as an unwelcome one.

"*All* faculty instructions?" Romanov purrs, echoing the wolf. His cruel face goes smooth and his pretty eyes turn wicked. "Well, well. That requirement places matters in rather a different light."

The wolf slices my enemy a look that simmers with warning. "I trust I needn't remind you, Mr. Romanov, that your own status at this Academy hangs by a thread."

My enemy's gaze slices toward me and his mouth crimps with displeasure.

"Thank you, Lucius. I am aware," Romanov says icily.

This is useful intelligence, and clearly my enemy is not pleased that I now possess it.

I am still pondering how best to use it to my advantage when the wolf says firmly, "This is enough discussion for the moment. I see that Dez was kind enough to take my shift in the kitchen. We can all continue getting to know Maxim over dinner."

"Yeah, no." My dragon queen plants her hands on her hips and draws every eye in this room. "That flying Godzilla's not setting foot in this *domus* until he explains why he's really here. Because the last time I saw him, he was threatening to kill all my guys and drag me off with him to Siberia to make dragon babies. Somehow, I doubt he's showing up here now because he's suddenly jonesing for an Academy education."

I square my shoulders and step fully into the room, because clearly no one is going to invite me. She lifts her chin and glares straight at me, silently daring me to deny the truth.

Our gazes lock like clashing swords. My dragon trumpets and beats his wings.

Ours, she is ours. And she is fertile, Maxim. She is fertile!

My dragon can be most single-minded and persistent.

Well, in this pursuit, so am I.

"I will not dishonor you or the bond between us with a lie," I tell my mate, low and fierce. "Soon you will rise, and then I will claim you."

"Yep, there it is right there." Eyes flashing with ire, she spears a glittery fingernail in my direction. "That's what I'm talking about."

A wave of accusing heads snaps toward me.

Now, one and all, these others are rank with suspicion.

I cannot contain my scowl. "Once your superheat is upon you, my Zara, you will no longer oppose me."

"Hey." Another of her mates, one who has been silent, emerges from behind a desk piled with books and hurries to her side. "You can't talk to Zara like that. Heat or no heat, she always gets to choose."

He is young, this one, with a mop of purple curls falling over his brow and a scholar's spectacles perched on his earnest face. He is no fighter, no match for my dragon. But his loyalty to her is absolute, and that is his weapon. Fiercely protective, he plants his big body at her side.

She reaches to claim his hand and draw him close, shooting me a look that dares me to protest.

A whiff of his sage-and-lavender soap floats past me, mingled with her mating scent.

This is the one whose clothing she is wearing.

My lip curls up to bare my teeth in a snarl.

It is shifter instinct, for which I can hardly be blamed (since I am a shifter), although the effect is lessened without my fangs, which a dragon only reveals when he intends to use them.

I have always envied Romanov his fangs, which are very fine, very permanent, and which contribute to his ruinous appeal.

But this bespectacled boy, to my displeasure, looks unimpressed by my display of aggression. He looms protectively over our queen's petite frame and frowns at me as though I am an alchemical formula he firmly intends to master.

"Thank you, baby," my sovereign murmurs, rising on tiptoe to kiss his cheek.

Oh, she loves this one, how she loves him. Her love for him is written in her voice. No one has ever spoken so tenderly to me. I wonder what he has done to earn it.

Perhaps if I observe him long enough, I can learn the way to win my queen's angry heart.

"You wanna win my heart, big guy?" Zara snorts. "For starters, stop threatening my warlocks, you asshole. And, for fuck's sake, *stop* talking about my fucking heat. I'm more than a fucking uterus, you got that?"

I blink at her in surprise. For it appears she too is reading my mind. It is the mate bond, no doubt, its pull between us already so potent.

Still, this kind of exposure is inconvenient.

And it is risky.

Even my thoughts, it seems, I must guard in this strange and hostile place.

The hard-faced blonde on the settee pushes out a disgusted noise and shoves to her feet. "No offense, but if you guys are gonna talk about Zara's heats and shit, Dez and I are chowing down in the library."

My ears prick at the idea that there is a library. My dragon loves adding antique books loaded with ancient wisdom to our horde. As for myself, never permitted the luxury of anything like a formal education, old books are a rare treasure, greatly to be coveted.

Seeing she has gained my attention, this boyish girl gives me a wary look. "Hey, uh, I'm Racetrack. That's my girlfriend Dez in the kitchen. We're exclusive, so don't get any ideas."

Truly, there is no danger of that. I have many ideas, but they all relate to Zara.

"I am Maxim. And there will be no ideas." If they were shifters and of my clan, I would scent them to establish my dominance. But they are not, and I cannot smell my queen's passion or her mating scent upon them, so it must be as they say. These two are not even of her harem.

"Yeah, we're not in the harem," the girl called Dez pipes up. "But we share Zara's roof, so we're her courtiers."

"You're my friends," Zara says firmly.

Dez is the little dark-haired one who has not spoken, but who has hovered in the kitchen doorway watching me this whole time.

And it appears she too has just read my mind.

When I slice her a guarded look, the strange girl taps her temple and winks. "I'm Valyrian, like Ronin. My gifts are telepathy and precognition, yeah? Don't let it freak you out."

Then this Dez is another telepath I must be wary of. Until now, I have had little exposure to any arcanes who are not of my clan, except for that disastrous summer with the Romanovs.

Already I am beginning to feel out of my depth at this Academy.

But I am determined not to show it.

"Yeah, and I'm Mogadon. So don't fuck with me." The one called Racetrack gives me a hard look. "You'll find out why soon enough. That's assuming you last the night."

Apparently I will learn her arcane gift later. Is this one threatening me or warning me?

"I will last the night," I say shortly.

"Hmmm, don't be so certain." Romanov sneers at me like a fairytale villain. "It's Purgatory for the new freshman, Maximka. Which means it's hunting season."

"Bring it on, Romanov," I growl, my voice thick with dragon. "My beast and I relish a good hunt."

"Oooookay then. You boys have fun with that." Racetrack gives us both a wide berth and beelines for the kitchen.

Dez's keen stare flickers between Romanov and me. Suddenly she hugs herself and gives an unexpected giggle.

"Don't let this lot get you down, cobber," she says to me, with a sympathetic smile that eases a little of my discomfort. She is the only person who has smiled at me since I arrived. "Bark's worse than the bite with this crew. You're gonna find that out soon enough."

She gives me a knowing look I can't decipher, passes a plate to Racetrack, then ducks after her into the kitchen.

"Speak for yourself, Desdemona." Vasili gives the kitchen a sour look. "I don't suppose you can take this dragon with you to the library? Assuming Lucius won't let us pen him in the yard like a dog."

"There's no need to be so uncivilized, Mr. Romanov." The wolf divides his stern gaze between the two of us. "There are matters the rest of us sorely need to discuss. That discussion includes Mr. Rasputin."

"Hang on a sec." My queen releases her consort's hand and strolls toward me.

My heart kicks in my chest and my skin tingles. My senses spin with the creamy sweetness of her scent.

But her jaw is tight, her eyes sharp with suspicion. She jabs an accusatory finger in my chest. Even that brief contact makes my cock spike. I barely refrain from dragging her into my arms so she can feel her own visceral effect.

She consumes me.

I am consumed with desire.

"Last time we met, you were talking smack about my guys." Apparently unaffected by anything like what I am feeling, she tips back her head and scowls up at me. "Remember?"

"I said that I would kill them," I agree.

Behind her, Romanov exhales an eloquent breath.

Her dangerous eyes narrow. "That still your plan, big guy?"

A wave of comprehension breaks over me. She wants my word that I will not harm her lovers. She is that protective of them.

Well, I am prepared to say what I must.

"I swore an oath," I say gruffly. "An oath not to kill while I am on Academy grounds, unless I myself am attacked—or unless you are." This last was not asked of me, but was an addition of my own crafting. "But only so long as I am on these grounds and behind these wards."

"Huh." My sovereign tilts her head to study me. I am dismayed that her suspicion of me persists, even after hearing what I have sworn.

"Mr. Rasputin has read the Academy Codex," the wolf announces, "and given his sworn word to honor it. As long as he shares our home, that oath precludes him from posing any physical threat to anyone here—unless, as he indicates, he is attacked first."

"Oh, I say, now *there's* a thought." Standing like a king in his outlandish finery in this well-appointed room with its high ceilings and antique furnishings and blazing fire, this room whose pretty comforts are so unlike the barren confines of my dragonlair in the tundra, Vasili bares his teeth at me in a poisonous sneer.

I ignore this threat because my mate still lingers before me, close enough to touch, filling the air between us with pheromones and mating scent. My cock lunges against my zipper like a chained dog, the barb weeping precum that drenches my crotch.

She is new to shifting, she cannot yet imagine how deeply and fiercely her body will welcome mine—

"You gave your word, huh?" My queen hoists her teal brows and folds her arms across her tantalizing breasts. "Exactly how much is *that* worth, Maxim? Just because you swore, we're supposed to believe you?"

My brows rush together in a scowl. "Yes."

Does she doubt my sworn word? Does she think so little of my honor?

Again the wolf comes to my aid, striding across the floor to loom at her side, scholarly in his tweed jacket and tie. "He swore on his dragon, Zara. That's an oath no shifter would ever violate, no more than I would if I swore on my wolf. In this particular matter, strictly within the agreed parameters, we may trust him."

"We'll see about that." Bracketed by her lovers, she studies me.

Holding my gaze, she slides an arm around the wolf's rangy frame to draw him close on one side, while she tucks up against the curly-haired boy in spectacles on the other. The boy nestles up against her without hesitation. Lucius, more cautious and reserved, pauses before he wraps a firm arm around her waist to claim her.

I think she is testing me, to see how I react to seeing her with her lovers.

My dragon does not like to see another shifter so close to our mate, it is true, but he has an abiding respect for scholars of all breeds. For that reason, and because we have sworn, he is tolerant of this wolf.

Within limits.

The curly-haired boy, my dragon thinks, smells sweet. The boy is resolute in his queen's defense. Yet, under our stare, he is blushing like a girl.

Perhaps this boy will submit to us, and serve us, and thus be allowed to live.

I will only kill them if I must.

"Yeah," Zara breathes, and I recall with a start that my mate has shown some aptitude for reading my thoughts. "I don't think trust is on the menu right now. He might've promised to behave while he's here. But he's still up to no good."

"That's it, then." The Brit with the black mane—Ronin Pendragon, the warrior—strides forward to stand shoulder to shoulder with Lucius. "If Zara doesn't want him here, he's history."

I square my shoulders and stand my ground.

Because I know what he does not.

"I'm afraid it isn't really a matter of whether Zara wants him or not," the wolf says softly. "The simple truth is that she needs him."

She pushes out a scornful snort.

"Blood of Christ. Why on earth do you think I argued so fiercely for his admittance once he turned up here in the first place?" Lucius sighs. "Above and beyond the fact that the witching world needs every trained warlock we can possibly muster, and he is the Sagittarius scion and the only fully manifested male dragon shifter to be extant, to anyone's knowledge. In the end, I welcomed him under this roof and into our cohort because Zara *needs* him."

"How's that, then?" Pendragon says curtly. "She's got all of us, hasn't she?"

The wolf opens his mouth, but I growl before he can answer. "She needs me to survive her superheat."

"There's that word again." Zara wiggles free of her mates and pushes forward to confront me, poking me again in the chest. I wonder if she senses the way her body craves any excuse for contact with mine. "You keep saying it. I wanna know what it means. I wanna know right now."

"Superheat?" I fold my hand around hers and press her palm flat to my chest, inside my battered leather jacket, with only my threadbare tee shirt between us. "Do you not know, my Zara?"

Her hand is small and soft and yet so potent. She hurls lightning with this hand. She could summon her lightning now and slay me where I stand. My heart beats hard with more than danger.

I burn to press her hand to the surging heat behind my zipper.

"Tell me," she breathes, her gaze locked on mine.

I could drown in those shimmering eyes of hers and die a happy man. Silently, I tell her this. Under all her suspicion, the ghost of a smile flickers across her sweet lips.

"Hmmm, there's a romantic lurking under all that dragon, isn't there?" she whispers.

Miraculously, she doesn't pull away. I flatten my palm over the back of her hand and work to steady my breath.

"I can be a romantic if that is what pleases you," I tell her. Under her touch, my dragon rumbles with pleasure.

"What pleases me now is for you to be honest." Her tongue traces the lush bow of her upper lip as though she's tasting the word. "Tell me about this superheat."

It surprises me that she does not know, only until I recall she was not raised among our kind. Instructing her in our ancient ways is part of what I promised Lucius Aries I would do here.

In truth, instructing her will be my duty and my pleasure.

"When a dragon queen meets her dragon king," I tell her, "there is a… biochemical change, do you say? Her heats become more frequent. More prolonged. More… intense."

"*More* intense?" She gazes up at me, looking both appalled and intrigued.

"And harder to break." Still pressing her hand to my chest, my fingers thread through hers. "In her heat, she becomes more… demanding. Harder to satisfy. But her pleasures, when they come, they are… electrifying."

"They're already electrifying, mate, believe me," Pendragon mutters, hovering close behind her. "Guess you'll pick that up under this roof soon enough. She's a lightning witch, isn't she?"

"And a lightning dragon. They are very rare." Proudly I admire her, the way she revealed her gift when she breathed lightning in Vegas. "When she rises in her mating flight, when she takes her pleasure in dragon form, she will be a goddess."

Without warning, Vasili looms at Pendragon's side.

Like the serpent he is, my nemesis has slithered into striking distance in lethal silence.

This is the closest he and I have stood since his exile. The closest we have stood since that night I watched in secret, with my heart leaping in my throat and my pulse throbbing between my legs, while he wrapped his pretty lips around the Italian captain of the Romanov yacht and sucked the man's soul out through his cock.

When I told Nikolai Romanov what I saw his son doing, Nikolai fired the captain on the spot. Hours later, Vasili was on his way to Icarus in disgrace.

I have always wondered whether that captain considered his punishment worth the prize.

Under Vasili's tongue and lips, he was in ecstasy.

Vasili's ice-blue eyes, rimmed and sultry with cosmetics, lock with mine. Under that seductive mane of silver hair, his face is delicate as a woman's, all high cheekbones and straight nose and pointed chin poised above the graceful sweep of his throat. The dark spice of his scent winds around my dick like a knowing hand and strokes me.

This is a reaction I do not expect.

I flush under an unsettling flood of heat. For the first time, I must fight to sustain my enemy's stare. One gilded eyebrow arches above his hostile eye.

Suddenly I am beyond thankful he is no telepath.

"I suppose you're going to claim she has to mate with a dragon?" he sniffs. "No other breed of shifter will do?"

My chest swells and my head lifts with pride. "What other creature could match her in the skies?"

And I am the last of my kind.

Vasili's gaze shutters with malignant intent.

Zara huffs out a breath and drops her hand. My dragon keens in protest. The loss of her touch burns in my chest like acid.

Yearning to pursue her, I clench my fists at my sides.

"Let's get a few things straight." My queen plants her hands on her hips and tilts her chin back to challenge me. "Like Neo already told you, who I mate is my choice. I'm gonna control this thing. This effing *superheat*. It's not gonna control me. I'm gonna control what happens to my own body. And if you wanna hang around me, big guy, you're gonna help me with that. Since I guess you're our big expert now on dragon shifters."

I cannot understand at all why she wishes to resist her nature. Still, she is determined. Despite my confusion, a reluctant admiration for her resolve steals through me.

Well, after all, she is my sovereign. I suppose I can understand her desire for control.

Even though, in this case, that desire for control will be futile.

There is no force under heaven that can control a dragon queen's heat.

I would say this to her, because I have already said I will not lie to her. But I am interrupted when Racetrack and Dez file past us into the hall, both carrying green bottles of Italian beer and steaming bowls of some spicy dish that smells deliciously of chicken and peanuts, with chopsticks thrust through the fragrant food.

I have not eaten since I arrived. But food has never been plentiful in my life. I learned long ago to ignore my hunger, even when it gnaws my gut.

Still, my interested stomach gives an audible rumble now that betrays me.

"I do believe that's the dinner bell," Lucius says lightly, turning toward the kitchen. "I dare say we'll all feel more like ourselves with full bellies. And we haven't dined together as a family since the three of you returned. We'll get Mr. Rasputin settled in his room after dinner."

My room should be Zara's room, but I am wise enough not to fight that battle now, with all of them ranged against me.

And my interest is captured by what the wolf just said. That we will dine as a family. Is that what they are to each other—my queen, her teacher, her mates?

Are they… a family?

My chest burns with a new ache that is foreign. My own concept of family, honed and whittled by a lifetime of solitary hardship and sudden violence in my mother's lair, has been rather… different.

Zara gives me a long searching look I cannot interpret. A furrow appears between her brows and her teeth sink into her lower lip.

"Okay, big guy," she says softly at last. "Let's get you fed. We can talk about the rest of this mess later."

She does not wait for my assent before she leads a general exodus from the room. When no one objects audibly to my presence despite another venomous glare from Vasili, I follow along with the rest to the kitchen, careful not to stray too close.

But my sovereign's bold declaration that she will resist me, that she will resist our mating and this powerful bond between us, hovers in the air between us like the sulfurous reek of dragonsmoke.

Chapter Fourteen
Neo

"Don't they have food in Siberia? He ate that kung pao chicken like he was fucking starving." My fated mate is pacing before our bedroom fire like a caged tiger.

She's been doing that since we holed up here in our room after dinner, Ronin and Zara and me, while Lucius helps Maxim get settled and walks him through his orientation packet. Vasili's off sulking somewhere, God knows where. He's been a basket case (like, more so than usual) ever since that dragon showed up.

And, pretty much, so has Zara.

"I mean it. He ate like he thought we'd take his food away. It's like he's feral or something." My cherished one pauses in her pacing long enough to frown at me, propped up against the headboard of our platform bed with my Honors Science of Witchcraft textbook spread open across my lap, since I'm still trying doggedly to bone up for our midterms.

"I mean, do they do that in Siberia? Starve people?" she demands. She might not like Maxim very much right now, but I can tell the thought of him suffering really bothers her. "The guy's all skin and bone."

"And dragonfire," Ronin mutters.

He's sprawled in her window seat, looking delectable but overheated, shirtless and barefoot with his pants unzipped (which makes me so horny). I can't help it, he's like explosively hot, all ripply ribs and drum-tight abs, it's so fitting that he literally has flames tattooed across his chest. But I'm still not totally over him ghosting me, so I don't act on it. Right now he's brooding and sharpening one of Vasili's knives, the one Vasili gave Zara during that whole queen killer stalking episode.

That knife normally lives in our nightstand drawer, and I almost forget it's there. I figure its sudden appearance now isn't really a good thing.

"And muscle," I add, going back to the dragon. "He's, you know, all sinewy?"

He's kind of intriguing, actually, the new guy. Obviously I know he's a dragon shifter, like Zara is now, which is so awesome. I can't wait to see her shift, even though I can tell she's nervous about doing it, because she's not on board with the idea of a mating flight with Maxim, like, *at all*. But right now the new guy reminds me more of a cheetah than a dragon, all long and lean and hungry, with sharp angles and starving eyes.

I guess I'm a little more accepting of the idea of a new guy than the others are, because I've always known I'll have to share her. Just like I do already. Our queens in the witching world are pretty much all polyamorous.

You could say I was raised for this.

I'm from a big political family with a famous last name, and my father leads the Arcane Senate. It's an elected post, but he keeps on winning it. The exact same way I'm supposed to do myself someday to carry on the Mercury legacy.

"Mmmm, you like that dragon, don't you, baby?" Zara's face softens in a fleeting smile that's just for me, which I can't help returning (with a blush) before she starts pacing again.

"This is a big bed." I shrug. "Even with Vasili's long legs taking up half of it and Lucius' wolf growling and fighting in his sleep."

I wish she'd stop pacing and crawl into this bed with me.

Actually, I kinda wish they both would.

They're gonna need to take the initiative, because I'm still aching and bruised and heartsore and torn up inside from being left behind. Ronin always senses what's going down with me, so I figure he's trying to give me my space and show he respects my feelings before he (inevitably) fucks me into a blissed-out sex puddle. I'm actually still trying to decide how hard I'll make him work for it before I finally give in.

But Zara's clearly way too restless to settle.

"It's a *crowded* bed." Ronin divides a pointed look between the two of us, then returns to scowling over Vasili's blade. "Those eastern religious warlock clans are homophobic as fuck. Just like Vasili's old man. Not really sure Maxim's going to fancy sharing you, love."

"Well, that's a deal breaker for me. Anyone who wants me needs to want all of us. And vice versa, because you all get a say. We're a package deal, and that's final." Flushed and irritable, Zara peels out of my sweater.

My heart stops beating. Heat pools in my dick.

Wow.

Underneath she's only wearing a bra, one of the yummy black lace push-up ones Vasili had shipped for her in his last lingerie box from Paris.

And I bet she's wearing the matching thong under her leggings. It's definitely *not* the innocent white silk and cotton skivvies of the regulation Academy uni. But they're both rebels—both my fated mate and Vasili.

Neither one of them really does innocent.

Or regulation.

I love the way Zara's full breasts spill out of the cups. Her boobs are even fuller than usual, it seems like to me. The way the outline of her rings and her swollen nipples juts against that black lace, yeah, that just makes my mouth water. Her skin gleams with a fine sheen of sweat.

Ronin and I both stop what we're doing to drink in the sexed-up, punk-rock pinup girl vibe she gives off so effortlessly. Jesus, my junk's standing straight up under my sweats.

I swallow hard and shift my hips on the bed.

Ronin gives a low growl that's almost a whine. That's his heat rising for sure.

But I know he's fighting hard to wait for the rest of our guys before he gives in.

"Not to mention," she adds, still pacing, while the firelight laps at her curvy body and the wild mane of curls swinging down her back, "there's that whole… *breeding* kink that dragon's rocking. I'm not having kids anytime soon. Not till after I graduate and we get this whole queen thing sorted out, like, at minimum. And he doesn't seem willing to wait. So Maxim being straight? That's actually the least of his problems."

"Um… couldn't he be… bi?" Carefully I mark my place before I close my textbook. Because I definitely saw the way he was looking at Vasili tonight, even if no one else seemed to notice. He was looking at Vasili with those flaming eyes of his like he wanted to light him on fire.

I get that they hate each other and all, because they've both made that pretty obvi.

But I definitely don't think that's dragon's straight.

Even if he'd like to be.

At the *very* least, he's bi-curious. Just like I was back in the day, when I was an awkward virgin secretly crushing on Ronin.

"After what that bloke did to Vasili?" Ronin grunts, sharp with contempt. "Not bloody likely. Probably afraid he'll catch the gay living in this house."

I don't know what Maxim did to Vasili, and Ronin doesn't seem inclined to say, but Zara hums and looks thoughtful as she paces. I guess they have secrets from me now, the three of them, due to all that time they just spent without me.

I try not to mind, I really do, but it's upsetting. It hurts being left out.

It hurts.

"I dunno," she mutters, sweating freely as her own heat rises. "I hear you, I do, and I'd say there's pretty much zero chance that he's anything *but* straight…" She shoots Ronin a wry look "…if not for the way he's been eye-fucking you."

"Me?" Ronin snorts. "Come on. Everyone eye-fucks me. I can make a straight bloke queer. Even if only for five ticks. Just look how I corrupted poor Neo."

He's totally telling the truth, because he was the notorious and unattainable Sir One and Done at this Academy until Zara came along. He'd do anyone once, but he never went back for seconds (except, it turns out, with Vasili. They were a regular thing, but the two of them kept it totally secret and pretended to hate each other, which is a typical Vasili way to operate.) Anyway, I know more than one straight guy on the class roster whom Ronin persuaded to sample the D that seemed to enjoy the experience. Half those so-called straight guys whose male cherry he popped are still sneaking him looks and mooning over him.

But now Ronin's committed to us.

Of course, he hears all this through our bond. He shoots me a smoking look from under that curtain of hair that heats my blood like a Bunsen burner in the alchemy lab.

Even in the window seat, which is pretty drafty, he's sweating and fidgety, skin gleaming in the firelight.

That's one more sign of how close he is to his heat.

"Hey, I corrupted him first." Zara gathers her heavy hair up in one hand and fans the back of her neck with the other. "Neo was a virgin till I got to him. Weren't you, baby?"

I push up my glasses and frown. Normally it makes me feel all warm and wanted and kinda sexy when they tease about corrupting me. That kind of teasing usually ends with them corrupting me more.

Tonight I guess I'm still feeling a little too sensitive about being babied.

"You didn't corrupt me. Neither of you. It was my choice. I wanted to be with you. *Both* of you," I say firmly. "Anyway, we're talking about Maxim. Not me."

I make sure to pronounce it the way he did tonight. *Mak-seem.* Leaning hard into the second syllable, which is so exotic with his Russian accent. At the sound of his name on my lips, my tummy gives a little flutter.

Suddenly I find myself wondering if Lucius is still orienting him. I wonder if the new guy's lonely, nervous, maybe even a little scared in the big downstairs guest studio which is the only vacant bedroom in the house.

Maybe, before I go to sleep myself, I should just check in on him? It would be the neighborly thing to do, and I'm pretty sure no one else is going to.

"Yeah. *Maxim.*" Restlessly Ronin tosses the knife and catches it. "Anyway, sure, he was looking. That dragon's got big eyes. I bet he's wanted a lot of things in life he hasn't gotten. Not a bloody felony to look, is it?"

"He said in Vegas he wants you sharing our bed," Zara murmurs, low and languid. I know how much she likes the thought of that. Even when she doesn't want to admit it. "That's a lot more than looking."

I glance between them, waiting for one of them to clue me in on what went down in Vegas, because I've still only heard the bare bones of that story.

Ronin chuckles grimly and shakes his head. "Not gonna happen, is it? Not with the way Vasili feels about the chap."

Okay. Looks like I'm destined for total ignorance unless I pry the backstory out of them. But I figure they're protecting Vasili's privacy, since he and I haven't exactly been all warm and fuzzy.

If I want to know what happened with Vasili, he's the one I'll need to ask.

Ronin's still tossing the knife and swinging his bare foot, and Zara's still pacing and fanning the back of her neck. Through our mating bond, I can feel her heat spreading out from her center and throbbing like a slow second heartbeat in her divine pussy. I barely took the edge off that heat of hers today. She's probably going to need, um, two dicks inside her at once tonight to break her first spike. Like double penetration. She's really into that.

Maybe, tonight, even three dicks inside her. You know, in all the different places?

And I'm betting Ronin's more than ready for a DP with Lucius and Vasili to get him through his own first peak.

I don't receive DPs. Or give them yet either. Because I'm the baby and everyone thinks I can't handle two dicks inside me.

Lucius and Vasili won't even fuck me.

Much less bite me.

All of a sudden, I'm angry all over again. I've been angry since the three of them left, even though I told myself I was past it since Zara promised she won't leave me behind again.

Now I realize my anger isn't so easy to dismiss.

And, somehow, I know Lucius is fighting the exact same battle. When he finishes with Maxim, there's no way our proud and aloof lone wolf prof's going to come crawling up here to bed with his tail between his legs and bend tamely for Vasili, especially now when V's being a total jerk over Maxim.

There's literally no way.

Which means Lucius needs me downstairs.

With him.

"Okay then." Hastily I gather my textbook against my chest and scramble down from the high bed, ignoring the little rolling staircase Zara uses sometimes to get her petite body up here.

Ronin and Zara both look at me expectantly. Oh God, they're right on the edge, both of them.

And if I don't get out of this bedroom in the next thirty seconds (or less), all three of us are going to wind up in a sweaty naked tangle on that carpet in front of the fire.

Anger or no anger, my dick sits up and takes instant interest in that prospect.

But Lucius. He needs me.

And even if he doesn't, I'm way too agitated to stay in this room and be sweet baby Neo tonight.

Fortunately I'm still wearing sweats and a tee, so I toe into my loafers and push a hand through my messy hair. "I'm just gonna go, um, check up on Lucius."

"Can't believe he's not beating down this door already." Ronin's gaze tracks Zara's pacing form like a cat with a toy. "He's our alpha, I know he missed us, and he knows we're both horny as fuck up here."

"Um, I'll go find him." Feeling totally guilty for just leaving them like this, I beeline for the door.

Anyway, where the heck's Vasili? He's Zara's alpha too, and he's Ronin's boyfriend, and the three of them are all thick now. He has to know the state they're in. Am I the only responsible person in this harem anymore?

Well, if I am, it's only because no one wants to give me a mating bite. Or else I'd be in heat like the rest of them.

My agitation mounts and my steps quicken.

"Neo, baby?" Zara calls after me. Under the pulsing burn of her heat, the sharp edge of her concern presses into me. "You're gonna come back tonight, right?"

"I need to find Lucius," I say, which isn't really an answer. "If I, uh, see Vasili on the way, I'll send him right in."

"Just hold on a tick, love." Now Ronin's uncoiling to his feet, and I know I have to get out of here, I have to, before I give in to both of them and their heats and abandon Lucius to his cold and lonely bed.

"Neo?" Zara's concerned and bewildered and fretful in her need. "Are you okay?"

Now I've made my beloved worry, which is the last thing she needs right now. Guilt adds its weight to the emotional load I'm already carrying.

I practically run to the door and wrench it open.

"I'm sorry," I blurt out to both of them without turning. "I really am. I thought I could just do this, pretend we're all back to where we were before you left, but we're not… and it turns out… I can't."

I rush into the hall and slam the door behind me to cut off their startled questions.

Damn it. Damn it. Damn it.

At this hour, the house is all hushed and shadowy, the fire in the great room dwindled down to coals, with just the dim amber cone of the downstairs hall lamp and spears of gray light from the almost full moon knifing through the various windows to pierce the shadows. As I creep along the upstairs hall, the sleepy murmur of voices seeps under Racetrack's closed door, where she and Dez are holed up.

Vasili's door is open and his room is dark. God only knows where he's gotten to. He tends to hide when he's broody.

Downstairs, more muffled voices float from the library off the great room, where it sounds like Lucius is still walking Maxim through his school schedule. Under the asthmatic wheeze of the basement furnace, the patient drone of my teacher's voice makes me smile.

I could wait for Lucius in his downstairs bedroom, where I'm pretty sure he plans to sleep tonight. But I'm not really in the mood myself to lie alone waiting in his cold bed.

It only takes a sec to figure out what I really want.

I'm tired of being sweet baby Neo.

I'm *so* tired of it.

I'm tired of being the guy everyone babies and no one bites.

Quickly I collect some supplies from the first aid kit in the kitchen and retreat back upstairs to my room at the end of the hall, the room I hardly ever use anymore except for storage. It's cold and dark in here without the fire, barely lit by the moonlight streaming through the leaded glass doors that open onto the snowy balcony.

The whole space smells kind of musty and mothbally, but it suits my cranky and disgruntled mood.

I leave the door open and the bedroom dark, but hit the switch in my half-bath. The old-fashioned bulb flickers on. The sputtery glow lights up the vintage black-and-white mosaic floor and the solid bulwark of the sink under the mirror. I line up my supplies on the sink's wide sill, give my hands a good scrub with a sliver of my lavender soap, then use cotton and iodine to disinfect my left earlobe.

I'm going to pierce my ear.

I've been thinking about this for a while. Zara's got six piercings rimming her whole left ear, plus her sexy nipple rings, and Ronin's got that heavy ring through the head of his dick that makes me salivate.

And both of them have been bitten. Clearly, they're not afraid of a little pain. Those piercings prove it.

And I'm not afraid either.

In fact, I'm not even going to use a numbing potion. I deliberately left the little vial downstairs in the first aid kit.

I fetch the silver hoop earring I bought off Dez a while ago and sterilize it carefully. Then I sterilize the needle I've also got ready. So far, the prep isn't all that different from setting up for an alchemy experiment in the science lab in the Dean's tower.

But now comes the tricky part.

I hesitate, then peel off my tee shirt, because it's one of my favorites and maybe I'll bleed a little. I take a sec to study myself in the mirror. My face frowns back at me, brow furrowed with concentration under my mussed-up curls, eyes resolved behind my glasses. There's the dark shadow of the hickey Zara sucked into my neck today when she fucked me. I'm all bulked up and muscly from my hours in the gym, but no one's here to appreciate it. My black sweats are riding low on my hips and the waistband of my boxer briefs is showing, but there's no one here to notice.

I push my glasses firmly into place, pinch the edge of my earlobe between two fingers, place the needle's sharp tip carefully where I want it. Then I suck in a deep breath, hold it, and jab the point into my tender flesh.

"*Ow!* Oh, crap!" I gasp.

I jabbed so hard I almost peed my pants.

Cripes, the needle didn't even go through. I'm not even sure it broke the skin, because I'm not bleeding.

I drag in another deep breath, take a fresh hold on my throbbing earlobe, and give another good jab.

"*Ouch!!*" I yelp. That prick was so hard it made my eyes water. And that needle *still* hasn't gone through. "Oh, damn it."

Through tear-filled eyes, I peer into the glass. Now there's a tiny red dent where I jabbed. Well, that's progress, isn't it? Next time, I just need to jab harder.

With renewed purpose, I position the needle, pull in a breath, push out a noisy huff, and—

"Mercury? What the actual *fuck* are you doing to yourself in here?"

The whiplash curl of Vasili's voice spins me around with another gasp. Adrenaline's pumping through me from the pain I've already inflicted, laced with determination to finish the job. Now the sight of my terrible enemy (which he was, you know, until just recently) lounging in my doorway like a malignant David Bowie in the floating staircase climax scene of *Labyrinth* gooses me with so much adrenaline I feel ready to summon lightning myself.

He's obviously been outside, because his long black coat with the high furled collar is swirling open around his tall body. Cold night air's still seeping from the folds. Snowflakes glitter in his silver hair and his cheeks are ruddy with cold.

I figure he's probably been out flying, because he does that sometimes when he's restless. It's just one of those powers that makes him so scary.

Yeah, I'm mad at him too. But we're not actually lovers, so I don't feel betrayed by him the same way I do by Zara and Ronin. His choice to leave me behind doesn't sting and rankle the same way. Instead, I'm just miffed enough at him that I finally found the courage tonight to kiss him, the way I've wanted to do for weeks.

Of course, it figures that when I finally took the plunge, I was so furious I just hurled myself at him and laid one on him with absolutely zero technique.

He probably hated it, being sloppy-kissed like that, by me of all people.

He's probably been secretly laughing at me and my shitty technique all night.

Embarrassment brings heat flooding to my face. My tongue tangles in knots. All of which means I can't answer him.

"Well? Don't tell me you're just going to stand there blushing?" Faced with my conflicted silence, his glacial eyes narrow. His gaze veers to the needle I'm still gripping, the disinfectant on the sink, and finally the little silver hoop I'm starting to think I'll never manage to insert.

"Ah." Comprehension flashes across his pretty face. My shoulders bunch up and I brace for him to mock me.

"I'm piercing my ear," I say, totally unnecessarily, because clearly he's figured that much out.

"Hmmmm," he murmurs, looking thoughtful.

"Everyone else has one… practically," I rush to add, because I remember suddenly that *he* doesn't. "I want one too. Maybe more than one."

His clever eyes flash with amusement or, more likely, malice.

"Best to start with one." He considers, head cocked, lips pursed, then gives a little huff. "Well. If you want your ear pierced, I'll do it. But not like this. Up."

"Up?" It's all I can manage, to repeat his last word. Because nothing he's saying makes any sense.

His lips curve in a small wicked grin. "Your derrière, darling."

"My… derrière?"

"Oh, for the love of God," he groans. "Hoist that luscious ass of yours *up* on the sink. I'd lift you myself, but you're such a brute." He pouts. "You'd put my back out."

A startled giggle fizzes out of me. I can never be sure with him, but I think he's joking. I think he's joking *with me*, which he literally never does.

An unexpected dart of happiness arrows through me. Biting my lower lip to hold back a grin, I brace my hands behind me and hoist myself up to sit. I'm a big guy, but this sink is ancient, it's probably been here since before the fall of Rome, it can handle my weight.

The shift in perspective brings us eye to eye. He has sexy bedroom eyes—I mean, you know, when he's not glaring like a psycho. They're all smoky lids and long lashes and wicked intent.

Holding my gaze, he slips the heavy coat from his shoulders. It drops to the floor behind him.

Underneath he's wearing his black silk turtleneck over his breeches. It's one of my favorite outfits on him, just the starkness and simplicity of it against all that delicate beauty, and the way the sleek fabric clings to his lean balletic body makes my mouth go dry. He drifts toward me, slowly peeling his sleeves back to expose his sinewy forearms. His stare roams over my naked chest and abs and shoulders in a way that makes my skin heat and my breath rough.

Nervously, I swing my feet. "Do you really think my, um, derrière is luscious? Because you never said so before."

"You don't need me pampering your Mercury vanity. But, well, since you're *injured…*" He smirks at my pin-pricked ear. "Every inch of your perfectly toned body is a work of art. Are you satisfied? Because of course I live for that."

I bite my lip harder, but I can't hold back the grin sneaking across my face. I still can't be sure, but it's just barely possible there's a little humor lurking at the corners of his mouth too. He pauses before my jutting knees and leans to one side to eye my medical supplies.

"Good Lord, you're untidy," he tuts. "First Boy, I am *shocked*. Where in all this ungodly mess is the numbing potion?"

"I'm not using any." I tilt my chin in a defiant jut.

His gaze swerves back to mine and his pale brows float up in surprise, which annoys me.

"My gosh, it's just an ear, Vasili." I try valiantly to ignore the way mine is still throbbing. "I bet Ronin didn't use a numbing potion when he pierced his dick."

"Hmmm, that's true." Vasili smirks. "I can confirm your naughty speculation since I was with him at the time. He had his cock pierced by a professional on the mainland. We went on a pleasure jaunt during summer holidays."

Huh.

Ronin's idea of a pleasure jaunt and mine are definitely not the same.

Just trying to pierce this ear is killing me.

"Zara told me she never used anything for hers either." I try my best not to sound defensive, but I'm not totally sure it's working.

"Why doesn't that surprise me?" he murmurs. "Well, darling, it's your funeral."

Without warning, his hands rise to my knees and nudge them apart. My throat flexes in a hard swallow.

But he's being gentle, he's not forcing, I can say no, I can stop this.

Instead, I let my knees drift apart under those twin wisps of pressure until I'm spread all wide and exposed in front of him. Of course, my dick chooses this moment to become extremely interested in the fact that Vasili Romanov finally has his sexy hands on my body. My junk stiffens and swells and shoves against my sweats, the outline embarrassingly obvious.

I squeeze my eyes shut and blush like blazes.

Why did I have to wear sweats tonight?

Hands still resting lightly on my knees, he drifts closer until I'm bracketing his hips with my thighs. I can't bear to look, but I can definitely sense him.

He's close. And he's watching.

I'm quickly losing interest in the idea of getting my ear pierced in favor of other things he could be doing to me with those hands of his.

"Mercury," he leans in to breathe in my uninjured ear. His dark familiar musk of caramel and vetiver fills my head. He smells exactly the way he does when he goes all alpha and rails our mates.

Eyes still closed, I swallow hard and scrape out the word. "Yeah."

"Be a love and get the needle ready for me." His silky mouth barely grazes my ear. "And stop biting your lip, *do*. Or I'm going to bite it for you."

My breath spills out in a shuddery rush and my eyes fly open in surprise.

"Are you… are you offering to bite me?" I whisper, with my voice all shaky.

Wow.

I never even thought of asking Vasili, what with us being enemies.

You know, until right now.

His breath hitches in my ear. Right now, I don't think either one of us is breathing.

He drifts back a little until our gazes meet. In his ice-blue stare, his pupils are blown wide. His lips part so just the sexy tips of his fangs are showing. He searches my hot face, and I'm *really* tempted to bite my lip again, just to see what he does.

"Now be good, darling, and stop teasing," he purrs at last, completely avoiding my question about biting me, in the velvety sex-drenched rumble of his bedroom voice. Because I do know what he sounds like when he's turned on. It's just that usually, it's Zara or Ronin or Lucius turning him on.

Not me.

"The needle," he reminds me softly. "Unless you've changed your mind?"

I'm not teasing, I want to tell him. *You can bite me. I... I want you to bite me.*

Instead, I duck my head and fumble with the antiseptic and resterilize the needle the way he wants. He should really wash his hands too, but I don't want him moving, I want him right here between my thighs. I want his fingers lightly kneading the medial muscles just above my knees the way he's doing right now. I'd actually love for his hands to drift higher, but I'm too shy to ask, and maybe if I did, he'd say no.

I clear my throat and hold up the needle. "Um, here?"

"Good boy," he whispers.

Oh my God. He's praising me.

A muffled groan leaks past my restraint. My teeth sink into my lower lip before I can stop myself.

A low curse rips out of him.

Much faster than I expect, he dives in to brand my mouth with a quick scorching kiss, a flash of sucking heat that leaves me gasping, a lash of tongue between my lips, the warning scrape of fangs over tender flesh.

It's over before I can reciprocate.

"Be careful," he hisses. "I'm warning you, First Boy. And I only warn once."

I'm still reeling and swaying when he snatches the needle, grips my chin hard to wrench my head to one side, pinches my earlobe between two cruel fingers, and stabs the needle through my ear with ruthless precision.

A sharp cry rips out of me. I struggle to stay still while he swiftly threads the ring through my throbbing ear and pinches the clasp shut.

"Uh... ow?" I breathe, seeing stars. *"Shit."*

"Well, you're the one who refused a numbing potion," he says thickly. "Now hush. It's all over."

The liquid heat of his mouth envelops my stinging earlobe in a burning kiss, sucking furiously like he wants to suck the pain out of me. His winter-cold lips feel better than ice on my abused and throbbing flesh.

"Oh my God, V." I drop the bottle of antiseptic I'm still stupidly clutching. It thunks over and spills into the sink and the sharp bite of iodine floods the air, but I don't give a shit. I grip his narrow waist in both hands and drag him close. "I don't know what we're doing here, but it's definitely—*not*—over."

He twists under my hands like the sea snake he is and his cold mouth locks over mine in a brutal kiss. His jaw flexes and his lips slant and his tongue lunges to meet mine. I moan and bite into his kiss with my own hungry mouth, our lips fusing together, our tongues fighting for dominance. His fangs are so deliciously sharp and he's right there, he's everything I've been aching to explore, and he tastes like the metallic tang of iodine and the juniper bite of that Russian vodka he likes.

You wouldn't think that would be a turn on, those particular flavors I mean. But they're sharp and aggressive and edgy and… unique.

Just like him.

His hand wraps around my head and spears through my hair to hold me. While his free hand, oh my God, his free hand dives between us and closes over the hard throb of my cock. With just my sweats and briefs between us.

A jolt of pleasure zags through me like a bolt of Zara's lightning.

His clever fingers wrap around my length and *knead*. And, God, he's *so* good at this, so good, so good I think I'm going to lose my mind and my load and come inside my sweats like I'm twelve or something. To keep that from happening, I want to beg him to stop.

I want to beg him never to stop.

But my body has a mind of its own. My hips burrow and rut into his grip. My hands wrap around his tight ass to grapple him closer.

"Mercury…" That low growl of his sounds like a warning.

"Oh my God, yes, like that." I suck his lip into my mouth, which presses my tender flesh into those two wicked points. What would it take to get him to bite?

But I want more from him than a love nip.

I want a real mating bite.

A shudder ripples through him, like he's just read my mind, even though neither of us are telepaths, so we can't do that without a mating bond.

"Why, First Boy," he breathes into my desperate mouth. "Who ever knew you could be so wicked?"

He must mean the way I'm bucking into his hand, my waist flexing and abs clenching with every snap of my hips, soft grunts exploding from my lips with every thrust.

"You did," I moan between kisses. I can't believe how good I feel with him jacking me off through two layers of clothes. "You always… you always watch me when I fuck."

"Hmmm, do I? I can't recall." He's teasing now (isn't he?) but his fist clenches in my hair to hold me still. The sting of having my hair pulled merges with the burn of my pierced ear and the incessant pulse of need in my dick.

It's too much stimulation at once, yet somehow this sensory overload is exactly what I need.

"You know you do." I writhe on the sink and pant for air like I'm having a damn heart attack as he nuzzles and nips his way down my neck.

He only hums against my skin.

Of course, he's not going to admit it. He's not going to admit the way he fucks me with his eyes.

Suddenly, that's something I'm determined to change.

I should probably be a lot more careful. He's Vasili, he's a snake, he could tear out my throat right now with those vicious fangs of his. For so long, he was my enemy. But tonight he seems content to drag his tongue and the points of his fangs down my skin, while he teases my dick through my sweats until I think I'm going to lose my mind.

"You smell like sage… and roses… and Zara… and innocence." His teeth scrape my skin. "Like something you're begging me to ruin and corrupt."

I guess corrupting me is going to be a theme tonight.

"V," I gasp, hooking my legs around his so he can't get away. "I'm giving you permission. You can, um, you can take off my pants and ruin me."

"Can I?" His mouth burrows into the tender spot where my neck meets my shoulder and gives a little nip. It's not even enough to break the skin, but I yelp and hump into his hand.

Lord, he's going to drive me insane for sure.

He releases my aching dick. My mood spirals from heady elation to crushing disappointment.

This is where he leaves me high and dry, where he voices his cutting Vasili laugh over how much I want him, his laugh that flays me to shreds.

I'm teetering on the edge of total despair when he gives my hair a last hard yank that makes me gasp, then drags my sweats down my hips in a single rough pull. Panting with relief and need, I kick off my loafers and squirm on the sink to help him and get my sweats down my legs and off me as fast as possible.

You know, before he changes his mind.

Now I'm only wearing my navy briefs, and he's still fully dressed, and I should feel self-conscious I guess, because my hard-on is, like, really obvious now and there's a big wet spot of precum spreading across my crotch.

But he only hums low in his throat, this awful warlock I'm so hot for, and skates his cool hands up my hot thighs to frame my bulge. Through the soaking cotton, his thumbs stroke up and down my length.

"Very nice, First Boy." His glittering gaze rakes over me, from my hands clutching the sink for purchase to my splayed thighs in my briefs and the spiral of red hair that licks down my abs to vanish under my waistband. "Very nice indeed."

"You can take those off me too," I rasp, meaning my briefs, even though my face is on fire with all this.

His head bows so I can't see his face. His cool fingers dip under the bottom of my briefs, like two inches away from my balls.

I whimper and squirm for more.

"What exactly are we doing here, Neo?" he whispers. Even though he almost never says my real name. I'm always *darling* or *First Boy* or *Mercury*. "Spell it out for me so there's no mistake. Because you've made it very clear you're already furious at me and Ronin and Zara for leaving you and Lucius behind. And I very much suspect our queen's fragile harem won't survive another of my catastrophic mistakes."

That might be the closest Vasili Romanov's ever come to admitting he makes mistakes. It actually blows my mind that he just made that admission to me. He's admitting he made a mistake—not by leaving the island with Zara and Ronin, but by leaving Lucius and me behind.

Which hopefully means he won't ever do it again.

And it means… it means a lot. My heart aches and swells.

I let go of the sink with one hand and cup his chin gently in my palm. I nudge just a little, and his head comes up until our gazes meet. His face is fractured and open, more open than I've ever seen it, except maybe when he's fucking our mates.

"Here's what we're doing," I tell him, my voice all low and husky. "You're making me come. You're making me come all over myself. It doesn't have to mean any more than that."

That's not all I want from him, sexually I mean, but it's honestly as much as I think I can handle. Vasili's always a lot to deal with, but especially when he fucks. Ronin's still the only guy I've ever been with, and I'm finally ready to admit I want to be with Vasili too. I, like, *really* want that. But I want it to happen with Zara and Ronin and Lucius all there, when it can help heal the cracks in our happiness.

His cruel eyes search my face. I manage a wobbly smile to reassure him.

I know what I want. I'm not going to freak out on him.

"Hmmmm," he says finally. "You're a very naughty creature indeed tonight. First the piercing, then that mating bite you've all but dared me to give you, and now… *this*…"

As the last syllable unfurls from his lips, his fingertips graze the sensitive skin of my balls. A cry shoots up my throat. He leans in to catch it with a slow sucking kiss.

"Yeah, *this*," I moan into his mouth, squirming as he strokes my swollen balls, trying to rock my hips into his teasing touch. "Come on, V. You owe me this for leaving. Now give it to me."

"So demanding," he purrs, licking into my breathless mouth. "I do believe I rather like this new you."

I like this new me too, especially when his whole hand snakes inside my crotch and wraps around the hot throb of my dick.

I jackknife into his touch with a yell and almost fall off the sink.

He gives a nice long groan. I'm all smeared with my own fluids, and he slicks all that moisture up and down my length and really starts stroking. His cool fingers are warming up fast and he's, like, *really* good at this. The fact that it's my horrible rival doing it, making me come apart in a writhing, moaning, panting, bucking mess on my bathroom sink, just makes this whole experience that much more mind-blowing.

It's pretty obvi that he's not planning to fuck me, since he's still one hundred percent got clothes on, and I should probably be embarrassed that I'm almost naked and bossing him around like this. But, gosh, he's making me feel *so* good. I've been weathering a mini sex famine since they left, and Lucius has been so gentlemanly and restrained.

I guess fucking Zara like I did this afternoon really opened the floodgates.

I grip the basin behind me with both hands and brace my feet against the sink and arch my back and fuck my whole body into Vasili's pumping fist. He wraps his arm around my lower back to brace me and dives in to suck a love bite into my neck to match the one I got earlier from Zara.

Oh crap. I'm going to come from all this in about five seconds. He's going to make me come inside my briefs like an awkward virgin. But it'll all be worth it… if only…

"Oh my God, V," I pant, his mouth sucking like a vampire at my neck, my head flung back, the guttering light bulb in the ceiling swimming in my eyes. "Will you *please—just—bite me*."

A ripple of alertness rolls through him.

"Why?" he rasps in a voice like sandpaper against my skin.

"Uh… no… no reason." I'm not expecting the question, so I handle it badly. "Just because."

"No." With unsettling speed, he unlatches from my neck to rear over

me like a rattlesnake, all narrow-eyed and wicked and still pumping me to a frenzy. "There's something more behind all this than your lust for my admittedly glorious cock. You want me to bite you—even though Lucius would be the far more obvious choice—and you won't tell me why. Until I understand you, I'm keeping my dreadful fangs to myself."

A wave of bitter disappointment crashes over me.

But he doesn't even let me process it, because now he's dragging down my waistband so my junk springs free, all swollen and lubed up and slick with the precum I'm pumping out for him.

He swoops down to encase the head of my dick—just the head, because he's such a fucking tease—in the wet silk of his mouth.

And the scrape of his fangs against that super-sensitive part of me pushes me right over the edge. I let loose with a raw shout that makes the walls vibrate. My climax boils out of my balls and up my shaft and erupts from my dick in spurt after spurt of explosive ecstasy.

Of course, being Vasili and now deeply suspicious of my motives, he just kind of siphons a few delicate sips off the top and then backs away and lets me come all over myself, hot jets of semen splashing my thighs and abs and chest, drenching the briefs still tangled around my hips, spattering his hand as he pumps me through it and prolongs my climax.

I'm still a shuddering, gasping, twitching mess when he swoops in to kiss me. His tongue plunges deep to coat my mouth with my own jizz.

"That's for lying to me about that fucking bite, and doing it so badly," he hisses. "Don't you ever dare lie to me. You're an appalling liar. Besides, you're supposed to be the honest one."

In a blink, I nosedive from blinding ecstasy to instant guilt.

"Oh, shit, V," I groan. "I—I'm sorry. Will you just let me explain—"

"Silence. I'll not hear a single solitary word from you until I know you're being honest." He drags a hand through the mess I've made all over myself and spreads it around to make me even messier. Jesus. I'm literally dripping in my own spunk. "And *that's* for leaving me frustrated and provoked and horny as fuck."

I sneak a peek at his crotch. Yeah, there's definitely a big mouthwatering bulge shoved up against the fabric. I've also managed to get a droplet or two of my come on his nice silk turtleneck.

Oh Lord, I've made a mess.

I mean, figuratively as well as literally.

"Vasili…" I say miserably. "Zara and Ronin… they need you upstairs—"

"I told you to be silent. I'm well aware." He licks my spunk from his fingers with a delicate tongue, while I sprawl panting and despoiled across the sink under his unsparing eye. Gradually, the combination of the taste of me on his tongue and the sight of me drooping and contrite (and corrupted) restores that wicked gleam to his eye.

"Now then," he says at last, sounding much more in control, "get yourself cleaned up and come to bed."

I blink at him and try to pull my head together. "Actually…"

He swoops to collect his discarded coat from the floor. "Or you can just come as you are, you naughty boy. I'm sure both Zara and Ronin will appreciate the effect. Although the sight of his star pupil all undone and ruined like this will probably give poor Lucius a stroke."

Before I can muster enough brain cells to answer him, to explain why this isn't as straightforward as he seems to think, he's vanished.

Which means I don't have the chance to tell him that nothing he's done to me tonight has made things right for him with Lucius.

And what I've done in here myself tonight, lying to Vasili so clumsily and rousing all his viperish suspicions, has just made that trust problem in my fated mate's harem a whole lot worse.

Chapter Fifteen
Zara

I sneak out of our bedroom at midnight.

This is all so wrong.

I shouldn't be sneaking around the ice-cold halls of the *domus* alone, hastily bundled back into my leggings and Neo's abandoned sweater which were the easiest things to find in the dark, while Ronin tosses and sweats and mutters with mating fever in our bed and Vasili sleeps beside him, rigid and unapproachable as a sphinx.

The Goblin King showed up tonight reeking of Neo, barely explained what happened to make him that way, then just got more and more grimly uncommunicative as the hours ticked by, with neither Neo nor Lucius showing up.

On the one hand, I could scream that I missed Neo and Vasili finally hooking up, even though they're allowed to, even without me being there, even if they didn't fuck. We're all allowed to be with each other however we want, you know, in all the ways, as long as it stays within the polycule. Those are the rules I insisted on and the guys agreed to, even if we're all still getting used to this whole poly relationship, and to each other.

On the other hand, the Goblin King apparently showed a surprising degree of restraint (under the circumstances, because Neo's *really* hard to resist when he's begging). Vasili left plenty of firsts involving my fated mate undone for the five of us to explore together.

On the *other* other hand (how many hands is this now?), this fucking superheat is looming.

Hormonally speaking, I'm off the charts.

As I tiptoe down the upstairs hall in my stocking feet, I finally have to admit all is *not* well in my harem. I'm really starting to wonder whether my fit of rebellion against this whole queen cage I'm locked into, plus the satisfaction of getting back at Xiao for betraying me, was worth what it's done to the five of us.

Ever since we got back, Neo wants something from us he's clearly not getting. I can feel it, whatever it is, and his longing for that thing is making me crazy. And Lucius is still so disappointed with all of us—but especially with Vasili—and so worried Vasili will be expelled and/or fired and our poly family will be broken. My wolf shifter clearly has his paws full trying to keep all that from happening.

I'm actually starting to worry that all of us could be expelled over that stunt we pulled, especially if the Senate and the AIB (the Arcane Investigative Bureau, which is the FBI of the witching world, but much scarier, and with fewer rules) can't cover it up.

Then there's the fact that we all need to pass our midterms.

Somehow.

With all this going down, it just doesn't feel right banging Ronin and Vasili into a panting, cum-sticky mess tonight. Not with half our guys hanging back and that amorous dragon lurking right downstairs.

Here's the bottom line.

I don't feel safe.

I don't feel safe perched on the edge of this goddamn superheat.

I don't feel safe fucking *anyone* with my lethal and unpredictable new powers. I definitely don't feel safe fucking without all four of my guys involved to ground me.

Which means this heat is *really* fucking with me.

And it hasn't even really hit yet.

Shit.

On the ground floor, I sense right away through our bond that my fated mate's asleep with Lucius in the master suite. Those two seem to be getting closer, and that makes me so happy. Neo blushes every time he looks at Lucius, he's definitely harboring a schoolboy crush on our teacher that he's way too shy to act on. I don't think they're fucking yet, because I'd feel it if they were. But Lucius seems really close to abandoning all that professorial restraint and decorum and finally giving in and just ravaging and ruining all that yummy Neo innocence.

I wish all five of us could share in their new closeness.

I wish we could all be together.

I wish we could all just go back to being the way we were.

Damn it.

We're going to get that back.

Carefully I give a wide berth to the closed door down the hall. That guest studio apartment across from the library is *terra incognito* right now, because there on the map be dragons.

That's where Lucius put Maxim.

Otherwise known as the root of all evil. Or at least, the root of all my current troubles.

My shifter senses are getting sharper, and the whole downstairs reeks like leather and brimstone from that dragon's mating scent.

Just a whiff of that dragonish scent is enough to wake that throbbing ache between my legs. My nipples tingle and pucker up tight under my sweater. My cunt ripples and clenches around my empty hole. My clit chafes and rubs against my thong, and my thighs feel damp and slippery.

Sweet Jesus, I need a cock inside me.

Preferably more than one.

But that's not happening without *all* my guys at this point. Because I figure it might take all five of them—all *four* of them, I mean, fuck, there are only four of them—to keep me from "rising" the way Maxim keeps threatening in my goddamn mating flight.

No way in Hell am I ready for that.

And I'm definitely *not* ready to start popping out dragon babies eleven months from now (since that's how long the gestation period is, according to my hasty and incomplete research).

Well, the *domus* gym's in the basement, and right now it's calling my name. Running off my hormones on the treadmill seems like the only viable option.

But one glimpse of the aqua glimmer from the heated swimming pool in the courtyard has me pivoting away from those scary basement stairs Vasili once chased me up with murder in his black heart. I scoop up my combat boots and veer through the great room toward the sliding glass doors.

I'm a water girl (even though I'm an air sign) and I still miss my rented safe house on the Red Sea coast that I lost when the Academy hoovered me up.

When I unlatch the doors and slip out, the crisp cold brings instant relief to the hot itch of the mating heat that's baking me from the inside out.

Gasping with relief, I crunch through the snowy crust and thread past the row of Roman pillars that rim the pool. I'm already peeling the sweater over my head when I hit the flagstone patio, where the steamy heat of the water melts away the snow. Under a silver moon that's only a sliver away from full, I kick off my boots, peel out of my socks and leggings, leave everything heaped on a pool chair. I'm still wearing my bra and thong. (I kept those on tonight, hoping I'd get to show them off for Lucius, who's surprisingly susceptible to lingerie.)

And they're definitely staying on.

I'm feeling close enough to naked with that dragon in sniffing distance.

"Sleep, dragon," I whisper, the lightning thick and humming in my throat. Violet sparks crackle at my fingertips and my hair floats around my shoulders. That's me summoning my magic.

I'm finally learning some real Compulsion from Lucius in Common Magics class, but my witchcraft works differently than everyone else's. When I'm casting, everything—always—is linked to the lightning voice. Anyway, sleep spells aren't too difficult, so maybe my makeshift magic will have some effect.

Even if it doesn't, because my technique is still erratic, this chlorinated water will mask my scent.

I hope.

Fuck this shit anyway.

I refuse to be afraid of my own fucking shadow in my own fucking house.

With a snarl, I sweep my arms overhead, vault from the deck, tuck my body into a jackknife in midair, and dive in headfirst. The warm water encases my skin and eases the bite of the winter night.

Underwater, I streak like a dolphin across the pool and surface gasping at the far end. My whole body's alive and tingling with energy from being back in my natural habitat.

Oh yeah. It's not a Red Sea reef, but I can definitely make this work.

I flip onto my back so I can backstroke over to where I started. Now I'm getting all nice and warmed up, so I twist into a breaststroke and do my next lap that way, which really kicks up my heartbeat. Eventually I settle into an easy freestyle that propels me back and forth across the surface in a powerful crawl I can maintain forever without effort. The exercise siphons off my simmering heat and burns away the restless energy that's kept me awake.

By the time I hook my arms over the edge and tip my head back against the rim to catch my breath under that floating moon, I almost feel like me again.

Like Zara the cat burglar, off the grid and on the run, with someone else's ass chained to the witching world throne.

My eyes are closed, my body floating, my head tilted back, my breath leveled out, my thoughts finally drifting toward sleep.

That's when I sense him.

Every nerve and synapse in my body snaps to high alert.

He's a hunter, he's stealthy, he's downright *sneaky*, and like the apex predator he is, he's managed to slither into the courtyard and decant his dragonish body into this pool without me hearing him, even with my newly enhanced shifter senses.

But he's close enough now that I can feel him. Without moving an inch, my eyes open a sliver.

I twitch with a jolt of alarm.

He's crouched in the water like a crocodile literally 6.5 feet away, submerged all the way to his nose, with a spill of pale hair streaming behind him as he glides toward me. His golden orbs are riveted on me without blinking.

Despite the warm water, my skin pebbles in a shiver.

Without lifting my head, I tell him, "That's close enough, big guy."

To my relief, that stops his stealthy advance.

"I am yours to command, my sovereign." His guttural voice scrapes through the gurgle of the artificial waterfall at one end that filters chlorinated water back into the pool.

"If only." I snort. "I'd like to command you to fly straight back to Siberia and leave me and my guys the fuck alone. But I know you won't. I've learned a few things about warlocks."

I close my eyes in royal dismissal (like that ever works). But I can *feel* him.

Sweet Jesus, can I feel him.

My entire body hums and tingles with, like, a whole new hyper-level of awareness.

Shit. This better not be that fucking mating bond.

I sense him the way I sense Lucius and Vasili, my alphas, even though this dragon hasn't bitten me.

And that's definitely not changing.

Fuck knows, my heats are already too intense. No way could I survive a third mating bite from yet another alpha.

"This is new to me also, my Zara," he whispers. "But, for me, our bond is welcome."

Cheese on toast. He's hearing my thoughts.

That's a mating bond thing.

And I know from just going through this whole bonding scenario with the rest of my warlocks that, if I accept this dragon as a mate, I'll be hearing his thoughts too.

"How do I turn it off?" I lift my head to glare at him.

"We cannot." His mouth is hard and cruel, but his smile is soft and wistful. "But it will grow easier to bear. When your beautiful belly is round and full with our eggs—"

"Our *eggs*?" I burst out. "You telling me I'm gonna lay *eggs* now like a fucking chicken? Well, that's a hard no. *Hell* to the no on that plan, buddy. I'm not a goddamn incubator. I got a degree to finish and a throne to claim. Not to mention four endangered arcane species I'm literally supposed to save from extinction."

"Yes, I know all of this. It is your destiny. I do not oppose it." He sounds so calm he maddens me. "You are Zarina Mikhailovna."

I push up straighter. "I'm who now?"

"Zarina, daughter of Michael, said in the Russian way. You are the dragon queen."

He dips his head, all sleek and silver in the moonlight, like in an old-fashioned bow. This heat must be frying my brain cells or something, because for a second there, this scoundrel actually comes off as respectful.

Even… kinda… reverent?

I hitch myself higher on the pool deck by my elbows and his eyes veer to my boobs, which are definitely on display in my soaked black lace push-up. Those vertical slits he has for pupils dilate wide.

For some damn reason (like, you know, this fucking superheat) my tits feel swollen and bigger than usual. My nipples are definitely tight and tingly and extremely ready to be suckled. *Hard.* I want his mouth on them so bad I'm aching.

I clear my throat and try not to think about my nipples.

C'mon, brain. Focus.

"How… how would that even work anyway?" I blurt out. "I mean the whole, uh, egg thing. For one thing, I'm massively on birth control."

His head tilts, like the notion of birth control is a foreign concept. "You take the pills?"

Thank fuck he doesn't sound judgy. Just curious.

"IUD," I say shortly. I can hardly believe I'm talking about my birth control with this dragon, like he actually has the right to be consulted. But I'm seriously deficient in my knowledge of dragon biology, and the books in the library don't go there, so he's the only one I can really ask. "At least, I *had* an IUD until the, uh, shifting. I don't know how this whole dragon thing works. Do I still have it?"

"Silver in the body survives the shift. All other implants are… dislodged and… discarded by the transformation." He unfolds to his full height, water sliding down his shoulders and chest. Like I noticed before, his nipples are pierced with silver. The same way mine are. And he just explained why my shift didn't change that.

I wonder if he likes having his piercings played with, the way I do. If he likes it rough, right on the edge of pain, the way I do.

Not that I'm planning to find out or anything.

A soft rumble rises from his chest that sounds like dragon laughter. I can almost sense that other presence inside him, the way I'm starting to do with Lucius and his wolf. That presence is ancient and crafty and remorseless.

But it… he… *welcomes* me.

He welcomes me in a way that makes my own inner dragon stir and uncoil inside my skin.

Stop, I whisper to her, that Lady Mothra inside me who breathes lightning. *Not yet.*

He is ours, Zara. A sleek feminine voice unspools like a silk ribbon through my thoughts. *We should claim our mate.*

Shit. Now my inner dragon's, like, talking to me?

Fuck.

I shove down a spurt of panic. I'm in control here. I'm definitely in control.

"I can help you," Maxim breathes. "I can help you control your beast. As I have learned to control mine."

I can't seem to stop looking at him. The water laps at the tight ripple of his ribs and the sinewy plane of his abs like a tongue. And there's enough greenish light sneaking up from underneath that I can clearly see he's naked.

Heat streaks through me like a missile and lights up my clit in a nuclear flash of need.

My eyes veer away before I get a good gander at that unique peen he's rocking.

Under the chafing rub of my thong, which is just inflaming the situation worse at this point, my pussy ripples and opens like a hungry mouth, ravenous for that wicked cock.

Fuck.

Me.

Hard.

"Yeah, well." I clear my throat, because my voice is dripping with sex. "My IUD is—was—molded plastic." You better believe I looked that shit right up after I shifted back. "And, for your information, the only reason I'm not totally freaking out about my BC right now is because I added a backup method after I started hooking up with my warlocks."

I *really* don't know why I'm telling him all this. How do I even trust any intel he gives me? Doesn't he have, like, an ulterior motive?

"I have told you I do not lie." Above his intense eyes, his brows rush together in a ferocious frown. "I will never lie to you, of all creatures living."

Reading my mind again through this bond I don't want.

Double fuck.

"Yeah, well, I get shots from the Academy clinic. That's my backup method." I might as well go ahead and ask. "You gonna tell me that's not copacetic anymore either?"

"I… do not know this word." His head ducks, like maybe he's

embarrassed by his less than perfect English. He doesn't need to be, because it gets the job done, even if he sounds a little stilted.

My heart softens for him a tiny bit.

"Copacetic just means okay," I tell him.

"Ah." Carefully he repeats the new word, his forehead furrowing in a way that is very slightly cute as he concentrates. "Poisons, potions, medicines, these effects are not undone by the shift. So these… shots? They should remain… copacetic."

I'm still suspicious, so I probe for more. "Even with this superheat? Even… with you? Assuming we ever did anything, I mean, just speaking hypothetically."

"Yes and yes." His lids drop over his crocodile stare. "In order to conceive our clutch, these shots must first end."

"Thank fuck for that." I heave a sigh and settle back in the water. "No offense, but those shots are my new best friend. I'm not into conceiving our, uh, clutch right now. Like I already told you."

He sinks down too, watching me carefully, eyes gleaming with reptilian interest. He's mirroring me like a damn predator.

"That is not what your dragon is telling mine. She is nearly ready to rise, my Zara." His head dips, yet his crafty gaze holds mine. "But your shots, they will guard you from conceiving. If that is what you fear."

"I don't *fear*. I just don't *want*. Not right now, anyway." My voice ratchets tight with frustration. "Look, obviously I get that I'll have to produce the next queen at some point. And maybe she'll be a dragon queen, and that'll help your clan out of a pickle. I get that you need more dragons, okay?"

Agitation crackles through me, and I make a real effort to rein it in, calling on all those control skills Lucius has been teaching me.

Because I don't like to think what'll happen if we're both in the water when I summon lightning.

My dragon—I mean *the* dragon, he's definitely not mine or anything—crouches in the water and just waits me out.

He can be patient, this guy, when he wants to be.

I dial down the volume with a sigh. "It's just I got a lot riding on me right now, Maxim. I'm supposed to save the arcane races from this extinction event, and I still don't know how, except it has something to do with my witchcraft and being a powerful queen once Messalina kicks the bucket. I dunno, maybe the whole mess has something to do with all the inbreeding. All twelve clans are doing it to preserve what little witchcraft we have left. But me? I'm not into that. I feel like maybe we need to stop it."

"You will learn. I will help," he says fiercely.

He's still hunkered low in the water. But his shoulders peek above the surface. My gaze snags on the pale scars that lick around his sun-bronzed skin from behind. I noticed those scars back in Vegas, but there was way too much going on at the time (what with my snake Hulking out and trying to kill the guy) to pursue it.

Now a dark suspicion arrows through me.

"Hey." I scowl. "Come over here for a sec."

He sinks lower, the way a hunting croc would do, until he's submerged to his nose again. His dragon eyes are wary, but he glides slowly toward me.

And, shit, my entire body feels him coming.

Under the waves, my skin floods with a wash of heat. Against the soaked strip of my thong, my clit pulses with need. My pussy clenches in a spasm so tight I barely bite back a moan.

"That—that's close enough," I gasp. "Now turn around."

For the first time, he hesitates. His eyes narrow to menacing slits. Something about my scrutiny is making him—the great big dragon—feel threatened.

I huff out a soft breath. "I'm not gonna goose you or anything. C'mon, turn around. I wanna see your back."

His head droops and his voice lowers to a hiss. "You wish to see my shame? So be it. That is your right as sovereign."

Before I can wrap my head around that, he pivots to give me his back. All that long blond hair is swirling in the way, so I gather it carefully in one hand—it's silky soft, so much softer than I expect—and ease it to one side.

From the base of his neck down, his narrow back is scored with the long pale slashes of old scarring. Those faded furrows crisscross and overlap and run all the way down under the water.

My tummy squirms with a sick feeling. I lay my free hand on his shoulder and he flinches.

This big tough dragon *flinches*.

At my touch.

"It's okay, big guy," I breathe softly. "I'm not gonna hurt you. I just wanna see. Okay?"

I hear the click of his swallow before he grunts his consent.

As gently as I can, my hand ghosts down his back to trace the furrows of all that scarring. Some of those scars are viciously deep, like they cut him to the bone. The mutilation runs all the way down his back and stops just short of his ass. Some of the damage feels like claw marks in straight solid rows. But some of the marks are curvy.

Way too clearly, he's also been whipped.

Brutally.

Like, with a bullwhip.

Someone hurt my dragon.

My voice lashes out in a dragonish snarl. "Who did this to you?"

His head snaps sideways so I can see his fierce profile.

But his gaze eludes mine.

The queen in me demands an answer. I snap out the command. "Who. Did. This. To. You."

"Siblings raised in the same clutch can be savage," he says curtly, with a complete fucking lack of emotion. "There is never enough food in the tundra to feed a clutch of starving dragons, so each must fight for his share. And I was… the runt of the litter, as they say."

I'm outraged and appalled as hell. His own siblings fucking savaged him and stole his food. No wonder he's skin and bone. Literally, how does this even happen in the twenty-first century? Even in goddamn Siberia?

"There's more to it than that. *Someone whipped you.* More than once." Goddamn it, I need to hear all of it. And somehow, I know he needs to tell me.

His head turns away from me, but I grip his waist to hold him right there. And, God help me, he feels good under my hands. He feels *so* fucking good.

Our mate, my inner dragon purrs. *Oh, Zara, how hard we shall ride him.*

Down, girl. I mean it. I clear my throat. "Who whipped you, Maxim?"

"My Lady Mother," he says tightly, biting off the words. "She scourged all of us. With her… her cat o' nine tails. With her cane. With her… bullwhip… when she meant business. To keep us in our place. So we would obey her. So we would never challenge her. Because I am the dominant male of my clan, I required more… correction… than most."

Sweet mercy. He says it so calmly. But this is the root of his shame.

His own mom beat him like a 1950s reform school nun and made him feel ashamed.

Like his suffering was his fault.

"Holy fucking shit. That… that is *so* not okay." The lightning lurks in my voice. I'm so upset I can barely get the words out.

That's child abuse.

It's fucking *child abuse.*

God damn it. His mom's a monster. If I ever meet his Lady Mother, I swear I'm gonna kill that bitch.

And where the fuck was Rasputin Senior lurking during all this?

"There is no… Senior." A little humor lightens his flat tone. "My mother does not wed her mates when she rises. Her way was always to mate them and then kill them. That is why I am now the last. My brothers, they are merely wyverns."

"Jesus. No wonder there aren't any left," I mutter. "Fuck, that's psychotic."

In fact, there's so much crazy to unpack in what he just said that I'm gonna need a bellboy to help me schlep all that baggage.

But here's the bottom line.

This guy was raised without a father, even a shit father like mine. He's basically been abused and brutalized by his whole damn family.

My heart aches like a bruise. I want to wrap myself around him from behind.

But I'm afraid of what will happen if I do.

Instead I release the wet weight of his hair to float free in the water and skim both hands gently down his back, letting him know without words that there's nothing shameful in these scars, not for him or for me.

He shudders under my touch and whines low in his throat. That's his dragon, I know it.

His dragon is… keening.

And fuck it, fuck this superheat, fuck me, fuck everything. I slide my arms around his waist and tuck up against the back of him. The shock of his body races all down my front, sparked by the scrape of my lace-covered nipples against his back, the press of the front of my thighs against the back of his, the nudge of his bare ass against my belly.

Need pulses between us, glowing red and hot in the moonlight.

But that's not what I'm doing here. I'm trying to offer comfort. I'm fighting like hell to keep my libido locked down and my motives straight.

In my arms, he's absolutely rigid. He's not touching back. It's like he's afraid of being touched. He's afraid of being touched from behind.

Well, no wonder, given the state of his back. Hasn't anyone ever touched him with love?

So much about him clicks into place in my brain.

Now an awful suspicion rears its head. I lean close and growl in his hair, "You know no one here's ever gonna do that to you, right? There's plenty to eat. I'm, uh, a benevolent ruler and I definitely don't go around scourging people. Even Lucius is, like, gentle under all that wolf."

Under my touch, his lean body vibrates with something like a chuckle.

"Lucius' nature is not gentle. He is alpha, and he is fierce, especially in defense of his pack. But this is as it should be." His tone shifts from humor to something more complex. "As for you, my Zara… you will rule as your nature demands. And I… I will find my place in your world. As you must do in mine."

That right there's my cue to stop touching him.

But I can't.

I flatten my palms along his belly, which goes a long way toward distracting him from the conditioned fear of having anyone (even me) behind him. He's all hot skin stretched over sinew and bone and dragon.

And I just know if I… ease my hands down a bit… I'll find that stiff barbed cock of his standing straight up for me.

Claim our king, and we will rise, my dragon queen hisses.

Yeah, no. We're not doing that. We're not fucking *rising*. I might not have much freedom or much control these days, but one of the few things I do control is my body. It's one of the last freedoms I have—the freedom to control my own actions and choose my own mates.

I'm not losing that. Not ever.

And this guy's not giving me a choice.

I bite my lip hard enough to sting (when did my incisors get so damn sharp?) I have to force myself—literally force myself—to lift my hands from this dragon's smokin' hot body and step carefully back.

"No one here's gonna hurt you," I repeat firmly, just for good measure. Then I hesitate. "Uh, as long as you're careful with Vasili."

"I am always careful with Vasili," he growls. "It is Vasili himself who is not careful with me."

He twists around to face me. And now I'm backed against the pool wall with a fully aroused male dragon shifter looming over me, roughly 1.8 feet away.

Which is a dangerous place to be.

I like it and I don't.

Spread your wings, my dragon whispers. *We will rise, and he will follow.*

A ripple of hunger clenches my cunt.

"Yeah, about you and Vasili," I say roughly. "Why'd you *do* that to him? Why'd you run and tattle to his asshole dad? That was shitty as fuck."

He doesn't answer. Not right away.

His lids drop over his secretive eyes and his face turns all shifty.

"This is, how do you say, ancient history? And it is between Vasili and me," he says at last.

He's still not lying, but he is evading. Vasili thinks Maxim was jealous. Who knows, maybe that gigolo yacht captain was fucking both those boys.

How old was this dragon anyway when all that went down?

"I was fifteen," he mutters. "Just barely. My dragon had not risen. But that Italian never touched me. If he tried, I would have killed him. And… and… Nikolai Romanov—Vasili's sire—he was the closest I ever came to a father."

That last sentence spills out in a jumbled rush, like something he never planned to share.

Which sends this hot mess spinning in a whole new direction.

My soles lower to the pool bottom and I shoot to my feet. "So, what, you wanted to get rid of Vasili and have his homophobic fuck of a father all to yourself? Jesus, Maxim. Don't you have any idea what that did to Vasili? Did you even stop to think before you ratted him out?"

That's why my Goblin King believes no one can ever love him. Because his father abandoned him over what Maxim told him.

God, this dragon pisses me right off.

But there's more to it than that. Under all my rage on Vasili's behalf, I'm smarting under the sharp sting of disappointment.

I was starting to think maybe the planet's last male dragon shifter was better than that.

Well, guess what?

I was dead wrong.

Scowling, the dragon too rises to his full height. Which means he looms over me, with the water barely covering that barbed peen I'm trying like fuck not to think about.

"There was—more to this matter than you know." Now he sounds downright sullen. "These are issues you would not understand."

"Why, because I wasn't raised in a homophobic fundamentalist culture? Because I come from such a Betty Crocker perfect family myself? Or because I'm just too stupid?" My voice and my power are both rising. Which means I want out of this pool and away from him.

Like, now.

At this point, he's a seething cauldron of emotions. Anger. Resistance. Determination. All swirling around some shameful secret he's desperate to hide. And of course the reason I know all this, the reason I *feel* this emotional shitstorm that's raging through him so intimately, is because we're forming a fucking mating bond.

Goddamn it. I could scream with frustration.

I don't want this bond with him.

I hate him.

I glare at him like I can shoot lightning from my eyes. Which isn't a gift I've manifested (yet). He glares right back with his own flaming eyes like some demented Smaug from *The Hobbit*. His ruthless Slavic face settles in stubborn lines.

"I do not wish to discuss Vasili Romanov," he growls. "I came to this place to be with you—"

"That was a waste of your dragon frequent flyer miles, buddy." I plant my hands on my hips and lift my chin. "I've already got four hot warlock cocks locked and loaded to get me through this superheat without any worries about me laying a clutch of eggs afterward like a damn chicken. Far as I can tell, having you close is just making it worse. You should go straight back to where you came from."

His voice drops two octaves to a snarl. "I will go nowhere without you. We will rule these mortal skies together."

He reaches for me. I sweep his arm aside, the flash of contact hard enough to bruise. Thunder grumbles in the cold winter sky.

"I'm only saying this once, dragon. Back off."

His eyes smolder with dragonfire. My own dragon is bugling for him and bating her wings in a frenzy.

Her inner voice scorches through me. *We crave. We need. We burn!! If you will not rise, then open your legs for him.*

To my alarm, his determined frown gives way to a crafty smile.

Because of course he hears every word.

Great.

Now he knows my own goddamn dragon's firmly on his side.

"Our dragons both desire this, my Zara." His pupils blow wide and his voice goes dark with intent. "I swear to you, I have never desired anything or anyone under God in heaven the way I desire you. You are my love. You are my fate. And I am not alone in this desire."

He closes the last few inches between us. My own traitor body is literally on fire for him, and fuck my need for control. I want him to shove me back against the pool wall, shred my thong with his dragon claws, thrust that barbed cock so deep inside me I can taste him in my throat, and fuck me till I'm drenched and dripping with dragon seed.

The word *no* flashes in my brain like a hazard light. I want him. I hate him. I need him. I fear him.

Most of all, I fear *rising* with him.

And I sure as shit won't do it alone.

Not without the rest of my warlocks.

Since we've already established that I'm not gonna summon lightning in this pool, and since he's way too close now for me to scramble out without him catching me, there's only one way out of this.

I fold my knees, plunge underwater, push off the wall with a powerful shove, and shoot past him into open water.

And because we're linked now, and my shifter senses are getting so keen, I *feel* him twisting and knifing after me through the waves. It's like a mock version of that mating flight he's jonesing for. But it's underwater.

And there's nothing playful about it.

I'm swimming for my life.

If he catches me, he'll fuck me.

He'll fuck me, and God, I'll fuck him. I'll lock the two of us in his room and I'll fuck him for days. I'll fuck him till I miss my midterms and we fail all our classes and this fucking dragon heat finally breaks.

I'll fuck away the last of my freedom.

I burst to the surface and suck in a burning lungful of frosty air. He's already on top of me, his sleek naked form arrowing toward me like a torpedo. I dive deep and dart away, my heel catching his face in a glancing blow that slows his momentum for a crucial sec.

I pit all my speed and strength in the water against him, I fight like hell to keep him from catching me or cornering me. But it's like fighting a crocodile. He's fast and he's strong and he's clever. I keep trying to maneuver to the side by the great room doors, because if I can get inside the *domus*, I've got options.

But clearly, he knows that.

And this flying reptile's determined to keep me out here.

Isolated.

At his mercy.

I'm getting tired and my pace is lagging, but the waterfall at the far end has possibilities. It's hard to hear or see under there, and it's shallow enough behind that I should be able to scramble out quick. I knife past the dragon's latest attempt to corner me against the pool wall, give his face a good splash when he surfaces for air, and shoot across the pool.

I'm midway through the waterfall when two hands close around my ankles.

Pummeled and buffeted by curtains of water pounding down on me, I twist and kick and thrash. I'm not shy about using my fists either, and I land a few solid blows (even blinded by this watercannon that's battering me) that make him grunt and swear. Somehow he's everywhere, all hands and limbs and swirling hair.

I'm getting disoriented and my chest is screaming for air like you wouldn't believe.

I claw to the surface with an explosive gasp.

Suddenly he's right in front of me, my tits crushed against his chest, his arms banded around my hips, his hands cupping my ass and dragging my pelvis to his. My legs strap around his hips and my pussy slots right up against that monstrous heat he's packing, with only the soaked strip of my thong between us. My hands fist in his hair and our mouths crash together so hard I taste hot blood mingled with the chemical tang of chlorine and the dark cinnamon burn of dragon.

It's teeth as much as lips.

It's bite as much as kiss.

His tongue lashes my mouth. My tongue swats his away. His lips punish and ravage. My mouth dominates and demands. He tastes so fucking good that a deep moan rolls up my throat.

And he swallows the sound down like he's starving for it.

I writhe against his strength. His cock slides against my slit. The rough prick of his barb sparks shattering spasms of need deep in my cunt.

I jam my hand between our struggling bodies and wrap my palm around all that exotic length. He's big, and he's hard, and he's… unique. I mean, he's really something. Gripping him is like gripping a devil's thick forked tail. Trying to be gentle, because he seems supersensitive there, my fingers skim over his hard tip and the stiff protrusions on either side of his swollen crown.

He bucks into my grip.

Clearly, he wants it harder.

Raw groans tear from his throat like I'm torturing him.

I don't have the first clue how that dick is supposed to fit inside me. But my hungry pussy's more than ready to give it the good college try.

The waterfall's pounding down on our heads, water's blinding us and drowning us and pouring into our sucking, biting, desperate kisses. Under all that churn on that surface, his hands knead my bare ass and wrench my thong to one side. A rough finger probes my pucker until I writhe into him with a wild cry. That's an invite he accepts, shoving that finger deep into my ass with literally zilch in the foreplay department.

My hole clenches and flutters around him and basically begs for more. I want him to wreck my hole like it's his cock inside me.

Our bodies are struggling together, the meager scrap of my thong still trapped between us. Inside I'm slick and creaming for him, for that barb of his that feels like it'll hurt when he fucks me. But it's a pain my inner dragon craves with a single-minded savagery.

My dragon queen is demanding to be fucked by her dragon king.

Right the hell now.

"Does it hurt?" I gasp between hard claiming kisses. "Tell me the truth."

We're linked, so he knows what I'm asking.

"Yes," he growls, his eyes lidded and burning. "Always. The first time—in particular. You will scream for me, my queen. You will scream when you take my cock. At first, you will beg me to stop."

Oh fuck. Oh fuck.

I whimper and moan and grind against him. My free hand claws into his back. His finger rides my ass and my cunt clenches around the chafe of my thong, craving him there too. I'm still kneading this barbaric dragon cock of his, rubbing him up against my slit, both blessing and cursing that skimpy strip of fabric that's trapped between us like a chastity belt.

This kinky little fantasy of mine arcs between us like an electric current.

A dangerous rumble rises from his chest. "If you were raised among dragons, such a thing would be no fantasy. In ancient times, our sires required their daughters to wear such garments until they were mated. This custom was all that kept them off our dragon cocks." He pauses. "Would such an arrangement… please you?"

In the state I'm in, even that kinky BDSM dragon fantasy turns my crank. Not that it's realistic, with five—I mean *four,* damn it!—four potent as fuck warlocks to savor and love in my bed.

"Forget the history lesson," I gasp. "Let's go back to me begging you to stop."

He chuffs out a chuckle and sucks hard on my lower lip. All the blood in my body rushes to that tingling suck. My ass clenches around him and I writhe in his grasp.

"You will beg, but I will prevail. I will insist, because I know your screams will turn to cries of pleasure." He presses his hot mouth to my ear and his voice roughens. "When we mate, my barbs will lock us together while I take my fill of your sweet pussy until you are overflowing with my passion. When a dragon comes—he is copious. And his release is—plentiful."

Sweet Jesus, he's not even inside me and he's gonna make me come.

My heels dig into the backs of his thighs and I fuck up against him. By now, we're both hot and panting.

He groans thickly in my ear. "When I am well pleased, as you will please me, my lock can hold for hours. In time, you will learn to sleep and wake and fuck and sleep again with me hooked and lodged deep inside you, warming you through our long Russian nights."

The mother of all orgasms hangs suspended over me like a wave on the brink of crashing.

Until his mouth claims mine in a savage kiss and he growls against my lips, "Then I will do the same with your sexy warlock Ronin. I swear I can barely wait to ruin both of you."

Oh, my freaking God, *yes.*

My big O crashes down like the waterfall that's drowning us.

It's a tsunami of violence and release and ecstasy.

I fling back my head and howl to the heavens in the lightning voice. The tingling jolt of the little lightning slams through me and blows the sodden hair back from our faces.

Fortunately, it's not the actual lightning, or else we'd both be barbequed. But my magic moment gives off plenty enough voltage to shock.

It's enough to dislodge his grip.

That's when my belated survival instinct (finally) kicks in. Shocked, breathless, trembling with climax yet horny as fuck, I shove him away and scramble out of the water. I'm dripping and next to naked in something like two feet of snow, but I don't give a shit.

Barefoot and desperate, I race through the courtyard with snow burning my feet and ice cutting my soles like the hounds of hell are hunting my ass. I claw the glass doors open, dive into the great room, slam the lock into place.

God.

That's it.

He can just cool his jets for a while out there. Before too long, I'll send one of the guys down to let him in—

But I'm still standing there, panting and shivering with my hands pressed against the glass, when the courtyard explodes in a blinding flash of light.

With stars and comets still streaking past my eyes, I watch the massive black dragon erupt from the pool with a soul-shattering bellow of rage and frustration and launch into the sky.

For half the night, that dragon wings and circles over the *domus* and the cowering Academy, tearing the fabric of everyone's sleep with his keening screams of loss and fury and loneliness.

Chapter Sixteen
Lucius

"Lucius?" Zara's whisper twines through my dreams, where my wolf lopes through the wintry forest and howls at the moon. "You better wake up. I think I screwed up. There's a problem with the dragon."

Although that isn't the sort of problem anyone wants to wake up to, my eyes are already open, pupils dilating to absorb the shadowy contours of my bedroom. Red coals still glow in my banked fire and the moon still floats in my window.

Not long after midnight then.

Neo and I have barely fallen asleep.

My sweet boy still slumbers where I've settled him, his big body curled under the blankets with me spooned around him, my arm cinched tight around his bare waist, my perennial erection tucked safely behind my pajamas (although it's also wedged shamelessly against his buttocks), my face buried in his soft curls so I can breathe in his scent of sage and Zara and innocence while we sleep. Oddly, he also smells quite strongly tonight of Vasili and… iodine?

He's a deep sleeper, this pupil of mine. His slow snores drone on without a hitch.

Zara leans anxiously over us, her tiny body swimming in her fur-lined Academy bathrobe, lips parted and breathless, towel-damp curls tumbled around her worried face.

She holds a burning candle.

This means she's blown all the fuses in the *domus* again, which still happens occasionally when my queen enjoys a particularly strong climax. Under my instruction, she's begun to make real progress controlling her lethal witchcraft. But she's nearly in heat (just as I am myself). Clearly, her control over her power is slipping.

"Sorry about the lights," she whispers. "Racetrack's in the basement at the fuse box getting everything switched back on. Uh, pretty much the whole house is awake—except Ronin. His heat's totally hit. Vasili's staying with him."

I'm concerned enough about all this that I've already unwound myself from Neo's warm bulk to sit up.

"Thank you. I see. I'll get up." Hastily I sweep my sleep-tumbled hair into a knot at my nape. It's really too long now to be practical, but the entire polycule objects to my cutting it.

The combination of my sudden activity and his fated mate's anxiety finally rouses Neo. Struggling awake, he mumbles thickly, "Zara? Babe, wha's a matter?"

His brawny arm spills from the blankets to grope for her.

She clutches his hand tightly in both of hers and lets him pull her in close against our bed.

It's his question she's answering. Still, her wide eyes cling to mine. "I almost fucked the dragon. *Almost* being very much the key thing."

In the wake of this admission, my concern mounts swiftly. "Why is the entire household awake? It's after midnight on a school night."

In truth, I'm hardly surprised that she and Maxim have been intimate (although I'm a bit surprised she stopped) since I expected nothing less when I welcomed him into this *domus*. A dragon queen requires a dragon king to carry her through her heat. Her powerful sexual needs are half the reason I argued to the Dean that we admit Maxim.

That decision means I'm solely responsible for Maxim's conduct.

I made a judgment call that, despite his barbaric upbringing, this junkyard dog would master his savage shifter impulses, just as I myself have done. Now I wonder if my optimistic assumptions have placed every student on this island in danger.

Zara applies herself to my question, but her face is shadowed with guilt. "They're all awake because Maxim woke everyone up."

I strive to project an air of calm for everyone's sake. "And where exactly is Maxim?"

My question is answered by the distant scream of an enraged dragon. I've heard such a thing only once, at a shifter solstice festival in my childhood, but it isn't the sort of cry one forgets. This is a banshee scream to send ice cascading down any man's spine. Even my wolf huddles low in a protective crouch.

Thank God that dragon is well away from this *domus*.

But, Christ, he's probably awakened half the Academy by now with his bugling.

"Yeah," Zara says softly. "He's up there. Just… circling. For a good hour now. I tried calling… you know, telepathically? But he won't come down. I didn't hurt him or anything, and we didn't actually fuck. But he wanted to—he *really* wanted to—and I wouldn't let him. Not without the rest of you. And I won't. Because I'm… I'm afraid of… *rising*."

At last, the contours of the current crisis take shape in my mind. I have further questions, of course, but they can wait. At the moment, Zara looks more defiant than actually frightened, because of course she's Zara.

"Let's talk about the subject of your rising later, my dear." Holding her worried gaze with mine, I relieve her of the fire hazard of that dripping candle before she sets the bed alight. I thrust the candle safely into the sconce on the nightstand.

Still gripping her hand, Neo pushes up to sit, his sleepy face firing with concern. "I should've been there with you. He should never have touched you without us being there. Oh God, babe, did he hurt you?"

Body of Christ, can that be possible?

I trusted Maxim, sympathized with his plight, allowed him into our very home, based purely on my own instincts and the strength of his word. I trusted his oath, sworn on his own dragon, not to harm my students.

What if I was wrong?

At the mere prospect of Zara being hurt, my wolf bares his teeth in a savage growl and claws brutally at my skin. I maintain a firm grip on him, because the last thing this household needs tonight is a second shifter rabid and raging.

"No, no, I'm fine," she says hastily, because of course she senses my wolf rising. "Really. But I think I kinda hurt Maxim, I mean, emotionally. I didn't mean to, Lucius. I really didn't. I… I promised him I wouldn't. He's— he's just so—alone—"

Her voice splinters.

With an exclamation, I leap out of bed and drag her into my arms.

She burrows into me gratefully, slim arms snaking around my waist. I press her face into my shoulder and tuck her compact curves tight against my body. I massage the silky back of her neck with a reassuring hand. She relaxes and snuggles into my touch with a sigh.

The creamy scent of roses and vanilla—her scent, my queen's scent, that scent I've missed so dearly, as I missed every single thing about her while she was on the loose—floats from her freshly washed hair.

Under the enveloping robe, I realize with a pang of concern, she's shivering hard enough to make her teeth chatter.

"Damnation, you're trembling," I say roughly. My palate tingles as my fangs threaten to descend. "Neo, stir up the fire, if you will."

He scrambles out of bed into the icy air in his briefs to comply, pausing only to press a tender kiss against Zara's temple and whisper, "Be right back. It's gonna be okay, babe, stay here with Lucius," as he rushes past.

"You're wearing pajamas," Zara mumbles to me, sounding bemused. Her cold face turns into the side of my neck. "I didn't realize you owned any."

"He has a whole drawerful," Neo says wryly as he wields the poker with purpose. In the hearth, a tongue of flame licks to life. "I think I've seen all of them."

Even in the midst of this crisis, I find myself blushing.

"You're such a gentleman," Zara murmurs, lips soft against my neck. "And he's so sweet and shy. Bet the two of you could use a little assist, couldn't you, Lucius? Just a little help to get you… over the hump?"

Her hands slip under my shirt to graze my lower back. At my mate's touch, goosebumps sheet down my back and tighten my buttocks.

Suddenly, I'm all alpha.

Abruptly my thoughts swerve from the still-bugling dragon whose intermittent screams continue to float through the *domus* to the more immediate imperative of my precious mate and her sexual needs. The wolfish musk of my mating scent floods the air. That scent is engineered to soothe, and she breathes me in deep with a little moan.

Under my pajamas, my shaft heats and swells. My fangs shoot down to fill my mouth.

Thickly, I manage to speak through them. "My dear, your hands are like ice."

"Ugh, sorry." Her face lifts and her teal eyebrows pucker. "I was in the pool. I took a shower to warm up, but I'm still kinda chilly."

She was in the pool?

The details of her disastrous encounter with Maxim begin to take shape in my mind.

"I want you to climb right into this bed with Neo and get thoroughly warm. That's the first thing." I make my tone firm enough to prevent either of them from arguing.

"Will you be getting in with us?" Her nails skate up my spine, spreading shivers and distraction in her wake.

"I will after a bit." *That's at least the third or fourth thing.* Firmly I disentangle myself from her clinging body, although separating from her is the very last thing I want.

But my duty beckons sternly.

Gazing down into her upturned face, I instruct both my students, "Now then. Into this bed with the both of you. I'm going to check on the others. Then I intend to phone the Dean."

"The Dean," she groans, bowing her face against my shoulder. "Same Dean who's still pissed at me for the whole stolen jet incident. Oh, groovy."

Obedient as always, Neo hurries up behind her, wraps his arms around her, and buries his gentle face in the side of her neck. "It's gonna be okay. We need to trust Lucius. C'mon, babe, let's get you all toasty."

Clearly still troubled, she toes off her slippers and lets him coax her into bed.

Despite everything, my wolf is fiercely satisfied to see my queen ensconced there in my bed where she belongs. Neo is already climbing in beside her and tucking the blankets around her legs.

Now they're both curled up in my bed, which is where they both belong. Truly, I yearn for nothing more than to climb in beside them and thoroughly ravage both of them.

Firmly I belt my smoking jacket over my pajamas and thrust my feet into my slippers.

I'm reaching for the candle when Zara lays her small capable hand over mine. I'm relieved to feel her skin warming.

Being tucked up in my bed with her fated mate is already working its own witchcraft.

"Lucius," she says softly. "I get that you're mad at us for leaving. I get that I hurt you—both of you." Her unhappy eyes veer to include Neo. "I never meant to, but I did, and I'm sorry. I'm so sorry."

My heart contracts under her earnest contrition. "My dear, it's best we discuss this later."

"I'm just saying you're our alpha. You're gonna have to fuck Ronin pretty soon to break his heat." Her voice goes husky. "And you're gonna have to fuck me."

All the blood rushes straight to my cock.

Perhaps, truly, the best thing for her right now is a hard fuck. Biologically speaking, if she won't accept Maxim, I'm the next best available option to break her heat. The biochemicals in my alpha shifter semen will trigger a strong and satisfying climax.

"Let me just check on the others," I rasp, my wolf thick and growly in my throat. "And phone the Dean. Quickly. Why don't the two of you, er, get started?"

Heat or no heat, this queen is not one to be intimidated by a growly alpha (more's the pity).

Her knowing gaze meets mine and her lush lips tilt in a cocky grin. "Because we're waiting for you, Lucius. Hurry back."

Rosy with blushes, Neo tucks his head against hers so his magenta curls tumble forward.

Dear God, my wolf is wild to mate with both of them.

I grip my candle and hurry into the corridor before I change my mind and abandon my duty entirely. As I pull the bedroom door closed behind me to conserve the fire's warmth, the lamp near the vestibule flickers to life. A cone of saffron light spreads across the great room.

Apparently, Racetrack has successfully concluded her business with the fuse box.

Dez is puttering around the kitchen in her flannel pajamas, whisking what appears to be a generous pot of hot chocolate for the entire household over the reluctant gas burner. God willing, she and Racetrack will suffer nothing worse from this imbroglio than an interrupted night's sleep.

I pad over to the glass doors and peer anxiously into the heavens, but the dragon is not currently visible. I can conceive of no way to draw his attention short of climbing to the roof and signaling him with a flashlight. Perhaps he and his thwarted libido are better off out there where they currently reside.

This is particularly the case with another alpha preparing to break his queen's mating heat.

Leaving the dragon to his own solitary if thoroughly disruptive devices, I climb the stairs to the second floor with heavy steps.

I'm deeply concerned about Ronin, and deeply aware of my neglected duty to him as his alpha (not to mention the fact that I'm desperately in love with him, which is an emotion distinctly related to, but still separate from, my consuming lust to fuck him).

But my unresolved issues at present lie largely with Vasili.

Until I can learn to trust him again, until I know I can rely upon him to be my responsible colleague, my mature alpha, my trustworthy ally, and my steadfast partner in keeping Zara safe (including from her own reckless instincts), I simply cannot accept him back as my lover.

Even if our estrangement is destroying me. Even if our estrangement is risking the happiness of our queen's entire harem.

Trust is a hard line for me.

Without trust, truly, we have nothing.

In Zara's pretty bedroom with its painted frescoes and curtained bed— a room which has also been my own bedroom in recent weeks—I find the situation precisely as she's described.

Ronin is deeply asleep in our tumbled bed, naked but quiet, reeking with the musk of Vasili's release and his own. The air is saturated with the heavy caramel and vetiver of Vasili's mating scent.

That scent makes my wolf burn to rut into Ronin (who clearly needs sleep more than fucking, at least until his next peak hits).

That scent also makes me wild to bend for Vasili myself.

Sexually speaking, Vasili is emphatically my alpha. Tonight he looks every inch the part as he prowls, scowling and intense, before the crackling fire in those sinfully erotic breeches he insists on wearing solely to torment me (or so it often seems) and not a stitch more.

Sensing my quiet but determined entrance, he gives me a shuttered look. He's uncharacteristically disheveled, cosmetics smudged around his shadowed eyes, hair wildly tousled as though Ronin's been fisting it while they fuck.

"Stay away from Ronin," he says briefly. "You can have your turn later. He's sleeping until the next spike. With any luck, he'll sleep till dawn, if that flying donkey of a dragon ever stops braying."

"I'll happily share in his tending." This is a rather circumspect turn of phrase to describe the way I'm burning to despoil my mate in that bed. But I pitch my voice carefully low to avoid disturbing him now. "I can return later to let you sleep. For the moment, I have Zara with Neo in my room, and her needs too are pressing."

"Hmmm." With a heavy sigh, Vasili drapes himself over Zara's desk chair, which he's dragged near the fire, and stretches his elegant bare feet on the hearth. "Thank you for taking care of her, at least. I can comprehend— reluctantly—why you imagined you wanted that dragon at this Academy, given Zara's newfound ability to shift into one herself. But was it truly necessary to welcome Maxim Rasputin, of all men living, into *our home*?"

Under his anger, a minefield of pain lies buried.

To avoid triggering it, I carefully refrain from noting that Maxim Rasputin will also very likely soon be sharing our bed. That's assuming Zara, who's always been unpredictable and wildly impulsive, will accept him. Since she's refused him tonight, even in the crisis of her rising heat, I am no longer certain what she'll do.

Since I dare not risk one of Vasili's more malignant reactions to the prospect of Maxim sharing our bed, I retreat to my less controversial motives for the dragon's admittance.

"I appreciate your troubled history with him, Vasili. Truly, I do. But you were both children when you knew him. That jealous boy who hurt you has matured into the last fully manifested male dragon shifter the witching world possesses. We need him as much as he needs us. And *I* need to know you understand this imperative. I need to know you're able to see beyond your own personal grievances."

I can't say the rest aloud. That Vasili owns my body and has ever since the night he buried his vicious fangs in my flesh. That he holds my heart in his cruel careless hands. That he's my love and my alpha and I don't know how I'll ever survive without him and I'm desperately afraid to try.

But I whisper what I can of all this through our mating bond.

I need you to be careful and mature and responsible with Maxim. I need you to put aside your hatred and your resentment and your bitterness.

I need to know I can trust you, Vasili. Please show me I can trust you.

And it's a measure of my desperate uncertainty over this critical outcome that I don't dare wait for his reply.

With a last agonized look at the sleeping Ronin, that other mate I ache to comfort, I retreat from the field of combat with what composure I can muster and supply my stalwart assurances and apologies regarding the dragon's conduct and welfare over the staticky landline to the Dean (who is indeed awake, considerably irritated over the entire unseemly disturbance, and threatening to send Maxim back to his irate parent). Apparently, the dragon's mother virulently opposes his admission and has been phoning the school nonstop to demand his immediate expulsion. This fate is one I manage to deflect—at least temporarily. Certainly Maxim deserves the chance to prove he is more than the savage beast currently bellowing overhead and terrorizing the entire student body in their beds.

Fortunately, the Dean accepts my argument. Having preserved the dragon's place in this Academy for the time being, I return in haste to my queen, who needs me.

Chapter Seventeen
Zara

Wrapped tight in Neo's arms, I've finally stopped shivering.

The two of us are cuddled up together in Lucius' narrow monastic bed (since he lived chaste as a priest for years before Ronin and I came along to tempt him from the path of virtue). I'm still bundled in my robe with the fire crackling, the little nightlight in the half-bath glowing, and the dragon's haunting screams gradually dwindling.

That's when Lucius returns.

By now, I've praised and admired Neo's sexy pierced ear, salivated over the yummy details he provided about that pornfest between him and the Goblin King that went down before I went off with my dragon… I mean, *the* dragon… and whispered to Neo by firelight the whole story of everything he's missed with Maxim.

My sweet bookworm is intrigued by the unique peen aspect in particular and has asked many questions.

He's never judged me, not ever, and my fated mate seems to think it's perfectly understandable that I refuse to risk losing control of my own body for the sake of some wild bout of dragon sex. He especially appreciates that I refuse to do it without all the guys involved (or at least consulted) first.

Possibly not even then.

Because Maxim is… a lot.

He's a lot to wrap my head around.

Not to mention that whole combustible World War III scenario he's got going on with Vasili is one helluva lot to handle.

Lucius slips into the bedroom quietly, closes the door behind him, and shoots the lock. That simple act makes me all tingly and breathless. It's the wolf in him, the hunter, cutting off his prey's escape.

Even though he'd never, ever hurt us.

"Ronin's sleeping soundly," he reports, somber, while he adds wood to the fire to keep things toasty (not that he needs a fire for that). "I dare say I've left Vasili with a few hard truths to process in that fiendish brain of his. I've also provided sufficient assurance to the Dean to postpone anyone's immediate expulsion—for now. However, I do think the two of you should sleep here tonight, at least until Maxim returns."

"Oh, we're definitely staying," I murmur. "And we're staying *all* night. But I don't think we'll be doing much sleeping."

I wiggle out from under the pile of blankets Neo's tucked around me and kneel on the bed. Now that I'm finally warm enough and things are as much under control in this harem as they're gonna get tonight, my real heat is kindling.

Yeah, it's fucking early. It's *days* early, damn it. How is that even fair?

Anyway, my heat's definitely here.

I unbelt the robe I'm still wearing for warmth and push it off my shoulders. The fur-lined garment slithers down my body like a slow caress, every brush of friction literally painful against my hypersensitive skin. I'm so warm now I'm practically steaming. All my senses are heightened, shifter-style. My vision is sharpened so I can see through shadows, my nose is flooded with the smells of sage and wolf and woodsmoke, my hearing is boosted into overdrive and extra acute.

I can hear Dez murmuring something to Racetrack in her bedroom about prophetic dreams (because Dez gets those) and an alarm clock. I can hear the restless tread of Vasili's pacing upstairs and even the slow rhythm of Ronin's sleeping breath. The Goblin King must have fucked the shit out of him to put Ronin out like that.

Damn.

It really sucks that I missed it.

But this room, our room, the room where I've just bared my body for my mates, is gripped in spellbound silence.

Before the fire, Lucius is frozen in place like a crouching wolf, his sherry-gold eyes riveted on my naked body and glowing red with need. My hands glide down my torso, grazing my skin, until my fingers brush the swollen nub of my clit. At the first spark of contact, I moan with an electric jolt of need.

Lucius growls deep in his throat and his fangs descend.

Lying still at my side, head propped on his folded arm, shining eyes gazing up at me in worship, Neo's holding his breath.

Inside my skin, my dragon purrs with approval.

"I think I'm changing," I whisper to both of them, both my mates, low and deep. "I think it's my dragon. I sense and I crave and I feel… *everything*."

"It's okay, Zara." Neo pushes up to sit and trails his big hand slowly up my inner thigh. "You can let go with us. We've got you."

Need licks at my cunt like a fiery tongue. A gasp spills out and my stance widens to welcome him. When his fingers graze the tender folds of my slit, I'm already slick and dripping. I groan and rub into his touch.

"Oh shit," he whispers. My innocent bookworm who hardly ever swears. I'm afraid we're ruining him, but he seems eager for that.

Neo rises to his knees behind me, which really makes him loom. His arms slide around my ribs, his cotton-covered bulge tucks up against my ass, and his hands cup my bare tits. Due to my heat, they feel fuller than usual, areolae tender and puffy, nipples taut and swollen around my piercings. When Neo tweaks and teases, I writhe in gasping need.

That's more than enough to drive Lucius over the edge.

A low snarl rips from his throat.

Carelessly my wolf shucks his English lord's smoking jacket (though he's actually Hungarian) and tears off his mannerly pressed pajamas in record time. Underneath he's all raw rangy strength, not gym rat buffed like Neo or whippet-slim like Vasili, he's like what you imagine an alpha wolf in a human body would be. His powerful chest is furry, but all that fur tapers to a narrow tongue of hair that licks down his abs. His chestnut curls are twisted into that knot at his nape, which adds a whole other note that's both civilized and exotic.

He also has the thickest cock of any guy in my harem. (Have I mentioned this? Because it's, like, this major obsession for me.)

Right now, it's jutting straight out for Neo and me from that thicket of dark curls between his thighs.

"Oh God," Neo whispers, all shuddery in my ear. "Is this actually happening? I mean, will it really be all three of us?"

"Yeah," I say, thick and husky, one arm rising to wrap around his neck. My other hand's still buried in my hungry cunt. "It's gonna be all three of us, baby. And Lucius? You keep those fangs out."

My wolf barks a short laugh, bounds across the room in what looks like a single animal leap, and lands on the bed on all fours. His eyes glow red as embers. His big-ass fangs are fully distended and sexy as fuck.

Lucius growls deep in his chest and rumbles, in a voice that's barely human, "Spread yourself wide for me, my queen, so I can ravish your succulent quim."

Shit.

Even his old-fashioned vocab turns my crank.

My pussy ripples and clenches, all slick and dripping with need. I writhe against the monster bulge of Neo's cock (still wearing briefs for modesty's sake) that's shoved up against my ass.

I don't want him modest.

I want him shameless.

And I want him naked.

Neo's breath quickens in my ear. While my fated mate holds me steady and nuzzles my shoulder with his soft lips and rolls his cock slowly against the crack of my ass, I spread my cunt wide for Lucius with unsteady fingers.

And I'm so turned on by exposing myself for him this way that it scares me, given all the shit that's going down with my heat.

My wolf's eyes flame. He bares his teeth in a bestial snarl. I speak in a rush before he can pounce.

"Lucius," I whisper to him, my first alpha, this teacher and mentor I trust above all others to keep me safe. "Whatever happens, I need you to help me control it. Don't let me rise."

His gaze veers from my exposed pussy to my naked face.

His stare locks with mine.

My fear pulses between us through our bond.

"Don't be afraid, my queen. You will not rise tonight. Your rising will be for *him*," Lucius says, thick and guttural. "Your dragon king. Tonight you are, in all your delectable entirety, for me. Your wolf king. And for our sweet boy."

My eyes flutter closed and my breath spills out in relief. Because I know I can trust him.

With him, I can trust.

My head falls back against Neo's shoulder. My fated mate turns his face so our lips meet and cling in a slow hot kiss. He tastes all sweet and minty from his toothpaste, but Lucius has been scenting him while they sleep, so my bookworm smells like wolf.

He also smells like Goblin.

God, both my alphas have been all over him.

Which is such a major turn-on.

Lucius' tongue drags up my slit in a long lick.

I jolt and snarl a curse into Neo's mouth. His arms tighten around me and his fingers find the rigid peaks of my tits. He tugs my rings hard enough to sting, just the way I like it. Currents of tingling pleasure shoot down the front of my thighs.

Dark and savage with purpose, Lucius laps at my clit while I writhe against his tongue and struggle to hold myself spread for him. My empty cunt pulses, desperate to be filled. When Lucius' mouth closes over my engorged nub and sucks hard, Neo swallows my scream in a deep open-mouthed kiss.

"Oh fuck," I whimper, back arching and pelvis pumping into Lucius' ruthless suck. "Fuck, fuck, fuck. I need your cocks inside me. Both your cocks. Want both of you to fuck me till we break this fucking bed."

Both my guys are on board with that plan.

Because Lucius is keeping my hands occupied and Neo's holding me up, it's up to my wolf to reach past me and drag Neo's briefs down his hips.

Neo's dick thwacks audibly against my ass.

At the sound, Lucius' head jerks up, lips and goatee shining with pussy juice, eyes fierce with wolfish hunger. His gaze devours every inch of us, Neo and me, naked and entwined. He's my alpha and I'm in heat, so this is deeply satisfying for Lucius on multiple levels. Plus he's wanted this with Neo forever, and I can feel how excited my fated mate is, how totally ready he is to go wherever this thing with the three of us takes us.

"One of you tell me what you want me to do," Neo whispers. "Or both of you tell me. I don't mind."

Which has to be like the hundredth reason why we're all in love with him. He's easy to love. He makes it *so* easy.

"My boy," Lucius groans through his fangs. "Mount your queen. I want to watch her ride your magnificent shaft."

For Lucius, that's talking dirty.

"What about you?" Neo says breathlessly.

Even while my fated mate tucks his cock obediently between my legs and starts stroking my dripping slit till he's all messy and coated in my juices.

Way too impatient to wait, I reach between my thighs to guide him. God, he's so hard he's pulsing in my hand. I flex my hips to slide all that dick up and down my soaked slit. His pelvis twitches in short thrusts he can't hold in while he pants and moans in my ear.

This whole time, Lucius crouches in front of my hips to watch the action go down (from like three inches away) with his unblinking stare.

With my back pressed tight to Neo's chest and his hands gripping my hips to steady me, I pause with his big dick nested tightly between my folds and his plump purple crown, glistening with both our juices, peeking out between my thighs.

"Wanna taste?" I whisper to Lucius.

With a groan, he dives in to wrap his fangy mouth around the tip of Neo's cock. Just the tip, because that's all he can reach from this angle. But he's doing it for the very first time, because these two still haven't gotten past first base. (I say this because of how primly Lucius was buttoned up to his chin in those *Downton Abbey* pajamas when I woke these two up.) He clings so desperately to his professorial propriety.

And I love to mess him up.

A ragged cry tears from Neo's lips. His muscled body burrows desperately into the back of me, which also feeds another inch of him into Lucius' mouth.

"Oh my God," my bookworm whimpers in my ear. "I'm gonna come too soon. I can't—I can't—"

"Easy," Lucius breathes to both of us. He backs off Neo's glistening dick in favor of slow swirling circles around his tip. Every time his tongue passes over the top of the circle, Lucius swipes over my clit with a hot lick.

"Sweet Jesus," I pant, doing plenty of twitching and rocking myself. *"Lucius."*

"The way you taste," my wolf breathes, warm breath spilling over my sopping folds and my throbbing clit. "The way you both taste. *Ambrosia.*"

Fuck. I need a cock inside me before I explode.

By this point I'm definitely projecting. Both of them groan out loud at the visual.

"Please," Neo gasps.

And Lucius already said that's what he wants.

I widen my knees and reach down between us to fit Neo's cock to the mouth of my channel, and Lucius backs off just enough to let me do it. Then I sink down and Neo pushes up and his fat dick slides right into my slick pussy.

A sharp cry bursts from my throat.

Neo shudders and groans into the side of my neck like I just knifed him.

For a sec I just stay suspended like that, completely impaled on his cock, while Lucius drinks in the sight of us and reaches between his own legs to give himself a few rough pumps that make both Neo and me moan. My prof's junk is all engorged and ruddy with hunger, precum already leaking from his slit, tiny droplets trapped and glittering in the tight nest of his pubes.

It's so rare for my wolf to forget he's our headmaster and just let everything go in our bed.

Usually, it's Vasili buried balls-deep inside him and hissing his vicious demands and just domming the hell out of him in his heartless way (the way only the Goblin King can do) that pushes Lucius over the edge.

Tonight I want Neo and me to be the ones that drive Lucius wild.

Slowly I slide up Neo's cock until just his tip is still lodged inside me. Then I sink back down, circling my hips in a lazy swivel and working his shaft like a pole dancer and hitting all those achy places deep inside me that clamor to be filled. Neo's already given himself up totally to whatever I want. His muscled quads form the scaffold that holds both of us upright as I undulate up and down his dick. I reach back to grip his thighs for balance, which arches my back and shoves my tits forward.

Neo keeps cradling my tits as they jostle with our thrusting, and he's absolutely ruthless with my sensitive nipples, pinching and playing with my rings till I whimper and mewl.

But it's Lucius who's killing me.

He's back down on his belly, all wolf-like, dragging his tongue over my clit and getting in long licks of Neo's dick every time it slides out of me. With every swipe, Neo groans in my ear. He's alternately gasping my name and Lucius', and I honestly think I'm losing my mind.

Neo's rod is massive (I might've mentioned?) and usually he's more than enough to fill me. But my dragon queen is awake and thrashing inside me, she wants *out*, and I know it's gonna take more than one dick inside me tonight to keep her chained up in there and satisfied.

"Lucius," I moan, rocking my clit into his tongue. "For cripes' sake, fuck me. Fuck both of us."

And this perfect Old World gentleman lifts his head, fangs fully exposed but brow furrowed anxiously, to search out Neo's gaze. "Would you mind terribly, er, sharing the space?"

"Oh my God, are you kidding me?" Neo gasps between short desperate thrusts. "Do you not get that I've got… like… this massive crush on you? Just the thought… of your dick touching mine… makes me wanna blow."

Lucius' face is a study in brutal craving and agonized restraint.

I legit can't take this backing and forthing anymore.

I'm in full flaming heat, for fuck's sake.

"Cheese on toast, Lucius," I groan from the heart. "Will you *please*. Just. Fuck me."

His nostrils flare and his eyes flame. "Your wish. My command."

With no further fucking ado, he lunges to the nightstand, wrenches the drawer open so hard it crashes to the floor, and upends like half a bottle of lube into his cupped palm.

We don't typically all sleep in here together. His bed's too small, and he likes having his private space. So I'm intrigued as hell that he's got lube squirreled away conveniently close to where he and Neo have been bedding down.

Hearing my thoughts, Neo snorts a breathless chuckle. "It's mine. I made sure he knew it was in there. Trying to encourage him to corrupt me."

"Oh shit," I gasp, my pussy clenching around Neo's cock. "Baby, you're so naughty."

"No encouragement required," Lucius grunts, barely verbal at this point with his wolf so close to surfacing. He slicks lube down his length till he's glistening and gives himself a couple of hard pumps, eyes riveted on the sight of Neo's dick pistoning into me, scholarly face contorted with pleasure.

Watching Lucius fist his own dick, my fated mate groans long and low. His grip on my tits gets rough and the pace of his thrusts picks up. He's getting off on the sight of Lucius getting off, he's starving to see our headmaster like this, the way all the students in the school secretly fantasize about, but only we get to see.

My finger dives between my legs and swirls through the moisture of Lucius' spit. My hips snap into Neo's in short hard strikes. My needy cunt clamps around my bookworm's cock and my rear channel twitches.

Roughly Lucius bats my hand away from my sweet spot. "No coming. Not until I'm buried inside you to the hilt, my queen."

"Then serve your queen and fuck me," I rumble, all deep and echoey, in the lightning voice.

The hair rises from my shoulders and the shadows shift to violet. It's the glow of psi fire igniting in my eyes.

That right there's my power rising.

But Lucius will keep me safe.

He engulfs me with his hard body. His furry chest chafes my nipples. He halts our desperate rutting and fits the head of his cock roughly against Neo's at the soaked mouth of my channel.

As these two particular swords in my harem cross for the first time ever, Neo groans in agonized pleasure. I whine with breathless need.

My head drops to appreciate the visual.

Because this I definitely gotta see.

Lucius pushes into my already well-filled hole one breath at a time, so *very* slow but, God, so fucking ruthless I want to scream at the pressure. He's splitting me so wide and filling me so full. This might've been easier with Vasili who's not as thick but, so far, the Goblin King hasn't seemed inclined to share his personal space in my cunt with anyone. I think he's still a tiny bit self-conscious about his guy-girl technique, since he's so new at it, though he has zero reason to worry. Still, when my snake comes calling down there, he wants my pussy's complete attention.

And what the Goblin King wants, he always gets.

"Stop thinking about Vasili," Lucius snarls through his fangs. "I'm the alpha filling your sweet quim tonight."

My guys don't get jealous much, not of each other, but having two alphas isn't the norm for this exact reason. It'll be even trickier if Maxim joins, because then it's gonna be three alphas sharing this bed.

Oh God. Just the thought of three alphas makes my pussy clamp tight around these two cocks to milk them dry.

"And stop thinking about that goddamned dragon." Lucius punishes me for all this distraction with a brutal thrust that seats him fully, balls-deep inside me, with a savage grunt. A breathless curse wrenches out of me.

Lucius' cock wedges tight against Neo's. The hot silky sacs of their balls nestle together against my perineum.

"Oh my God, Lucius," Neo moans. "I can feel you. I can feel every inch of you. Oh Lord."

My shy bookworm is totally still inside me, absorbing all these novel sensations, letting Lucius settle into both of us with short rocking thrusts. Every stroke makes my overfilled channel ripple and spasm around all this cock.

"My dear boy," Lucius whispers, head lifting from our joined bodies to pin my fated mate with his gaze. "Are you mine at last?"

"I've been yours for weeks," Neo pants, sweet as fuck. "Yours and Zara's. Always."

A floaty euphoric warmth sweeps through me. It's that feeling you get being happy, you know, because the people you love are happy? In poly circles, there's a word for it.

It's called compersion.

God, Lucius and his wolf look more than ready to pounce on Neo and rail him right here. I'm pretty sure that'll happen later.

And I literally can't wait.

"Go ahead and kiss him," I tell Lucius with a smile. "He likes your fangs."

Over my shoulder, their mouths crash together in a raging kiss that hits my clit like a bolt of lightning. I wind one arm back around Neo's neck and grip Lucius' hip with the other. I work my way cautiously up all that cock, then wiggle my way back down again. Which makes them both gasp and swear.

Although, in Neo's case, what he actually gasps is, "Oh, sugar."

I hide a grin in Lucius' shoulder and nip his skin with my sharp baby shifter teeth, which makes his wolf whine. We all take turns setting the pace. Sometimes it's me working my eager cunt up and down all those inches while they both quiver and groan and my inner dragon purrs with pleasure.

Sometimes it's Neo jerking short and fast and eager against all our friction and fighting like hell to keep from spilling too soon, while I voice my pleasure with sharp high cries and Lucius' wolf grunts and mutters.

But mostly, it's Lucius driving the action with fierce hard thrusts that make all of us sway against the impact and fight to stay upright on the bed. He pins my hips in his commanding grip and I palm the rhythmic clench of his unstoppable ass and Neo squirms and whimpers and fucks into me from behind.

My heat is spiraling…

All that cataclysmic pressure…

Building…

My climax rushes toward me like a sea of molten lava boiling from the planet's core. Like the dormant volcano that made this island rise from the sea all those eons ago is flaming back to life.

Here. Now. Tonight. Inside me.

I'm gripping Lucius hard enough to bruise, and the sheer force of his will is keeping my lightning in check. I engulf his mouth with mine, sucking on his bestial fangs. His tongue lashes into my mouth to swipe at mine. With an impatient tug, I drag his hair free from that mannerly knot so it tumbles around his fierce face in wild waves.

Neo's plastered against my back and ass, both of us slick with sweat as he hammers into me with frantic need. And I can *feel* him, I can feel the aching maw of his need… his desperate need for…

A bite.

A mating bite.

That's what he wants. That's what's been bugging him. My sweet baby's feeling left out. He's longing for a goddamn mating bite.

"Oh Neo," I gasp. "Oh baby."

My brain swims with sudden understanding, poisoned with a bitter flood of guilt. If I hadn't been so wrapped up in my heat and my dragon and my need for freedom—all *me me me*—I'd have figured this out weeks ago.

Poor Neo.

My head falls back against his shoulder. He groans and pumps into me.

Lucius isn't linked to him, so he can't feel what I feel. But suddenly my inner dragon is snarling and pacing and bating her wings.

Ours, he is ours, she croons in my head. *This tender creature is ours. Claim our mate!*

Lucius is fucking both of us so savagely it's like he's going to split me open. My pussy throbs and burns, but Jesus, he's gonna get me off like an atom bomb. He's growling with every thrust and his wolf is lurking in his brutal face. He's my alpha and his fangs are right there, he's definitely got what it takes to bite Neo.

But my dragon queen is trumpeting her own fierce possession of our fated mate.

Lucius flings back his head and bellows. The fiery flood of his climax kicks and spurts deep inside me, drenching and claiming both of us in the deepest possible way. As his own big O hits him, Neo goes totally rigid and hollers in a very unNeolike way they can probably hear all over the whole damn house.

I'm dripping with jizz and drenched in my own cream.

I'm coming so hard I almost wet the bed.

I scream to high heaven, my voice edged with lightning, but Lucius grounds me the way he always has. The heady spice of my Mogadon pheromones floods the air and makes all three of us high and dizzy.

So it seems like the most obvious and natural no-brainer type thing I've ever done in my whole life to twist in my mates' arms like the dragon I am and sink my teeth deep into my fated mate's muscled shoulder to give Neo the mating bite he craves and deserves and is damn well begging for.

Because he's mine. He's always been mine. If anyone's biting him, if anyone's claiming him, if anyone's giving him this most basic thing he needs, it's gonna be me.

I'm his alpha.

I'm his queen.

He's mine.

Lucius exclaims in shocked dismay. The bond between us pulses with sudden dread.

That's a weird reaction I totally don't get, and right now my dragon has no patience.

Lucius (foolishly) tries to pull me off Neo, but my inner dragon snarls and snaps at him, and his wolf backs right off.

My dragon bates her wings and screams in brassy triumph.

My jaws lock hard into Neo's brawny shoulder to stake my claim. Neo's exuberant shout of triumph, laced with pain (because a mating bite's no joke, that shit hurts), just about takes the roof off and definitely makes the earth quake.

Desperately he crushes me against him. His whole body shudders violently.

After taking two mating bites in the recent past myself, I definitely know the drill. I ease off to lick and nuzzle into the bloody half-moon bite I've just left in the silky pale skin stretched over his deltoid muscle. I'm lapping up the blood and administering the clotting agent in my shifter saliva.

"Oh Zara," he whispers, all soft and broken, into the mess of my sweat-damp hair. "Oh babe. You make me so happy. I'm just so incredibly happy."

"You deserve it, baby," I say between tender kisses and long licks over his bite. "Anything you need, even if I'm all clueless and self-absorbed like this time and I somehow don't offer, you only need to ask. I promise I'll pay more attention next time, sweetie."

His blissed-out sigh makes me smile.

They're both going soft now, their cocks slipping out of me. Along with, like, a *lot* of come. Their spunk and my own juice are dripping down my thighs in rivulets to spatter the sheets. I feel absolutely filthy and extremely well fucked and my inner dragon is completely smug with satisfaction.

Neo sort of collapses on the bed and drags me down to tumble across his naked hunkiness.

I grab Lucius' hand and pull him down with us in a steamy tangle of limbs and hair and sex.

My girly parts are swollen and hot from all that friction, but fuck if I want to get up and deal with it now. Anyway, with all these warlocks to accommodate, I've got, like, an industrial-strength pussy.

I always recover fast from our fuckfests.

Firmly I tuck up against Neo's side so I can keep tending his bite. Lucius ranges himself along Neo's other side, all frowny and protective, his eyes shifting back to sherry as they roam slowly over our entwined bodies, Neo's and mine, in that quiet possessive way I love.

Lucius scratches his own shifter itch to tend and heal by nuzzling Neo's newly pierced ear.

My bookworm slings a brawny arm around each of us and snuggles happily between us. His happiness warms me up better than the fire whose gentle heat is lapping at my back.

"I'm so happy," he sighs out loud, so Lucius too can hear, just in case someone still hasn't gotten the message. "Will I go into heat like the rest of you?"

"I think you might, baby," I murmur, because that seems likely, though I really don't know for sure.

The idea of sharing that with the rest of us seems to please him. Even though we don't actually *all* go into heat, because no one's ever bitten Vasili (no one would dare).

But clearly my Neo's been feeling excluded. And now he's not. Whatever comes, I'm determined to give him every smidgen of alpha care he's ever gonna need. I'm never gonna neglect him. I won't ever leave him wanting.

Not even with this mounting distraction of my own superheat.

"Oh my dears," Lucius sighs, his yummy baritone all ragged with sex and thick with foreboding. "Merciful Christ, we're taking a terrible risk."

"I don't follow." I rest my cheek on Neo's chest and smooth the tumbled curls away from Lucius' pensive face. "Why can you and Ronin and me all get mating bites, but Neo's not supposed to?"

"Because you and I have shifter DNA, and I never meant to give Ronin a mating bite in the first place." Lucius studies our bookworm with broody eyes. "As I've endeavored to explain to him, Neo's DNA is pure Kryll. There's simply no predicting how his physiology will respond to the biochemicals in a shifter's bite."

"I don't care." Neo sounds rebellious, and I realize this plot twist isn't exactly a bookworm newsflash. He and Lucius actually talked about this, probably while I was off in Vegas spreading my wings and getting back at Xiao.

Which suddenly doesn't seem to matter, like, *at all*.

Neo's way more important.

"Shit." Alarm skitters across my skin and clenches my heart in a fist. My tummy kinks and knots with dread. "Lucius. Are you saying my bite could actually… hurt him?"

"Quite simply," Lucius murmurs, heavy with worry and regret, "I'm saying I don't know. Truly, my queen, it would have been better if you'd never bitten him."

Chapter Eighteen
Maxim

I will be the first to admit it. My romantic encounter with my queen could have gone better.

This morning, I am an unwelcome outsider in an alien land.

In these few hours I have spent in this deconsecrated church where classes are held, I have quickly realized I am the only pureblooded shifter, along with Lucius Aries, in this entire Academy.

This means I am the only dragon in Mistress Agrippina's Genetics of Witchcraft class.

Clearly, my new classmates despise me. This may, or may not, be due to the fact that I surely upended this entire population of junior witches and warlocks from their beds, sweating and half-suffocating with terror, by screaming over their roofs in my dragon form, then circling and bellowing with rage until dawn.

For this, I make no apology.

My queen is in full heat, my dragon is in full rut, and my queen has refused to accept my attentions.

In truth, I could be doing far worse than circling and bellowing in this condition.

I am seated now in the very last row of Mistress Agrippina's classroom. It is a tidy, industrious sort of place. Pristine snow piled on the windowsills sparkles in the afternoon sun. More sunlight slants across the old-fashioned rows of desks, barely occupied by a smattering of uniformed students. The ancient floorboards under these new Academy loafers that pinch my feet are scuffed and worn with age, but the wood gleams a rich russet in the sun. The air smells pleasantly of books and chalk and fresh wood shavings from the mechanical pencil sharpener bolted to the wall.

I gather this seat is, how do you say, prime real estate? Judging by the snide remarks and stink-eyes I am receiving, it is a privilege to which my fellow classmates seem to feel I am not entitled.

But I will sit nowhere else. I will not endure an enemy at my vulnerable back.

Every time in my life when I have endured true pain, it has been inflicted from behind. It took a great deal of resolve to overcome a lifetime of deeply conditioned instinct when I gave Zara my back last night. But my sovereign was determined to see my scars.

Even to touch them.

She seemed not even to find them shameful.

In fact, that moment when I flinched at her touch was when she softened and became gentle. That moment was when she let me close.

That was before my accursed past with Vasili reared up again between us.

So far, this class schedule Lucius has given me has kept me apart from Zara, which is frustrating. It has also kept me apart from Vasili, which is fortunate.

However, this Academy is far too small to keep us apart for long.

Slumped over the desk beside me, noisily popping her gum and scribbling verses that look like poetry in her notebook, lingers the strange prickly girl named Racetrack from our *domus*. But she is of little comfort. She has made clear that she only sits beside me because she promised her girlfriend she would look after me, so the new boy will not be hazed (although I was quick to assure her I am no child who needs sheltering).

Well, no matter.

Apparently, this Racetrack is a creature of her word. She has stayed stubbornly by my side all day, keeping all the others at bay, even though plainly she resents this duty.

Ronin Pendragon sprawls three rows away. He arrived at class quite late, and he is a considerable distraction. In the black blazer and crimson tie of the Friday uniform, with his silky hair pulled in a sleek tail, he lurks in our midst like a hunting jaguar.

He is such a blatantly sexual creature he is dangerous.

I find myself wondering, with some agitation, if Zara has told him what I confessed I want to do to him.

If she has, he does not seem intrigued by my forbidden fantasies. He does not even seem mildly interested. If anything, he is the opposite. To him, I am nothing more than that detestable creature who once wronged his precious boyfriend.

But today his heat is riding him. He is restless. He is distracted. He is fidgety. His pupils swallow his feral eyes, and a sheen of sweat glitters on his skin. Clearly Lucius (whom I now understand to be his alpha) should be tending him.

If the wolf will not? Well, I too am alpha.

Zara has already mated this Pendragon, even if only in the common law way of the witching world. He will be part of whatever she and I build together.

I wonder how opposed he would be to my mating bite.

"For fuck's sake," he mutters, a baleful outburst I do not expect. He sears me with an irate glare from his feverish eyes. "Keep it the fuck to yourself, yeah?"

Saint Sergius guard me. This warlock is reading my mind.

Given the tangle of lust and brutality that dominates my rutting dragon, my thoughts must feel to this sensitive telepath like a violation.

I struggle with a confused impulse to apologize. According to my culture, it is shameful, unmanly, immoral, unspeakable—especially for him at the, er, receiving end—these things I wish to do to him.

But this apologetic instinct is far less powerful than my sinful impulse to drag him into an empty classroom and bend him over one of these desks.

In truth, that treatment is what he requires.

I… I have never… taken a man. In my clan, it is never done, two men together, except shamefully and in secret. But Zara has been very clear already that the thought of me with this one pleases her.

I would please her.

I would please them both.

"Oh, bloody hell." This time, Ronin's explosive curse draws the schoolmistress's ire. He shoves his chair back with a noisy scrape and thrusts roughly to his feet. "That's it then."

"Mr. Pendragon." The elderly professor gives him a severe look over the top of her half-moon spectacles. "Has this particular DNA sequence done something to offend you?"

"Sorry, Aggie." Ronin scoops up his backpack and strides for the door, but not before shooting me a narrow look through his tiger eyes that sends all the blood rushing to my dick. "Not feeling all that chipper."

"I'm sorry to hear of your… indisposition," she says calmly, with a look that suggests she understands exactly what condition is troubling him. "Take the hall pass. And go to see the nurse straightaway."

I doubt he has any intention of that, he is probably going straight to his alpha for a fuck, although he does swipe the lanyard from its peg before he ducks out.

"Nice job, Romeo," Racetrack drawls. "You always this fly? Looks to me like you're 0 for 2 in the romance game."

This is some obscure American sporting reference, but I grasp the gist. She is Mogadon like Vasili, she is not even a telepath, but she has eyes, and she has lived with these warlocks and their heats.

Still, I feel compelled to defend myself and my masculinity from this implied slur.

"I have done nothing to him," I mutter, resentful.

"Yeah, riiiiight." She snorts. "*Yet*. You're hot for him. Just like almost everyone else around here's hot for him. And he just smelled it on you."

"I am *not*—"

"Oh, for shit's sake." She pops her gum and rolls her eyes. "Don't bother with the whole denial thing. Believe me, I know *all* the signs. Too bad he's not into you, huh? Heat or no heat."

Suddenly I find I cannot meet her knowing gaze.

Around me, my fellow students hiss and snigger. They are still pale-faced and hollow-eyed from their sleepless night, but I feel no guilt. I myself have not slept, but I am no stranger to exhaustion.

This entire Academy situation is not comfortable, but I am no stranger to discomfort.

Once my new classmates decide they hate me more than they fear me, this situation will become dangerous.

But I am no stranger to that either.

Doggedly I keep my gaze pinned to the old-fashioned blackboard. There are no computers on this island, not even a functioning cell phone, due to the magical wards that guard this Academy and conceal its existence from the mortal world. Blackboards and journals and dusty spell books are the norm here. But I do not mind.

If not for these hostile students, I might be able to find this place… pleasant. In time, I might even find it delightful.

But I am not likely to be tolerated here long enough for that.

If I am not expelled for my own misconduct, my Lady Mother will surely find some way to ruin me.

Carefully I pretend that I understand this frail witch with the steely voice and the cloud of white curls spiraling down her straight back who now returns to teaching this class. She is demonstrating the genetics behind the Theory of Genetic Exhaustion, which tries to explain why the population of the witching world is slowly dwindling.

But I am struggling to follow the science.

I understood Lucius better in our History of Witchcraft class. He spoke of other theories behind the arcane races' near-extinction, and I was able to follow much of this, despite never having set foot in a formal classroom in my life. I paid particular attention to the Theory of Royal Culpability, which blames our endangered species status on the weakness of our ruling queens. They are weakened despite centuries, if not millennia, of inbreeding.

This situation is just as Zara says. All the great witching families are inbred now, in our desperate effort to preserve the last frail threads of witchcraft that linger in our arcane DNA.

At least this theory is less far-fetched than the competing theory that we spring from alien races who visited Earth in the time of the Roman Empire. The Theory of Royal Culpability is the theory I have always believed.

When Zara ascends her throne, we will halt the witching world's decline. Somehow. And my dwindling clan of dragon shifters will be reborn.

Now, however, with this Genetic Exhaustion business, we are on difficult terrain. This professor is scribing endless rows of letters across the board with her chalk stylus, she is droning on about transcribing DNA into RNA and translating RNA into protein and how these phenomena apply to the witching world. I know this class is important, because witchcraft is an inherited trait. We have always bred for it.

But with all this talk of dominants and recessives and mutations, I am at an utter loss.

"In accordance with the central dogma," Mistress Agrippina lectures at a louder pitch that somehow seems meant for me and the inattentive Racetrack in the back, "adenine transcribes to thymine, and guanine transcribes to cytosine…"

She might as well be speaking ancient Greek.

Dragons are gifted with languages, but this is not a language I know. I am fighting to conceal my confusion and frustration and incipient panic, because if I cannot master this material, I know I will not be permitted to remain here on this island with my sovereign. I will be sent home to my Lady Mother where, of all possible places, I do not wish to go.

I know nothing of science, nothing of genetics. Yet I am reluctant to reveal my ignorance.

In my world, ignorance is never tolerated.

It is punished.

The deep gong of the church bell comes as a welcome relief. Even though I have been dreading all day the next block of time in my academic schedule.

I push to my feet, but I linger, strategically gathering my books and stowing the leather-backed journal Lucius has given me into my shabby backpack. I am letting the room empty out before me, so I will be the last to depart, with none of these hostile students at my back.

Chattering easily to each other in a way I have never experienced in any interaction with my own peers, my classmates idle out the door in twos and threes, textbooks clutched to their chests, casting wary or sullen looks in my direction.

Still, no one attempts to speak to me.

Once they are all safely gone, even Racetrack abandons me, muttering something about meeting Dez for study hall and something else about me staying out of the boys' john unless I want to get my dragon ass kicked. Although I am very slightly sorry to see her go, I do not respond. I will surely not thank her for this superfluous companionship I did not request.

No doubt this is why, when she finally leaves, she too looks annoyed.

Well, so be it. I am not here to "make friends" with these young witches and warlocks.

I am not like these others.

I do not have "friends."

This classroom has now emptied, except for the professor, who is erasing her chalkboard with a vigor that belies her many years. I hoist my backpack over one shoulder and trudge for the door. I do not welcome the class I have next.

I am nearly in the corridor when the professor calls, "A moment, if you please, Mr. Rasputin."

Despite her courteous phrasing, this is not a request.

I circle warily, so my back is not exposed, and approach the old schoolmistress in her Academy robes with caution.

"I was reviewing your file before class," she says, in a tone that could be gentle, if not for the steel in her canny eyes. "As I do for all new students. Your academic transcript is missing. Have you a copy I might consult?"

My shoulders rise in a defensive clench. Lucius was supposed to explain my situation to the other faculty, but Lucius has had a great deal on his mind. He is going into heat himself (as an alpha, I know all the signs), and he is worried about Vasili, and he is distracted—as we are all distracted—by Zara and her looming superheat.

Well, there is no help for it.

This formidable old woman expects an answer.

"There is no transcript to show you," I say shortly. "I have attended no formal institution before this one."

"You've studied with private tutors, in that case?" At my silence, her aristocratic face sharpens. "There is no shame in it, Mr. Rasputin. Your tutors would have provided letters of reference outlining your academic progress to the Dean. Might I review a copy of those?"

"There were no tutors." My voice is too gruff, but I am self-conscious about the state of my education in this elite establishment. "I am… I have only taught myself. From the books in the family dragonlair."

"You taught yourself?" Surprise flickers in her elegant face, along with a flash of pity that raises all my hackles. "All the elementary spells and potions? The scientific foundations of witchcraft? The histories of the arcane races?"

"I taught myself to read. I studied the major languages. And I read the clan lore and the dragon histories in our lair." Despite my effort to rein in my aggression, my voice hardens and my chin juts. "The rest I will learn here. I am a quick study."

It is rude to speak so curtly to an elder, but I do not want anyone's pity. Nor do I care to answer her inevitable questions about why I am self-taught, or why even now I am enrolled at this Academy in defiance of my Lady Mother, who never gave me leave to abandon the lair.

Already I am backing away, although the schoolmistress has not dismissed me.

"Mr. Rasputin." Her tone makes clear that she expects my obedience.

I have tried everyone's patience enough already, and I do not wish to be sent away from my queen. So I stop (reluctantly) and wait.

"I cannot stay," I say as politely as I can manage. "I have another class. I will be late."

"I'm going to recommend a Genetics tutor," she says, gently but quite firmly, so I know this is no recommendation but more of a command. "The brightest pupil in this school is Neo Mercury, the First Boy on the Dean's List. A member of your cohort at Villa Augustus, I believe?"

My mind summons up an image of the boy with the soft curls and the scholar's spectacles and the gentle eyes. The one who calls himself my queen's fated mate. I am envious of that one, envious of the way she loves him.

She does not flee from that one.

The way she fled from me last night.

"I already have a tutor assigned to me by Master Aries," I say stiffly. I am very close to open rebellion over the tutor he has chosen, but Mistress Agrippina does not need to know this.

All the same, her tone turns tart. "I fear Mr. Romanov's patience as an instructor of remedial magics leaves a great deal to be desired. You require instruction in the central dogma of genetics at the very least, Mr. Rasputin, before you can advance to more sophisticated studies in this class. I recommend you approach Mr. Mercury."

I do not lie, but I can evade.

"Thank you for the suggestion," I tell her, and slip out before she can suggest something worse.

Already the deep church bell that orders the hours in this place is tolling. This Academy is barely inhabited in any case, and the corridors in the cloister are now emptying of the schoolgirls in their tidy plaid skirts and the schoolboys with their neat ties and pressed blazers with the Academy crest. Quickly the last students vanish into the classrooms that surround the glassed-in conservatory garden.

The whole complex is arranged in a quadrangle, so at least I cannot get lost.

I consult the schedule folded in the pocket of my Academy blazer and plod reluctantly through the echoing open space of the student commons, which used to be the church nave. My dragon frets and complains over this unfamiliar uniform we are wearing. If he had his way, we would wear nothing.

In deference to his sensibilities, I loosen the tie that is strangling us, but I dare not remove it and add a deportment violation to my growing list of shortcomings.

Slowly I climb the spiral stairs that coil up and up to the choir loft.

In the loft, the organ and its bank of pipes have long been removed. These walls are lined instead with bookshelves stuffed to groaning with an inviting collection of arcane tomes and grimoires. A heavy table on a colorful Turkish rug dominates the space, surrounded by a comfortable cluster of wing chairs, a giant globe, the heavy disc of a bronze astrolabe, and a Roman coin collection among other fascinating curiosities. The appealing dry smell of ink and parchment permeates the still air. This loft now functions as the school library, and my dragon loves books and trinkets.

But I cannot muster my usual interest in these matters. It is here I am summoned for the daily independent study I have dreaded since the moment I saw the ordeal in my schedule.

At the massive central table under the row of stained-glass windows, lounging in an enormous wing chair that rears behind his slender frame like a bating dragon, my enemy is waiting.

And if I thought Ronin Pendragon appealing in his Academy uniform, then Vasili Romanov is lethal.

I do not understand why he does not wear faculty attire, but his status here is strange, neither teacher nor student, and Lucius has spilled the secret that Vasili is on probation, which means he may be terminated.

It must be odd for him, and uncomfortable, but Vasili is not one to invite this sort of intimate observation.

A spear of winter sunlight lances through a cobalt pane of glass. It gilds the mop of hair that grazes my enemy's knife-sharp jawline and frames his cruel face like a helmet of ice. His dangerous hands, adorned with black nail polish, drape over the chair arms. Under his stylish blazer, his red tie is tugged loose at his throat, but even that is graceful. His legs are crossed and propped arrogantly on the table. He is wearing combat boots with cherry-red soles.

"You're *at least* five minutes late," Vasili announces with poisonous glee, glancing dramatically at his bare wrist with his smoky cat-eyes. (He wears cosmetics as skillfully as a runway model, but he is not wearing a watch.) "If you intend to make a tiresome habit of this sort of tardiness, Mr. Rasputin, I shall be forced to assign detention."

At the thought of being subordinate to him in this or any other way, I suffer a spike of resentment.

But I am late, and he would be within his authority to discipline me, and I do not wish to be sent away.

Zara refused me last night, it is true. She took her pleasure writhing against my cock, and it is this knowledge alone—that I pleased her, that I provided the release she needed, that I made her climax—this knowledge that kept me sane while I spiraled and screamed through the heavens.

I pleased her once, and I swear I will do it again.

She is wary of me, and of her superheat, but I will prove that I am worthy.

"Well?" Vasili drums his fingers on the table in mounting impatience. "Aren't you going to deploy some snarky attempt at dragon wit to slay me, Maximka?"

I twitch with another flash of irritation. I hate when he calls me that. It is a boy's name, a child's name, like when he calls me *malchik*, which means *little boy* in our mother tongue. And he is doing it now to provoke me.

To provoke him in turn, I show restraint.

"Mistress Agrippina detained me after Genetics class." Calmly I lower my backpack to the table and drop into a wing chair of my own. "Are you aware that you have a large wad of chewed gum sticking to the sole of your boot?"

In an eyeblink, his haughty mouth drops open in a gasp of absolute horror. With gratifying speed, his boots thunk down from the table, he shoots to his feet, and I earn a brief reprieve. While I snicker to myself, he produces an alarmingly sharp knife from beneath his blazer (note to self: he is armed) and rushes to the trash can to deal with this apparent disaster.

When he returns to the table, he is sulking.

By now I have produced my leather-bound notebook and a pencil, and I am resigned to receiving whatever dubious wisdom he is capable of imparting.

"Well, that was revolting." With a delicate shudder, he drapes himself over his chair and crosses his elegant legs, but at least he does not return his feet to the table.

The knife has vanished, but it is somewhere. Being Vasili, I also suspect he has more of them.

He studies me.

I wait.

My pencil hovers over my notebook.

The pressure of his stare crawls over me.

I work to keep my breath even, my face impassive, my heartbeat slow. But even in this drafty loft, my shirt beneath my blazer is damp with sweat.

I am in rut, and he is alpha, and part shifter, so it is very likely he recognizes the signs.

Slowly, one eyebrow arches above his wicked eye.

I brace myself to withstand some scathing comment about how thoroughly Zara has rejected me. Because I am certain that is what she has told him. What I do not know is whether she has also told him how hard she climaxed, writhing so beautifully against my cock.

"Very well, *malchik*," he says softly. "I have you for two hours, and again after dinner. What do you wish to study?"

I lower my pencil and frown at him. "You are asking me?"

He huffs out an impatient breath. "I'm not Valyrian. I can't see inside your stubborn dragon head. And since you're an alpha like me, I imagine you'll learn best if you're the captain of your own vessel, academically speaking."

I do not plan to provoke him, but the words spill out as though the Devil himself has possessed my dragonish tongue. "Do you not mean, the captain of my own yacht?"

A new tension invades the space between us.

The very walls seem to hold their breath.

The last time I saw this man years ago, he was naked. I saw his pretty mouth and his sinful hands make another man writhe in ecstasy.

And I… I watched the entire scandalous encounter in profoundly shocked silence, with unfamiliar and alarming emotions churning through my body, the bitter tang of betrayal flooding my mouth… and my own rigid cock gripped tight and throbbing in my fist.

I barely understood the mechanics of what I was seeing.

I was barely more than a boy myself.

But I did not budge from my hidden vantage until this man who is now before me made that sailor cry out and spill in his mouth.

The entire encounter occurred with Vasili's back to me, although I could tell even from behind that he was pumping himself, just as I was. I have always wondered (when I allowed myself to wonder) what Vasili Romanov looks like when he—

"Be very careful, darling, *do*," he purrs. (Secretly, I am deeply grateful he is Mogadon, and no telepath like Ronin.) "I value my position at this

Academy, and I fully intend to keep it. But, with very little effort on my part, I can make your life at this institution so wretched you'll wish you'd never been born."

I doubt he could be any more terrible (even at his worst) than my loathsome brothers.

Not to mention my Lady Mother.

But my dragon is restless in the presence of this strange alpha. He has not yet decided whether Vasili should be viewed as an enemy or… something else.

To keep my dragon quiet, I answer calmly. "Will it be worth your own expulsion to make me suffer? If you would risk being forced to abandon our queen for my sake, then you are not the alpha she deserves."

Vasili coils in his chair like an asp.

"Rest assured, I am going nowhere." Each of his words falls softly as a drop of venom between us. "It's Purgatory, which means you're the new boy and subject to the requisite hazing by the entire student body, and no one would ever be able to prove I'm to blame. I'd positively relish your misery, *malchik*, so I'd advise you not to test me. And I only warn once."

Well, let him warn. I am indifferent to the prospect of my own misery.

Misery is too familiar a state for me to fear it.

What I truly want is to ask if it hurt him when his father sent his lover away.

I have wondered, sometimes, if it was love between him and that sailor, or only passion. In truth, I have wondered more about Vasili and that sailor in the intervening years than I care to confess.

So, once again, I avoid these questions.

It is true that I must learn from him, if I can. The Dean has made clear that I will only be allowed to remain if my grades merit my place.

"If you are asking what I wish to study, I do not wish to study Genetics," I say, because all those letters and proteins and codons made my eyes ache, and also because Mistress Agrippina has advised that I learn that subject from Neo.

"Well, that makes two of us," Vasili murmurs. "It's a frightfully tedious subject. Is there anything you *do* wish to learn?"

I dig into my backpack and produce a heavy tome that I thunk down on the table between us. "I wish to learn this."

"Foundations of Witching World Law." He eyes the volume with a glimmer of interest. "Why that subject, in particular?"

"We will need this knowledge when Zara ascends." This is my tacit admission that we may both be at her side when that happens. He will be hard to kill, this enemy of mine.

And I… I did not always wish to kill him.

That summer on the Romanov yacht, I wanted anything but that. He was three years my senior, and I admired him. He wasn't the warlock then that he is now, but still, he was a force of nature. I admired his confidence, his wit, his fashionable sophistication, his utter lack of scruples, his terrifying skill with a blade. I envied him his father, and I wanted to be his brother, in a way I could never claim true kinship with those hateful worms who crawled from my mother's revolting nest. I wanted to be his friend.

And, in absolute truth, I even wanted—

"I am aware of no current plan to add you to our harem," he huffs, with a little flash of spite. "Despite your histrionics in the pool." So she did tell him. At least, she has told him some of it. "However…"

I eye him warily. Truly, he is capable of anything.

He gives my wary face a playful pout. "Well, darling, I did promise Lucius I'd teach you. I suppose this subject is as good as any."

Sly humor gleams in his ice-blue eyes. He would look at me this way sometimes that long-ago summer. He did it just often enough, between bouts of mockery and days of avoidance, to keep my wistful hopes of friendship with him alive.

I know he cannot read my mind, he is Mogadon and I am shifter, and we are not mated (of course). Yet I find I must lower my gaze to the textbook to avoid meeting his. I do not wish him ever to guess how much he hurt me that summer.

In silence, I nudge the book toward him.

"Hmmmm." His narrowed gaze probes my face, but I keep my eyes on my notebook and inscribe the date in my careful script. At last, he says, "Shall we start with the body of law that governs the royal succession?"

His choice of topic pleases me, but I merely grunt.

I always knew he was clever, but I never knew how much. He begins to speak, without notes, without preparation, without even glancing at the text. Quickly the truth becomes apparent. His intellect is sharp as a surgeon's scalpel or an assassin's blade. He explains to me what I barely understood before today, about Messalina the weak Aquarius queen and her dead bitch daughter Cybelle and how now there is no Aquarius heir, because Messalina is barren and aging. (Possibly he is wrong about that, about the current lack of an Aquarius heir, but I will choose my moment to tell him, when Zara too can hear.) He speaks of Zara's brother Damien, Cybelle's intended mate, who terrorized this school to the point of tyranny, until the late queen killer struck and murdered the poisonous couple.

And he speaks of Zara, who never sought to take anyone's place.

When Cybelle died, Lucius and Ronin kidnapped Zara to bring her here. She wished only for her freedom. Yet now she must give up that freedom she craves like oxygen to become the Gemini queen.

He is a gripping storyteller, this enemy of mine, although I will never pamper his colossal ego by telling him.

Still, I am riveted.

I am riveted by his words.

And I am riveted by him.

I am taking notes to begin, when he briskly outlines the Byzantine clauses in the matrilineal law of succession that govern how the throne passes to the eldest scion of the next-most-purebred witching house if the line of the dominant witch dies out. This has happened before, since Aquarius queens did not always rule. The Aquarius clan replaced the ruling Cancer clan, whose purebred line has long been extinct.

But my pencil soon slows.

Now my reluctant tutor warms to his subject. He prowls and paces and gestures while he talks, which leaves me free to watch him at my leisure.

He was always a pretty boy. But now he is truly striking.

He is taller than I am, taller than anyone here, he is slim as a saber and supple as an eel. The soft light pouring through the stained glass makes his skin glow like alabaster. That pure light caresses his high cheekbones and narrow nose like a lover's touch. I admire the wicked fangs that peek between his lips.

But I am wary of his witchcraft.

Since the day my dragon manifested, no one has ever held me at his mercy, the way this warlock did so effortlessly in a gas station parking lot.

"…When that tiresome hag Messalina finally kicks the bucket," Vasili is saying, "she'll be the last of the failed Aquarius line. And all the Aquarius witches, at least in recent generations, are weak. After the Aquarius clan, the Gemini are the closest to a purebred witching line in existence. Mick Gemini leads that clan, he married his own cousin to keep the bloodline pure, and Zara is their only surviving child, which makes her the Gemini scion and…" Abruptly, Vasili's gaze narrows. "Are you listening to a word I'm saying, Maximka?"

"Yes." And it is true. I doubt anyone ever ignores him when he speaks.

"Well?" One hand scrolls through the air in an irritable gesture. "Do you have any questions?"

I do, but they are questions I must never ask.

"Hmmm." Vasili looks displeased by my silence. "If not, let's move along to the laws that govern Zara's legal relationship, as queen-in-waiting, to the Arcane Senate. In principle, the sitting queen leads the Senate, but it's largely a ceremonial function. The queen's greatest significance to the survival of the four races is genetic, symbolic, and magical—"

"I do have a question." I did not mean to ask, but still the words burst out. "Did you ever see him again?"

He slices me a sidelong look like a thrown razor. "See *whom*?"

My mouth is dry, but I will not veer away. "The sailor. The one from the yacht."

A heartbeat ago, he was halfway across the room. Suddenly he is rearing directly over me, malignant as a scorpion. I jolt back in my chair, body tingling with instant alarm.

I never dreamed he could move so fast.

Clearly he has become a well-trained fighter, in addition to all these other lethal gifts he has honed.

Swift as a rattlesnake, he coils and strikes. "Are you truly the witless beast they're all calling you after last night's melodramatics? Or are you actually *trying* to provoke me, Maximka? Because that would be unwise."

My dragon spreads his wings and hisses with menace, but I keep a firm hold, although adrenaline is spurting through my body, and the aggressive musk of Vasili's Mogadon scent is making my head spin.

I push my heavy chair back to put distance between us. But my nemesis is having none of it. He darts in to trap me, cold hands pinning my wrists to the furniture like manacles. He fences me in with his rapier-slim body.

If I were one of my poisonous brothers, I would spray his face with blinding venom.

But I am no wretched worm of a wyvern. Besides, I would never do that to him. I wanted to hurt him all those years ago, the way he hurt me, even if he never knew it.

And I did.

I hurt him in ways I did not even intend.

"I am Maxim now," I tell him, low and careful. "And it is no provocation. Did you see him again? I want to know."

His venomous gaze searches mine for trickery or deception. I keep my eyes steady on his. I might deceive, but I never lie. Being this close to him… have I ever been this close to him?… it is triggering every hunting instinct my dragon possesses.

But it is not hunting my dragon desires.

Vasili's delicate mouth hardens with suspicion. "Why do you want to know? Wasn't it enough to know you stole my father's love—such as it was?"

"After he sent you away, your father sent us all home. I never saw him again." That memory burns and aches in my chest, because it is true. I longed to claim Nikolai Romanov for a father. I hoped he would offer to foster me at their *dacha*. The Romanov marriage is famously not a happy one, so I hoped Nikolai would desire my mother, who is as beautiful as she is deadly.

That summer, I hoped for everything.

But Nikolai Romanov was never a fool—except where his son is concerned. He saw me (in my then-dragonless state) for the deadweight I was, saw her for the monster she was, and sent us all packing.

"Besides," I hear myself say, though I know I should keep silent, "this was never about him. Your father is not why I did it."

"I knew it." His eyes narrow and his nostrils flare. "I fucking *knew* it. Notwithstanding all your outraged sensibilities and your antiquated morals, you wanted Paolo for yourself."

This is precisely why I should never have spoken. My alarmed gaze slews past him to the stairwell, but it is empty.

Thankfully, there is no one in this loft except the two of us to hear.

"Fuck, it's true, it's actually true!" he carols, poisonous with gleeful rancor. "I knew it. I fucking *knew* it—"

"Vasili," I say gruffly.

"What?" He scowls at me.

"Shut up."

I know this is a mistake the moment I say it. The only commands Vasili Romanov ever tolerates are those he issues himself.

"Why?" He gloats. "It's true, isn't it? Little Maximka, the precious princeling of the swaggering Sagitarius clan, secretly likes the D—"

Truly, there is only one way to stop him from speaking these horrible truths, here in this public place where anyone can come along and hear.

I lunge up in my chair and seal my mouth to his.

A shocked exclamation spills out of him before our lips collide. He is utterly toxic, and his fangs are fatally sharp.

But fangs are erotic to a dragon.

And he has the softest lips.

His lip gloss tastes like cherries, tart and sweet, and I lick a long swipe over his astonished mouth before it occurs to him to stop me. He is still pinning my arms to the chair in a twinned vise I cannot break (because it turns out he is stronger than he looks). But I sweep my leg behind his to make his knees buckle. He spills into my lap with a muffled curse, which lets me deepen the kiss. My tongue plunges deep into his mouth, past those deadly fangs that inflame me so dangerously, to tangle with his in a dance we were always meant to share.

He is like kissing a demon, he is vicious and treacherous, but that is perfect for a dragon.

He is perfect.

He is even more perfect than I always dreamed he would be.

He is hissing and writhing on top of me, he is fighting to gather his legs under him, and this chair is in real danger of tipping, but I do not give a single shit. Let us fall. Let us splinter this chair to kindling. Let the whole world burn. God, let anything happen, as long as I can finally have this with him. I moan into his mouth and arch into his slim body.

My rut flames up with a blast of heat, fierce and savage. My dragon is roaring in my skin, provoked beyond bearing by this triggering proximity to another alpha. When alphas come together, either they fight or they fuck.

My dragon is an unrepentant primitive. And he, at this moment, demands both.

Lord, if Vasili would only do to me what he does to Ronin, and apparently also to Lucius, and probably even to that innocent-looking Neo. My cock is starving for his wicked touch. My thrusting pelvis collides against his.

And that moment of stolen contact sears me to the bone.

Behind his stylish trousers, my rival alpha is concealing a raging erection.

Saints of the northern steppes guard me.

He is as hot for me as I am hot for him.

Grunting in savage triumph, I pump against him in hard brutal snaps. Our cocks crash together through our trousers.

I swear if there is a God in Heaven, even if I burn in Hell for this, I will make him spill for me—

He releases my arms and wrenches free from my kiss with a gasp. I am already reaching for him, ready to rip every stitch of that proper prep school uniform from his maddeningly elusive body.

That is when his vicious backhand connects with my face, with all his coiling viperish strength behind the blow.

My sight is obliterated in a flash of crimson pain.

That blow rocks me back in my chair, reeling with a force that makes my ears ring.

"Ouch, damn it," I groan, one hand rising to grope gingerly at my throbbing cheek. "Jesus Christ, Vasili…"

"What the fuck?" he pants, dragging an unsteady hand across his lips. All his lip gloss is gone (no doubt it is now smeared all over me) and his hair and clothing are all disheveled from my touch.

He is all undone, all due to me.

Despite the terrible peril of this moment, I am ferociously pleased.

"What the fuck *was that*?" he demands, somehow both icy and raging, righting his clothing with sharp furious tugs. "Some pathetic, homophobic attempt at mockery, what?" He pauses for my nonexistent answer, then rushes ahead. "You're exceedingly fortunate I only slapped you. And I may well still crush you against the floor like a cockroach. I asked you a question, and I fully expect an answer. What. Was. That."

"Not… not mockery." Shaking my head (which makes my face throb worse), my ears still ringing, I push unsteadily to my feet.

Warily he backs away, keeping plenty of distance between us. I am so hard for him, so absolutely rigid, that I have to shift about awkwardly and adjust my physiology down below.

A flash of comprehension widens his gaze.

"Oh dear God, you're in rut," he says in absolute disgust. "Of course. *That's* what all this nonsense is about. You and that rutting dragon of yours are so pathetically horny you've lost your scaly minds. You're both so far gone that even a queer boy like me, with a cock and a hole, briefly holds some perverse appeal, despite the fact that you're fucking *straight*. I'd advise you to find some girl to fuck, but I can't imagine who'd have you."

I want to say no, you're wrong, there is more than that between us, Vasili. There is so much more.

But I am frozen by the icy contempt that frosts his tone. I forced myself upon him when, all too clearly, he does not want me.

Now I am shamed into silence.

"Just stay away from Zara. Stay away from her and all my mates. Consider yourself warned. She isn't ready for this—for you. None of us are ready." My enemy flashes me a final venomous glare, buttons his jacket tight around his narrow waist, and spins away. Now I can barely hear him. "I'm not certain any of us will ever be ready."

Our lesson is not yet over, but clearly he is finished with me for the day, if not for all time. What will I do if he refuses to tutor me for insulting him like this? Will they send me away? Back to my Lady Mother?

If they do, surely it will be no more than I deserve.

Briskly he sweeps his books and notes into a stylish leather satchel. This gives him a handy excuse to avoid looking at me. I know he is sharply aware of me, the same painful way I am aware of him, as I stuff my notebook helter-skelter into my backpack and bolt for the stairs. My thoughts are tangled in knots, my cheek is throbbing like blazes from his blistering backhand, and he did not even answer my question about the sailor.

I am already on the stairs when I stumble to a stop. Truly, I have made such a catastrophic mess of this entire shameful encounter that I might as well spill the rest.

Hesitant, I glance at him over my shoulder. "Vasili."

Wary as fuck, he slices me a dangerous look over his satchel. "Maxim."

At least I have achieved this small victory. He no longer addresses me like a child. I drag in a bracing breath, steel my gut against the blow, and set the truth free.

"It was never the sailor," I tell him gruffly. "It was you. For me, it has always been you."

He snatches in an audible breath.

His jaw drops and his eyes ignite. Something fractures in his face, and something fractures in my soul.

If I were not in this church, I would spread my wings and take flight. Caged by this mortal structure, I launch furiously down the stairs at a run. I flee to spare him the need to reply.

I flee to spare myself the whiplash pain of my shame and his scorn.

I flee to spare my dragon and myself the certain scourge of his rejection.

Chapter Nineteen
Zara

"Cheese on toast! Are you fucking *shitting* me?"

I'm sitting on the kitchen counter, still wearing my uniform, with my stockinged legs swinging while Vasili shucks oysters for the big pot of *bouillabaisse* Ronin's whipping up for the *domus* dinner. The yeasty smell of baking bread wafts from the oven, and my tummy's definitely ready to rumble.

Now, in my total fucking shock over the news grenade my Goblin King just casually lobbed, I almost fall off the counter. "You mean to tell me that dragon actually *kissed* you? And you fucking *slapped* him for it? Shit, Vasili."

Of course, the fact that we all figured Maxim was mostly straight, and majorly homophobic to boot, has been one of the primary obstacles (but definitely not the only one) to him joining our polycule.

Not to mention one of the primary obstacles to me, you know, rising.

If my dragon—I mean, *the* dragon—is going to go around kissing my warlocks now, that puts him in a whole new category of possibility.

Which begs the obvious question.

Even though I pretty much know the answer.

I swing my feet and ask anyway. "So, uh, why'd you slap him?"

"You'd do better to ask him why he kissed me," Vasili says, wielding his knife to pry open an oyster with a ruthlessness that would make any crustacean's blood run cold. "That wretched worm was mocking me and I won't stand for it. He fondly imagined he could torment me as he pleased and that I'd be helpless to retaliate due to Lucius' charming ultimatum. I merely disabused him of the notion. Somewhat violently."

"Well, I hope you didn't overreact." Because Vasili's no joke when he's violent, and that dragon's seen enough violence in his life. My own face is already stinging in sympathy. "Did he slap you back? Because he'd be entitled under the terms of that promise he made to Lucius. Since you swung first."

"He *kissed* first." Vasili shucks a fresh oyster with an extra-vicious twist. Which totally leaves me wondering if Vasili kissed back. My snake is a goddamn sphinx when he wants to be, and I can't read him at all right now. He's being *very* cryptic. "The inciting offense was sufficient, believe me. He completely demolished my lip gloss."

"Real kiss then, huh?" I probe.

"Hmmm." His mascara-coated lashes effectively screen his eyes as he assaults another oyster. I think the critters are still alive and cringing in that briny bucket he's pulling them from (even though they're not, like, sentient), and this has to be a traumatic way to go.

Death by Goblin King.

"And after you hit him, he didn't swing back?" I nudge a little more. I'm getting more and more interested in this whole fascinating kiss. The more evasive Vasili gets, the more determined I am to tease the whole truth out of his dark and snaky heart.

Vasili doesn't even hum this time. Which I'm taking as a no. Maxim took the hit and didn't hit back.

Ronin and I exchange a meaningful look.

"What makes you fancy he was mocking you?" Looking sexy as fuck, all barefoot in distressed denim and one of his silky button-downs, Ronin's sampling the soup with a wooden spoon and pillaging Lucius' spice rack in a hunt for oregano.

Except now he's paused the proceedings to give Vasili his full attention.

Vasili sneers at the terrorized oysters. "What else could he possibly have meant?"

"Same thing a bloke usually means when he kisses a bloke, yeah?" Ronin says dryly. "I think Neo's got it right. That dragon's hot as fuck for you."

"Dear God, don't be absurd." Vasili lowers his knife and arches an eyebrow in icy disdain.

I seriously envy his ability to do that nifty one-eyebrow trick, but I'm way more focused on what Ronin just said to get sidetracked by my snake and all that sexy.

"What's so absurd about it?" Calmly Ronin drops a massive tangle of clawed crab legs (looking horribly like a giant spider) into the pot. "I've been mulling the whole bit over. He pitches up on your yacht a lonely little runt and, well, you're you. Lad probably got an instant raging crush on you, but he couldn't act on it due to all that religious bullshit. All tormented and guilty and whatever. Then he sees you fellating your Italian, gets jealous as fuck, tattles to your dad—"

"Jealous?" Vasili scowls. "There was very little to be jealous of, I assure you. Aside from his colossal cock, that Italian was barely interesting, believe me. Besides, Maxim was a teething infant at the time."

"Oh, c'mon. He was fifteen, if I've got the age gap right," I chime in. "Hardly an infant, Goblin King. I was fucking at that age. Shocker, I know."

"Early bloomer." Ronin grins at me, then shifts his gaze back to Vasili. "Bloke's probably been fantasizing about you ever since, and feeling conflicted as fuck about it. Either way, based on what just went down in that library, he's definitely got the hots for you now."

"Oh please," Vasili murmurs, dismissive in the royally imperious way only the Goblin King can be. "You've simply got dick on your delectable mind, darling. You're in heat and you're delirious."

"Oh, I dunno." Ronin wipes his hands on a dish towel and saunters over to me. He slides between my spread thighs to pin me against the cupboard behind me. "Have I got dick on my mind, love? Or could it be I'm obsessed with your succulent pussy?"

Right on cue, my succulent pussy sits up and says howdy. My simmering heat kicks up and my mating scent wafts out. My legs drift apart to invite him closer.

My warlock pulls in a long breath, rumbles with interest, and leans in for a slow kiss. His tiger eyes are all lidded and lazy, the way he gets after Lucius rails him, and I'm betting Lucius probably fucked him right through his latest peak after class. Which hopefully means he'll peak again later.

Right when I do.

"Mmmmm." I rest my hands on his lean hips to prolong the moment. "Dick or pussy? Could be both, because why choose?"

"I quite fancy the way you think." Ronin's hot hands skim up my bare thighs, and suddenly it's feeling like maybe dinner can wait till later.

There's only a tiny sliver missing from the fat moon floating over the courtyard through the kitchen window. Lucius and Neo double-dicked me right through my first spike last night. I needed a long soak in the bath this morning to baby my well-stretched and -pounded girly parts.

But I'm pretty sure I'm ready for round two.

Vasili keeps brutalizing those poor shellfish like a wrathful kitchen genie, but he's definitely watching. Over Ronin's shoulder, our gazes meet. His pretty eyes glitter with spite and temper. He's still wearing his school uni which looks killer on his slim sexy body, blazer and tie discarded and sleeves all rolled up.

Yum.

These two warlocks are sexy as fuck at all times, but even more so when they cook for me.

I sneak a peek at the old-fashioned wall clock over the double fridge. Lucius is late getting home again, but Dez and Racetrack are right next door in the great room, where Neo too is studying. He's all worried about our midterms, and he's basically studying for all of us.

I'm wondering if maybe there's time for a quickie when I hear the front door slam and the stomp of snowy boots.

Lucius is quiet as a church mouse (or a stalking wolf) padding in and out, so I know who our new arrival must be. Even before my inner dragon uncurls and lifts on her hind legs, bugling in welcome, wings flaring as she tries to rise.

Shit.

That's some powerful dragon shit right there.

But I'm in control, damn it. Not this dragon heat.

Ronin's amber eyes lock on mine, because of course he's picking all this up. At the island, Vasili falls suddenly and dangerously still, because we're also linked. And they're both getting a major rush from that heady spurt of pheromones my horny body's kicking out. My shifter Spidey senses kick in, and now I'm hyperaware of Ronin's hands on my thighs, inches away from that sudden dampness that makes my panties stick.

"Hiya, Max," Dez carols from the great room. "Didya have a good… oh, crikey, what happened to you?"

"Purgatory happened to him," Racetrack mumbles. "Obviously. Didn't stay outta the guys' john like I said, did ya?"

Even Neo exclaims, and I can totally feel the spike of concern that blips from my fated mate. My head snaps toward the kitchen door.

Because Maxim definitely knows I'm in here, and I don't think he's gonna be able to keep away. We're both super-focused on each other right now.

Vasil's eyes narrow to cyanide slits. He abandons his shucking knife and reaches for the real one strapped to his inner arm like he has every intention of hurling it and pinning our dragon to the wall.

Maxim slinks into the kitchen looking totally disreputable.

I haven't seen him since the pool last night, but I know he's been in class all day. Somewhere along the way, he's picked up a big shiner and a fat lip. Ribbons of long pale hair spill from his sleek braid, and the shoulder of his blazer is ripped open.

"Sweet Jesus." I swing toward Vasili with concern and outrage spiraling through me. "I thought you said you slapped him, not beat the living shit out of him."

"I did." Vasili too looks startled. My snake can lie like the Devil and he always gets away with it, but this time his indignation in our bond feels genuine. "I mean, I didn't. Look, this is *obviously* some transparent ploy for sympathy—"

"Vasili is not responsible," Maxim says shortly. "There were seven of them. They ambushed me when I was returning from class."

"*Seven* of them? What the actual fuck?" Just hearing those unfair odds pisses me right off. Yeah, he's a dragon and all, but he wasn't when they ambushed him. "Christ, I know they haze the newbies, but not like this! I bet it was those little shits from Villa Tiberius. They're the remnants of Cybelle's old court, so they've kinda got a rivalry with us in Villa Augustus."

"It was just a few stones they threw at me—"

"*Stones!*" I'm outraged as hell. "They fucking threw stones at you?"

"Just enough to stun me and knock me down. Then a few kicks and punches." Maxim shrugs and looks uncomfortable. "If they had not cornered me in these unfamiliar streets, I would have done better. Before I could retaliate, the cowards took to their heels."

"Too right," Ronin says grimly. "It was a bloody hit and run. Rotten little shits were pissing themselves with fear you'd shift."

I know he's not a big dragon fan, but even Ronin looks indignant on Maxim's behalf. My warlock's still standing between my spread knees, hand resting on my bare thigh as he frowns at our battered shifter, and I definitely don't want Ronin moving. I'm not done with him yet.

But I do want a closer look at the damage on Maxim.

"Come over here, big guy." I use my queen voice so the dragon won't argue.

Slowly Maxim sidles over, giving Vasili a wide berth and keeping a wary eye on Ronin. This guy's like a feral dog (and my classmates fucking threw stones at him! Goddammit, I'm gonna go *Thor: Love and Thunder* on someone's ass.) But right now I find myself sitting very still and even holding my breath, like any sudden sound or move will spook the guy into bolting.

Tucked between my legs, Ronin shifts warily. I whisper to him though our bond, *Stay here for me. And be nice to him, Adam.*

Ronin shoots me a look that's smoking with amber heat. *Just how nice to him d'you want me to be?*

That's one visual my impending heat definitely doesn't need, because it triggers another rush of warmth under my prim schoolgirl panties that I'm pretty sure they can all smell.

Very nice, I purr. *I want you to be very nice to him. Think you can do that?*

Ronin rumbles a sex-drenched sound low and deep in his throat. I swallow hard, spread my knees wider, and hold Maxim's guarded stare with mine.

"That's it, big guy," I murmur. "No one here's gonna hurt you. I just wanna see."

When he's a foot away, he hesitates, those slitted eyes shifting to Ronin in a way that manages to look both somehow ashamed and deeply suspicious. Without meeting his gaze, Ronin edges sideways (still very much between my thighs) to make room.

Oh yeah.

This is gonna be good.

Those dragon eyes veer back to mine. I give Maxim a sexy smile and beckon him close with a crooked finger. He squares his shoulders and edges between my knees. Moving slowly so I won't spook him, I hook a hand in his belt and ease him in even closer. Ronin's facing him now, so that tucks Max's hip right up against Ronin's dick, which I'm sensing my sexy Brit doesn't mind at all.

Hell to the yeah.

Okay, I gotta admit it. I *really* like having both my warlocks tucked between my thighs.

Very carefully, I graze Maxim's jaw with my fingers. He's all raspy and glittery with blond stubble and he needs to shave (or not, because the effect is hella sexy). His dragonish scent of brimstone and leather sneaks into my nose and makes me sweat.

Now he keens a little under his breath, which I figure is his dragon vocalizing. My inner dragon croons in sympathy, kind of a bird trill rising from my throat.

Jesus.

I didn't even know I could make that kind of sound.

Everyone glances at me with interest. I shove down a ripple of unease and clear my throat.

"That's it," I whisper, holding Maxim in place with my hand looped in his belt. I angle his head so I can check out that black eye, which looks like the worst of his facial bruising. A thick silky tendril of hair slips over his eye and gets in my way.

"Help a girl out, Adam," I breathe.

Ronin grunts and reaches to help.

But even that little bit of movement makes Maxim flinch.

"Easy, mate," my warlock says, way more softly than usual. I figure Ronin's picking up a lot telepathically, like the fact that this great big scary dragon is actually afraid of being touched.

Maxim steels himself, and Ronin gently strokes back that wing of fallen hair, which reveals the curvy sweep of silver studs piercing the cartilage of Max's ear… and a big fucking goose egg rising near his hairline. That has to be from one of those stones.

They were fucking throwing stones at my dragon's head.

My inner Godzilla snarls and paces with murder in her scaly heart.

I growl under my breath and probe the damage with care, which Maxim tolerates with his whole stoic tough guy persona. Ronin leans in to look, while Vasili watches in sphinxlike silence the whole time from across the room.

"Lord, that looks awful," Neo says from the kitchen door. Dez and Racetrack crowd in behind him. "Want me to get the first aid kit?"

"Yeah, baby, bring me a numbing potion," I tell him. "And a piece of sirloin from the freezer."

Because that old-fashioned shit works better than witchcraft to bring down the swelling.

Dez and Racetrack watch from the door while Neo fetches the first aid kit and rummages around in the freezer. Our freezer's packed with red meat, because Lucius' wolf craves it and he can't always get out to hunt.

In an impressive display of multitasking, Vasili seizes another terrified oyster and starts butchering, while simultaneously dividing his attention between the dragon tucked up in my personal space and the mouthwatering vision of Neo's muscled ass molded in his chinos as our bookworm bends over and scrounges around in the meat drawer.

Completely innocent of Vasili's carnal desires and the general distraction he's causing, Neo emerges from the icebox with his glasses frosted and a frozen steak wrapped in cellophane in hand. He's coming up behind Maxim with the steak, the meds, and a look of concern written all over his earnest face when Maxim stiffens right up.

"Don't go behind him, love," Ronin says softly to Neo. "Just bring the booty to me."

Figures a telepath like Ronin would sense what it took me too long to figure out on my own last night, which is that Maxim's afraid of letting anyone near his poor scarred back.

Neo circles around and gives Ronin the goods, no questions asked.

Because my fated mate's good like that.

I'm ready to put that steak to use, but it's Ronin who gets the frozen meat—still in its cellophane wrapper—situated over Maxim's swollen eye. The dragon endures this patiently, groping to hold the filet in place, while Neo hovers and Ronin sifts through the first aid kit and I start feeling Maxim down for other damage.

The dragon's not too comfy with all this attention, but Ronin distracts him by sliding a feather-light finger around the studded rim of Max's pierced ear, which makes the big guy shiver.

Ronin leans close to whisper, lips brushing the dragon's ear, "These are nice, Max."

Maxim swallows hard and his uncovered eye gets all lidded and heavy.

That's Ronin being sweet to him for me.

"Maybe I'll show you mine sometime," Ronin murmurs, with a wicked look and a sexy sideways smirk at me. "Though I've only got the one. Think you'd like that?"

That right there's a visual to make my toes curl.

While Max is (understandably) distracted and stammering, I'm unknotting his tie and unbuttoning his shirt. Underneath, the sinewy heat of dragon builds a slow fire in my cunt. Ronin's got his traffic-stopping ass wedged against my inner thigh, my skirt's riding up till my panties are almost showing, and Maxim looks way more interested in all that exposed skin I'm flashing between my red plaid skirt and my thigh-high black stockings (and, quite possibly, Ronin's thickening dick pressed against his hip) than he is in those sore spots I'm discovering all over Maxim's ribs.

"Dammit, I swear I'm gonna take the roof off that fucking Villa Tiberius," I mutter, dabbing plenty of numbing potion on his bruises. "No one fucking touches you—*any* of you—Purgatory or no—"

"It is nothing," the dragon says gruffly, though I can tell the potion and the steak are helping. "They knocked me down with that stone to the head, then they got in a few kicks before I could rise. They were lucky. That is all. Next time, they will be less lucky."

"Why didn't you shift into your dragon and flambé them?" Neo asks, sounding genuinely curious.

I'm glad he asked, since I'm mulling the same question.

"Because I do not wish to be sent away." Maxim lowers the steak and his golden eyes lift to mine. "When my dragon is loose, he can be… willful. And this I cannot allow. My place is here with you, my sovereign."

My inner dragon purrs for him, and I barely manage to swallow another of those weird vocalizations. The last thing we need right now is for me to start making bird sounds. Honestly, my lightning's enough to handle, and I was just starting to get a grip on it with all those skills I've been learning from Lucius when this whole dragon thing came along.

"You're allowed to defend yourself, big guy," I state firmly. My hands are still resting on his bare waist, and I'm not in any big rush to let him go. "I'm not saying go all *Game of Thrones* on this Academy, like in the series finale or anything. But if you're in over your head, you know, let 'em see your inner Mothra."

A hint of that sexy Rasputin grin slips past his guard. "I will show mine when you show yours."

Now he's talking about my goddamn mating flight.

Fuck.

I scowl and cross my arms over my chest.

"Well." Rudely Vasili upends his cache of murdered oysters into the soup with a noisy splash that makes us all twitch. "I'm going straight to the *thermae* to rid myself of the appalling stench of shellfish—if I can. Kindly don't forget our tutoring session in the library after dinner, Mr. Rasputin. And don't even *think* of being late, or I'll make you suffer."

Maxim stops buttoning his shirt and slides him a long look. Vasili sounds far from inviting (to put it mildly). Geez, he's really gotta work on that whole teacher-student approachability thing. Still, I get the definite feeling Maxim's… relieved… that the Goblin King's still willing to put up with teaching him.

Kiss or no kiss.

"I will not forget," the dragon says quietly. "Or be late."

Vasili interrogates him with his eyes (which is basically a mini-Spanish Inquisition, minus thumbscrews, but still not comfortable, like, *at all*). Finally he gives Max a curt nod and slithers off.

But he doesn't get very far before Lucius appears in the kitchen door, still wearing his sober winter coat.

His grim face and quiet voice rivet us all where we stand (or sit). "I'm sorry for being late for dinner, my dears. I trust you'll forgive me for making you all wait. I fear there's been… a development."

My prof isn't easy to rattle, so that note in his voice gives me a cold chill.

"What kind of *development*?" Vasili asks, narrow-eyed, speaking for all of us.

Lucius' wary gaze shifts to me. "A development concerning Zara's accession to the witching world throne."

Well, fuck.

Chapter Twenty
Vasili

"Sweet Jesus. A *rival queen*? And she just, what, issued a goddamn press release?"

Zara's abandoned her dinner halfway through her bowl of Ronin's exceptional *bouillabaisse* in favor of stalking around the great room and cursing, while the rest of us huddle around the big table and stare at each other like imbeciles.

"Not quite a press release, my dear. It's only an old rumor that's surfaced rather suddenly in *The Witching Inquisitor*." Lucius slips his handkerchief from his tweed coat and pats gently at his damp temples.

Clearly his heat is starting, precisely when I've predicted it would, based on the phase of the moon when I bit him.

Of course, he's fiercely resisting our impending fuckfest, also precisely as I predicted. Later he's probably going to try locking me out of his bedroom like a medieval virgin on her wedding night.

Not that any lock's going to keep me out.

I'm his alpha, he's in heat, and Zara's current crisis is literally the only reason I'm not already launching myself across the table and dragging the poor dear off to his bedroom for a good hard fuck.

Normally Zara would be an active participant in my little X-rated fantasy (as well as the subsequent fuck). Tonight, she merely scowls at the magazine clenched in her fist. "Yeah, well, that so-called old rumor just made the goddamn cover."

"The *Inquisitor* isn't even a proper newspaper," I sneer, thoroughly offended on her behalf. "It's a filthy rag. A scandal sheet. Everyone knows the publishers accept money to print any old rubbish."

"But everyone in the witching world reads it." This heartening contribution comes from Neo, the senator's son, who frowns and pushes his glasses up his nose. "Honestly, this isn't good. And it's definitely not a coincidence that this rumor resurfaced right after what just happened in Vegas. Whoever paid to print this piece chose their moment *really* well. They're striking while Zara's perceived as weak… and maybe, you know, deficient. Even if it's only a provocation, she can't afford to ignore this."

My queen isn't normally one to pace. Because she isn't normally indecisive. She's an action heroine, and I simply adore that about her.

But she too is teetering on the edge of her heat.

In this condition, she has kilojoules of energy to burn.

Tonight she's all but wearing a path in the floor as she circles the central hearth, firelight glowing in her eyes and dancing on her skin, with one hand slapping the rolled-up news rag against her thigh and her Hollywood face pensive.

In fact, this printed scandal that Lucius has just produced at the dinner table between ravenous mouthfuls of freshly baked baguette (because his heat is also making him peckish) is so unexpected I'm rather tempted to pace myself.

"Bloody hell, Lucius, how's that even possible?" Ronin blurts, his own soup forgotten some time ago. "Haven't old rumors been, like, overtaken by events? Messalina's the last Aquarius bitch, and Zara's the Gemini scion. The Senate already voted. She's fucking *next*."

Seated at the head of the family table, Lucius opens his mouth to answer. He's allegedly gotten all his insight from the paper, just flown in on the latest supply plane. But he's also the Aries scion, and the entire Aries clan is rich as Midas. It's Old World money, stodgy and respectable, completely unlike my own clan's ill-gotten gains.

For these reasons, I've long suspected Lucius has his own sources of intelligence on the mainland.

"It is possible because Messalina is not the last Aquarius bitch." This information emerges unexpectedly from the dragon (of all creatures) who's seated across the table from me, and who hasn't even glanced at the paper, because darling Zara's been hogging it (admittedly, she's entitled) ever since Lucius plucked the rag from his briefcase.

Maxim has already downed at least three bowls of soup at a furious rate, with a protective arm crooked around his bowl as though he fully expects to fight for every drop. At the rate that soup is disappearing, Ronin will shortly need to make more.

Next time, someone else can shuck the damn oysters.

True, I suppose Maxim can use the extra calories to beef up that lean but not unattractive (if I'm being honest) starvation chic physique.

"That's exactly what it says in this paper. Even though Cybelle's dead, and the bitch didn't have any siblings. What I wanna know is how *you* know that, big guy." Zara sashays straight across the room to hover over the dragon.

My, my. Our queen looks deliciously fuckable in her short plaid skirt with her blouse half-unbuttoned and her hair tied up in pigtails.

Despite her preoccupation with that news grenade whose trigger pin this infuriating dragon has just casually pulled, I notice she's still careful not to lurk about behind him.

Truly, I'm more than a bit dissatisfied with my own observational skills, which are typically exemplary. That damned kissing dragon has had me so flustered and so distracted that it actually required that little byplay in the kitchen—specifically Ronin's telling comment about not approaching Maxim from behind—for the cliché lightbulb to illuminate in my fiendish brain.

As a child, Maxim was abused.

Of course he was.

I vaguely recall from our charming family holiday that his entire clutch of brothers is hideously scarred, because that sort of thing is rather difficult to hide during a summer holiday on a yacht, but I merely took it as evidence of some grotesque communal dragon sport and never gave their shared mutilation another thought. (Yes, darling, I know. I'm horribly self-obsessed. In my own defense, I was barely eighteen at the time, and struggling to come out to my homophobic father as gay.)

Maxim finally stops vacuuming up his soup and dabs his rapidly healing mouth with his linen napkin. Of course, he's pure shifter, which means his injuries are healing at a furious pace. Table manners seem largely foreign to the Siberian kissy monster over there, but I've noticed he watches us all quite carefully, and imitates what he sees with some skill.

He may not be formally educated, but I'll admit (privately… if I must) that he's not a *complete* idiot.

"Cybelle was Messalina's only known child," Maxim says to Zara. "The fruit of a legal and legitimate union with her harem. However, there is more than rumor to suggest she had a bastard in secret—a daughter—when she was very young. This supporting information is, how would you say, classified? Only the Arcane Investigation Bureau has access."

"Fuck. Me." This is Racetrack's eloquent contribution, mumbled through her crusty baguette.

We've abruptly fallen silent enough in this *domus* that I can practically hear the snow fall in the moonlit street beyond our window.

This juicy dragonish tidbit certainly explains a great deal about our latest predicament. While each of my queen's courtiers is digesting that tidbit in his or her own way, I savor the fact that our dragon's just inserted his taloned foot into his sexy mouth.

"Now you're really gonna need to explain to me how you know that, Max," Zara says softly. She's leaning over the table, her glittery fingernails tapping a restless tattoo on the surface. "How you got access to classified AIB files. And why the fuck you kept it to yourself till just now."

He looks up at her, and his slitted pupils dilate. He may be accustomed to protecting his secrets (nearly as well as I do, so one mustn't hurl stones).

Still, he clearly grasps that our queen will judge him now by his honesty.

"I learned from my mother," he says curtly, with an utter lack of sentiment any sociopath would envy. "Sometimes she kills for them—the AIB. She kills for pleasure. She savors the hunt. But she barters her kills for secrets, which are a dragon's favorite treasure. This secret is one I overheard years ago. Long before I came to you."

"You kept all that pretty quiet, big guy," she breathes.

"I meant from the start to tell you. I was waiting for… the right moment." His dragonish face turns crafty. "For that moment when I knew you would trust me."

Her aqua eyes narrow to slits. "You mean you were waiting till we fucked."

"Yes," he agrees, with no attempt whatsoever at modesty. "I knew it would not take long."

Truly, this entire situation is intolerable.

They're clearly forming a mating bond, even though she doesn't want one. The latest indication of that detestable bond is the way my precious girl takes one long look into those crocodile eyes of his and inexplicably concludes this reptile is telling the truth.

Her willingness to believe him is a pill too bitter for me to stomach.

"And you actually believe the AIB tells the truth to *her*—your monstrous mother? Their glorified wet boy?" I sneer.

Now his uncanny eyes shift to me. "It is your father who told her. For it is he who leads them."

For perhaps the only occasion in my life, I'm actually stunned silent. My immediate impulse is to scoff at this preposterous allegation.

Except that I can't.

All my life, I've certainly suspected that my father does… oh, something or other… for the arcane government. Something very lucrative (obviously) that he never speaks of, and that no one ever asks about.

From time to time, it has crossed my diabolical mind to wonder whether it might be something he provides to the AIB that supplies the abundant family fortunes.

Of course, I haven't wasted a single brain cell thinking about that bloodless machine of a man who sired me in quite some time. Now it seems entirely plausible, knowing the man as I do, that Nikolai Romanov *would* inevitably lead whatever shadowy organization is currently lining his pockets.

While these thoughts are streaking along my cerebral superhighway, Ronin scoots closer on the bench and slips a discreet arm around my waist. One never cares to betray weakness, but I drop a stealthy hand to his denim-clad thigh under the table and allow myself to lean into the familiar comfort of his touch.

You doing okay there, bad boy? Zara whispers through our bond.

In deference to my prickly sensibilities, she hasn't rushed to my side, because she knows I'd despise appearing vulnerable in front of that dragon.

But her clever face is concerned. I'm the complete focus of her attention. If I want her bent over in our bedroom with her panties wrapped around her ankles, she's mine.

All mine.

In *all* the ways.

And I always do want her.

I'm barely even surprised, I tell her. *However, I fully intend to exorcise any residual family demons by fucking them out of my system later. Consider yourself forewarned.*

Not scared of you, Goblin King. Her pretty lips tilt in a smug smile. *I think you might actually be losing your villain superpowers. Because that promise sounds more like an incentive than an actual threat.*

Let's just wait and see how we manage, shall we? Feeling more like myself, I smirk at her, then shift my gaze to Lucius.

My big bad wolf sips his Hungarian red and looks thoughtful.

At last, he admits, "Of course, I too am familiar with these rumors of a bastard queen. It's an old legend, and one that has long lain dormant. I stumbled over the anomaly years ago in Messalina's academic file. According to her transcript, our sitting queen spent her junior year abroad in the Academy exchange program. Unfortunately, the exchange school she supposedly attended burned down years ago, and all its records with it."

"Hmmmm, the plot thickens," I murmur.

"Holy cow, Lucius." Neo pushes a worried hand through his soft curls. "Are you saying she might have used that whole ruse to conceal a pregnancy? Because my dad's privy to all the political dirty laundry in the witching world, and I've never heard even a whisper of anything like this."

"As the sitting queen, she certainly has the power and the influence to protect her secrets." Lucius perspires and broods into his wine. "It's conceivable she herself arranged the destruction of the exchange institution, once she became queen, to protect her alibi and cover her tracks."

"I don't get it. Why would she bother doing all that?" Zara straddles the bench next to Neo and steals a swig of wine from Lucius' glass, which he permits with a tolerant smile. We alphas enjoy pampering our mates, and he'd feed her by hand if she'd ever allow it. "I mean, she needs an heir, right?"

"Cybelle *was* the legal heir until the murder," Lucius reminds us. "Cybelle was unfortunately a weak heir and a weaker witch, which was surely among the reasons Messalina bore no other offspring to her sizable harem. She worried obsessively about challenges to Cybelle's rule."

"However, as I seem to recall mentioning to *someone*, illegitimate offspring can't ascend, according to centuries of witching world legal precedent." I skewer Maxim with a pointed look and wish it were one of my hidden blades. This is the very point I took such pains to explain to that flying dinosaur during my inspired lecture in the library. Immediately before my so-called student kissed me like he wanted to ruin me and transformed the entire lesson into such a calamitous debacle. He could have told me what he knew then about this classified information in the AIB's vault, yet he chose to remain silent.

For that deception, I intend to make him sorry.

The truth is, I dislike secrets intensely, unless I'm the one holding them.

"But if that's the case, if this rumored bastard can't ascend, and if the rumor itself is years old, then why the fuck did it just make front page news?" Zara demands. "That makes zero sense."

Obviously she's never been particularly enthusiastic about being chained to the throne (which is one of the things Anti-Monarchist Vasili 1.0 appreciated about her in the early days, even when otherwise I hated her guts). She essentially had to be coaxed by Lucius and Neo and her own tender conscience into agreeing to give up her freedom to save the four races, *et cetera*. She may have accepted that royal mission, but it hasn't certainly hasn't stopped her from harboring a not-so-secret resentment against her royal chains.

Well, if she didn't chafe against her constraints, she wouldn't be Zara.

"As to that, my dear," Lucius says mildly, "your antics in the skies above Las Vegas were not particularly well received by the Arcane Senate or the AIB, both of which have had to tidy up the matter. In the internet era, that hasn't been easy to do. They're still turning up the occasional TikTok or Instagram post and having to discredit the entire affair as a casino publicity stunt. In truth, they've had to produce an extensive disinformation campaign, to which your father has wisely contributed."

"Yeah, well, that's big of him. Considering that whole fiasco was actually my dad's fault." Zara snorts. "Talk about disinformation. It was literally entrapment. He lured my ex into the open, sprinkled the intel where he knew I'd find it, fucking tried to kidnap me, and then when I resisted, he decided to have me unalived—to put it in TikTok terms. I'm still not getting how any of that's my fault?"

"Oh, it's our fault for rising to the bait." I sigh. "How horribly tedious."

Truly, I'm starting to swing around toward appreciating Lucius' point of view on this entire wretched affair. If only we'd taken him (and Neo, with his political instincts) into our confidence in the first place and trusted them, quite possibly we would have ferreted out the trap.

Then this whole messy circus could have been avoided.

Including the bothersome intrusion of this kissing dragon into our bucolic and polyamorous happiness.

Lucius pats at his perspiring brow and slips out of his tweed coat, while I watch him disrobe with a degree of focus that's nearly psychotic. At this point in his cycle, he's so aroused he won't even meet my gaze.

Well, no matter.

He'll bend for me tonight, and we both damn well know it.

"There have always been those," he tells our queen, still doggedly avoiding my stare, "who say you're too headstrong, too impulsive, too reckless, too undisciplined to hold the throne. For those who doubt, these rumors of a hidden Aquarius queen possess a certain pernicious appeal. For all their magical weakness, at least the Aquarius are… well behaved."

"But what about this so-called rival?" Zara tosses the magazine on the table. Instantly my hand snakes out to claim it. "There isn't a pic or even a name in this article. Just this comment that some news outlet in Mongolia resurfaced the story. Assuming another candidate even exists, who'd actually want to take my place? And would they be strong enough to do the whole witching world messiah thing?"

Lucius tugs his tie loose and looks fretful. Clearly, the poor dear is having a hot flash. "Truly, the existence of any rival at all is impossible to confirm. As I've said, it's an old rumor, with just that single fresh clue to this so-called rival's whereabouts—Mongolia—a clue which seems rather too obvious to be believed."

"You think it's a setup? Someone wanting to lure Zara out from behind the wards… to blooming Mongolia?" Ronin scowls and tightens his arm around my waist. "Bloody hell."

An electric frisson of alarm hums between us. Based on the well-publicized evidence of Zara's latest exploits, a clever and determined adversary might certainly be tempted to bait their trap in a way that plays on our little queen's famously impulsive and headstrong nature to lure her into the open.

Out from beyond the wards, where she's vulnerable.

My chest tightens and the air floods with a sudden spike of my Mogadon pheromones, until the room simply reeks of aggression. Lucius bares his fangs, Maxim snarls into his soup, Ronin growls under his breath, and even Neo looks fierce. As for my girl, she looks… dangerously thoughtful.

Good God. I hope she isn't actually considering rising to this clumsy bait. That's certainly not how this little game is going to play out if I have anything to say about it.

Which, of course, I do.

"Mongolia, huh?" Zara says slowly. Her eyes narrow with interest. "Never been there. Normally I'd say wild horses couldn't keep me away."

Our entire cohort holds its collective breath.

"Zara," Lucius growls through his fangs. "I am undertaking certain inquiries on your behalf, but these things take time. It's really rather difficult to ascertain—"

"Relax, Teach." Her tight mouth softens in a wry grin. "I'm not about to hijack the jet and go haring off again—as much as I'd like to. I kinda learned my lesson about busting out of this joint and sneaking off on my own and leaving you guys behind the last time."

The tight clench of alarm in my chest loosens. The room's honed tension loses the worst of its edge.

"Thank Christ for that," Lucius sighs, his fangs retracting. He pats at his brow with his handkerchief.

"So I guess that means we wait—for now—and see what your mysterious inquiries turn up." Zara tucks her knees up to her chin, props her chin on her folded arms, and looks positively mutinous. "What am I supposed to do in the meantime? Just keep studying for my midterms like everything's hunky-dory?"

"Actually, studying for your midterms would be an admirable start." Lucius gives her a severe look which, knowing the precious girl as I do, will thoroughly dampen her pretty schoolgirl panties. "Demonstrate through your actions that you take your royal responsibilities seriously. And, for the love of God, kindly forego any more unsanctioned adventures in the outside world. Do these things, and perhaps this public discontent will die away on its own."

"That's one way to handle it," my queen says slowly. She unfolds to her feet and resumes her pacing. "Or we could take a more proactive approach."

Lucius looks alarmed all over again, but I'm intrigued.

"Tell us what sort of scheme you have brewing in your diabolical mind, darling, *do*," I purr.

"Well, I'm not flying off to Mongolia, for fuck's sake, but I *am* gonna hold my own arcane press conference right here at Icarus," she announces. "I'll officially announce that I'm accepting the whole queen gig. I've never done that, everyone's just assumed, and clearly it's time to put any doubts to rest. And I'm gonna do it live on WNN."

"You're going to make your television debut on the Witching News Network?" I'm instantly delighted by the entire notion. "Well, all publicity *is* good publicity, as they say. I dare say you'll make prime time."

"Would they even let you do that, cobber?" Dez asks. She's helping Racetrack clear the table, since RT has cleanup duty tonight, but she waits to hear Zara's reply.

"I'm not asking for permission," Zara says curtly. "I'm the fucking queen."

"You're the queen-in-waiting," Neo says, with an apologetic look at his fated mate. "There's a difference, babe. Your legal authorities are pretty limited until you actually ascend."

"You planning to ask, like, the current queen?" Racetrack pipes up from the kitchen. "About your whole press conference master plan?"

"Yeah, no." Zara snorts. "The current queen hasn't exactly been making overtures my way, has she? For all we know, she's in on this rumor resurfacing. She could actually be plotting to put her hypothetical bastard on the throne. And the Aquarius reign's running the four races straight to extinction. So, no, we're not asking."

"But would WNN even run your gig without her say-so?" Dez wonders.

"We're a constitutional monarchy with an elected Senate, not a dictatorship, right, Lucius?" Zara shrugs. "I'm like the Prince of Wales. Right now I may be powerless—you know, politically. But clearly, as we've seen, I'm newsworthy. Like Vasili said, if I call a press conference, we'll probably make prime time."

"But you haven't much fancied that whole queen bit, have you, love?" Ronin points out. "You're not tempted by the notion someone else could shift this whole burden right off your shoulders?"

"Not in this sneaky, underhanded way." Zara scoops up her own dirty bowl and silverware and hands them off to Racetrack, then starts collecting the rest of the dirty crockery in a highly unqueenlike fashion. "If some mystery chick turned out to be an aboveboard candidate who wanted the best for the four races, wouldn't she just come forward and say so? Or if she's aboveboard and *doesn't* want the throne, she could come forward and say that, and bury all these rumors."

"Our little queen makes a fair point," I muse. "I've already skimmed the relevant article, which is sensationalistic and poorly written, of course. Beyond that rather glaring attribution to an unnamed source in Mongolia, the piece contains nothing more of merit.

Ronin's still leaning against my shoulder and reading it himself.

Now I'm newly distracted by the aggravating way that rutting dragon across the way keeps eye-fucking my boyfriend.

Doesn't he realize Ronin only flirted with him in the kitchen because that's what Zara wanted?

It's not as though Ronin reciprocates his interest.

I glare at the dragon and, holding his stare the whole time, lean in to drag my serpentine tongue along the rim of Ronin's ear. Needless to say, this is an intimacy my boyfriend accepts with a sexy murmur.

I'm marking my territory, as it were.

"Nope." Standing in the kitchen doorway, Zara folds her arms and pops one sexy hip. "If this rival exists, I don't trust the bitch. This is a huge important deal for the whole witching world. Whose ass sits on that throne—it fucking *matters*. I might not have seen that at first, but now it's pretty fucking crystal. The future of the arcane races could literally depend on it, and I'm gonna go with my gut."

"I'll have to clear your notion of a press conference with the Dean," Lucius frets, and raises a hand when she starts to protest. "Yes, Zara, I must. At the very least, the Dean will have to approve a damned WNN news crew passing through the wards. And your statement will be stronger, and viewed more seriously, if you have this Academy standing behind you."

My royal darling doesn't like being told what to do, but she trusts Lucius, and her chin dips in a reluctant nod. "Yeah, I guess that makes sense. But if she won't play ball, you tell her I'm not giving up, and she won't like what I try next. Like Neo said, we can't afford to ignore this. The arcane races are literally dying. That means the succession's too important."

"At least pass your midterms first," our headmaster pleads. "If I tell the Dean we'll schedule the event for minimal academic upheaval after midterms next week, and that your academic performance will demonstrate your commitment, I may be able to secure her consent. This is a reasonable request, my dear, and you know it."

"Fine," she sighs. "That's Wednesday night then. Five nights from now. Right while I'm dealing with my fucking heat. I'll agree to it because it's you asking, Lucius. But you talk to her, okay? I mean, it's probably after her bedtime so, like, tomorrow? Tell her I'll pass the goddamn midterms—I swear to fuck I'll pass them, Neo will help me study, won't you, babe?"

"We can start tonight," Neo says happily. Because he's happy when Zara's happy.

For him, happiness truly is that simple.

Whatever was troubling him last night, when I pierced his ear and made him blow his load, seems to be no longer an issue.

Hopefully he isn't regretting what he let me do to him. Because once I get Lucius and Zara and Ronin through their heats and this damned press conference in our rearview mirror, Mercury and I have some unfinished business of our own to conclude in Zara's big medieval bed.

"Fine." Now that her mind's made up, our girl's already powering toward Neo's study nook in the corner, where he's commandeered half the textbooks in the entire *domus* for his monster study sessions. "But I want this shindig set up. And I'm gonna need all of you to help me make it happen. I wanna make Wednesday night prime time on WNN a total goddamn spectacle."

Hmmm, that sounds promising.

So my queen wants a spectacle, does she?

Well, she's certainly come to the right warlock.

To begin, she's going to need something a bit more… dynamic… than a mere press conference. Something a bit more, shall we say, high concept? Fortunately, with all that accession law and arcane precedent fresh in my mind after delivering my underappreciated lecture for that ungrateful dragon's benefit, I already have a concept taking shape for this Wednesday night spectacle that will command the entire witching world's complete and unwavering attention.

Chapter Twenty-One
Maxim

Ancient Accession Rituals of the Witching World

I labor to peck out the title of my essay with two fingers on the antique typewriter in the *domus* library.

Because I am self-taught, my handwriting is not what it should be (for instance, legible). Vasili has taken one disdainful look at my first handwritten attempt and announced that the only way he will deign to grade my essays is if I type them.

And, as I have observed, computers do not function behind the island wards.

The flat *tap!* as each letter flies up to strike the carriage echoes through the silent room, barely lit by a lick of fire in the grate and the branch of candles flickering on the old-fashioned table where I am working. Zara has been practicing her lightning on the roof with Lucius, because lightning magic will be part of her midterms.

And she is holding nothing back.

Consequently, the power seems to be out all over the island tonight.

Vasili is draped over the big Victorian wingback by the fire, completely absorbed in whatever antiquarian tome is spread open across his lap, one booted leg dangling over the upholstered arm in a way that silhouettes the supple line of his thigh against the fire. It is as though he is inviting someone to kneel beside his boot and nibble their way up that long leg of his.

Even worse, I am virtually certain he is wearing a corset under his Renaissance velvet coat, which is truly so distracting I can barely type.

But it is surely Lucius he is wearing lingerie for tonight, and not me. Lucius has been working feverishly with Zara all night, but our headmaster is definitely in heat. After the way Vasili was devouring Lucius with his eyes at dinner, I expected Vasili to shove our headmaster facedown over the dining room table and start pumping into him before we could even clear the room.

Abruptly Vasili's head snaps around to pin me with his contemptuous stare. With a start, I realize I have stopped typing.

I am staring at him.

"Searching for the correct choice of word, Mr. Rasputin?" he bites out, every syllable chiseled from ice. "Need I remind you that I expect to see an adequate five-hundred-word essay before you're excused for the night?"

With a sigh, I return to my two-fingered pecking at the round metal keys and my labored description of the ritual combats our ancient queens once undertook when they ascended. At least Vasili is still willing to teach me these things.

Truly, I cannot imagine why I ever kissed him, why I gave way to this forbidden impulse and indulged this forbidden temptation and committed this forbidden sin, except that I am in rut myself.

Tonight, we are both very careful to keep our distance.

A dark whiff of ambergris twines into my nostrils, and my dragon rumbles with interest. I sneak an upward look, as I toil over my English, to see Ronin Pendragon idle into the den.

He is still wearing the ripped jeans and silky shirt he wore at dinner, when he whispered in my ear and admired my piercings. Only now that shirt is unbuttoned halfway down his chest, which gives me a searing eyeful of that black dragon tattooed across his tawny skin.

I swallow hard, because suddenly my mouth is dry. It is as though he has branded his body, branded himself specifically for me and my dragon to possess.

In truth, it is far more likely that he is branded for my sovereign and her dragon queen.

Since he does not even like me.

Covertly I watch between my painstaking keystrokes as he idles across the room, so supple and predatory he makes my heart pound, to where Vasili is reading by firelight. He leans over the back of Vasili's chair to read over his shoulder. My teacher reaches back absently to slide a hand down Ronin's leg.

"Are you all right, darling?" Vasili murmurs, so tender for such a terrible warlock. "How's your heat?"

"Good for a bit yet." Ronin sifts an affectionate hand through Vasili's moussed and layered rock-star hair with an easy familiarity I marvel at. "Lucius fucked me so hard earlier I can still barely walk. You reading about royal coronations?"

"Hmmm." It is obvious to both of us that Vasili is deeply absorbed in his reading. Still, he is a good alpha, even if he is only part shifter. "Do come and fetch me if you need a fuck."

It still shocks me that they are so open, all of them, with these forbidden passions. I have to remind myself repeatedly there is no custom or religion here that forbids it. Our own queen is known to be bisexual, but her last female lover betrayed her, and she has taken no female lovers into her harem. (I have already concluded the other women who share this house are only with each other and seem to have no interest in the men.)

Trying to keep my mind on my business, I coax out a question mark (the key is reluctant and sticking), manually return the carriage, and prepare to embark on a fresh paragraph.

This task proves very difficult, because now Ronin Pendragon is drifting in my direction. Moving slowly, he circles the table, the fingers of one hand gliding across the surface.

And all I can think about is how sinful those fingers would feel gliding across my skin.

Softly he steals up beside me.

I concentrate fiercely just to type and not to stiffen.

No worries, mate. His silky tenor slides through my thoughts. *Not going to trouble your back.*

"It is… no trouble… when I permit it." The words are thick in my throat, but they are true. I enjoyed Zara's touch on my back last night, once I accustomed myself to it.

Would I be permitted, then? If I wanted? Ronin asks.

I sneak an upward look at Vasili, who appears to be utterly engrossed in his reading, just as he has been all night. Yet I am under no delusion that my viperish teacher is unaware of any tiny detail that transpires here between his cherished lover and his hated rival.

I clear my throat and say hoarsely, "Yes."

"Good dragon," Ronin whispers.

My beast purrs for him.

Ronin trails the very tips of two fingers lightly up my biceps to graze the deltoid muscle. I have changed from my torn uniform into the familiar comfort of my worn tee shirt, so the heat of his touch scorches my bare skin.

He is ours, Maxim, my dragon puffs through a ribbon of steam. *We have been waiting for this one. It is no sin for us to claim him.*

My dragon knows nothing of morality. He cares nothing for propriety. He possesses nothing like a conscience.

He is a creature of animal instinct and visceral need.

I swallow hard and focus on finishing the sentence I am toiling over, before the thought flies out of my head entirely. This becomes even more difficult when those two Pendragon fingers sneak under my worn sleeve to trace the flex of my triceps and glide over the thin line of one of my scars.

Goosebumps sheet across my shoulders and my breath snags.

Now typing is completely out of the question.

I can barely even breathe.

"Easy," Ronin whispers, so softly, under the fire's crackle. "You're all right."

"Yes." I bow my head under his touch. My dragon, too, lies down for him.

We submit together to this graceful touch that strokes over the bridge of my shoulder, covered by the worn cotton, then glides across the naked back of my neck. I am thankful beyond words for the concealing barrier of the table between us, because a tingling heat is rushing to my groin. Does he know… does he know how much I want him… how much I want him to share what I will have with Zara…?

I'm a telepath. His warm voice in my head is amused. *There isn't much I don't know. But there can never be anything like that between us, love. Not unless you and Vasili—*

"Finished with your essay?" Vasili's serrated voice curls through the air like a whiplash. "Let's see if what you've written is any good."

"Yes—I am—nearly finished." Hastily I tap out a few closing words while Ronin drops his hand and recedes out of reach with a secret smile that only distracts me worse. I sense that he enjoys teasing me like this, teasing both of us, watching both of us lose our minds over him.

Truly, this man threatens to cause more trouble than Helen of Troy.

With all this tension bristling in the air, Vasili and I will be launching flights of flaming arrows at each other and rolling out the Trojan horse in no time—

"Stop ogling him and bring that essay here," Vasili snaps.

I am dutifully unrolling my typed essay from the carriage when the electric whiff of roses and arousal floods into the room, accompanied by the quick echo of my sovereign's hurried step. My entire body tingles with the charge of her presence.

Zara blows into the room like a hurricane.

My dragon coils up to sit and trumpets a welcome.

My queen is always a revelation, no matter what she wears. Tonight she is glorious. Her teal curls are swept up in a regal pile on her head. Platinum lightning bolts flash in her ears. She has abandoned her innocent schoolgirl uniform for attire that screams sex. Her showgirl curves are poured into a strapless electric blue latex dress that clings to her lush breasts and tiny waist and barely covers her curvy hips, paired with sleek go-go boots fashioned from silver leather.

She isn't wearing stockings or a brassiere.

I am not even certain she is wearing panties.

Abruptly I lose all interest in my essay. Ronin growls under his breath and undresses her with his burning eyes. Even Vasili closes his book and sits up with a predatory gleam in his basilisk stare.

"Everyone get dressed," my queen announces. Her eyes spark cobalt with energy and her bubblegum lips curl in a grin. "You too, Maxim. We're going to a party."

"What party is that, darling?" Vasili drawls. "I'm already wearing my party dress."

"Yes, you are, bad boy." She swanks over and drapes herself sexily across his villainous lap. "You look *very* pretty tonight, Goblin King. Way too pretty to waste on a Friday night at home. The cohort at Villa Hadrian is having a birthday bash for Mallory McSnicker. RT just told me. She and Dez are both going."

"The Hufflepuffs." My teacher sneers, which is not easy to do while he is also simultaneously purring because Zara is nuzzling his neck. "Those hapless halfwits have never thrown a proper party in the history of the Icarus Academy. They're hardly going to begin now, playing *Sixteen Candles* for Mallory McSnicker. Besides…" Without warning, his spiteful gaze swerves to skewer me. "I'm not taking the Siberian kissy monster to the freshman dance."

"The… what?" My face burns with an uncomfortable heat.

Saints of the northern steppes. I am blushing.

"You heard me." Vasili sweeps me a look of utter disdain. "For all I know, you'll kiss me again."

"If I do, you will kiss me back." Now I am provoked and scowling. "Again."

The next time, I swear to him in ferocious silence, *I will not kiss you. It will be you who kisses me.*

"Mmmm, big guy, sign me up for that," Zara murmurs, squirming in Vasili's lap in a way that must be giving him a ferocious boner.

I wonder if she is hearing me through our bond.

I clear my throat and open my mouth to ask.

"Silence!" Vasili's eyes flash atomic with rage. "Mr. Rasputin, utter one more scurrilous syllable and I'll clap you in detention." His nuclear stare shifts to Zara and he softens. "Sorry, darling, but I'm staying in."

"But why?" Zara looks adorable when she pouts.

If she were in my lap, I swear I would fuck that pout right off her.

"Need you ask?" Vasili slides a slow finger along the upper swells of her breasts, which makes her shiver and floods the air with our queen's mating scent. "Aside from the fact that I can think of nothing more tedious than another Hufflepuff party? Lucius is going into heat. He's resisting it, of course, but nature will find a way, *et cetera*. In case it's escaped your notice, all is not exactly sunshine and roses between Lucius and me these days. He's been holding me off. Tonight, that's going to change."

"Shit." Zara's pout vanishes and the witchy light in her eyes dims. "You're right, of course you're right. I was thinking it would be good to show my face in public after that magazine piece. You know everyone on this island's seen that rag by now. I want to show the whole school we're strong as fuck, and we're not going anywhere, and anyone who goes up against us should be fucking terrified."

"Too right," Ronin mutters.

He slips up beside me to appreciate the sight of Zara and Vasili entwined and overflowing from the wingback—my nemesis wrapped in rose velvet and sneering horribly at me with the tips of his fangs peeking through glossy lips, my sovereign sleek and confident in electric blue latex and kilometers of suntanned skin.

"Anyway," Zara sighs. "I can't pry Neo away from his books until after midterms. And Lucius would never go to a student party. You're right that he'll need you here tonight, Goblin King. I should've thought of that, but I'm not really thinking straight myself. It's all these hormones. We'll all just stay in—"

"I will go with you to this party, my queen." I seize my moment like a gift from God and arrow across the room to press my essay into Vasili's suddenly reluctant hand. "This one can grade my essay and tend to Lucius' heat."

Vasili gives me a poisonous look. "I beg your pardon, Mr. Rasputin—"

"Your strategy is a sound one. And you should not stray far from at least one of your alphas tonight, my sovereign." I gaze down on the sight of my half-naked queen tumbled across my rival alpha's lap. "There is your own heat to consider, yes? So if you wish to go to this party, I will take you." I turn to include Ronin. "I will also take you."

"It's not a bad notion to be seen," Ronin says into the fraught silence my words have opened. "For all the reasons you've just mentioned, love. With Dez and Racetrack and Max and me, you'd have half your court beside you."

"This dragon," Vasili says coldly, "is *not* a member of your court."

"I share the queen's roof. That makes me one of her courtiers, by accepted custom." I try not to sound argumentative and even manage a sly smile as I cleverly use his own argument. "This fact was in your witching world law lecture, Master Romanov."

"Hmmm." Vasili pouts at our queen curled in his lap. "Well, that may be. But he's certainly *not* one of your alphas."

"He could be, though… couldn't he?" Ronin pads past me to crouch at Vasili's feet. "If she decides she wants him, he's in. Lucius has already accepted him, or he'd never have brought Max here. Lucius literally brought him into this *domus* so Zara's dragon and Max's could fuck. And you know Red's happy with whatever Zara fancies. We're all mainly waiting for the two of you—you and Max—to figure your broody alpha shit out."

"Darling, you're in heat yourself." Vasili heaves a long-suffering sigh. "Both of you are off-the-charts hormonal. Why am I the only one who seems to comprehend this biological fact? For all his numerous shortcomings, this flying designer handbag is an alpha. Therefore, it stands to reason that you're both hot for him. It's basic biology."

While I hold my tongue and try not to look offended (even though he called me a flying handbag and claims it is only hormones that make these two want me), Ronin toys with the laces tied in a pretty bow above the alluring bulge of Vasili's breeches and smolders up at both his lovers with smoking eyes. Looking thoughtful, Zara licks her luscious lips and leans in to nuzzle Vasili's ear.

I have the distinct sense that these two are working together to placate their irritated alpha.

Or, possibly, they are working to reassure him.

At last, my nemesis heaves a sigh and flourishes an exasperated hand. "Oh, very well. Date him if you *must*, darlings. Only until your heats pass and not a moment longer. If you fuck him, either he gets tested first, or everyone wears a condom."

My heart hammers with shock.

Then my spirits shoot up with a cautious spurt of optimism. My dragon launches to his feet with a surprised bugle.

This is so much less than I want.

But it is also so much more than I have dared to hope.

Ronin hides a grin of triumph by resting his forehead against Vasili's knee. He captures Vasili's restless hand and presses a lingering kiss to his boyfriend's inner wrist. This, Vasili allows him to do.

As for my Zara, still tucked up in my enemy's lap, she sucks in a noisy breath and looks as though she is about to protest that she wants to do any such offensive thing as date me.

Much less fuck me.

For my part, I wish to protest the condom. There is no need. I am not diseased. And mine is not a cock that takes kindly to such encumbrances.

"How. Ever." One flash from Vasili's icy eyes freezes the hot words that hover on Zara's lush lips and vaporizes the cold protest on mine. He spears me with a warning finger and glares straight at me. "That dragon is *not* part of this polycule. He will never be part of it—never be one of us—unless we all explicitly agree, Lucius and Neo included. Which, at the present time, we all too clearly *don't.*"

Chapter Twenty-Two
Ronin

When Zara struts her stuff into the Hufflepuff bash like the badass queen of the witching world she is, with half her court lined up at her back, I'm still swinging like a yoyo between anger over this rumored queen bullshit and total fucking shock that Vasili's actually willing to grant "friends with benefits" privileges (even temporarily) to his hated rival.

Honestly speaking, I never for a tick expected he'd actually agree.

I was just hoping to hurry things along a bit, for everyone's sake. To get us through Zara's superheat, it's bloody crystal she needs dragon cock.

Whereas Lucius wants the world's only male dragon shifter to have a proper education, which will only happen if that dragon stallion and our dragon queen find some way to rub along together.

Plus, yeah, I'm not quite ready to admit it, but I'm starting to feel a wee bit of a gooey spot in my own tattered heart for this scarred and scrappy stray we seem to have picked up.

And despite all Vasili's sneaky efforts to guard this particular secret from me—his telepathic and deeply bonded boyfriend—he hasn't stopped thinking about that dragon, one way or another, since Max flew straight into our shared life together, literally breathing fire.

So because we're a polycule—and not the open-ended kind, we don't have random fucks drifting in and out of our bed—we're all waiting on Max and Vasili to figure out their shit. (That's assuming they can.)

Well, gods know I've done my bit to help matters along.

Right now, it's Zara who's got my full focus.

Villa Hadrian's the biggest residential college at Icarus, but the cohort here's pretty mediocre in the witchcraft department. They're basically the Hufflepuff contingent (at least according to Vasili, who's definitely our resident Slytherin). But this crumbling ruin of a Roman villa perched high on the harbor cliff, leaning over the edge like it's about to lose its balance and topple into the foamy sea, is barely inhabited and the closest thing this island has to an actual haunted house.

Consistent with that whole house-of-horrors theme, they've got an actual ruined speakeasy in the basement, dating back to the reign of terror of some long-ago headmaster who tried to outlaw booze and frolic. Centuries before that, this basement was a fucking dungeon.

If you look close enough, you'll probably still find bloodstains soaked into the flagstone floor.

This cheerful place is where the Hadrian lot have their keggers.

Tonight, this spooky basement with its cobwebby rafters and shadowy corners looks even spookier than usual, due to the power being out all over the island. The Hufflepuffs have stuck dripping candles to every available surface for lighting and dragged a bunch of steel barrels with burning garbage inside the joint for heat. Someone's dug up an old-fashioned, battery-operated boombox that's cranking out axe-murder metal (because when you've got a good thing going thematically, you might as well lean into it).

The liquor's flowing from the bootleg bar, and a bunch of kids are already packed into the open space grooving to the edgy Halloween tunes among rows of crumbling pillars, mountains of dusty packing crates whose contents everyone's forgotten, and the eerie as fuck cavy grottoes that function as rainwater cisterns for the villa.

Right away, I've got my eye on those bullies from Villa Tiberius, lurking like cockroaches near the bar.

Pretty sure they're the buggers who ambushed Maxim. If those fucks go anywhere near him or Zara tonight, I'm going medieval with my witchcraft. I'd rather fancy blistering some Aquarius arse.

Not that my girl needs me playing defense.

Zara's carving a confident path straight through the dancers to the gift table where the birthday girl's hanging out. Whenever anyone gets a little too close for comfort, violet sparks snap from my girl's fingers. Which pretty much means my classmates are falling over their own feet trying to clear out of her way in the crowded space.

It suddenly occurs to me that maybe Zara's accidental lightning strike, the one that downed the Academy power line and knocked this whole rock off the grid, wasn't actually an accident.

After what happened to Max today, I wouldn't put it past my girl to give this whole island a wee warning.

Just to remind them what kind of electrical havoc a pissed-off Gemini queen can wreak.

I'm not guarding my thoughts, I rarely do with her, so Zara tosses me a laughing look over one sleek bare shoulder as we edge through the mob. Candlelight flashes on her wicked lightning bolt earring and pools in her big Betty Boop eyes.

"I'd *never* do such a thing," she calls above the grinding beat. "I'm not a hooligan, I'm a law-abiding queen. I have to set an example. And shame on you for thinking I'd go rogue."

"Whatever you say, love," I call back with a grin.

Have I mentioned I fucking love being mated to such a badass?

Our queen eels through the scrum, careful to protect the gift-wrapped box she's thrown together with a nice repurposed gift for Mallory McSnicker, who's a shy Luna Lovegood sort and never causes any trouble (though she had a pesky crush on me freshman year, which I never requited—no challenge to it—so the birthday girl's not one of my one-and-dones).

As soon as my queen dials down the amperage so I won't get a jolt, I wrap an arm round Zara's latex-sheathed waist and tuck her up against my front to avoid getting separated from her in this mosh pit.

Then I reach back to get a good grip on Maxim's hand and tow the skittish dragon after me through the tight crowd.

In my periphery I've got a glimpse of Dez and Racetrack peeling off, Dez already shimmying to the tunes and really showing off her moves in her sparkly party frock, while RT snags a pair of longnecks from a big bin full of ice.

Maxim presses up behind me (which I don't exactly mind) and mutters in my ear, "This is chaos. Why is this appealing?"

"Just a bunch of kids blowing off steam before midterms." I tighten my grip on his hand so he doesn't freak out over all these clueless fucks violating his personal space. "Don't you have parties like this in Siberia?"

The look on his face makes it pretty fucking clear they don't.

At least not in the part of Siberia this bloke hails from.

His slitted pupils are all telescoped wide, and his mouth is set in a ruthless line, and the healing ring of his black eye adds a nice touch of violence to the whole effect. He's got his blond hair raked back in the sleek braid that gives his cold Nordic face that Russian *bratva* vibe. Yet despite the leather jacket and spiked belt and shitkicker boots he's thrown over his ripped jeans and that form-fitting charcoal tee I'm ready to peel off his sinewy frame with my teeth, he's jittery under all that attitude.

Tonight he's my date. Mine and Zara's.

Vasili said so.

To be honest, I'm starting to feel a bit protective of the chap. Like I'm catching feelings or some shit.

Surely not.

Zara finally wiggles her way through the crush and gives her gift and a warm hug to Mallory. While the two girls chat, Max and I hang back and scope out the scene. Yeah, those Villa Tiberius bastards are out in force, most sporting some sort of Aquarius bling—a tee shirt, a bit of statement jewelry, an exposed tattoo. These chumps were Cybelle's old court, so it's not too surprising they're all kitted out with Aquarius gear. It's not even treason since Messalina's skinny ass still warms the throne, and she's (supposedly) the last Aquarius queen.

But the sheer prevalence of all that in-your-face Aquarius bullshit is a blatant insult to Zara.

It tells me she's right as fuck about showing our faces tonight. Clearly they've all read that shit in *The Witching Inquisitor*.

Which means they all need a proper reminder that Zara's the queen-in-waiting. Except she's not fucking waiting. She's embraced her fate, she's the next fucking queen, and she's not backing down an inch.

She's forcing that whole succession issue.

She's upping the stakes.

That's something the whole witching world will see in spades on Wednesday.

Now that Zara's set up shop, more of the Hadrian lot start drifting past, all finding some way to chat up my girl and generally signaling they're not openly in league with the Tiberius gang.

At least not yet.

The thing about the Hadrians is, they're survivors. They'll wait and see how this whole queen vs. queen throwdown goes down.

Then they'll back the winning side.

While Zara makes nice with Mallory and the Hufflepuffs (because it's good to have allies, especially when you're on their turf), I keep a proper grip on Maxim, who looks like he's ready to slink off and hide in a corner. Clearly this dragon isn't used to school parties (since he doesn't seem used to school). Just as clearly, he's not too chipper about having me hold his hand in public, which maybe feels a bit too *Little House on the Prairie* for the bloke.

So I free the dragon, but I tuck him up next to me and loop a casual hand through the back pocket of his battered jeans in a way that isn't remotely *Little House* but still says *Private Property: Hands Off* to stake my claim.

He shifts about a bit under my touch, but at least he holds his shit together and doesn't freak out openly over me touching him, which is important if he's auditioning to join the harem.

Maybe he's not comfy admitting it or putting a label on it, but he likes my hands on his body. He definitely doesn't seem as skittish about his arse as he is about his back.

And I don't exactly mind the tight flex of his glute under my straying palm.

I get lots of attention myself at these social things, like a proper Leo. Given my history, I'm an urban legend at this Academy. Not to mention my snug leather pants and half-open shirt and roaring dragon tattoo and all this hair spilling halfway to my butt are pretty much guaranteed to catch the eye.

Which means my proprietary grip on Max's arse is generating plenty of interest.

After tonight, half this school's going to fancy he's another of my one-and-dones (even though I don't have one-and-dones anymore, not since joining the harem).

But I don't give a single flaming fuck.

If I can just coax this surly dragon and my temperamental boyfriend to kiss and make up, then persuade Zara to okay the whole setup, pretty sure Maxim Rasputin's going to be the next addition to the Gemini queen's harem.

Because we need him.

We need his strength.

We need the last male dragon shifter as one of the Gemini kings.

The fact that Zara craves dragon cock to fill her needy pussy and I'm more than a bit interested in filling an orifice or two myself with that exotic junk he's rocking?

Let's not get distracted. Those are just bonus bennies.

The music shifts from that grindy Halloween axe-murder shit to some techno with a decent beat. Now Zara's swiveling her sexy hips in that little dress while she admires Mallory's birthday haul. My girl's hot as fuck tonight, with her heat looming.

I'm starting to feel a few good licks of heat myself, pulsing in my balls, streaking like sunbursts from my dick up my abs and down my thighs.

That's my own blooming heat kicking in.

Next to me, Maxim's laser-focused on Zara. Those dragon eyes are all narrowed and his slitted pupils are blown wide.

I lean in close so he can hear me, though his shifter senses seem pretty keen, I get my lips up against his pierced ear (and, yeah, maybe I have an ulterior motive for that). "Wanna help me get her out on the dance floor, love?"

His golden eyes veer to mine. All of a sudden, he's all hunter, fixated and intense as fuck.

"Yes," he growls.

"Man of few words. I quite fancy that in a bloke." I grin at all that sexy, give his tight ass a squeeze, slide my hand out of his pocket, and sidle up behind Zara to wrap my arms round her waist. Her creamy scent's just flooding the air, way more potent than the stale odors of spilled beer and potato chips creeping from the bar or the stink of kerosene blasting from the burning barrels.

That potent hit of her Mogadon pheromones wraps round my dick like a hand and squeezes.

Fuck. Me.

Looks like we both need a fuck.

I open the door in my mind to Max so he can sense what I'm sensing. This sort of shit's easy for me, since I'm Valyrian, and that dragon's so focused on both of us he's not even resisting all this intimacy.

I match the sway of my hips to Zara's and say over her shoulder to innocent Mallory, "Happy Birthday, Hufflepuff. Mind if I take our queen off your hands for a bit?"

"For your information, Ronin, I'm a Gryffindor. Don't let the name fool you." But Mallory's a sweet kid, even with a family moniker like McSnicker, and she turns away from my forever unattainable self to give Zara a wistful smile. "Have fun, you two. Or, should I say, you three? Or five? Just be careful tonight, okay? I mean it. That Tiberius gang's sharpening their knives."

"Thanks, Mal. Enjoy yourself tonight. We definitely plan to." Zara pivots smoothly to face me and wraps her arms round my neck.

I growl and tuck her sweet pinup girl curves up tight against my boner. My heat's definitely choosing this exact moment to wake up after being fucked into a sex meltdown by Lucius. Too bad both the alphas who usually fuck me through my heats with their biochemically optimized shifter spunk are all the way cross town tonight.

Bollocks.

Wonder how hard I'd have to work to persuade Maxim to do the honors?

"Just so we're clear," Zara says pointedly as I coax her onto the floor, "*I* still haven't agreed to the dragon. Aside from that fucking superheat I'm still not ready to roll over for, he knew about that fucking rumor and he fucking kept it quiet. Who knows what else he's hiding?"

"Yeah, he did keep it close to his chest. And it's your call," I tell her, because that's always been true, from Day fucking One. "You gonna mind if I play with him a bit? Since Vasili gave his okay?"

"Hmmm." Psi fire flares in her eyes. "No, Adam, I don't mind if you play with the dragon. I even asked Neo for you before we left. He knows you're in heat. He's all good with it."

And that's your cue, love, I tell the watching dragon, who's been listening in this whole time. *No touching her, leastwise till she trusts you. But you can touch me all you like. And our girl, she likes to watch.*

He's still a bit shy in front of the crowd, what with all that religious baggage he's toting about. But Zara's hot as fuck. She raises her arms overhead and sways for me, her smoking stare never leaving mine, my hands all over her lush ass so I can fit her up against my boner.

The first light brush of Max's hands against my waist from behind is all tentative, like he's afraid I'm going to push him away. But Vasili said yes, and now Zara has, and Neo. And Lucius said yes to all this the day he brought Max home.

We've checked all the boxes.

Fuck if I'm pushing him away. He's got a place with us… someday… if he and Vasili and Zara ever work out their problems.

Which, admittedly, is a pretty hefty *if.*

You feel so nice, Max, I whisper to encourage him. *And our girl's watching.*

If there's one thing you can bank on with Zara, it's that she loves seeing her guys in action. Her confidence and generosity are part of what I love most about her, what we all love. She doesn't need to be the center of every scene, even though as queen, she easily could be.

Instead, she wants that for whoever needs it most at the time.

Right now, she's got my heat top of mind, plus the fact that Max is lonely. Her witchy eyes are totally riveted on the two of us. When Max shimmies up behind me till we're all breathing musk and dragon, then nudges his cock against my ass, Zara's pupils flare wide and a breathless moan spills from her parted lips.

I lean down to catch that sexy sound in my mouth. My tongue plunges deep into my girl's slick cinnamon-flavored mouth for a long lick.

Her eyes fall closed and her hands coast down her body, fingers spreading to caress her tits on the way down.

Fuck, that's hot.

Me, with my heat kicking in? I'm pretty fucking fixated—on her, always, everyfuckingday—but also on Max and that shifter boner he's packing. I got a good look at his gear back in Vegas, and he feels fucking potent tucked up against me, all forked and hard and barby. Especially when he slides his hands under the bottom of my button-down and spreads his palms over my bare abs.

My dick shoves against my zipper and a groan rips from my throat.

"Ronin," he whispers in my ear, all strained and hoarse. "Am I… is this… permitted?"

"Fuck, Max, yeah." I plaster Zara up against my front, all curves and sweat and latex, and grind my ass against the hard lean lines of the dragon behind me. "Let me feel you."

Let us both feel you, love.

It's crowded and chaotic and dark as fuck on this dance floor, everyone bumping up against everyone, and those flaming barrels are kicking out major smoke. Under all that camouflage, he bends to rub his face along the side of my neck. He needs to shave (or not, I fucking love his glittery gold stubble) and he's rubbing his mating scent into my neck and growling and, gods, now he's bloody licking the sweat off my skin and nipping a line of slow hot kisses up my neck.

He's tentative at first, still afraid I'll push him away, but the feel of his mouth on my body makes my dick ache. Then he finds a spot he likes, right where my neck curves into my trapezius muscle, and sucks a love bite into my skin.

My teeth clench and my hips punch forward. Zara tucks up against me and rides my cock, her leg twining around mine, my hand locking under her naked thigh to help her balance. Her silky skin's so hot with her temp spiking that her heat burns my fingers.

Bollocks. It doesn't feel like she's wearing panties.

If she isn't, all she needs to do is unzip me (because I never wear anything underneath) and I can push a few inches inside her and get in a few pumps, right here on this dance floor, without anyone much noticing.

"No, I want them to notice," she says, thick and throaty as she rides my cock in time with the heavy beat. "If I wanna fuck my warlocks in front of half the witching world, who's gonna make me stop? I'm your fucking queen."

Have I mentioned I'm in love with this girl?

Because I totally bloody am.

I'd burn the world down for her.

For all of us.

"Gods on the mountain, that's hot as fuck." I swallow hard to clear my throat. "Go ahead and unzip me, Max. You know you want to. No one here's going to stop you."

He's still sucking on my neck, I'm going to have a blasted hickey, and if I let him mark me, gods, I'll never hear the end of it from Vasili. But Max groans against my skin and slips my button and slides down the zipper of my leather pants, just the way I tell him.

He breathes hard against my skin and wraps a hot hand around my throbbing cock.

It's pretty obvi he's never done this before, not with a guy, but he's so eager to do it with me that it overrides all that first-time shyness lurking under his tough-guy persona. And I'm so hot for it myself I almost spurt in his hand.

Shit. My head falls back against his chest with a groan. I pump into his fist and drag Zara's sexy body closer to both of us.

"Cheese on toast, that's so hot," she pants. "The two of you."

My dick, with Max's hand wrapped around me and stroking, shoves up against her crotch. I'm still not feeling any panties under that latex dress, and every brush of her inner thighs against my cock makes fireworks go off in my head. She's wiggling in time with the beat and she's massaging her tits through her dress and being pretty blatant about it, yet not any more blatant than some of the other action going down around us on the floor.

Her pierced nipples are jutting up against her latex.

And because I'm a telepath and she's in heat, I know just how badly she wants me to play with them.

With a grunt, I find the zipper between her shoulder blades and give it a tug, just a few centimeters for now, in case this all turns out to be a really bad idea. Her bodice releases just enough to spill more of her juicy Hollywood curves into the open. At this point, the dress barely covers her nipples. She arches her back and pushes into me, so I reach in and get a handful of her breast, all pale under her tan line. I savor the silky warm weight of her in my palm.

No one else can get a proper eyeful, not really, not with her trapped against my body and my hand over her breast. But it's no secret to anyone watching what's going down.

"I don't give a shit," she growls, her lids lifting just a slit to burn me with her stare. Periwinkle fire's pooling in her eyes and the soft tendrils slipping from that chic twist on her head are starting to float. "They need a potent fucking queen on that fucking throne, and that's *me*. And only me. This is part of my power, Ronin. You and my warlocks, all fucking me good, you're part of what's gonna save us."

Righty then.

Guess we're all good with the PDA.

Behind me, Maxim groans and rocks his wiry body into my back while his hand builds an earnest rhythm up and down my shaft. He's a bit awkward, he's learning what I like, and he's still afraid I'll shove him away. I can feel all that fear still lurking inside him. But he's really eager to please me, and that's hot as shit. My hole flutters and clenches and generally wants to be filled.

Yeah, my blooming heat's pretty much raging. If not for his jeans and my leather trousers, which are currently wide open but still clinging to my hips, I'd be feeling that dragon cock of his up close and personal. I'm riding his hand and cupping her tit and I want the two of them to get closer too, I want the two of them much closer.

I want all three of us much closer.

I buck into the hot friction of Zara's slippery thighs. Between the glide of Max's hand and the scent of Zara's pussy, my cock's weeping, and we're all getting good and slick.

I find the tight peak of her pierced nipple and give my girl a pinch. "Will you kiss the dragon for me, love?"

Her eyes open wide and violet fire spills out.

"I want to feel your mouth on my body, Adam," she snarls. "Right where your hand is. Do that, and I'll kiss the dragon."

Bloody hell, she doesn't have to ask twice.

I grip her thigh, drag her hard against my body, and tug her bodice down another inch so her gorgeous breast is fully exposed, her nipple blushing pink and swollen around her ring. I swoop in to capture that sweet bud between my teeth and suckle hard, just as hard as I know she likes it.

Her head falls back and her sharp cry slides through the music. "Oh, fuck, Ronin, fuck."

Max dives in, and she throws her arm around his neck and pulls him close. Their lips crash together above me in a messy kiss. I flick her nipple and work her ring with my savage tongue.

Between her thighs, she's all sticky from both of us, and I rut blindly into all that slick heat. My cock's bumping up against her soaked bare pussy, and if I can find the right angle I'm bloody fucking her right here on this bloody dance floor the way she bloody wants.

She and Max are still sloppy kissing, he's jacking me with one hand and fisting her hair with the other. His barbed cock shoves up against my crack, and it's literal agony, with our trousers still between us, not to have him filling me.

My hole's just aching to clench around all that dick.

Zara surfaces from the kiss and drags in a gasp.

I lift my head to appreciate the sight of her with her mouth all puffy and breathless from dragon kisses, her hair falling down in spirals round her pretty flushed face, her eyes wheels of purple fire.

In the murky spill of candlelight, through coils of oily smoke, half the student body's getting various degrees of naked as they writhe alongside us to the grinding beat.

The other half's just sexy dancing and drinking and watching the three of us go at it.

I actually think it's our heat driving all of them over the edge. Because group orgies aren't typically the norm at an Academy bash.

"Whose cock d'you want inside you, love?" I drag my tongue up Zara's sweating neck. "Because you're definitely getting at least one of us."

Max's dragon rumbles in my ear. Suddenly the twin pricks of sharp fangs scrape my neck.

He's not normally fangy, not at all, so he must be like Lucius.

He's like my alpha.

He has fangs, all right. Apparently they descend from his palate when he wants a wee nip.

My pulse spikes with a spurt of adrenaline and a massive wallop of lust.

No biting, love. I shove the hasty thought into his lust-clouded head. *Not tonight, and maybe not ever. We've got to discuss that shit with all six of us.*

He snarls a protest, but I stand my ground. *I mean it, Max. You bite me and you'll launch Vasili into orbit. Not to mention I've got more than enough heat to deal with already, you feel me?*

His raspy sex voice makes me shiver all over. "Not tonight then. But soon, Ronin Pendragon. Soon I will give you my mating bite."

I can deal with *soon*.

Long as I don't have to deal with *now*.

Max lifts his head and searches out Zara's sex-drunk face. Between his parted lips I get a glimpse of those fangs he's rocking, not as massive as Lucius' but definitely bigger than Vasili's elegant incisors. These days, shifter fangs give me an instant hard-on. In my cock, my heat pounds and rages.

Bloody hell. I need a fuck.

"Tonight," he hisses through his canines, eyes all flaming, going full Vlad the Impaler. "I swear to you. Tonight you will accept my mating bite, my Zara."

"Yeah, about that." Zara's tongue traces her kiss-swollen lips, even as her eyes linger on his incisors. "Not so much, big guy. Right now, I'm with Ronin. We gotta agree on that whole no-biting rule, or we're just not gonna get along. That's a permanent thing we'd all need to negotiate, which I still haven't decided I want. And I definitely wanna see that dragon cock in action before I decide whether to take it on myself."

Her lidded gaze finds mine. Shared need flares between us like a lit match. "Will you fuck him for me, Ronin? I know you want to. Your heat's spiking. He's auditioning for a starring role in our alpha lineup. Will you fuck him and let me watch?"

Chapter Twenty-Three
Lucius

Sweet Neo is fast asleep.

My star pupil has finally fallen heroically in action at his post.

To be precise, he's slumped over the desk in his study nook. He's thrown one brawny arm over the desk as though to prevent some adversary from dragging him away by brute force from the treasure trove of textbooks and grimoires he loves so much, all spread open beneath him. His reading glasses lie discarded over his spell book. A vivid wing of magenta hair tumbles over his eyes.

Carefully I stroke those soft curls from his sleeping face.

Still, he doesn't stir.

My boy is a deep sleeper. But his sleep tonight seems to be particularly deep. Often these days, since we've gotten so close, my nearness or even just my scent will wake him.

I bend to pull in a long breath of his own fresh soapy smell. I savor the innocent odors of sage and lavender, mingled with Zara's vanilla musk and the gamy reek of wolf and the woody butterscotch of Vasili's mating scent.

To my intense relief, Neo smells no differently than usual, even to my wolf's keen nose. Nor is he feverish, he's cool to the touch.

I hardly dare hope this means we've dodged a bullet, that my prize pupil isn't preparing to undergo some physically disruptive and potentially destructive biological transformation as a result of Zara's impulsive mating bite.

The terrifying truth is this.

It's far too soon to say.

Although, surely, he will be disappointed if he doesn't at least go into heat.

As though he's following my thoughts, Neo sighs deeply in his sleep. Even his sigh sounds heartbroken. I consider bundling him up and carrying him off to bed. But truly, I don't wish to wake him. He needs his sleep to recharge that formidable brain he's been taxing with his studies and to process that truckload of shifter biochemicals Zara inoculated him with by biting him.

However, that's hardly the real reason I don't want to wake him.

If I gather him into my rapacious arms, this luscious boy to whom I'm so sexually drawn, this young lover with whom I'm so scandalously entangled, he's going to trigger this damnable mating heat I'm barely holding at bay. Neo still hasn't given himself to any man but Ronin, I barely managed to resist taking him last night (since we both shared Zara instead), and I have no intention of subjecting my virginal student to the brutal passions and relentless stamina of my wolf when we're in heat.

On this point, I am utterly adamant.

There's also the fact that it's Zara, and not I, who is his alpha now, she's made that clear. This means that, at the very least, I should be negotiating all this first with her—as a matter of shifter ethics.

Then there's Vasili, who seems to be poised on the verge of ruining our innocent First Boy. He's been obsessed with Neo, one way or another, for quite some time. These days, that old death-to-my-enemy obsession seems to have turned enemies-to-lovers. This, too, I must respect. As cautious co-alphas, Vasili and I have been giving each other a great deal of leeway as we navigate our queen's new harem.

All of this means that, truly, Neo is best left where he lies. His strong young body can easily cope with a little stiffness from a few hours spent sleeping in a chair. No doubt Zara will come tripping home soon with the others to collect him for bed.

Quietly I pad around the darkened great room, adding fuel to the central fire and banking it well for the night, finding a thick afghan and draping it with care over Neo's broad shoulders. The electrician won't be able to finish repairing the power line until daybreak, so the house tonight's going to be frigid.

Before the others return, I'd dearly love to lock myself and my wolf safely into my bedroom. Still, I pause for a long moment to sniff the air.

I'm sniffing for the telltale scent of my own alpha.

I'm sniffing for Vasili.

Of course, this entire house reeks of his scent, of all our scents commingled. But my shifter senses are keen, and I can always sniff him out. (The better to avoid him, my dear.) Matters between us are far too unsettled, given all his probationary drama, our bitter brawling over Maxim, and the tidal wave of hurt and anger and wrenching disappointment that's still swamping my own battered heart due to his betrayal, for me to give way to him and this infernal heat.

To my surprise, my troublesome alpha's scent is not at all easy to detect.

What I smell more than anything is the spicy reek of patchouli. I've been burning cones of it, with perhaps an overly lavish hand, in a desperate attempt to cover up my own mating scent. Because now there's a third alpha male in the house, the unpredictable Maxim—a fully manifested dragon shifter in rut, God help us—and I live in active dread of triggering the young alpha with my own heat.

It seems most unlikely that Vasili would respect my clearly signaled wishes and leave me to struggle through the pinnacle of my heat alone… at least until I can get my paws on Zara and Ronin, who are safely mine to ravage.

But, somehow, that appears to be what's happened.

Vasili is simply nowhere to be found.

Perhaps he's out flying, as he often does when he's restless. Perhaps he's gone off with the others to the student party after all. Perhaps he's having a rare moment of uncharacteristic deference to my wishes and he's going to let me make my own decisions about managing my own heat.

In any event, I'm not waiting around for my formidable alpha to materialize. Grasping the lit candelabrum from the dining room table, I make a swift circuit of the house to ensure no unattended candles are left burning (fire hazard) and that all doors and windows are soundly latched (security risk). My students all have keys and can let themselves in.

At last, swiftly, gratefully, I retreat to my ground floor bedroom.

I'm irritably aware that I'm creeping about my own house like a burglar, practically on tiptoe, since there is no need to alert Vasili—if indeed he's lurking anywhere about—that I'm barricading myself from him.

By now, my need is raging and clawing at my resolve like a rabid wolf. I'm rigid and unbearably swollen in my trousers.

God save me, this wretched heat is intolerable.

I'm already planning an emergency session with a generous application of Neo's lubricant and my hand, followed by a long hard run on all fours through the forest, to work off the worst of it.

At last, I blow out the candles and flee into my patchouli-scented bedroom. With a vast sense of relief, I bolt the bedroom door firmly in my wake.

The spartan confines of my sanctuary enclose me in welcome comfort. The narrow bed with its fur coverlet and fresh linens neatly made up by Neo this morning, the tidy pile of books and papers beside my decanter of Hungarian *palinka* on the desk, the bearskin rug snarling at me from the floor before the hearth.

My fire is burning low and shadows pool in the corners, but this dim light is ample for my shameful purposes. I lower the candelabrum to my trusty desk, then allow myself to lean against the solid surface and bow my head with a low groan.

Dear God in Heaven. Thank Christ I'm finally alone. Alone to relieve this unbearable heat—

"I'd advise you to peel out of those professorial trousers you're wearing unless you want me to tear them off you, pet. And be lively about it, *do*."

The horribly familiar whiplash of my alpha's voice has me gasping and spinning, my heart lodged firmly in my esophagus to throttle me, my pulse beating hard and fast in my groin.

"You've kept me waiting long enough." Vasili's razor-sharp stare slices my rabbiting heart to ribbons. "You know I despise being made to wait."

Of course, this sly snake I've so rashly and unwisely mated has been lurking here in the shadows, lying in wait for me to stumble into his den, and relying on my own overabundant use of incense to mask his scent!

Now he's looming between me and the door, a tall and deadly shadow in his Renaissance coat and breeches, lace spilling from his cuffs, boots silent in the thick pelt before the fire. Needless to say, every stitch of this creature's civilized attire is strategically chosen for theatrical effect.

He'll barely have to unlace.

He'll strip me naked and fuck me raw while he's still fully clothed with his boots on. With every pump, he'll drive into both of us how desperate I am to take what only he can give me, how needy I am for his heartless domination, how thoroughly I've abased myself to this shameful passion for my former student.

At least, he'll stay clothed the first time.

The mere thought that there will be a next time, and a next after that, and so on, that he'll cheerfully fuck me unconscious if that's what it takes to break my heat—the thought clenches my balls in a spasm of need and shoves my aching shaft against my zipper.

"Mr. Romanov." Desperately I summon every shred of my academic authority. "I'm afraid you don't have an invitation to visit my bedroom tonight."

"Since when have I ever needed one?" His lip curls in a sneer that reveals his sharp fangs, which only worsens the plight in my trousers. "Darling, I promised you an absolutely relentless fuck, and you should know me well enough by now to know I always deliver on that sort of promise." His velvety voice unravels in a sexy snarl. Then his mouth curls in a teasing grin. "Now stop clutching your pearls and come over here and kiss me properly. That heat of yours is so intense you're making *me* sweat."

"Dear God, how can I possibly make you understand? I… I can't simply bend for you as though… as though nothing has changed. Not when *everything* has changed." My voice sinks to a wretched whisper. "Don't you understand how terribly you've betrayed me?"

"Hmmmm." His gilded head lowers in thought. "Surprisingly enough, I do understand—although, admittedly, I was a bit slow at first to grasp where you're coming from. This relationship the two of us have fallen into, well, it's complicated as fuck. You're my alpha in the classroom and in the office, while I'm your alpha in this bed."

"Yes, that does seem to be the crux of our dilemma." Blood of Christ, my chest is splitting open and my heart is lying in fragments. Now that we've finally embarked upon this dreaded discussion, I can muster no further excuse to delay breaking our bond.

If I can.

"Shit." Sharply his head lifts to find me, still clinging to the desk behind me for fortitude. His gaze narrows and his brow furrows. Obviously he's sensing these thoughts I'm struggling to hide, through this mating bond I'm determined to renounce. "I freely admit this dynamic between us is confusing as hell for me. It has been from Day One, hasn't it? Surely it's the same for you."

At least my clever snake of an alpha is willing to be honest about that much.

A little of the tension eases from my shoulders. I release my death grip on the desk.

"It's certainly nothing either one of us planned to happen." I heave a morose sigh. "In all honesty, that night you bit me could have ended tragically, with one of us tearing out the other's throat, instead of with you wringing out of me the strongest damn climax I'd had in years."

"Hmmmmm," he hums, low and rich as a purring cat. "I remember. Having you submit to my bite like that… and then my body… it's one of my fondest memories."

He glides toward me like an adder winding across my bearskin. Hastily I raise both hands, palms out, to ward him off.

"But that's all it is now," I burst out in desperation. "It's history! I'm talking about the present. I'm talking about the deliberate choices you made, you and Zara and Ronin, the night you snuck out of this *domus* and abused your faculty privileges and stole that damn aircraft—"

Impatience flickers in his imperious face. His breath spills out in a huff. "Yes, we were rash. Yes, we were foolish. Yes, we rushed off and got ourselves into horrid amounts of trouble and endangered Zara and by extension the future of the entire witching world without first consulting your august faculty personage—"

"Damn it, this isn't about my faculty personage." Clearly this entire effort is hopeless. Desperately I make a break for freedom, determined to whisk past him and straight out the door. I'll sleep in my office at the church tonight, and every night if I must. "I don't trust easily, and you betrayed that trust. Thus, I find that your betrayal is not possible for me to forgive—"

"*Do* let me finish, Lucius." Deftly he sidles to block my escape. Only two steps away, he towers over me.

Damn it to hell, he's still between me and the door.

"Damnation, Vasili—"

"I rushed off to Vegas," my impossible alpha slices through my protest "without recognizing that my position and responsibilities at this Academy have changed, that you were trusting me to live up to duties I still refused to accept, that my choices could hurt *us*. So if that's what you've been waiting for… for me to admit I was in the wrong…"

For the first time, his confident voice wavers. His hands spread and his mouth tilts in a wry smile. "Well, I'm admitting it. I've accepted your dreadful improvement plan, haven't I? I'm tutoring that fucking dragon practically twenty-four/seven, when all I desperately wanted the night he slithered in here was to piss all over him and light him on fire. Both for that rotten trick he pulled on me years ago, and for moving in on Zara and Ronin and coveting what we have here now, what he's had all his life, but what I've never in my life had before—which is a fucking family, Lucius. *Our* family."

Finally, on the last word, his voice splinters.

Only once have I ever seen him weep. That was the night he bit me.

The secret truth is that I'm horribly susceptible to this terrible man when he's upset.

And the instinct to comfort him, this frighteningly powerful and utterly lost young warlock who was my student and my charge for years, is overwhelming.

"Vasili, my dear…" Beyond doubt, it's dangerous to venture close to him, especially now when I'm already so vulnerable to his blandishments. Yet I find myself taking the risk. "Maxim doesn't want to take that away from you. He's barely daring to hope for a very little of it for himself."

His arm slashes through the shadows like a rapier. Wrath hones his voice to an edge like a saber. "Let's leave Maxim out of this. I'm sick to death of Maxim as the dominant subject of conversation in this *domus*. Tonight is only about the two of us. You and me."

With serpentine swiftness, he darts inside my guard. One hand brushes my cheek with fingers hard and sleek as talons. I flinch at his touch, even as my need for him rages like a bonfire.

I flinch because I crave his touch so desperately. But love is something he's never looked to find.

He takes my flinch for loathing.

His delicate face fractures. His spurned hand falls away.

"What more do you want me to say to you, darling?" he whispers, every syllable ragged and broken. "Because I have no aptitude at all when it comes to these pretty graces that flow so easily from others, all humility and remorse and promises to do better. I won't do better. I'm a snake and a villain and I'm rotten at being anything else. But I'm—I'm trying my damnedest to—make things right."

My entire being, body and soul, is aching for him. I can barely speak, but I scrape around the bottom of my battered heart and dredge up a few words from the rubble. "Well, certainly, it's to your credit—in the end—that you finally acknowledge your responsibilities as an alpha—"

"Fuck my responsibilities as an alpha," he says rudely. "Good God, I was raised Mogadon. I barely even know what it means to be shifter. Lucius Laszlo Aries, the reason I'm trying so desperately to make things right between us is because I'm fucking in love with you, all right?"

His voice dwindles to a scrap of a whisper, as if he's terrified to let anyone hear. "Darling pet, I'm so utterly and disastrously in love with you."

These words are so unexpected I can literally make no sense of them. He loves Ronin deeply and always has, and I've heard him confide like a secret his love for Zara, which is new and therefore fragile—this love for a woman he never imagined himself capable to feel.

But he and I have been rival alphas in this *domus* for so long. Our entire history has been one of wary circling and the baring of teeth. I had only begun to lower my guard and dare to trust him when he left.

That's what made his betrayal all the more wrenching.

These words of love I never believed he'd be capable of uttering—not for me, his co-alpha—God, this confession only deepens my endless craving to be possessed and despoiled and ravished by this complex and treacherous rival.

My body burns for him.

My soul bleeds for him.

"Blood of Christ!" I cry. "Why must you tell me this *now*, of all possible times? Oh, perhaps you do… believe… you love me. But how can I ever again trust you?"

He searches my agonized gaze with his own probing stare. We're linked so tightly now that my agony is his.

God help me, I can hide nothing from him. My secrets are his secrets.

"Ah." Slowly his brow smooths and his lips part to reveal the tips of those pretty incisors I'm so wild for. Clearly, he's just experienced some sort of revelation. "Well then."

Far too swiftly to avoid, he snakes in to snatch my agitated hand and presses it to his chest.

Beneath my palm, his furious heart beats hard and fast.

Under all his baroque finery, his body is a siren song luring me to ruin on the rocks. Dear God, this is madness, tormenting ourselves this way.

I groan in absolute despair. "Vasili…"

"Darling pet," he breathes. "Don't you see? You and your wolf are holding my heart in your carnivorous paws. I'm not asking you to trust me. I'm trusting *you.*"

All my resolve breaks like a dropped and shattered plate. My fist knots in his velvet coat and drags him close. He dives in to seize my starving mouth in a vicious kiss.

Saints in Heaven, he has undone me. This declaration of love from my intolerable alpha has disarmed all my defenses. I can deny him nothing. I can deny myself nothing. I am finished with denial.

I am ruined.

Fiercely I clutch at his clothing. His arms sweep around me and drag me up against his body. Underneath he's wearing a corset that cinches his waist and flares his hips and generally makes me desperate to cut him out of it with one of his own knives. But he's ready for me (because I've done that before, to his intense displeasure). He seizes my wrists and pins my hands behind me and bends me back and kisses me like he's going to crawl down my throat and gut me.

He tastes like juniper and he smells like sin. His tongue plunges and pillages, his lips suck and savage, his fangs are a constant menace that makes kissing him a game like Russian roulette.

Like no one else, he is dangerous to kiss.

My own fangs descend for others but retract for him, making myself vulnerable, letting him inside. My wolf whines and rolls and bares his belly in submission. The room reels around me until I'd surely fall on my backside if not for his strength holding me up. He finds the knot of hair at my nape and tugs it loose to spill down my back, because for some reason, that seems to be always how my mates want me, untidy and undone.

"For the life of me," he breathes between long drugging kisses, "I can't decide whether to take you hard and fast against the wall, snarling and fighting me the whole time, or whether to bend you over your proper professorial desk and pump into you slow and long and make you come all over your student papers. Now… it seems… I'm feeling indulgent. Shall I let you decide?"

Finally he releases my wrists, steadies me on my feet, and allows me to surface for a desperate gasp of air.

I gather my legs under me, pull in a long inhale to slow my pounding heart, and do my damnedest to clear my head. I grip his lapels in my unsteady fists and bow my head for a breath against his chest. He strokes my fallen hair and nuzzles the top of my head. The dark spice of his mating scent envelopes me.

Damnation. I can't even speak. This dreadful creature has stricken me speechless.

For once in his infernal life, this alpha of mine is actually behaving as a proper alpha should.

He is steadying me.

Supporting me.

Loving me.

I can still scarcely believe he's admitting it. But he has, and now this endless menace needs something from me. Something that I alone can give him.

My forgiveness.

I lift my head to find his face looming over me. If I didn't know him as I do, I would find him terrifying. Without doubt, this warlock with his telekinesis and his levitation and his knives and his shifter recessives is the strongest Scorpio scion we've had in centuries. He lies like Lucifer. He wreaks more mischief than Loki. He's cunning and sly and unscrupulous. His ethics are appalling.

But, well, he's Vasili.

Why not admit it? I'm in love with him. We're all in love with him. Perhaps, in time, even the dragon will succumb.

"Oh, I wouldn't hold your breath waiting for *that* day." His eyes turn murderous and his face turns lethal. "Your love, I will kill for. But his, I will never abide."

Ah well. Perhaps Maxim is a challenge best left for another night.

My hands slip under the decadent folds of his coat and glide over the satiny sleekness of his corset. The ruthless cinch of fabric closes down his spine. I find the tight knot of lacing above his tailbone and tease the laces loose.

He hums with appreciation and his eyes fire with lust.

"Very well," I breathe. "I'll give you ten minutes to make me feel like you need me. Regarding the location for our exertions… might I suggest, for a novelty, the bed?"

Chapter Twenty-Four
Zara

"You've got nine minutes to make me feel like God," Ronin growls. "Because I'm bloody going to need some proper foreplay if I'm going to take on that dragon cock. I'd suggest the two of you get started."

Oh hell to the yeah.

I'm locked together with my warlocks in the horror show basement of the Hadrians' haunted house. And this isn't a dance floor anymore, not since the three of us started going at it and somehow infected this entire party with the fever of our mating heat.

Now we're marooned in the middle of a full-on orgy.

Mallory's getting the birthday of her life.

Two of the Hadrian guys have the birthday girl spread across the gift table, and she looks dazed but definitely happy about what's probably gonna be her first three-way. There's a whole tangle of that Tiberius crew—all genders—getting down and dirty right next to us. Skin's on display and clothes are getting shucked on the speakeasy's gnarly floor. Over by the bar, I'm seeing a lot more of Dez and Racetrack than I'm used to, they were like the first two to succumb when I started blasting the joint with Mogadon pheromones (not deliberately, but I figure that's what's happening).

That's when all the psychic amperage of Ronin's arousal and mine started lighting up the island's emotional grid and turning on anyone in the place with a telepath gene in their witchy DNA.

Dayum.

Did *we* do this? As in, the three of us?

Let's just say… love is in the air.

But I'm not really focused on any of that. Not with Max writhing against Ronin from behind, and Ronin suckling my nipples and not-so-dry-humping me, and my latex dress barely covering my ass, and my warlock's pierced cock nudging up against my pussy (because, yeah, I didn't wear panties to the dance).

"Fuck, Zara." Ronin's head swings up to rivet me, those intense eyes of his burning with amber fire. He's cranking out full-force *fuck-me* vibes to every telepath on the whole island.

Max looms behind him, dragon eyes glowing like golden orbs, vertical pupils narrowed to slits, because he's turned on as fuck-all.

And I love that he's all over Ronin in public.

Maxim is overcoming his fear and putting that homophobe shit right in the rearview mirror where that trash belongs.

And they're just so hot together, both my guys, Ronin all black-haired and tawny and Maxim so Nordic blond and dragonish and both so fucking broody.

My question's still crackling in the air between us like an electric charge.

But Ronin doesn't leave me hanging.

"Yeah, I'll fuck him for you." My warlock sweeps a spill of hair out of his blazing face. "Long as I can fuck you too, love. Assuming the other guy wants it."

"Yes," Maxim growls through his fully distended fangs. (OMG, he has fangs! I'm dying a little inside, because I have a not-so-secret vampire fetish.) "Here?"

He's a man of few words, this dragon of mine, when he's on the hunt.

"Uh." Ronin's gaze rakes the heaving sea of nudity around us, including the extremely sketchy floor. "Give us a tick."

He scoops me up in his arms, which plasters my whole front against his whole front and makes my dress ride up, so my lower half is getting breezy.

Well, ass, say hello, world.

I'm probably mooning the whole room. At this point, literally no one cares.

I wrap my arms and legs around Ronin as he shoves brutally through a scrum of tangled bodies. Maxim stalks after us, shucking his leather jacket and peeling his shirt over his head with a careless hand. This maneuver gives me a front-row seat for those barbell-pierced nipples and washboard abs he's rocking.

Cheese on toast.

Ronin gets us off the floor fast, which gives the three of us a little more personal space, but he doesn't go far. He plants my back against the wall, snugs my legs around his hips, fills his hands with my bare ass, nails me with those topaz eyes, and growls, "You ready for me?"

"Uh-huh." Shit, he makes me breathless. "Born ready."

My latex is all rucked up around my waist, and my pussy is slick and bare and needy, and his cock is nudging up against my swollen folds. He's so rigid he's gonna spill in about two pumps.

Maxim lurks behind him, predatory eyes riveted on all this action, and he's not waiting around for an invite. He leans in to suck on Ronin's sexy neck, which he literally can't seem to leave alone, and I really hope he remembers not to bite. Jesus, we're really trusting him and his dragon not to lose it.

Then Max gets his fists wrapped around the lapels of Ronin's silky button-down. He rips the whole shirt open with a single hard clench.

Oh fuck.

Flying buttons ping against my skin like stinging hail.

Ronin braces my back against the wall and sheaths his cock deep inside me with a single thrust. My mouth opens in a breathless yell that mingles with his guttural snarl. Our voices sink into the grinding techno beat that's pulsing from the boom box.

God.

Damn.

He's buried so deep inside me, I can taste the musky salt of warlock in the back of my throat.

My heat sparks and ignites an inferno of need. His heat's like gasoline poured on the flames. My inner dragon screams and thrashes in a frenzy. And Max's dragon—suddenly so vivid in the mating bond that flashes to life between us—trumpets and flares his wings in full rut.

Maxim bares his fangy teeth (which I adore, though suddenly now I'm also craving Lucius) and reaches between us to peel the latex off my boobs. Now the bodice props up my girls like a push-up bra. The dragon's hands are rough and hungry as he kneads my curves and works my nipples. That action sends double zings of sensation shooting through my synapses to add to this sensory overload I'm drowning in.

My first climax roars through me before I'm even halfway ready and drenches Ronin's cock in pussy juice.

Teeth bared, face tortured, he grunts and pistons through it into the pulsing vise of my cunt. Before I've even floated down from the Cloud Nine climax I'm parked on, his cock kicks and floods my basement with liquid heat.

Ronin bucks and bellows like a branded steer. Maxim grabs a fistful of Ronin's long hair and devours his mouth in a hard claiming kiss that muffles his yell.

Normally we'd both last a lot longer, Ronin and me, but we're both in heat.

Plus neither one of us is anywhere close to done.

When he lowers me to the ground, Ronin's whole body still trembles with need, and my legs barely hold me up. Max is already stripped down to his ripped jeans, and I can tell he's barely holding off his shift. He's reacting like he's already our alpha, so Ronin and I are definitely setting him off.

Well, he better fucking hold it together.

I'm not doing that whole mating flight.

Not tonight.

I refuse to lose control.

Max gives me a drunken look, eyes fiery with rut, then twists to shove open a door beside us that I haven't even seen. I catch a glimpse of some kinda drug den or something in there, lava lamps oozing and pulsing with colored light, rough walls covered with fluorescent acid rock tapestries, psychedelic cushions scattered over a 1960s shag carpet, and two girls and a guy on the floor in full fuck.

Whoa.

That Tiberius girl's getting double-dicked by a couple of Hadrians and I am *here* for it.

"OUT!" Max thunders in his brassy dragon bellow.

Geez. He practically knocks the lamps over and blows the tapestries down with that dragonish roar.

Mother naked, the three Hadrians come tumbling out and literally fall through the door into the full-scale orgy going down on the dance floor. Max grabs my wrist, practically hurls Ronin into the den—still hard, sex-drunk and swaying, leather pants open and clinging to his hips—then swings me in ahead of himself and slams the door behind the three of us.

The whole joint reeks with the skunky smell of pot, but who cares. It's fucking private.

Max barely gets the bolt shot (which the earlier three apparently failed to manage) before Ronin and I are on him, unbuckling his spiked belt and unzipping his distressed denim and shoving his pants down his hips. Underneath, our dragon's a tiny European speedo kinda guy, but his barbed cock is straining the fire-engine red fabric, his crown already shoving into view to say howdy. His crotch is dark and sopping with dragon precum.

Jesus. My mouth is watering.

Ronin drops to his knees, peels off in record time that last little tease of a garment our dragon's still wearing, and cradles all that cock in both hands. Clearly Ronin wants a proper look at what he just rashly agreed to take on.

And, God knows, Max is well worth seeing.

The dragon leans back against the door, eyes falling closed, and groans like Ronin's gutting him. Ronin himself is pornographically hot with silky hair spilling down his bare back, sweat gleaming on his golden skin, cock jutting through his leathers and glistening with his come and mine.

"I'm gonna suit you up," Ronin murmurs to the dragon. "But I'm honestly not sure how well the condom's gonna hold."

Max's eyes slit open in a ferocious frown. "I am not diseased, and I do not lie. I was tested before I left Russia. Do you think I would ever risk her safety? Or yours, my mate?"

Well, all righty then.

He's not our mate, obviously, but I gotta admit this dragon's hella sexy when he's all broody and protective. That's probably my heat talking, but you can't lie to a telepath. Ronin can sense he's telling the truth, and so can I.

And clearly Ronin's on board.

I'm just starting to weigh my options (all good ones, from where I'm standing) when Ronin grabs my hand and tugs me down next to him. He wraps a possessive arm around my waist to tuck me up tight against his side.

This setup totally works for me, because A) this carpet's thick and soft, and B) I'm finally ready for an up-close-and-personal of that dragon cock myself.

Just in case you're wondering, the dragon's… huge.

I mean it.

Even without those fleshy barbs on either side that make Max's junk look like a devil's forked tail. He's thickest in the middle and narrow at the tip, where he's flushed and plump and drizzling, like, a *lot* of precum.

Seriously. I've never seen a guy pump out that much.

"Dragons are a critically endangered race, my Zara," he rasps. "We are the white rhino of the witching world. Our extinction may already be inevitable."

My gaze flies up to find Max brooding down at me. His hand wraps in my hair, now all tumbling down from that classy twist I had going. He frees the whole mane with a hard clench that sends it cascading down my back. His oblong pupils slit with pleasure.

"Yeah, you're endangered—I mean *we* are, which still feels weird for me to say—and that's definitely something we're gonna work on." I cock my head. "But *that's* why it's Niagara Falls down here?"

"It is nature's way of… increasing the odds. When I take you, I will fill you, and my lock will hold my seed safely inside you." Max's broody stare shifts to Ronin. "Both of you."

Oh shit. That's hot.

Ronin's careful fingers skim over those two sharp barbs. I'm linked up with him—both of them—pretty tight, and I'm relieved to realize Ronin's feeling way more intrigued than alarmed by that anatomical hazard sign Maxim just hung out there.

"How's this bit work then?" Ronin traces a careful finger around Max's pointy parts.

"They fold in when I… enter." Max's voice gets thick and husky because of the way Ronin's stroking him. "So there will be no impediment… at the outset. Then the barbs engage… to give me a tight lock… so that I can… fill you. This will cause pain, but if you are… aroused… it will hurt less. And this mating may take… some time."

Holy. Fuck.

My heat blazes up like a sulfur fire. My cunt is dripping in full flood and my thighs are slick with Ronin's come. I swipe a hand between my legs to collect the moisture (because we're gonna need a lot of it) then slide my grip down that barbed cock of Max's from crown to base to lube him up.

He's fiery hot to the touch, but so is Ronin. They're both fire signs. Ronin hurls flames with his hands, and Max's dragon breathes fire.

I'm an air sign, which means I fan the flames.

When I stroke the dragon, both my guys moan in unison.

At least that dragon's telling the truth about his barbs folding in, because the downstroke's totally not an issue.

But too much upstroke in a hurry?

That could be a real bitch.

"I will always tell you the truth, my sovereign," the dragon rumbles. "But I may not always tell you everything I know."

Well, shit.

"That's one hell of a warning, big guy." I scowl up at him. "Are there things about this mating you're not telling me?"

He hesitates. "Be more specific. With your question."

"Jesus, it's like we're fucking Aladdin's lamp," I mutter. "If Ronin fucks you tonight. Let's start there. Are there things you're not telling us about that?"

The dragon's head lifts and his eyes flame. "Only that I hope I will please him enough that he will fall in love with me. The way he is with your other ones. And that his love for me will make *you* love me, my Zara."

Fuck if that wallop of honesty doesn't make my chest ache like someone just swung a sledgehammer at my heart.

Does he honestly think I could never love him for his own sake?

"Wow… I, um…" I slide a glance at Ronin. "Sure you're up for all this, Adam?"

Ronin, bless his heart, is so sexed up right now he's up for anything.

"Fuck, sign me up." My warlock leans in to wrap his lips around Max's fat dick. But, before he takes him all the way in, he hesitates.

"These barbs of yours gonna engage in my mouth if I blow you?" he mumbles around all that cock.

"That depends," Max growls low in his throat. "On how well you please me."

Okay, that does it. I want in on this action.

I want *in*.

My inner queen dragon wants him inside *us*. But we're absolutely not going there. At least, not tonight. Instead I lean in to lick a long stripe down Max's shaft, while carefully avoiding his barbs. He tastes like hellfire and brimstone and Ronin.

I guess he tastes like dragon.

And one swipe from my tongue makes Max groan and my inner dragon keen like I've just gutted them both.

Why do we delay? my inner monster moans. *He is ours, Zara. He and all the ones that will follow.*

Wait a sec.

Is she telling me there are gonna be *more*? More dragons? Or just more mates to follow the four I've already got and this new one I'm all too clearly in the process of acquiring?

I'm hoping that whole concept of more isn't a flash of precognition but more, like, an aspirational statement.

Either way, now is not the time to tell me about *more*. My hands are literally full with the ones I've already got.

Ronin's still nuzzling and licking Max's swollen crown and lapping up the steady drizzle of precum dripping from his tip, which is hot as fuck. I wrap one hand around Ronin's cock to pump him nice and slow. At the same time, I cup and fondle the tight sac of Max's balls.

They're both losing their minds. Both my warlocks.

I love this.

Ronin and I share a lot of cock, because he *really* loves giving head. And so do I. The two of us together can get Neo and Lucius and even our sly and difficult Vasili to blow their loads in less than a minute (as timed on my dive watch) when we put our minds to it.

Now our lips meet around Max's cock. We share slow sucking cum-sticky kisses around his crown, our gazes locked and pulsing with psi fire, Ronin's arm looped around my waist to help me balance, his hand wrapped around the base of Max's shaft to hold him steady. Max kneads my head and Ronin's and whispers hoarse broken words in what has to be Russian.

Any time either one of us touches his barbs, he moans.

Those pointy babies, jutting out where his cock forks, are hella sensitive.

Pretty soon Max is rocking and thrusting and basically desperate to get his whole cock in someone's mouth. But if he does, he's gonna lock. Maybe, it sounds like, for a good long while.

And Ronin and I both need cock inside a whole other hole.

Pretty much now.

I can't even look at the sub-basement window set high in the wall. That moon's barely a sliver shy of full, and my inner dragon is more than restless.

She's in full-scale rebellion.

If I even see the moon, pretty sure I'm gonna shift.

Then I'll rise. And Max will follow. And I'm just not ready to lose my shit in some mindless frenzy of a mating flight.

"Soon," Max says thickly. "Soon you will be ready, my queen."

Steady on, Ronin whispers. *She gets to say when.*

Crap. It's the goddamn mating bond.

We're all linked.

All freaking three of us.

"Look." Ronin drags his mouth free with a moan. "Here's how this whole scene's gonna go down. You come right over here, love."

He pretty much peels Max off the wall and coaxes him down on his back on the pile of psychedelic cushions on the floor. Clearly Ronin wants to be on top, so he can control how much of that barbed cock he's going to take.

I'm happy to follow Ronin's lead this time.

Since he's, uh, taking one for the team.

I peel Ronin out of his leather pants, find a packet of lube in his pocket (because he's always prepared like that, he loves a good fuck), and fill my palm with the stuff. Ronin tears open a second packet and does his own prep, because it's pretty obvi that whole end of things is totally new to Max. While Maxim watches with fire in his eyes, I wiggle out of my own dress. Now I'm wearing nothing but a pair of silver go-go boots, my nipple rings, and my lightning bolt earrings.

And I've never felt more like a lightning witch queen.

My hair floats in a cloud around my shoulders and static sparks along my skin. I climb onto the cushions and straddle Max's hips.

He reaches for me hungrily, but I lean back out of reach. "Uh-uh, big guy. I'm just getting you all ready for Ronin."

Which definitely isn't the answer he wanted.

But he grits his teeth and accepts that it's my call.

So I wrap both hands around Max's shaft and start lubing him up. He fists the cushions while he writhes and thrashes under my hands and between my legs like a moray eel caught in a net. His hair comes loose from that braid he ties it in and spills across the cushions like golden silk.

"Zara, my queen," he says through gritted teeth, "you have tasted me. Allow me at least to… return the favor… while I fuck him."

Oh sweet Jesus. That's what I'm talking about.

The air floods with a sudden flowery rush of my mating scent.

Now that Max and Ronin are both nice and slick, I climb off the dragon so Ronin can take my place. It takes more willpower than I expect, almost more than I have, not to start teasing my aching cunt with the head of that dragon cock.

But if that cock gets anywhere near my pussy, it's mating flight time.

My breasts are full and tender too, so I dip my fingers between my legs for more of Ronin's jizz and tease my nipples, which makes Max groan and Ronin curse.

"My queen," Max growls. "Let me taste you."

Oh *hell* yeah. I waste zero time scrambling over the cushions, swinging myself around so I can still see Ronin, and straddling the dragon's head. That's all I need to do, because Maxim's hard hands are already skimming my thighs, his thumbs spreading my aching folds.

"I'm gonna taste like Ronin," I gasp, just in case he needs a warning. "He came a lot."

"Good," Max growls, his breath skidding up my sticky thighs. "You will also taste like you. And I am claiming both of you."

His tongue swipes up my slit and I almost climax on the spot.

Jesus.

Freaking.

Christ.

I am *so* freaking ready for this dragon.

"Oh shit, Max," I whimper.

His tongue lashes over my clit in a long lick that makes me yell. Then he dives in deep to spear my hole. My snatch clamps around his tongue like the organ is his cock and he's already riding me.

He snarls against my core, a deep vibration that makes my cunt clench, and starts tongue-fucking me like it's an Olympic sport and we're in medal contention.

Stars explode behind my eyes.

I fight to keep them open, because this whole scene that's about to go down is epic.

It's definitely something I wanna see as well as feel.

Ronin climbs up Max's body like a panther, straddles his hips, gets a good grip on our dragon's cock, then lowers himself, one slow inch at a time, onto all that lubed-up length.

I honestly don't know what's more amazing to watch.

The always incredible sight of Ronin taking cock, his tattooed body arching back to grip Max for balance, slowly fisting his own pierced dick while he does it.

The look of gritted concentration on my warlock's face while he bites his lip and figures out his new lover's barbs and angles and tries not to blow.

Or the fierce pleasure that makes the dragon's lean body shudder and writhe beneath us as he groans good and loud and eases into his first male fuck.

Sure, Max might've been hesitant at first. Now that he's decided to go for it?

He's all in.

And I surely appreciate his enthusiasm.

I know exactly when the barbs engage to lock Ronin in place, which that wicked tool of Max's wastes zero time doing. I know not only because I feel the sharp stinging jolt of the barbs engaging through our bond, but also because Ronin hisses and Max moans.

"You okay, Adam?" I breathe, going still myself, as if that could possibly help.

"That's, uh, intense," Ronin says slowly. "Bollocks."

He looks like he might want to back off all that cock, but backing off is clearly not an option. The way those barbs work, Ronin can only take him in deeper.

Damn. Damn. Damn. What if this was all a huge mistake?

It goes easier if you… submit, Max whispers, hesitant, through the bond.

Which is the first time our dragon has done that.

Talked to us like that through the bond.

"Submit, is it?" Ronin rocks gently, fucking himself slowly deeper on all that cock, even if what he'd really prefer is the opposite. "Easy there. Not going anywhere, am I? I'm all for you right now. I'm all yours."

I guess he can sense what Max needs, with that coaxing fuck and that soothing tone. I feel it right away when they both relax, because Max starts purring against my cunt, and Ronin's movements soften from stiff to fluid.

"That's it," Ronin breathes. "That's better. D'you like the way this feels? Because I sure as fuck do."

The sudden reek of leather and brimstone inundates the air.

That right there's Max's mating scent.

He's scenting both of us.

Now that I know, Max whispers through the bond, *I will never let you go. Both of you. You are my mates.*

Which could definitely be problematic, since Vasili hasn't agreed to mates. Even if Lucius and Neo are both kinda expecting this (because that's what you get with a polyamorous queen, it's supposed to help the whole witching world when I level up), Vasili's still just barely agreed to temporary dating-slash-fucking till we're through our heats.

Max growls and reaches behind me to grip my ass in both hands. Then he snaps his hips into Ronin. All three of us sigh and moan, mingled with the rhythmic slap of flesh on flesh.

"Gods, Zara," Ronin pants, his sleek skin glistening with a sheen of sweat. "You look so fucking hot riding his face it's unreal, with your pretty eyes on fire and your hair all floating. You going to come for us, love?"

"Pretty sure that's a yes," I gasp.

Max is still fucking me with his tongue, thrusting deep inside to find my sweet spot. My whole body is ebbing and floating in this total sea of sensation. I rock into our dragon's mouth and play with one nipple while my other hand dips to find my clit.

Oh yeah.

That right there's gonna do it.

I'm gonna go off like the Death Star in that *Star Wars* flick.

"That's right. Just like that. Let's see you lose your soul to us." Ronin plants a hand on Max's chest and leans in to claim my mouth in a hot kiss.

Sparks flare at the contact. One of the oozing orange lava lamps sputters and goes dark.

My clit and my pussy both ripple and pulse with the shock of another climax that makes me arch in a scream.

Outside the window, lightning flashes and thunder grumbles.

Max spasms under both of us with a soul-deep groan. I feel what Ronin feels as spurt after spurt after spurt of dragon seed fills his hole.

That whole dragon ejaculation goes on. And on. For. Ever.

Ronin throws his head back and pumps into his own fist, abs flexing, thighs straining, teeth bared, with all that inky hair swirling around his gorgeous body. He's gleaming with sweat when his rhythm stutters and his body goes rigid. He roars and paints my tits and belly with creamy jets of warlock spunk that drip down my torso in the most deliciously filthy way.

"Shit," I breathe. "That's so freaking hot."

Ronin snarls in agreement.

And none of us are anywhere *near* done.

Because Ronin's at the peak of his heat and he's still hard. My inner dragon's pacing and lashing her tail and wanting to rise. Max's cock is still hooked deep inside Ronin.

In fact, this entire building is pulsing with sex. Based on the vibes I'm getting from the big room, not to mention the cries and moans leaking through the door over the music's sexy grind, most of the students at this Academy are fucking.

"Damn," I whimper. "Is this really happening?"

You are their sovereign, Max whispers through slow licks of my dripping cunt. *Your pleasure is their pleasure. You honor them by sharing it. This is, how do you say, a sacrament?*

Huh.

It's like I'm more than a queen. Like a priestess. Or a goddess.

Or something.

I slick a hand through the creamy mess of Ronin's jizz and swipe a dripping finger around my clit. Ronin dives in to drag his tongue over my soaked tits, then gives me a sloppy open-mouthed kiss that coats my tongue with the familiar tang of his seed. Finally he starts suckling my nipples for real, tugging and twisting my rings to make me gasp, hips grinding into Max like this time he really means it.

Every time Ronin's pelvis flexes, I hear the wet suck of dragon cock inside him.

I've pretty much inundated Maxim's face, but he laps at my cunt the whole time like he's starving for it. Now I basically fall off his face (guy's gotta breathe) and plaster myself against Ronin, kissing him and writhing against him and smearing his mess all over both of us. Max spreads my ass cheeks and drags his tongue from my hole up my crack (so much for breathing). When that slick organ probes my pucker—which is uber-sensitive like the rest of me due to this heat—I shock myself into a third climax that makes sparks race over the cushions and crackle up the tapestries.

That little O of mine sets Max off again. His hands clamp around Ronin's thighs to lock him in place while Max fucks into him and snarls and spurts inside him. Through this mating bond with both of them, I feel every damn pump like a mini-explosion.

"Mine. Mine. Mine," our dragon grunts, timing every syllable with the upstroke. "Both of you. You are mine. Say it."

"We are his," my inner dragon hisses. With *my* fucking voice. *"Just as both of you are ours."*

"Fuck." Ronin sucks my lower lip into his mouth with a sharp nip that makes me gasp. "Yours. Both of yours. But *only* if Vasili's on board, Max. I mean it. You'll have to learn to live with him. To love him."

"And Lucius. And Neo," I add, thankfully in my own fucking voice again. "We're an all-or-nothing kinda deal."

Max and/or his dragon roars and bucks harder between my thighs. He's either coming again, or he/they never stopped coming the first time.

"Think I'm full up," Ronin moans. "But, gods, don't stop."

This might seriously be one of the hottest fucks I've ever experienced.

And that's, like, really saying something.

Ronin's cock is jutting against my tummy and he's just too sexy to resist. I grip him in my fist and give all those slick inches a few hard pumps to make him good and ready. Then I angle him right and sink down and take him deep inside, till his Prince Albert bumps against my cervix.

He's plenty big, but I'm so soaked with his come and Max's saliva and my own juice that he slides right in.

My cunt locks around him like I'm barbed myself, which is hopefully not something that's gonna happen once I start shifting. I make one of those dragon keening sounds (shit, she's getting so vocal!) and Ronin gasps out a curse and clamps his hands over Max's around my ass.

Together they push me onto Ronin's cock, which also pushes Ronin down on Max's.

Then the three of us are rocking and flexing all together in a shared rhythm, finally, finally, *finally* getting it just right for all three of us. Max's leathery smell of dragon and Ronin's ambergris and my mating scent swirl together with a blast of my Mogadon pheromones, all thick and heady in the air. I'm arching back, supported by my mates' joined hands, and Ronin's suckling and licking and tugging on my tits.

His pistoning cock fills me so good, so tight, so perfect. He's mine. And he feels so damn good.

Clearly Max's dick is working magic for Ronin.

Next time, I'm pretty sure, Max's dick is gonna be working magic for me.

I don't even know where my last big O left off or where the next one started. I'm basically one continuous O at this point, we all are, Ronin's spunk still smeared over my boobs and belly with more slipping out of me and dripping down my thighs, the kick and spurt of Max's magic moments pretty close to constant (which I can feel through our bond like it's me he's buried in). Ronin blissed-out and half-conscious but still climbing one last peak.

When Ronin erupts inside me with a wordless shout, the frisson of his breaking heat jars through me like one of Neo's earthquakes. My head falls back and my mouth falls open around a lightning scream that lights up the sky outside the window behind us.

In fact, I'm still staring at that window when the glass shatters…

…and a bottle of liquid capped with a burning rag hurtles through the air…

…and the bottle bursts against the opposite wall…

…and the tapestries ignite in a solid sheet of flame.

Chapter Twenty-Five
Vasili

There, darling. I've gone ahead and said it.

I've fallen in love with Lucius.

You might find it peculiar, I suppose, that it comes as such a revelation. After all, he and I have been fucking like feral dogs for weeks.

Sometimes the two of us share Zara or Ronin (or both), but often it's just Lucius and Vasili. The wolf and the snake. Me bending him over the desk in his office or shoving him up against the wall of the shower or just rutting brutally into him in the heated darkness of Zara's curtained bed, muffling his ecstatic cries with my hand while our mates slumber peacefully.

But somewhere along the way, our brutal fuckathons… evolved.

Our torrid teacher-student affair, well, it *expanded*.

It became me seeking him out for advice in dealing with some thorny disciplinary issue in one of the classes I've started teaching. Me asking him to review my lesson plans before I submit them to our deeply suspicious and not overwhelmingly supportive Dean. Me looking to him for insight sorting through some shifter behavioral complexity as I learn to embrace my recessive genetic legacy.

In every one of these exchanges, every time I've needed him, he's generously and thoughtfully and tirelessly given me precisely what I need.

To be honest, I think now I've always loved him.

What's changed since we began this entire co-alpha arrangement (which is extremely rare, so he tells me, since alphas typically don't cohabitate) is that I've finally learned to…

Trust him.

"I can't bear the thought of losing you, pet," I tell him roughly, while the mood's upon me, before I turn sly and guarded again. He's nestled in my arms, both of us lying sideways and facing each other on his monastic bed, his dark tumbled curls reeking of wolf and Zara and Ronin and Neo—all the mates we share in various ways between us.

He's already eased my coat off my shoulders. Now his patient hands are teasing open the laces of my corset.

"You won't ever lose me now," he whispers, under the crackle and snap of the cozy fire we've rekindled in his hearth. That fire is the only source of light since we've drawn the curtains for warmth. This snug little room has become our intimate secret. "Not as long as you're honest with me, my dear one. I can bear anything from you… all your tricks and your tempers and your arrogance and your cruelty. Anything except treachery."

There's a warning buried here for me, glimmering in the depths of his lovely sherry-gold eyes. But just at the moment, I'm in no mood to hear it. He's mine again, after resisting and distrusting and evading me for days.

He's *mine*.

If I were a wolf myself, I'd simply howl in triumph.

I've already unraveled his sober tie and unbuttoned his starched shirt. My wicked fingers are tiptoeing like spiders over the pale skin of his naked torso and combing through the soft fur that covers his powerful chest. His wolf is loving the attention, loving me, loving the thought of me spreading the two of them wide on Lucius' prim and proper bed and claiming them so thoroughly that this other new alpha (ah, he means the dragon, that wolf is wise to be suspicious) will stay well away.

Now I tease open the caramel leather of Lucius' belt and gently nudge the button of his trousers through the slit. His breath stutters on his lips. His heat is raging fiercely, it's a fever in his blood.

Yet he seems desperate tonight for my tenderness rather than my lust.

"I'd find it easier to lay your fears to rest," I murmur, "if we could come to some accord regarding that bothersome dragon."

"Honestly, there's nothing to discuss." Lucius sounds breathless but determined as I ease down his zipper. "I regret your unfortunate history with him. Truly, Vasili, I do. But you must strive to forgive him for the sins of his past. Zara needs him in the harem. When the full moon rises, she *will* shift and rise, no matter what she thinks with her rational mind she wants. She's already perched on the very brink of her superheat. We simply must have a dragon to break it."

"Must we?" Lucius is wearing paisley silk boxers under his houndstooth. I purr over the discovery. Truly, he is *such* a delicious Old World gentleman under that savage beast. "Any dragon will do?"

"Well, Maxim is the only fully manifested male dragon shifter—that we know of—to be extant." Lucius frowns. "If it were absolutely necessary, his wyvern brothers could possibly suffice—"

"No, they couldn't. They're horrid." I shudder with a moue of distaste and tease open the slit in his boxers.

He's trying to concentrate on my question and probably deliver a lecture like the dutiful professor he delights in being, but his thick cock is outlined so delectably under the silk that I'm determined to distract him.

Still, there is the little matter of my question to address.

"Once upon a time, the Russian shifters were all dragons. Firedrakes, ice dragons, lightning dragons, sea serpents, and others whose gifts have been lost in the crumbling pages of our histories. And they were a mighty race indeed." Lucius' brow furrows as my naughty fingers dip into his boxers. "A plague killed many of them in antiquity. Then, in the last century, the Marxists hunted them down relentlessly and chained them in the gulag and worked them to death."

"Yes, that fate befell some of my own ancestors," I say. "That's how the full shifter branch of the Romanov line was extinguished."

"Oh, indeed?" The history professor buried under my wolfish mate looks attentive. "Finally, Anastasia Rasputina—Maxim's unfortunate mother—well, she herself did the rest, mating and then murdering every sire who rose to break her heats. Almost as though she herself were determined to eradicate the last of her own race. Now… Blood of Christ, Vasili, I'm… trying to concentrate…"

"Yes, pet, I know." While he's distracted with his history lesson, my terrible hand has dipped past his paisley silk to circle his luscious thick cock, his pulse throbbing under my fingers in his veiny girth, his length jutting hot and eager from the thicket of dark curls between his thighs.

Typically, he likes to be used rather crudely—oh, he'll deny it, but it's true, he loves when I debauch and despoil and debase him. Tonight, out of deference to his bruised and tender feelings, I'm determined to cosset his fine sensibilities like a medieval virgin on her wedding night.

While I tease out of him all the little historical secrets I need to disentangle in order to resolve our queen's current dilemma.

So my cool fingers stroke his eager length as reverently as the rare treasure he is, this lovely mate of mine, while my free hand slips between his restless thighs to cradle the hot tight bulge of his balls.

With a gasp, he parts for me, one hand circling my wrist as though his priestly conscience is begging me to abstain.

Even as every carnal cell in his body is begging me to ruin him.

"Take off your trousers for me," I whisper, ignoring his modest attempt at protest. "So I can ravish you properly. And tell me more about our little queen's superheat. Does it have to be a dragon that breaks it?"

Obediently he abandons my corset, which he's largely unlaced by now in any event, slips his trousers and boxers down his thighs, and neatly folds them at our feet. "It has to be a shifter… who flies."

"Hmmmm." Now this is all very interesting.

But my mate is sweating with mating heat, and the alpha in me is becoming rather distracted by all this mating heat myself.

It really does require considerable discipline on my part (and not *that* kind of discipline, darling, *do* try to elevate your mind) to orchestrate my little inquisition as I nudge Lucius onto his back and eel my way between his parted and now quite deliciously naked legs.

"And does it require a mating bite to break a superheat?" I inquire. Just before I swoop down to lick a long stripe from Lucius' base to his tip, which makes his dick jump and his wolf whine for more.

"Vasili…" Lucius' sensitive scholar's hands flutter about in distress before he cradles my head.

"Yes, pet?" I lick a slow circle around his flushed and eager crown. "You were saying?"

"The—the mating bite." The poor darling sounds half-strangled as I nuzzle and kiss his slit. "Typically, yes, an alpha will bite during a mating flight. The difficulty is that… Zara herself may be alpha… she's already bitten Neo, even though—merciful Christ—"

Of course, I already know she's bitten Neo. I saw the bite this morning in the shower when he bolted past me (blushing, of course) to ensure he'd be well away from his horrible rival by the time I stripped down myself. Lucius leaves twin punctures when he bites, but Neo has a pretty half-moon on his shoulder.

And it surely wasn't that dragon who bit him. The two have barely interacted.

Well, this entire development certainly explains why Neo wanted *me* to bite him last night. He simply wanted a bite.

Anyone's bite.

Even mine.

If I'd been thinking clearly, I would have bargained the bite he wanted from me for the fuck I want from him.

But I wasn't thinking clearly, I was preoccupied and fretful over Lucius and our prolonged estrangement. Now, very likely, it's back to fucking Square One in my seduction of the shy but stubborn Mr. Mercury.

Lucius is still earnestly trying to explain his qualms about Zara biting Neo, and he'd willingly deliver an entire lecture on that subject if I only allowed him.

But this is not the information highway I need him traveling along tonight.

Besides, there's his heat to break.

"Never mind about our First Boy at the moment." I sit up between his legs to slip out of my corset like a snake shedding its skin, then let the gossamer silk shirt I'm wearing beneath slide from my shoulders. His gaze coasts down my naked chest and torso. His fangs descend and his eyes begin to pulse that delicious evil red.

"Mmmmm, there you are." I purr. "Where's your lubricant?"

"Er… nightstand." His wolf is thick in his voice. Good. I don't want him thinking anymore tonight.

"Be a good pet and fetch it for me."

While he does this, I toe off my boots and peel out of my leggings, one leg at a time, as elegantly as a lady's silk stockings. In fact, I make an entire burlesque performance out of it. (I truly can be the most dreadful tease.) This technique proves to be quite effective and diverts my mate nicely from the troublesome subjects of Neo and shifter genetics and, well, anything really that isn't *me*, all sleek and scented and more than ready to give him the tender fuck he seems to be craving tonight.

I don't say another word until I have two fingers buried to the third knuckle inside him; my normally restrained and reticent headmaster has already spilled twice down my throat and once (deliciously) all over his own abs; and his mannerly tenor is hoarse from bellowing. It's a good thing the house is empty, except for the notoriously deep-sleeping Neo, or Lucius would have woken every soul under this roof.

Of course, I find all this deeply satisfying.

"Now about these mettlesome mating bites," I murmur, between slow sucking kisses to his balls that make him gasp and whimper. "It's possible, clearly, for an alpha to bite another alpha, because, well…"

I gesture gracefully (with my free hand) toward the obvious evidence (to wit, the two of us).

"It's extremely rare," Lucius pants and writhes, because I'm scissoring my fingers to open him wider. "Every queen in history has had a single alpha… at a time… in her harem… until Zara, who's now taken two… and may soon take a third. In fact, for an alpha actually to *bite* another alpha at all was unheard of, until *you*… Vasili, oh dear God, will you please…?"

"Unheard of? Well, it's really too bad no one ever bothered to inform me." I pause the proceedings long enough to lube my soon-to-be-quite-naughty cock, because truly, I'm nearly at the limit of my own considerable endurance. "And yet, in Zara's case, she herself possesses quite obvious alpha tendencies—given Neo's current predicament—despite the fact that she's been bitten by *two* alphas herself. Which was apparently sufficient to switch on her own shifter recessives and summon her dragon. Truly, it *does* make one wonder…"

"About what?" If you can possibly imagine an elegantly naked Old World Hungarian gentleman with flowing Renaissance curls, impatiently waiting for his lover to fill his well-stretched hole while simultaneously looking deeply suspicious, well, that would be Lucius at this moment.

"Nothing, darling." I bend his legs toward his shoulders to give me the optimal angle, fit my own impatient cock to his sweet pink pucker, and ease in a slow inch to get him used to the fit. "Nothing at all."

"Vasili—"

"Do hush. There's a good pet." I reinforce my edict by swallowing his suspicious questions with a deep open-mouthed kiss that tastes of his arousal (which is my contribution to the flavor) and the fruity bite of his *palinka*.

I swear to God, he is the most *delicious* fuck. You can hardly imagine how scrumptious he is. He never bent for anyone until I came along, and even now he rarely lets me ride him flat on his back the way you'd ride a woman. Oh, he likes it, but he's shy about liking it.

Yet he's more than allowing it tonight. He's practically begging for it.

And he's so gloriously tight.

I fuck him slowly, leisurely, languidly, my hips swatting gently into him for as long as the two of us can possibly hold out. I alternate long hot kisses with blissful interludes when I merely gaze into his eyes and whisper his name while I pump into him.

I want him to feel, not just know, that I meant what I said to him.

I love him.

Whatever happens with the witching world throne and this rumored rival and the looming extinction of all our races, I've never loved a man as patiently, as protectively—as gently, really, as a vicious reptile like me is ever capable—as I love this one, this other alpha I've bitten, seemingly against all the rules.

It came as the most delightful shock to winkle out through our bond tonight that he loves me in return. He actually loves me. Of course, this is why he's been so fiendishly difficult about being left behind.

Well, we won't be doing that again.

"We'll make new rules… the five of us…" Lucius murmurs between kisses, because now we're bonded so tightly he's reading my mind as well (except for a few dangerous little thoughts I've tucked safely away out of sight). "Even the six of us… if you'd only allow that, my dear…"

I'm hardly prepared to entertain the six of us as a conversational topic tonight.

"No! We'll live beyond all rules," I hiss though bared teeth. "Fuck the rules."

His hole is fluttering around my cock and, heavens, he feels simply divine. Now my pace is quickening, flesh slapping against flesh, my hips snapping into him with a force that makes him grunt with every stroke.

He may imagine he wants it gentle, but I'm his alpha, and I know what it takes to shatter his heat.

Ruthlessly I pin him to the mattress, trap his arms above his head while he flexes and snarls beneath me, and rail him like I'll never get deep enough. "There are no rules—my despoiled and darling pet—there are no rules in this world for creatures like us."

"No rules," he pants, his accent thickening the way it does when he's losing himself. "Oh—oh God—oh God—"

Imagine my surprise that it's this anarchic notion—the somehow shocking concept of all of us living polyamorously and scandalously without rules—that drives my scholarly headmaster over the edge.

His hole clamps tight around my cock and ripples and milks me in a way I'm utterly helpless to withstand. He whimpers and shudders and spurts hot gobbets of wolf seed all over both of us, while a high cry spirals from my own breathless lungs and I empty myself endlessly, fathoms deep inside him.

We come in unison until we're both shaking and spent and senseless.

I'm collapsed limply over my mate in a mess of twisted sheets and drying semen, feebly trying to convince myself to get up long enough to clean us both up and give him the aftercare he needs after a long fuck, but drifting inexorably toward sleep despite myself, when that absolutely ungodly trumpet of a scream wrenches us both violently upright and tears the peaceful night and our intimate interlude to shreds.

It's the scream of a berserk and raging dragon.

Chapter Twenty-Six
Zara

Fire races up the wall of the Hadrians' drug den-slash-fuck palace like someone's just doused those acid rock tapestries with kerosene and lit a match.

Oh, wait.

That's because someone just fucking *did*.

Ronin and Max are still physically locked together, due to that whole barbed cock situation. But either Max's anatomy retracts in a crisis or Ronin just steels himself to withstand the damage, because the three of us tear ourselves apart and tumble free across the cushions.

"What the *fuck*?" Ronin rolls to his feet and bolts naked to the door, throws the bolt and wrenches it open, and barks into the big room, *"Fire!"*

Which might be the only warning anyone gets, because I'm pretty sure this whole island would fail the fire code inspection.

Max coils upright with a snarl and twists around to help me up, only I don't need help. I'm already on my feet and lunging.

Not for the door.

For that fucking broken window.

"Bloody hell, Zara, wait—" That's Ronin, who knows me and knows what I'm capable of.

But I'm way past waiting.

For weeks now, I've been walking around like a ticking time bomb with a teal Godzilla bating and pacing and snarling inside me. I've barely been able to keep her bottled up in there. I've been holding back my shift by my fingernails.

Now the moon's pouring through that empty frame, and it's nearly full, and I am *done* resisting that cosmic force.

I am done holding back.

Someone just fucking tried to flambé my warlocks. Someone like those pissy little Aquarius ass-kissing shits from Villa Tiberius who already threw stones at Max's head.

I.

Want.

Blood.

I'm scrambling across the cushions, naked except for my go-go boots, with my hair streaming behind me and the fire licking at my spine. That same heat is burning inside me, a cone of fire in my core that's spreading up and out like a mushroom cloud. My speed picks up, like there's a strong wind under my feet that's lifting me.

In fact, when I push off with my back foot and lurch through the air for that empty frame, I lift right off the ground with a lightning scream that deepens in mid-yell to a full-throated brassy roar.

I burst through the window in a blast of nuclear heat and spread my wings in a powerful downstroke that pumps my dragon body high above the haunted house on the hill.

I catch a crazy skewed glimpse of the rocky cliff and the churning sea way below and a sky full of stars and moon high above. Icy wind howls past my scales and my tail lashes the air. My body's off-kilter and uncoordinated, my flight feels awkward and far from confident, and my proportions are definitely wrong. But I'm fueled by a cold white rage that lends strength to my wings like an atomic reactor that's consuming every atom of emotional fuel I'm hurling into it and converting that fuel to pure energy.

I part my jaws and bellow in the lightning voice.

Thunder crashes and lightning forks from my mouth to rip the sky.

All my senses are telescoped. Tiny voices shout tiny words from tiny bodies far below. My ears swivel to pick up the chemical hiss of extinguishing spray. My long tongue snakes out to taste the acrid tang of smoke and the metallic burn of chemicals.

And despite the fact that it's pitch black (because the power's still out all over the island), my dragonish eyesight is hella sharp. The shadows that cloak this rugged island with its wooded slopes and the steep stairs of the village streets seem more gray than black.

Directly below, the heat signature of that room I just left pulses a fiery orange.

Well, hey. Look who's seeing now in infrared.

A flicker of movement snags my gaze like the predator I've become. Three, four, five little darts of orange scatter along the cliff behind the villa.

Life forms.

Bipedal.

Fleeing their ugly mischief.

THEY ARE MY ENEMIES!

My jaws yawn in a resonant bellow that roars through my serrated teeth. Lightning forks from my mouth and gouges a smoking crater from the earth. Those tiny glowing figures scatter, their tiny screams rising to a terrified pitch.

Good. Let them know how it feels to fear.

But I'm still learning to use this new power. To direct it. It's different this way, tricky, imprecise, when I can't use my hands to cast. I've got these taloned forearms (yay, arms) but I already know they'll be useless for casting.

I angle my wings to sweep around for another pass, but these enemies of mine are crafty. Now they're racing back to Villa Hadrian. They'll hide like rats inside the walls. I'd gladly tear those walls down to reach them and eradicate them from the planet.

But.

The whole school's hiding in there somewhere. Hiding from the monsters. Mallory and the Hufflepuffs. Maybe even Ronin hasn't gotten clear. He could be fighting the fire.

I howl my frustration and fury at the moon.

A sleek black form slices over that pearly disc, flashing past against the cold white light. Wings spread and jaws part around a roar like bronze thunder.

Our mate.

I croon to him, my beloved, my dragon king, the one who will rise to my mating flight.

A savage lust, even bigger than I am, thrashes and claws at my dragon form.

But my mate too has spied our enemy. He angles his massive body and plummets past, a column of crimson flame already pouring from his lungs to blaze through the night, though he's still well beyond range of his target.

But he isn't slowing. Those vile cockroaches who tried to hurt my mates will reach the villa first.

And my mate, in his rage, will ignite the whole building.

I trumpet a warning, but he's way beyond reason. Screaming my frustration, I tuck my wings tight and plummet after him, jaws parting to release a warning fork of lightning that crackles harmlessly beneath him.

He is utterly relentless. He will kill for me without mercy.

Even when killing is not what I want.

Words are difficult in this form. But I reach for mine.

Maxim! I howl through the bond that I know lives between us. *Don't!*

His words roll through me, distorted by rage. *They would harm you. Harm Ronin. I will slay them. I will slay them all!*

Fuck.

He won't listen. I'm smaller than he is, by quite a bit. But I'm also quite a bit faster and way more agile.

I fold my wings tight and arrow after my enraged mate.

Wind screams in my ears and burns in my eyes. I slice down from above just as he's rumbling up a good firestorm. I slam into his scaly back with teeth-jarring force.

A spear of pain twists through my mouth. At the moment of impact, I've bitten my forked tongue. My mate's wings batter me with hammering force as he bellows and claws to stay aloft. Pain buffets me, but I ignore it and scramble to get a good grip.

He can't do this.

He can't.

I won't let him.

He'll kill innocent people, young witches and warlocks who don't deserve to die. Witches and warlocks we can't afford to lose.

They're my people. My subjects. Whether that's what they want to be or not.

They're mine.

I won't let them die.

But Maxim is far beyond listening.

We're in free fall. Our tangled bodies bate and writhe, both striving to stay aloft, him struggling to shake free, me clinging to his back like a burr and trying to get a grip on the scruff of his neck. He snaps his teeth and roars at me, but I won't let him go.

Down is up.

Up is down.

My whole fucking world is total fucking chaos. Still, somehow, I manage to deflect him from the house.

But that victory comes at a price.

Because now the ground is rushing up to meet us.

We're way too close to pull up. We're going to crash. Way too hard, way too fast, plummeting way too far to survive.

My mate bugles in alarm.

Now we're both thrashing to get free. But somehow my wing's trapped under his. The claws on his forearm are snagged painfully in the fragile membrane stretched between my wing joints.

We're just way too late—

A slim shape flaming with heat streaks past us like a damn meteor. I catch a single wild glimpse of a cold furious face and the gleam of silver hair and (improbably) a rose velvet frock coat fluttering madly in the wind.

Vasili.

Because Maxim isn't the only one of my mates who can fly.

I've felt this bone-crushing vise of telekinetic force before, closing around me like a trash compactor. Back when the Goblin King and I were lethal enemies. This time, he isn't actually trying to crush me like a bug.

Vasili's throwing every erg of his scary witchcraft into arresting our uncontrolled descent.

Unfortunately… or fortunately?… we're so close to the ground I've only got an eyeblink to wonder if he can actually pull off this crazy stunt. Because two tons of falling dragon (or however much we weigh) is *a lot* for one warlock to handle.

Even a warlock as powerful as the Goblin King.

Max collides with the ground with skull-crushing force. A millisecond later, I come crashing down on top of him.

That jolt knocks the wind clean out of me and jars every bone in my body. My skull rings and vibrates like the church bell in a gale-force wind.

My chest heaves.

My lungs scream.

Desperately I struggle to drag a few wisps of oxygen into my achingly empty airway.

"Well, *that* was certainly diverting," Vasili says coldly, as I heave and retch. "I trust you enjoyed your first date with my queen and my boyfriend, Rasputin. Rest assured there won't be a second."

I barely manage to lift my head enough to piece together a blurred glimpse of my snake's bare feet, pale and bloodless on the snowy ground. I guess he got dressed in a pretty big rush.

Though at least he's wearing pants.

Which is more than I can say for Max and me.

Because the shock of impact knocked us both out of our shifts, and we're both bipedal again. Which means we're both naked.

I've got just enough sense left in my addled brain to register that Max is groaning and squirming underneath me. That means he's still in one piece (for better or worse, damn his headstrong dragon hide, and how *dare* he fucking ignore me?) He's still in one piece, even after crashing harder than I did and then having dragon me land right on top of him.

Darkness is eating away at the edges of my world. That's tunnel vision closing in, so I'm gonna be lights-out in twenty seconds at best.

But Ronin's racing across the snowy ground behind the villa to meet us, swearing breathlessly, wearing his leather pants and boots, with an armful of what looks like our clothing clutched to his bare chest.

At least he survived the fire, unscathed but definitely pissed.

That's good enough for me. More than good enough. A crippling surge of relief washes over me.

"We really gotta do something… about those pissy little shits… from Cybelle and Damien's old court," I manage to mumble. Damn, I sound drunk. "This is just… a temporary reprieve."

Then the night closes in.

I let it swallow me.

Chapter Twenty-Seven
Neo

That dragon doesn't look half so fierce when he's asleep.

Of course, it's hard to look fierce when you're naked (practically) although both Ronin and Lucius seem to manage it. God knows Vasili looks terrifying naked or dressed.

But it would be way worse if he wasn't so darn pretty.

Our new mate Maxim definitely looks very serious, stretched out on his side like a giant cat in our big platform bed, facing me in the soft morning light that seeps through the frosty glass, with his eyebrows scrunched together, one arm flung over his messy head, and half the pillow bunched in his fist.

I'm happy to see the last of his bruises from that street fight healed up, all shifty-swifty, during the night. This dragon runs hot like Ronin, and at some point overnight he rolled away from Ronin's feverishly hot naked body and snuggled right up against me.

He's still doing that, actually, he's got one arm looped around me and his hand parked nice and steady on my hip while he sleeps.

Which is… nice.

It's chilly in the bedroom with the fire gone out, and there's nothing like a fire sign mate in your bed to keep you all toasty.

He's too thin, I can feel that really clearly, because under the blankets he's only wearing like the world's tiniest pair of briefs (leopard print, which made Vasili sneer horribly and murmur snide asides about going on safari and visiting the Animal Kingdom, when we all six piled into Zara's big bed after everyone got cleaned up and all the excitement finally died down). I snuck my arm around Maxim's waist right away once he started snuggling, and I can feel every single one of his ribs plus his hip bone jutting under my hand.

That just makes me want to feed him.

I make homemade buckwheat pancakes for Saturday breakfast, it's kind of a *domus* tradition, and I wonder if he'll like my recipe.

I'm still thinking about breakfast when those fiery dragon eyes of his suddenly flare wide. For a sec he's all bleary, then those vertical pupils zoom in on me and dilate.

His brow furrows and his mouth opens.

"Ssshhh," I whisper, barely breathing out the sound. "Everyone's still asleep. They all really need it after last night."

He blinks and looks pretty muddled, so I scooch closer to him and put my mouth right up against his ear.

"Hi," I whisper.

"…Hello," he whispers back after a sec, all raspy with sleep.

"You don't remember much about last night, do you?" I give his confused face a sympathetic smile. "That's okay. You and Zara were both pretty out of it when Vasili brought you home."

He scowls, and suddenly he's Mr. Ferocious again. "Vasili brought us? How?"

"Uh, he carried you. One at a time. And, you know, flew?" I hesitate. "Complaining the whole time about how he isn't a taxi service and it was totally a one-time thing so no one should get used to it, yeah, but the important thing is, he did it."

Maxim looks startled by all this information.

Cautiously he turns his head to where Zara and Ronin are wrapped up in each other behind him. They're smothered in sleeping alpha, because both Lucius and Vasili wanted to sleep really close to them and basically both on top of them after what could've happened to our mates last night.

This means all four of them are essentially sleeping in one big yummy pile.

"Hey. It's okay if you don't remember," I whisper. "It must've been really overwhelming bonding with Zara and Ronin both together at once last night, like super intense, even before that whole near-death experience. And when you all came back here, Zara was still totally out of it, and you just refused to be separated from either one of them, and Ronin was pretty insistent that you shouldn't be. So Lucius finally said we should all just sleep in here—you too, no matter how much Vasili seethed and hated—and that was how we all finally settled down and went to sleep."

His eyes search my face, from my tumbled hair to my scruffy jaw, and take their time doing it.

The way those lidded dragon eyes look at my mouth makes me all warm and tingly.

"I hope this does not… offend you?" he says slowly. "That I too have claimed your mate? Zara said she has asked and you have given your consent. But I—I should have asked you myself. I meant no… disrespect."

"Hey, none taken." I let a little sigh slip out. "We're fated mates. That's something special that only we have. Zara and me. We're in each other's natal charts and everything. I've known for years we'd be together, just like it's written in the stars, even if it took her a little longer to accept our whole fated mate situation. But what it means is, I feel what she feels. I love who she loves. I need what she needs. And what she needs in her life right now, right at this exact moment, that's you. So that means you get me too. We're like a matching pair of socks. You don't want one without the other."

"Is this outcome truly as… easy to accept… as you say?" Now he sounds straight-up cautious. When he's suspicious, his eyes narrow and turn all sly and shifty.

"For me, yeah." I shrug, unoffended. Heck, I'm into Vasili (secretly), and they don't come any more sly and shifty than him. "I'm the easy one in this relationship. Ask anyone. If Zara wants you, if Zara needs you, that's good enough for me. Only it turns out Ronin wants you too so that's, like, a bonus? Because I'm with him too."

"The way you explain the arrangement, this all seems far too simple." He shifts around in our bed and frowns. "After all this… struggle."

"Does it?" I get that he's skeptical, I really do, but I've learned a few things since we started this harem.

I've learned that Lucius takes care of everyone.

I've learned that Vasili complicates everything.

And I've learned that my job is to make things simple.

And the way I do that with Maxim is by laying my hand really gently against his face, so I don't scare this big tough skittish dragon who's potentially bi-curious but also potentially a little bit homophobic (which has to be so confusing for him). I stroke my thumb over the sharp slant of his cheekbone and rub my palm against his blond stubble and, when he doesn't freak out or stiffen up, I lean in nice and slow to fit my mouth against his.

Most of the time, his mouth looks cruel and ruthless. But when I kiss him, his mouth is warm and soft, yet firm at the same time, like Ronin when he kisses me. Max tastes like brimstone and he smells like sun-warmed leather.

He takes control of the kiss the same way Ronin does, spearing his hand through my hair and cradling my head and angling his mouth against mine until I open for him. And then he just kind of plunders and lays siege to me until I'm giving him my tongue and squirming closer to him under the blankets and trying not to moan and wake everyone up.

When he finally lets me up for air, he doesn't really let me go. He just eases off with slow sucking kisses that make my lips tingle and make me want him not to stop.

But I do find his hand under the blankets and press his palm against my dick, which is already throbbing and hard for him under my briefs, so he can feel how much I'm into the whole idea of him. He wraps his hand around my shaft nice and tight to knead me and gives this sexy dragonish growl—

"Hush," I whisper, breathless. "You'll wake them up."

"Someday very soon," he whispers just as softly against my mouth, "when you ask me to touch you, I will not be quiet. And I will not stop."

"There." I give a happy sigh and smile against his lips. "Now I've claimed you too."

A sudden tingle of awareness races through me that definitely feels like Zara.

I break the kiss with Max so I can get ready to kiss her too. She pushes up to sit behind him.

"Pretty fast moves on my fated mate there, Max." Her tone's a lot more flinty than I expect my cherished one to sound, since she's in the middle of falling in love with him herself. But I guess maybe she doesn't totally accept that yet. "You gonna ignore what I want you to do with him the same way you ignored my direct fucking command as your queen when you tried to fry my whole fucking class to a crisp last night?"

Vasili rears up beside her, fully awake and terrifying, and trains his glare on the poor dragon.

"Yes, *do* go ahead and tell us, Mr. Rasputin," he hisses, stony-eyed as a gorgon with snakes coiling in his hair, "exactly how prepared you are to sublimate those brutish dragon instincts of yours to the greater good and help the rest of us save the witching world. Because if we aren't all singing from *that* particular sheet of music in perfect fucking pitch, I'll send you straight back to Siberia on the next supply plane. And, superheat or no, our queen will gladly help me do it."

Ronin rolls over on his back with a heartfelt groan.

Beside him, Lucius rises up on one elbow and looks concerned.

"Um, wow." All eyes swing to me and I blush hotly at all the attention, but I sit up too and face down the stares. Because clearly somebody in this bed needs to be on the dragon's side. "That's, uh, a lot to deal with before anyone's even had their coffee. How about we all get up and see about those pancakes?"

Chapter Twenty-Eight
Zara

"Not quite so fast letting him off that hook, baby," I tell my fated mate, who looks so rumpled and flushed and happy that I really hate to rain on his parade. "I wanna see that dragon squirm a whole lot longer."

Max rolls over to face me and mutters, gruff and sexy, "You did not see enough of my… squirming… last night?"

He's all sexed up from kissing Neo and (obviously) feeling him up under the blankets, his blond hair's loose around his shoulders, his angular cheeks glitter with tawny stubble. And all it takes is the sound of that dragon's voice and the memory of his so-called *squirming* under Ronin and me to set off my fucking heat.

Again.

God damn it, I can't spend this entire weekend fucking.

I literally can't.

I've got midterms on Monday that I need to pass and a succession ritual on Wednesday that I need to plan.

"What I remember more than your squirming," I narrow my eyes at the cause of all my problems and cock my head, "is your fucking *flaming*, Maxim. And your not stopping when I told you, which meant I had to physically stop you myself. And your not listening, and how we both almost *died* as a result. All that's kinda overshadowing our horizontal gymnastics."

Max scowls and pushes up on his elbows, which sends the blankets cascading down his sexy chest and exposes his sexy nipples. Now he just looks stubborn (and sexy). "For protecting you, my sovereign, and for protecting our mate, I will make no apology."

Vasili hums a little behind me. He actually sounds like he appreciates the sentiment, even if my snake is coiled as far from that dragon as he can possibly get and still be in the same bed.

All the same, the two of them *are* in the same bed (even if I have no idea how we all got here, since I was in La-La Land at the time). Somehow, this development feels like major progress.

If I was in a claiming mood, I mean.

If I was actually officially intending to pick up another mate.

Which I'm not.

Think that ship might've sailed a bit ago, love, Ronin murmurs, just for me, because he can draw the telepathic curtains around us whenever he wants. *This dragon's bonded with us—you and me—he's bonded really hard. Looks like Neo won't be far behind. Even if Max hasn't bitten us yet.*

Ronin hasn't even taken a mating bite from Vasili, because it's a point of pride for the Goblin King that Ronin fell in love with him without needing a mating bite, way before Vasili even knew he had enough shifter in him to give one. So it's a really big deal that Ronin's hinting (even super privately) that he'd maybe accept one from Max.

Which just makes me more pissed at that stubborn fucking dragon.

"Okay, big guy." I assert my dominance by rolling over and straddling Max's hips, buck naked of course, since that's how I always sleep these days. But I'm extra careful to keep the thick duvet between me and that barbed dragon cock my hoochie's howling for.

Max's gaze slides down my body. His nostrils flare, either because I'm scenting or because he can smell all that pussy juice my girly parts are pumping out. I'm, like, really slick down there.

And he knows it.

"Look." I swallow hard and get serious. "Here's the thing."

He grips my waist with his hot hands and growls, "Tell me this thing. I am listening."

Sweet Jesus, why does this dragon have to be so fucking sexy? *Why?* My life would be so much simpler right now if he wasn't.

Next to him, Neo laces his brawny arms behind his head and grins at me and watches the whole show with appreciation. He clearly likes the way I look with Max, like he won't mind seeing a lot more of the dragon's hands on my body.

That's assuming I don't kill the big guy first.

"The thing is," I tell Max firmly, "it's not just me and the guys you're protecting, okay? When I do that succession ritual on live TV, I'm taking a vow to protect the whole witching world—right?" I shoot a look at Vasili, who's gonna be choreographing-slash-directing the whole performance for me like a theater production, though he hasn't filled me in yet on everything he's planning.

"Hmmmm." My snake's watching us too, really closely, but he's got the blinds lowered in his head, so I can't pick up what he's thinking.

Given my looming superheat, my Goblin King's looking extra yummy. His silver rock star mane is growing. It's falling past his jaw now and halfway to his shoulders, framing his imperious beauty and icy eyes like a punk rock halo.

Yep, it's a really good look on him.

Of course, he's been cagey and secretive as fuck about his feelings for Max since that whole library kiss fiasco.

But, you know, that's Vasili.

He's the quintessential Scorpio. Still waters run deep, etc.

My gaze zooms back to the dragon. "That protection gig we take on as royals starts right here at Icarus, okay? If you're ever gonna be one of my kings, you can't go around flaming innocent people. And that villa you were so dead set on attacking was full of them."

His slitted pupils narrow. "My queen, they attacked you—"

"Stop 'my queening' me and listen up." I cup his scruffy jaw in my determined hand. "You can't throw out the whole bushel over a few bad apples. A bunch of students would've died, and you would've gotten expelled and probably arrested by the AIB and locked up for murder. And that would make it way harder for me to queen it when the time comes. So no more flaming—or attempted flaming—of innocent people. Got it?"

"Is this the only reason you will be displeased if I am expelled?" He looks like he's actually listening, with his Slavic face all grim and his brow all furrowed. "Because it will be harder for you to rule?"

Okay, so this is him wanting reassurance.

Wanting to know if all that's between us is witching world genetics and my superheat, or if I actually feel something for the guy.

Even though I'm pissed, my stupid heart goes all melty. I've always been a total sucker for anything my guys need.

Still, I gotta think about Vasili's feelings. It was only a few days ago that Ronin found him crying in the shower (a thought I guard *really* closely with those telepathic privacy barriers Ronin taught me to put up when I need to, because that's a vulnerability Vasili will definitely *not* appreciate me sharing, especially with Max).

"Jury's still out on that one," I say lightly. "You and the Goblin King gotta figure things out first, okay? Then we can revisit that whole issue about my feelings."

But I soften the blow by leaning in to give the dragon a super-quick kiss.

It's just supposed to be a peck.

But the millisecond our mouths meet, my inner dragon (who's been snoozing in there) wakes up and leaps to her feet with a roar.

Zara, he is ours. We must rise!!

No go, showgirl, I insist, as firmly as humanly possible with Max's hard hands sliding up my back and his warm mouth teasing mine open so he can slip me the tongue. *No rising.*

"You will rise tonight at moonrise, my Zara," he mutters between hot slow kisses that taste like hellfire and light me up like Fourth of July fireworks over the Vegas Strip. "You will no longer be able to resist. When you rise, so too shall I."

Fuck. Guess that's what you'd call a ticking clock.

"My, my. Don't be so insufferably certain you've got this one properly gift-wrapped and tied with a pretty bow, Maxim Rasputin." My snake sounds absolutely silken with menace. Especially since he's just slithered over Lucius and Ronin to straddle the dragon behind me—a position that is absolutely rife with potential.

Vasili's hands slide around my waist to draw me out of the kiss and plaster my back against the front of six-plus feet of Goblin King.

Hell to the yeah.

His skin is cool to the touch, because water signs run cool, and you can practically hang beef in this bedroom when the fire goes out. He's wearing a pair of silky sleep pants, which isn't usual for him (because we all definitely like him naked), whose stark black stands out dramatically against his pale skin.

I guess he wasn't super comfy rolling around in this bed buck naked with his archenemy.

I wind an arm around Vasili's tousled head and twist to give him a proper good morning kiss. I don't want him ever to worry about competition if a third alpha joins the harem (not that anything's decided). If Max is gonna go around flaming my subjects, there's no place for that dragon in this bed.

The Goblin King smells like caramel and tastes like malice, but his tongue snakes past his wicked incisors to twine around mine. His clever fingers steal over my breasts to give my nipple rings a twist that revs my engine and nearly rips an instant O out of my oversexed body.

"Fuck, Vasili," I gasp. My fist clenches in his hair.

It really is getting longer than I realized. His hair's almost grazing his shoulders. It's growing so fast I can almost *see* it grow while I—

"Good morning to you as well, darling," he murmurs, between delicate licks and razor-sharp teeth. "Let me just say I actually *do* agree with one little thing this flying tyrannosaur is saying."

Max pushes up to sit with an aggressive snarl.

Now I'm the BLT in a warlock sandwich.

Max is all toasty and my clit starts pulsing in a way that makes me even slicker down below. The two of them bristle at each other, with me tucked in between them and pumping out mating scent.

My inner dragon's just noticed my snake, in a way she's really only noticed Max so far, and she definitely likes what she's seeing. Vasili's playing with my boobs and undulating sinuously against my back, so his silk-clad boner nudges my crack. Maxim lets his fangs descend (and what a lovely surprise *that* was last night) and leans in to drag those twin points up my bare shoulder to menace my throat.

I moan and arch into his mouth. My head falls back against the Goblin King's shoulder.

And we're all so close they're touching too. The backs of Vasili's hands are grazing Max's barbell-pierced nipples. When Max's arms wind around my waist, his hands land on Vasili's hips.

Which is hella hot.

Sweet Jesus, these two have more chemistry brewing between them than the Academy's alchemy lab.

Max lifts his head. His dragon eyes lock on Vasili.

"Do you see, Romanov?" he rasps. "Already we begin to get along."

"Now, now, let's not exaggerate our moment of fleeting accord," the Goblin King purrs. "I'm merely saying I appreciate the fact that you were trying—however ham-handedly—to protect Zara. Rest assured I intend to punish those Tiberius pissants for attacking the three of you. I'll do it in a manner that suits me, and without causing collateral damage, since it seems I'm now a reformed villain." A pout lurks in his malicious voice. "Let's just say those little monsters have hurled their last Molotov cocktail."

"They are mine to punish," Maxim growls.

Vasili hisses like a rattlesnake poised to strike.

Well, shit.

And this was all starting off so well.

"Yeah, look, about those Tiberius guys," I say hastily, before Vasili buries one of his hidden knives in Max's eye or crushes Max's bones with his telekinesis for impertinence. "Believe me, those assholes are going down hard. They don't get a fucking pass for what they fucking did. But we gotta be smart about how we do it, and actually solve the problem instead of making it worse."

"What precisely did you have in mind, darling?" Vasili works his supple fingers over my nipples in a way that's *almost* tweaking Max too.

My dragon's breathing hard and he's flexing his hips, just a little, underneath us. He *really* wants Vasili to touch him. His need pulses laser-hot in our brand-new mating bond.

Which only makes me hotter down below myself.

I clear my throat and try to focus. "That whole Tiberius cohort are Aquarius courtiers, right? That means they do what Messalina tells them."

Lucius unwinds his arm from around Ronin's waist and sits up with a frown. He's wearing his *Downton Abbey* PJs again, probably because he's too modest to let his new student Max see him naked.

I'm starting to think my warlocks in general are all wearing too many clothes in this bed.

"Until last night, the Tiberius cohort left you largely alone, Zara," Lucius points out, "except for the usual standard bullying. And they've always given Ronin—and certainly Vasili—a very cautious berth. Clearly, something has changed for them. Some new stimulus has surfaced. It's even possible Maxim was their target."

"Another reason for me to kill them," Max grumbles. "Slowly."

Lucius raises his hand in a plea for patience. "I'm simply saying I don't believe we should be overly hasty in assigning the blame for this incident to Messalina, who's always been quite cautious."

"You think whoever sold that old rumor to *The Witching Inquisitor* put out a hit on Max and maybe me?" My mind leaps back to Vegas. "You think maybe that's what my dad was doing back at the Double Gem? Luring me in for the kill?"

Yeah, that actually computes. Because my dad's wanted me six feet under for years.

And a casino boss like Mick Gemini's always on the take.

"Truly, I can't say for certain. There could be another player entirely that we're overlooking. There's so much we still don't know." Lucius sighs. "I'll use the landline, if it's working today, to check in with my sources on the mainland. My plea to all of you is to stay close to home this weekend, forego any bloodthirsty acts of vengeance until we can at least confirm the identity of your assailants—since I gather you were unable to make a definitive identification of the specific individuals involved from the air— and, for the love of God, study for your midterms."

It totally goes against the grain for me to let it slide when someone tries to hurt my warlocks. But I know Lucius has a point. We do need to follow a rule-of-law type process.

Because if I don't follow the laws of my own realm, how am I ever gonna persuade anyone else to do the same?

"Yeah, okay." I let them all hitch up to my train of thought, including Max, so they all know where I'm coming from. "Lucius has the lead on tracking this shit down and getting us the intel we need to deal with the sitch. The rest of us gotta hit the books hard this weekend anyway."

"I'll make pancakes," Neo says happily, tossing back the blankets so he can get out of bed. "We need brain food to study."

Quick as a snakebite, Vasili uncoils from Max and me and plasters his sinuous body over my fated mate's buff and nearly naked one.

Now he and Neo are nose to nose.

Neo sucks in his breath and freezes.

"Mmmmm, breakfast," Vasili murmurs. "By all means, *do*, Mr. Mercury. I simply adore your… pancakes. I'll take mine with cherries and sour cream."

"Yeah, okay." My sweet baby turns tomato-red at this up-close-and-personal with his suddenly flirty frenemy. "Um, same as you have every week then?"

"What can I say? I'm *desperately* fond of cherries." Vasili dips his head and grazes his dangerous mouth over the half-healed crescent of the mating bite I've left on Neo's shoulder. "And the next time you're looking for a mating bite, darling, for pity's sake, don't lie to me. Just tell me what you want." His tongue drags across Neo's bite and makes him shiver. "Am I being clear enough for you, First Boy?"

"Uh-huh." My fated mate looks dazed, but his face is still flaming. "Um. I'll just get up now? For the pancakes?"

Vasili poises his mouth over Neo's, almost close enough to kiss.

Everyone in the whole bed pretty much stops breathing. Because these two haven't done the horizontal tango yet, though they got pretty close the other night based on what Neo told me.

"Say please," Vasili whispers. "For me."

Neo sucks in a shaky breath. I can feel his heart pounding through our bond. When he breathes out, his mouth and my snake's are close to brushing. "Please?"

Still straddling Max's lap, I'm ready to burst into flames on the spot.

"Well, since you've asked me so nicely." Suddenly Vasili rolls off the bed (to my intense disappointment, and I'm pretty sure Neo's) and saunters toward the half-bath, but not before I get a searing glimpse of the mouthwatering hard-on outlined against his silky PJs. "Mr. Rasputin, I'll see you downstairs in the library in precisely one hour. I've revised your study plan and graded your rather tedious essay. Don't even think of being late, or I'll make you suffer."

"I will not be late." Max is still sitting up, his arms looped around my waist, with me straddling his lean hips. Which means my boobs are pressed against his chest and his hands are stroking up and down my back.

But his head turns to watch Vasili's sexy body—I honestly wish I could put a sway that sexy in my own booty—till my warlock vanishes into the john.

Only recently has Vasili started storing some of his hair products and cosmetics and facial goop in there with Ronin and Neo and me. (Lucius likes having his own space downstairs.) Seeing the permanently aloof and wary

Goblin King settle into our shared space is a development that makes me really happy.

Max sighs and looks kind of wistful. He's following my thoughts and yearning for Vasili in a way that makes me soften toward him a little.

Still, I really need to know if I can trust him.

"No flaming, Max, I mean it." I figure it bears repeating. "At least not till we know what's what, like Lucius says. We need to know who's pulling the strings for that Tiberius crew. I wanna hear you promise. We good?"

I'm alert and sniffing for any whiff of resistance.

Instead, Max's warm palms spread wide across my chilly back and tuck me in close to his brimstone heat.

He lowers his head and leans his brow against mine. "I am yours to command, my sovereign. Even when I do not like the command you give me."

Okay then. That's kinda, you know, a tiny bit heartwarming? Even when I really wanna stay pissed at him a good while longer over that whole near-death experience.

Maybe there's a shred of hope for the big galoot after all.

Chapter Twenty-Nine
Neo

The moon's about to rise.

We all had an early dinner, because it looks like it's going to be a pretty lively night.

Zara made us all spaghetti with meatballs—even though it wasn't her turn to cook, and normally it's not her favorite thing to do—because she's trying to keep busy, and she's getting too antsy to sit still and study with her heat. I quizzed her on the major periods in our History of Witchcraft textbook while she cooked, with an emphasis on the Arcane War that happened in the witching world in parallel with World War II in the '40s. (That's the chapter she missed playing hooky in Vegas.)

Anyway, I'm pretty satisfied she's going to pass her midterm on that subject, at least.

Science of Witchcraft is Zara's weakest subject, and that's a whole other story.

I hope she'll be able to focus more tomorrow.

You know, after Max breaks her superheat.

"That's not a done deal, baby. We still don't know how this whole scene's gonna go down. Until we do, I'm not deciding, and I'm definitely not committing to a damn thing." Zara's pacing around and around the central hearth, wearing leggings and a hot pink tee shirt so she doesn't ruin anything expensive if she doesn't have time to strip down before she shifts. She's flushed and sweating, even though we cracked the sliding doors open to give her instant access to the courtyard and the open sky when she needs it.

She's also drinking a hefty snifter of Lucius' Hungarian *palinka* to try and relax a little.

I keep a close eye on her from my study nook and try to relax myself. She fucked all the nerves out of me before breakfast and again before lunch (that time with Ronin joining), then she had a fuckfest of monumental proportions with Lucius and Vasili (her alphas) right after dinner. V's also been all over Ronin and Lucius, who are both still in heat themselves.

Basically, everyone's been fucking except Max.

Because he isn't officially part of our harem.

At least, uh, not yet.

Now the dragon's been totally banished to his studio apartment down the hall, because Zara's worried he'll set off her shift if he's too close, and she wants to control when it happens.

I feel bad for him, so I spent some time walking him through the four base proteins in a genetic sequence and the magical traits associated with each. He asked me to tutor him in Genetics, and he's supposedly in there right now doing some basic DNA transcription exercises I set out for him.

I'd like to check on him again, just to see if he needs my help.

But I'm actually afraid to leave Zara so close to moonrise.

The rest of us are all right here in the great room with her. Lucius is quietly grading papers at the dining room table. Ronin is sprawled, shirtless and sweating, all over the sofa with his Common Magics spell book spread open across his lap, trying to practice his glamor magic (when his heat lets him focus). He's just turned Racetrack's hair pink, but I'm pretty sure she doesn't know it (yet). RT's wearing her vintage earphones and listening to music while she paints Dez's toenails on the carpet by the fire. Dez is flipping rapidly through the neatly lettered formulas on her Alchemy flash cards and muttering to herself.

Vasili's the one who worries me.

He's up to something.

I mean, he's pretty much always up to something.

Tonight he's standing right in front of the open door, even though it's cold and drafty as heck over there. He isn't even wearing a coat, just one of Ronin's silky button-downs that's open all the way down and a pair of jeans riding low on his hips, with a sparkly couture name spread across his perky bottom.

He definitely isn't saying much, and he's been atypically quiet all day, which is at least giving poor Max a break from that wickedly poisonous tongue and all that unrelenting Goblin King malice. V actually looks kinda warm, even though he's the only guy in this house who isn't either in rut or in heat.

Except me.

Because, yeah, I don't feel any different—physically, I mean—since Zara bit me.

My treasured one has been super attentive and super sweet with my bite, fussing over it and giving it plenty of licks with her shifter saliva to keep it clean, and she keeps asking me how I'm feeling. I actually love that she's so focused on me, with her own superheat about to kick in. But, like I keep telling her, it totally isn't necessary. Because I don't think anything's happening—you know, biologically—with me.

I'm really disappointed, even though I know Lucius is incredibly relieved.

But I'll deal with my disappointment later.

The winter night's falling fast over the courtyard, making the steamy turquoise gleam of the swimming pool stand out in the gloom. A pale glow silhouettes the *domus* roof on the opposite wing. That's where the moon's rising.

I definitely notice that Zara's very carefully *not* looking over there.

"My dear, you'll exhaust yourself pacing," Lucius says gently. "Why not try sitting down for just a moment to finish your *palinka*?"

"Can't," my beloved says curtly. "If I stop moving and siphoning off all this energy, I'm gonna burn up."

She takes a hefty swig of her drink and… just keeps swigging. She tips her glass back, her pretty throat rippling as she swallows and swallows. She doesn't lower that glass till it's empty.

When she finally does, she licks her lips and looks fretful. "So thirsty. Do we have any more?"

Lucius is watching her closely. "Perhaps a glass of water—"

"No!" she snarls. My cherished one, who's never snarled at Lucius since the day he bit her. Her husky voice is all distorted by the deep brassy rumble of her dragon.

"Bloody hell." Ronin sits up and tosses aside his spell book. (Racetrack's short hair is half pink, half lavender. She's not a girly-girl, like, *at all*, and I really hope he changes it back before she sees it.) "It happening then, love?"

Zara's glass slips from her fingers to the floor and shatters with a smash. Racetrack glances up sharply, plucks off her earphones, then scrambles up with a curse.

My cherished one wraps both arms around her middle and huddles around herself with a moan.

"Babe?" I push to my feet with a jolt of alarm.

Then I feel it.

Holy.

Crap.

Waves of arousal—like, really strong ones—rippling and pulsing all through her like lava.

"Stay away," she moans, hair falling forward to curtain her face. "All of you. If you touch me, you'll trigger the shift."

"Zara, my precious heart." Lucius is on his feet too, but he does what she says and keeps his distance. "Shall we just step outside together? It's all right to let go, truly—"

"Noooooo." My wonderful fated mate slides both hands between her thighs and starts massaging. That's where it hurts, where her heat is cresting. Her head jerks up, and I can't hold back a gasp. Her eyes look just like Max's, orbs burning gold with vertical pupils. "Have—to—control—this—"

RT takes one look at Zara basically masturbating on the spot and drags Dez to her feet. "We're, uh, gonna clear out and just leave you guys to it."

"Go," Zara growls in her dragon voice. "Hurry!"

Even though she's bi, Zara hasn't shown any interest yet in adding other girls to our polycule. Dez and Racetrack aren't in it and don't want to be. They're monogamous and, I'm pretty sure, one hundred percent lesbian. That works out for us guys too, because the gals are basically like sisters to us, and Zara's not normally into them in a sexual way either.

Which is why Dez and Racetrack are clearing out so fast.

Before Zara's hormones take over.

The girls take off upstairs, with Dez throwing a single wild look over her shoulder as they flee, checking out the glass doors and the fat full moon that's rising into view.

I'm just opening my mouth to suggest that V might want to get out from between Zara and the door when the Goblin King suddenly gasps, wrenches the door all the way open, and rushes out into the courtyard himself.

Which is kinda… unexpected?

Geez. He isn't even wearing shoes.

"Oh, fuck me." Ronin leaps to his feet like he's just been goosed. As he stares wildly after V's vanished form, his face goes absolutely electric with shock and some kind of dawning realization that I totally don't get. "Lucius, what the actual *fuck*?"

My gaze shoots across the room to Lucius, who's staring after Vasili with a look I've never seen on him before either. His face is set with kind of a grim resignation, mingled with… guilt?

Whatever's happening to V out there, Lucius is definitely in on it.

"What's going on?" Confused and upset, I come out from behind the desk.

Zara stops rubbing herself long enough to rip her tee shirt over her head and shove her pants violently down her legs. She isn't wearing anything underneath in preparation for this whole experience.

And I know this superheat situation isn't something she wants and is therefore horrible for her but, Lord, she's like something airbrushed and supernaturally perfect and ripped straight out of a high-end porno mag (you know, one of the classier ones).

Her gorgeous breasts are definitely riper and fuller, her areolae flushed so pink they're almost the exact current shade of RT's hair. Her nipples are taut and practically the size of cherries. Her skin's glowing Malibu gold, her hair's swirling and floating around her head, her smooth pussy's all swollen and glistening like a fresh split peach.

Her juices are so plentiful they're literally dripping down her thighs.

The entire room, and probably the entire house, is fragrant with her creamy floral mating scent.

One whiff of all those Mogadon pheromones she's pumping out has me peeling the sweater over my head and Ronin dragging down his zipper. Even though his conflicted stare keeps veering between Zara and the door V just bolted through.

All of a sudden, I'm absolutely frantic for a fuck.

And, clearly, so is he.

"Outside, my dear, quickly." Lucius sounds insistent but controlled, like nothing's happening here that he hasn't planned for (which is probably true), even as he rapidly unbuttons his sweater vest and shirt. "You don't want to shift in the house."

"I don't—want to shift—at all," she grits between clenched jaws. *"Don't—want to—fucking—rise—"*

Bang! The slam of wood against plaster echoes down the hall.

That's the sound of Max's bedroom door flying open.

Zara's eyes narrow in determination and defiance. Naked and snarling, she bolts for the glass doors at a dead run and dives into the courtyard.

She's barely outside when a nuclear flash lights up the night and sears my corneas.

I yell and cover my face, just for a sec. When I force my hands down and my eyes open, I catch a split-second glimpse through the glowing spots dancing in my vision of two powerful clawed legs and a blue-green tail, scaly and forked.

That's Zara in her dragon form, rising into the sky.

Max comes pounding into the room like an Olympic sprinter, not wearing a stitch of clothing, his hair streaming behind him like a battle flag. His reptilian eyes are on fire and, holy shit, he has fangs like Lucius. (Who knew?!)

That dragon slices one blazing look at Ronin, who's naked too at this point, and Lucius—the other alpha in the room—who's slipping his shirt off his shoulders and stalking toward Ronin and me like, you know, a hunting wolf.

Max snarls through his fangs at Lucius, whose own fangs punch down in response to the threat. Lucius' eyes flame red and he snarls back.

But Zara's rising in her mating flight (clearly) and there's no force on this planet that's strong enough to keep Max from chasing her.

He pelts right past all of us through the doors and leaps into the air. This time I manage to squeeze my eyes shut before a blast of light and heat sears my face.

When I take a peek, the courtyard is dark and empty.

Lucius grips Ronin with the savage violence I only ever see when his wolf is surfacing, jerks him roughly around, and shoves him brutally face down over the couch. I'm simultaneously tearing open my chinos (because I might as well take advantage of Lucius being in this mood, and Ronin's definitely going to be all over me) and rushing for the door (because I'm desperate for a glimpse of Zara up there) when a *third* freaking blast of heat lights up the courtyard.

"What is even *happening* right now?" I really don't like yelling and hardly ever do it, but I have to admit it relieves the tension.

Even when, you know, no one answers.

Lucius is about two breaths away from shoving his thick cock balls-deep inside Ronin with zero foreplay and fucking him dry. Because, uh, we don't keep lube in the great room. Normally I'd run and get some to help everyone out.

But this is not a normal time.

I burst into the cold dark courtyard, snow crunching under my loafers, and peer up at the starry skies. But Zara took off like a bolt of lightning, Max too, and they're already out of sight.

"Hey, V?" Shivering, I hug my naked torso and peer into the shadows, really wishing I had infrared vision the way Zara says she does in dragon form. "Vasili?"

Chapter Thirty
Zara

I feel like I've been dipped in fire.

I'm being burned alive.

Frigid wind howls past me, crystallizes the moisture in my eyes, and freezes the air in my lungs to ice. But underneath that superficial crust of cold, my blood burns and churns in my veins like molten lava. And whatever kind of dragon pussy I've got lurking down there under my dragon tail is like an erupting volcano of need.

I beat my wings harder, gaining height and speed, desperate to put as much distance between me and my dragon king as possible.

Because if he gets anywhere close, like within sniffing distance? There's no force in this universe that's gonna keep him off me.

And I'm literally burning for a fuck with that barbed dragon cock.

Faster, fly faster! my dragon queen hisses. *To win us and mate us, first he must catch us.*

Yep, this is my mating flight all right.

And for maybe the first time ever, I'm in total sync with my inner monster. She wants us flying like hell to make Max prove himself before he fucks us. And I want us flying like hell so we can just fucking outfly him.

I'm already fully extended, but my new dragon body isn't exactly used to this kind of exertion. This island gets buffeted by some pretty intense wind (because, you know, island) and the wards make it way worse. Every gust that hits my wings makes me pitch and yaw like crazy, and every crosswind makes me bleed speed and burn energy.

Which I definitely can't afford.

The dark bulk of the island spreads under me. Between puffs of cumulus skidding across the heavens in a raking wind, a sky full of stars and that fat orange moon opens above me. When I flick out my tongue, the icy air tastes tinny with the threat of snow. My scaly skin tingles with the promise of winter lightning. Strength and heat pulse through my powerful body with every wingbeat.

On one level, I feel amazing. And I'd kinda like to savor this whole experience.

But my mating frenzy is a raging fire that makes me frantic.

I need to control and channel this raw intensity.

Somehow.

I can't just give in and roll over and let my all-consuming hunger for that dragon cock make my decisions for me. I won't let this mindless hunger own me—

A sudden shadow falls between me and the moon. Pure instinct tilts my wings and sends me into a nosedive. Just a few feet overhead, a massive black shape hurtles past and buffets me with his backdraft. The deep bronze bellow of an enraged dragon splits the air.

Too close!

That sly and crafty would-be mate of mine flew swift and silent from the *domus*, stayed sneakily in my six where I couldn't smell or see him, and flew within a whisker of a freaking ambush. If my reaction time was a second slower, my mating flight would've been over before it even got going.

I scream my fury in a fork of lightning I let rip from my throat with savage purpose—not to hit him (no matter how pissed I am) but as a warning. With lazy grace, the infuriating ass cants his big body to one side and avoids my warning shot with annoying ease.

I tuck my wings in tight and dive.

He rumbles what sounds like dragon laughter and plummets in pursuit.

Like I said before, I'm smaller and more agile than he is. His monstrous size and those heavy horns curling on his head increase his wind resistance and slow him down. I'm faster than he is, but I'm already tiring, and I definitely haven't logged as many dragon frequent flyer miles. This guy's like a million miler on Dragon Air. So it's pretty obvi he's just flat out better than me at dealing with the crosswinds and headwinds and turbulence and all that shit.

At least for now. Till I get better than him.

Which I will.

Right now, he's playing with me. Maybe it's fun for him, ducking in and out of my visual range, suddenly sweeping up on me from underneath or dropping down on me from above and basically flying flaming circles around me.

But I think he's doing it to establish his dominance.

And that just pisses me right off.

He's fucking getting laid tonight over my dead and decomposing body.

I let loose with a rage-filled scream—

Suddenly he's *right there*. Right in front of me.

My dragon heart explodes with panic. Furiously I bate and backwing—

His giant body wraps around me, forearms and hind legs clamping tight, wings beating hard to hold us both aloft. His tail lashes around mine and drags my tail aside to expose that vulnerable hole I've barely even had a chance to check out on my own goddamn body.

Sweet Jesus. In dragon form, I'm a virgin.

How am I even gonna deal with that ginormous dragon cock?

Is my BC really gonna work when I'm in dragon form? What if he fucks me and I, like, lay eggs?

The sharp prick of his cock thrusts roughly between my legs. Raw lust pounds in my pussy. I can literally feel the mouth of my dragon hoochie parting and opening like a flower in welcome.

My inner queen croons, long and low, a sound like a moan that's literally drenched with sex. He makes a rumbly sound that's somewhere between a purr and a growl.

Doesn't even matter that I know it's gonna hurt. My body craves that sex-laced pain. I thirst to suffer for him.

Jesus, I'm so fucked.

Rage and panic sandblast my brain. I can't think straight. Rational tools like words and telepathy elude my frantic clutch.

I bugle in fury—that's me saying *oh hell to the no* in dragon form—and sink my teeth into his muscled neck.

He bellows in triumph and buries his fangs deep in my shoulder.

Pain and pleasure rip through me. My dragon cunt clenches. My hole floods with slick and drenches his tool. His cock prods for the angle he needs to sink deep and lock inside me, while I writhe and hump and claw at him and work my fangs deeper into his throat. The rich meaty broth of his blood, spiked with brimstone, explodes in my mouth. His jaws clamp around my shoulder to demand my submission. His tongue flickers over my scales and laves his punctures with dragon spit that burns like acid.

What are the odds that at least one of us, and possibly both of us, just gave the other a fucking mating bite?

Fueled by desperation, I stop gnawing on his throat and thrash free from his jaws. Maybe I can break his grip before his bite can, like, take. But, OMFG, the way his cock is prodding at my starved and throbbing hole—

The howling wind parts around a piercing scream. A scream of eardrum-shattering proportions.

It's not mine.

It's not his.

Which can only mean it's the scream of… a third goddamn dragon.

What.

The.

Fuck.

This monster I'm halfway fucking throws his head back and trumpets a rage-filled challenge. His eyes tinge red with bloodlust.

I twist my neck to watch a streak of glittering silver flash past. It *is* another dragon, it really and truly is. But this new arrival is, like, a whole different species from Maxim and me. This new guy's a coiling eel with a maned head, like a sea serpent, his sinuous body completely sheathed in ice and diamond scales that glisten with glints of cobalt and emerald. No forearms or back legs or limbs of any kind. He's a literal serpent. Except for just the prettiest pair of iridescent feathered wings you've ever seen.

He's a flying snake.

My tongue flickers out to taste the air, drenched with the feral stink of dragon. I can smell cock on that thing. He smells like caramel and vetiver.

Under a flowing silver mane like a wild stallion's, sky-blue eyes, lidded in glittery silver, meet my astounded stare.

How do you like the effect, darling? a familiar voice purrs in my head. *Is it a good look?*

Goblin King?? Both my words and my telepathy flood back in a tingling rush. *Sweet bleeding Christ! How…?*

I can't even start to wrap my head around what's happening here. Like how my snake just fucking shifted to an actual flying snake. And clearly now is not the time, because this big bastard of a dragon I'm almost fucking is roaring and steam's leaking around his fangs.

My snake has given me my words back. Now I hurl them at this horny black Godzilla who's clutching me like I'd hurl a bolt of lightning.

If you fucking flame at my mate, Maxim Rasputin, you can fly straight back to the domus *and pack your goddamn bags.*

Max roars and tilts his muzzle at the sky to unleash a torrent of boiling crimson flame. But he's very clearly *not* aiming at the white dragon.

He's obeying my command.

Even though he obviously doesn't like it.

He's obeying me the way he promised.

Vasili flows with liquid grace into a serpentine loop—leave it to the Goblin King to shift into a pretty dragon—and parts his jaws like some well-bred Jane Austen lady patting a delicate yawn. A blizzardy swirl of snow and hail pours from his mouth. He politely misses Max, but he's showing off.

He's some kinda ice dragon.

Which is perfect for a warlock shifter who's a water sign.

Then he eels down in a long fluid scroll of dragon toward the dark island below. The white dragon's taunting croon unfurls on the wind behind him, daring us to chase.

I explode from the black dragon's stunned and loosened grasp and plummet after my snake.

Max roars so loud he nearly shakes the stars loose from their moorings. Then he wings after both of us in furious pursuit.

Vasili's silver serpent is bigger than me, smaller than Max, and faster than greased lightning. He flows through the night like milk poured from a pitcher. He's magic to watch, and my queen is overjoyed to have two kings—the snake and the dragon—competing for our favor in this epic mating flight.

She doesn't even mind us chasing Vasili instead of Vasili chasing us. After all, my Goblin King's a little bit of a queen himself.

He always steals the spotlight.

Under the slender scroll of his serpentine body, the twisting maze of village streets flashes past. The Gothic bulk of the cathedral looms ahead, bell tower jutting into the sky like an erect phallus.

Guess who's got dick on her mind?

Vasili flows toward the tower. Max is breathing down my neck. I dive low to keep my freedom and wing hard after my snake with the last shreds of my failing strength.

Vasili streams into the belfry with a blinding flash of light. That's him shifting back to his warlock shape.

I fold my wings in tight and arrow in his wake. My nose is barely in the belfry when my dragon shape falls away in a flash that sizzles like a lightning strike.

I hit the snowy floor barefoot and race naked across the roof without slowing, under the peaked cupola, past the massive shape of the hanging bell where Lucius first fucked me and taught me to summon the lightning.

My snake has already slithered into the covered staircase and vanished.

Behind me, Max lands with a roar that morphs into a wordless human shout in a brilliant blaze of light. The quick *crunch-crunch-crunch* of human footsteps in virgin snow chases me into the dark tunnel of the stairs.

Around and around and down and down the coiling stairs I run, hearing Max's harsh breath and pounding steps raising echoes from above, but not hearing a peep from Vasili below. I burst from the darkness into the moonlight of the choir loft library where Max kissed Vasili so disastrously and—

A tall shadow darts from behind a bookcase and pounces.

Before I can even snatch in a breath, a cold mouth tasting like cherries presses against mine. Icy hands drag me behind the bookcase into a slice of darkness. Twin fangs sharp as scalpels press into my lower lip. A tongue dipped in juniper swirls around mine.

That's the taste of Goblin.

I wind my grateful arms around Vasili's neck and writhe against his naked body. His hands cup my ass and drag me up against the supple jut of his cock.

My closet monster wants him.

I want him.

This fiery heat is burning me alive and I want him to fuck me into that wall behind him until I shatter.

"My snake," I breathe against his silken lips, and he hums with pleasure. "How's this even happening, bad boy?"

"You didn't wish to be left alone with that dragon and your superheat," the Goblin King whispers, menacing my mouth with his pretty fangs. "Lucius and I merely ensured you wouldn't be."

"Lucius!" My brain races, putting two and two together in the obvious way. I've always been good at math. "He fucking bit you, didn't he? All those biochemicals in his shifter DNA triggered your switch, just like his bite triggered mine. But I don't see where?"

"Inner thigh." His snaky tongue licks into my mouth. "To hoard my advantage and keep it secret—"

"At last." A sandpaper voice scrapes my ear. "We finish the hunt."

The physical impact of a hard body sears into my back like a column of living flame. Max's ruthless arm locks around my hips like a dragon's tail. His hand dips between my legs. Brutal fingers slide down my wet slit. One coated finger shoves deep inside my cunt.

The sudden shock of penetration, coupled with the hard press of his palm against my clit, makes my heat spike. The contact wrings an instant O out of my overstimulated body.

I convulse and shout and shudder like he's hooked me up to jumper cables and switched on the juice.

My basement goes slick and my channel clamps down on his finger. My hips ride his hand like a dildo.

Max growls and wraps his other hand in Vasili's disheveled hair. My snake hisses like a boiling kettle. Their mouths crash together, these two alphas who've hunted me and hunted each other at the same time, in a blazing kiss.

I'm trapped between them and their luscious cocks, Vasili's long shaft jutting against my belly and smearing my tummy with precum, Max's forked tool jabbing into the crack of my ass and already dripping.

Yowsa.

These two swords are definitely gonna cross tonight.

"Your dragon," Max says thickly between kisses. "Vasili, he is beautiful. You are so beautiful and so perfect for me. Both of you. You are mine."

Vasili takes control of the whole flaming mess, all three of us sexed up and breathless and writhing with need. He steers our entwined bodies toward the big black leather sofa in the reading nook.

We topple into it in a pile with Max on the bottom, me squirming around to face him, my thighs closing around his hips, and Vasili behind me on top. My snake's cool fingers glide up my slit to sweep a generous swipe of my own slick over my pucker.

Hell to the yeah.

Both my inner dragon and I like where this is going.

The Goblin King grips a fistful of the dragon's hair and swoops in to kiss him like a striking cobra. I love that Max seems comfortable navigating Vasili's fangs, which has always been a sensitive subject for my snake.

If I had to guess, based on what I'm getting through our bond, I'd say my snake's fangs are actually turning on my dragon.

The same way they turn me on.

The flash of tongue between them, coupled with Max's hoarse groan, works my hips in a building rhythm against all those exotic inches scraping between my thighs. The dragon's dripping precum and I'm gushing and I'm not afraid of losing control anymore. Not with Vasili right here in the bond with us. I'm not afraid of that dragon cock either. Ronin loved it inside him last night. Max never went full cray battering ram with that thing the way I worried he might.

Vasili and Max and me.

We can all be a thing.

They're not gonna let anything bad happen with the three of us.

Not ever.

Between deep consuming kisses that are battles for dominance in the war they've been waging, Max flexes his pelvis into my cunt and growls, "You are mine and I am yours. Say it."

"Both of us belong to her." Vasili breaks free of Max's mouth and nuzzles the fresh mating bite on my shoulder. "But I'm the dominant alpha in her harem, *malchik*. You're subordinate to me and Lucius."

I kinda hold my breath over that ultimatum while Max grumbles and scowls. But we're all pretty distracted with more immediate issues.

That's three warlock alphas who've bitten me now, in case anyone's losing track.

Cheese on toast. I'm gonna be in permanent heat.

"Our sovereign." Max's mouth meets Vasili's over my bite (this is one of those more immediate issues I was just talking about), both of them licking the punctures and each other. "Will you take us both, my Zara? Both of us together to be your kings."

I suck in a breath and my heart starts racing. But I'm in no condition to hold up my end of this heart-to-heart till my guys break this superheat. My dragon's rubbing his forked cock up and down my slit, getting both of us good and soaked and ready. Every time one of his barbs scrapes my happy spot, he moans, and it's like a firecracker goes off in my clit.

Meanwhile, my snake is working a slick finger into my pucker. Fuck. I'm gonna come all over again from that back door action.

"Okay," I pant. "We'll talk to the other guys. We will. But I got a pretty strong feeling they're gonna agree."

"All of us share Ronin," Max whispers in my ear.

Uh-oh.

My snake quivers with a ripple of electric violence. Vasili's always been over-the-top possessive of Ronin, and Max is kinda the same way, there's something about Ronin that brings it out in our alphas.

Guess I better referee on this one.

"That does seem to be what Ronin wants," I remind the room at large. "If he's into it, we should go for that."

Of course, that's easy for me to say. I'm possessive as fuck about Ronin too, but for me, sharing him with another girl would be the deal-breaker. I love sharing him with my guys.

I arch my back and push my ass into the Goblin King's finger with a moan. He purrs with satisfaction and works in another finger.

But he still doesn't answer.

Be nice to the dragon for me, I coax Vasili through our bond. *You know you'll always be our snake.*

We all suffer through a loooong and angsty silence.

"I suppose I won't *entirely* object to having an occasional tag team partner," my snake says tightly. A river of relief floods through me. For once in his life, he's going to try to be reasonable. "That's assuming Ronin himself consents, because I won't have him pressured. But he's always been one to appreciate a proper DP. Rather similar to the thorough reaming our queen's about to receive."

"Oh shit," I whimper. I can't take this anymore. The combination of the foreplay and the anticipation are lighting me on fire.

I reach between us to fit Max's forked tip to the mouth of my cunt. We all moan in unison.

Vasili swears softly in Russian and replaces his fingers in my ass with the head of his dick. All three of us are pumping out enough moisture that there's plenty of natural lube to work with. The Goblin King grips my hips and eases me into a slow swivel that lets me start working both of them into my two tight holes.

Ooh boy.

Not gonna lie, those two barbs are gonna take some getting used to. They scrape and poke against my tender inner tissues in a steadily building irritation.

My rear passage simultaneously stretches and burns under the inexorable prod of Goblin cock, parting and pressing into my pucker.

I know this whole thing's about to get a whole lot more intense.

"And what of that boy who is our queen's fated mate?" Max says, all gruff and thick from the slow suck of my pussy enveloping his cock. "Do we share him? I saw in our bed this morning that you all desire to fuck that one. I confess, I can see the appeal."

Is this even the same homophobic dragon who got my snake thrown out of his parents' not-exactly-loving home? This stubborn and taciturn renegade Russian who just lusted over three of my mates?

"Yeah, Neo's gonna like that a lot—" My words choke off and I hiss with effort. Between the two of them, both working their determined way into my various places, that's a lot of pressure and a truckload of stimulation to process.

"And I suppose there is also that wolf," Max mutters.

"Oh, there is no *supposing*. Lucius is very much a part of anything and *everything* we build together." Suddenly my snake is all purring menace. "*That wolf* is completely non-negotiable, darling. He's part of this."

The dragon's eyes narrow. I can feel him cautiously processing the notion of adding a fourth mate to his male stable.

He'd never admit it, but I can tell Lucius intimidates him.

"Don't worry, big guy." I nuzzle Max's scruffy jaw. "The two of you can work out between you what kind of relationship you want. But you're really gonna like Lucius once you get to know him."

"Well, then, I will try." Admittedly, he sounds a little grumpy. "Even though I do not see at all how three alphas in a harem will work. I am the Sagittarius prince. How can I be subordinate to another?"

"How about you leave all that to me. We're all pretty much equal in this polycule anyway. That's an uber-hard line for me." I wiggle my way deeper onto his cock and impale myself on his shaft.

C'mon, showgirl, I encourage my pussy, which is now burning in ways that are both good and problematic. *You're an industrial-grade pussy. You are titanium. You were made for this.*

My titanium pussy still isn't sure about all this.

But it definitely helps that my climax is building.

Vasili's cock is so long that taking him, especially this way, always feels like he's gonna fill me till he comes in my throat. He's still only about halfway in, because he's waiting for Max (in a very unsnakelike way) so they can do this with me together. But he's, like, *really* talented at back-door action. He's patient when it's called for, but he's also relentless, with insane amounts of stamina.

My ass is already fluttering and clenching around all that length of his in a way that's setting the rest of me off.

I cup Max's face between my palms, slant my mouth over his brimstone kiss, and rock my cunt into that forked devil's tail he's got for a cock. Those twin barbs shoot out and lock in my channel with a *plink!* of impact that makes me yelp. The contact dredges out of him a deep groan.

The bond between us pulses with his fiercely satisfied possession.

"Now you are mine at last, my Zara," he grunts through gritted teeth. "You are both mine. You are mine. You are *mine*."

With every grunt, he works his way deeper. Every fraction of an inch of terrain he claims rips a cry from my throat. Stars explode behind my eyes with every thrust.

"Well, darlings," Vasili breathes, "it's about fucking *time*."

On the last syllable, he too seats himself deep, like he's embedded and taking root in my soul.

That soul-deep connection makes all three of us yell.

Suddenly, the pain I'm experiencing dissolves into smoke and drifts away. Any residual discomfort seems way less important than this typhoon of pleasure that's howling through all three of us.

Yeah, Max is locked in good and tight, but my titanium pussy's finally kicking in.

Which means he's starting to feel fucking amazing.

He and my snake are definitely doing me as a team, like twin pistons in a damn machine, one of them on the downstroke while the other's on the recoil. The Goblin King's getting plenty of forked friction through the thin membrane inside me that separates those two cocks, and he's starting to lose his mind a little from the pleasure.

Which actually loosens his notoriously unflappable tongue.

"Darling," he moans, so soft I can barely hear, his body plastered to my back, hips flexing fiercely into mine, face buried in my hair. "Do you… do you love me?"

My heart melts into an instant puddle of goop. Because how can he possibly still not know? My mouth pops open to impress on him in no uncertain terms that *yes*, I would kill for him, he's my Goblin King, he fucking *ruins* me—

But Max gets there first. "I have loved both of you as long as I have known you. Let the world end, and I will love you. There is no place you can go where I will not follow. What you love, I will cherish and protect. Your enemies are my enemies. For you, I will ravage and destroy."

Well, dayum.

That right there's practically a marriage vow.

My heart gives a sharp *ping!* as something essential I've always been missing snaps and locks into place. Like a missing piece of my soul made whole.

This is the moment I fall in love with the dragon.

He's loved me from the start. I'm his mate and his sovereign. I'm his everything. Under all my pride and rage and defiance, behind all his pigheaded stubbornness and breeding kink and his infuriating threats against my warlocks, I've always known I'm central to every choice he makes. Even when his unshakable certainty made me rage.

I'm the whole reason he's here. On this island and in our bed.

But it's Max owning the secret truth of his love for Vasili, despite their loaded history and all that homophobic baggage, that finally makes me love the big galoot back.

Vasili shudders like he's falling apart. His tempo stutters and splinters.

Hot damn. Max saying he loves him is gonna make my lonely love-starved snake blow his load.

And it's all the more impressive that Max says all this while he's hammering into me and straining with pleasure. While he's pumping out a steady drizzle of dragon spunk that my greedy pussy is hoovering up and sucking deep inside. He's flooding my basement with extremely potent Grade A seed, my uterus is absorbing all that jizz like a sponge.

I really hope my BC shots are up to the challenge.

My snake pumps fiercely into my ass, one hand clamped on my hip hard enough to bruise, the other fisted in my hair to arch my back and bare my throat like a sacrifice. Shrill cries wrench from his chest like the feel of me clamped and pulsing around him is breaking him.

When he goes rigid and his cock kicks and spurts deep inside me, I hurl myself over the cliff in free fall.

My mind reaches out by instinct for Ronin. Because he's such a strong telepath, I can reach him all the way across town. Right away, my warlock's love surges in welcome and wraps tight around me.

Even though he's… busy.

Holy shit, all three of them are busy.

If I'm reading this right, baby Neo's getting spit-roasted on the

Renaissance sofa by the two of them. Lucius is so deep in his wolf right now that he doesn't even feel guilty or apologetic about the imminent prospect of losing his load down Neo's happily accommodating throat. When Ronin's cock explodes in about five seconds in my fated mate's drum-tight tushy, that's finally gonna break his mating heat.

I'm sorry to be missing that particular action.

But all's well with all my kings—all five of them. All five of these powerful mates who will stand behind my throne and rule at my side.

And I'm kinda busy right now myself.

Besides, I know the absent three will give me the full blow by blow (hardy-har) later.

My floating mind slips back into my body with a snap.

My cunt clenches and ripples around Max's dick as he pistons hard and fast inside me. Static races and crackles over all three of our locked and straining bodies. I'm so full of dragon spunk that my lower belly feels warm and distended. His lock bottles up most of it, but he's still spurting inside me. My thighs are soaked with his juices and mine. My whole body's slick with sweat.

Vasili's silky mouth closes over the new mating bite on my shoulder in a way that makes goosebumps race over my skin.

Max's hot mouth locks around my nipple in a fierce sucking pull that shoots straight to my clit.

I arch back in their arms, both my kings, and scream to the heavens in the lightning voice. The whole room glows ultraviolet in the witchy light that spills from my eyes. Thunder rips open the night, a holocaust of light flashes platinum through the tall arched windows, and the church bell dongs once in a deep-throated hum.

I could shatter this church like an eggshell with one whack from my lightning hammer. But I don't. I'm in control. I'm in command. The lightning does my bidding and slams—powerfully, joyfully, harmlessly—into the winter sea.

The bell's still humming, the church sizzling with amperage, the whole island pulsing with Gemini power, when my kings smash my first superheat like a Molotov cocktail.

Bring on that so-called rival of mine and anyone else who questions my right to rule the witching world.

Bring.

Them.

On.

Me and my Gemini kings? The six of us—the snake, the dragon, the wolf, the telepath, the alchemist, and the lightning, all six of us together—we're unstoppable.

Chapter Thirty-One
Lucius

I finish grading the last midterm at midnight.

This endeavor on my part has been substantial, but essential. This is because the Dean has clearly indicated she will permit the considerable disruption of a WNN television crew inside the formidable island wards tomorrow if—and only if—every student in my cohort passes their midterms.

The fire in my potbellied stove has dwindled, the acrid scent of charred wood mingles with the dank smell of damp stone, and my office in the church crypt is growing cold as the tomb it is.

Eyeing the sarcophagus where the bones of my long-dead predecessor provide macabre but quiet company, I lean back in my desk chair and stretch to ease the cramped muscles knotted between my shoulder blades.

Perhaps I'll shed my tie and pants and blazer right here and allow my wolf out to lope through the snowy streets to the *domus*.

The moon is finally waning, which means our various heats are sputtering out. In a few days, Zara's monthly will arrive. She tends to be less energetic sexually during that time (although my own hunger for her is entirely unabated), so that tends to be a quieter and more restful interlude for our polycule.

I do hope it won't overly disgruntle Maxim, who's still settling into his new relationships with the group, when that incontrovertible biological evidence arrives to confirm our still-childless state.

Zara simply isn't prepared to start clutching dragonets. Or wolf pups, for that matter, although I find that singular prospect is not at all unappealing.

She's made her current position on pregnancy abundantly clear.

Indeed, I dare say none of us—including Maxim—is truly ready to assume the heavy mantle of parenthood just yet.

I'm switching off my desk lamp and tucking my tidy pile of graded examinations into my briefcase when a mannerly knock on my office door makes me smile. There's only one person who would come to fetch me home at this hour who'd knock so politely.

"Come in, sweet boy," I call softly.

Neo slips into my sanctum, still wearing his sober coat, his earnest face ruddy with cold, snowflakes melting in his curls.

"I couldn't stay away any longer," he explains with a shy smile. "And we all miss you, so Zara sent me to bring you home. If you're still working…?"

"Actually, I've just finished grading the last examination." I snap my briefcase closed and permit myself to savor the warm glow of belonging to someone. Indeed, I relish this unprecedented sensation of having several someones actually give a single flaming damn if I stay up working half the night. "I'm just packing up, Neo. Why don't we walk home together?"

Intense interest in his academic results kindles in his green eyes, although they're rather difficult to see, since his glasses are steaming. "Lucius… that essay on the dangers of contested succession in your History exam… I've been so distracted that it's been really hard to study. I hope you're not too, um, disappointed in my grade?"

He's so anxious about his grade that he's already rushed around my desk. He seems fully prepared to drop to his knees and clasp his hands in entreaty, as though I'm some sort of religious icon and he's praying to me for mercy.

Before he can fall to his knees, I slip my arms around his waist and urge him gently forward to straddle my lap between his muscular thighs instead.

"Well," I explain to his worried face, "the grades post tomorrow. But I dare say you'll keep your spot at the head of the Dean's List, First Boy."

"Really?" At once, he flushes rosy with pleasure.

"Yes, really." I can't resist the urge to adjust the glasses sliding down his nose, which then leads to me stealing one of his sweet, yielding, minty-tasting kisses. "Perfect score on your Alchemy exam, so well done you. In addition, Mistress Agrippina has awarded you extra credit for tutoring Maxim in Genetics. Even though he won't sit for exams until finals, that was a true kindness on your part."

"Gosh, it was nothing, he was just all worried about getting sent away, and I wanted to make him feel better." Neo straightens my tie and smooths my lapels and fusses over my rumpled late-night attire in his adorable way. "What about Zara? How did she do? She's really been worrying about her results, pretty much all night. You know she gave you permission to tell me."

Despite the somewhat questionable ethics of this entire situation (by which I mean, this scandalous relationship I'm now sharing with five of my own students), I know this to be true.

Zara keeps no secrets from Neo any longer.

"Well, she won't make the Dean's List," I say wryly. "Science of Witchcraft in particular is her Waterloo. Nonetheless, she's earned a solid pass in all subjects. Pass with distinction in History of Witchcraft and Lightning Magic. She's managing to do better in Common Magics as she catches up with her peers, after her late start midway through the academic year. Overall, really, I'm quite pleased with her progress."

"Oh, wow, that's so great!" He's so excited that he throws his arms around my neck and hugs me.

I allow myself to smile at his excitement and breathe in his clean sage-and-lavender scent (although he also smells quite a bit like Zara and Ronin and me, since we've all three been all over him, and rather insatiably).

I don't tell him I've already telephoned Zara's results to the Dean, so that she'd agree to lower the wards for that infernal news crew.

Time enough tomorrow to worry about that news crew.

"How are you feeling, my boy?" I ask instead. "How's your bite?"

"Aches a little," he says casually, rubbing his affectionate face into my neck to absorb a bit more of my mating scent.

His casual demeanor leaves me undeceived.

He's desperately hoping that lingering ache from his bite is a belated indication that his mating heat is looming.

In truth, that bite of his *is* healing rather more slowly than I'd like, despite Zara's commendable diligence in tending him.

Still, irrefutably, he isn't in heat. He was bitten days ago, yet he's cool to the touch. Someday soon, the sharp needle of certainty will burst his fragile bubble of hope.

"I'll take a look when we're back at the *domus*." I kiss him again, purely for the joy of it. We've all done so much fornicating in various configurations (although by no means all of them, not just yet) to get Zara through her superheat, Ronin through his, and me through mine—and Neo has been so sweetly and transparently delighted to accommodate my every advance—that I'm finally getting past this lurking sense of guilt over my inexhaustible carnal passion for this innocent student I've been teaching and guiding for years.

In fact, the incendiary notion of bending my star pupil over this desk where I've tutored and counseled him since freshman year for a quick hard fuck right now holds a powerful appeal.

But it's better tonight to wait, really, until we're all back at the *domus* together.

After all, the six of us are still navigating certain tensions.

I ponder those tensions quietly while I bundle up and lock up and tromp through the narrow streets through the silent swirl of snowfall, with Neo's gloved hand tucked in my coat pocket for added warmth.

Beyond any doubt, the worst of those tensions churn around the twin vortices of Maxim and Vasili. Those two are still navigating which of them will eventually bend for the other—both emphatically alpha, both damnably aloof and proud and arrogant, yet both very clearly enamored with each other— which introduces a certain electric tension to our cozy domestic arrangement.

Until they work through the delicate contours of the power dynamic between them, they've mainly indulged as a ménage (or a foursome) and kept Zara (and at times Ronin) firmly between them.

Admittedly, that choreography has worked out explosively well.

For all involved.

As for myself, my wolf and I haven't laid a paw on Maxim, nor will we until some of the more pressing matters in our shared bed are settled… which isn't entirely to say I haven't been tempted. I'm rather waiting to see first if Vasili goes into heat from that bite he insisted that I administer in secret to force his shift. The gambit certainly paid off in the skies the night Zara rose.

All the same, Vasili adamantly maintains that, sexually at least, nothing at all has altered.

Still, I harbor my dark suspicions. My alpha can lie like Lucifer when it suits him, and his telepathic barriers have remained suspiciously high while he and Maxim navigate the perilous complexities of their new arrangement.

Then there's the matter of Vasili and this dear boy trudging up the snowy lane at my side.

I steal a look at Neo's clean-cut profile, his head bent thoughtfully as he trots along. His new earring gleams in the electric light of a nearby streetlamp.

"How are things with you and Vasili?" I venture.

He flicks me a sidelong look through his spectacles. Then the words tumble out far too quickly. "Um, we're okay—I mean, you know, we're not fighting or anything?"

"I see." And I do see, rather clearly, all that still lies unsaid between my alpha and my prize pupil. "You do realize, I trust, that our snake has grown rather… besotted with you?"

"So, um, yeah," he mumbles, his face heating up. "That's an old-fashioned Lucius way of saying V wants to jump my bones and add, like, a Neo-shaped notch to his bedpost. If I ever gave in and just gave him what he wants, he'd be over me in a week."

"Isn't it possible that you're being a bit unfair to him, my boy? As well as rather unjust to yourself?" I ask gently. "There's quite a bit more depth to Vasili than he permits the world to see, and you greatly undervalue your own considerable appeal if you believe all he wants from you is the ego boost of an easy conquest. I suspect you're far more than a longed-for fuck to him, Neo."

He blushes to his hairline to hear the matter put so bluntly.

Still, he stays stubbornly silent.

"Is there something in particular you're waiting to see from him before you decide whether to trust him?" I probe with care.

"Well, for starters, how about an actual apology for being a complete and total shit my whole time at this Academy until the exact moment he fell for Zara?" Neo bursts out, pulling his hand from my pocket and whirling to scowl at me through the snowfall. "He's always been a villain and a snake, and excuse me for daring to question how fast he's shed his skin. I'm not a Valyrian telepath like Ronin and Zara, I'm just a plain old Kryll. I don't share a whole two-way double mating bite bond with him like you do. I didn't grow up with the asshole like Maxim did… practically. How am I ever supposed to be sure I can trust him?"

Even when he's furious, he's adorable, standing there barking at me in the street like an indignant puppy. I have to remind myself not to smile at his entirely genuine frustration.

Instead, I cup his flushed cheek in my gloved hand. "By giving him the chance, sweet boy. Just as you did with me."

"You're nothing like him," he mutters, ducking his head so his magenta curls tumble forward in his eyes. His hair is growing longer, because Zara enjoys that, we all do.

I tuck a thick wing behind his ear so I can gaze into his mutinous eyes. "Why not give him a chance to earn your trust. I'm well aware the two of you were mortal enemies once upon a time. But you've both changed, haven't you, since you chose to join this harem? Our queen needs us all to be in accord. All I'm asking you to do is to consider forgiving him for the sins of his past."

It's clear to me that my First Boy remains reluctant, but he's generous and forgiving by nature, not typically inclined to nurse a grudge, and genuinely eager to please. This means I have these fundamental qualities of his character in my favor.

Patiently I wait until, finally, he heaves a conflicted sigh that seems dredged from the depths of his soul.

"Okay then. I'll think about it. But only to help Zara. And only because it's you asking." He rubs his face affectionately into my palm, then resumes his climb up the zigzag stairs. "Anyway, we better get a move on. Zara's still finishing her heat. She thinks getting bitten by Max during their mating flight kinda… prolonged the whole thing? She's gonna want us together with her and the guys tonight."

My own step quickens at this delectable prospect.

Despite these simmering tensions and unresolved conflicts in our queen's harem, there's nowhere on this earth my wolf and I would rather be tonight than together with our mates—all five of them—in Zara's old-fashioned bed.

Besides, her succession ceremony will be broadcast live to the entire witching world in less than twenty-four hours.

Although my generously financed intelligence collection efforts continue, my inquiries to date regarding the identity and location of this mysterious rival have been spectacularly unfruitful. This means we're going to need all the trust we can possibly build among us, between now and tomorrow night, to defeat our still-unknown enemies.

I maintain this to be the case because, with a spectacle like the one we're about to broadcast, there's no way on earth they aren't coming for her.

Chapter Thirty-Two
Zara

Almost time to hit the stage, showgirl, I encourage my nervous inner dragon. *We can do this. I mean it.*

Angsty and on edge, we circle in the clouds. My dragon body chuffs out an aggressive rumble that makes thunder grumble and lightning flicker in the storm clouds that swirl around the jagged peak of Mt. Apollo. That's the highest point on Icarus Island, barely accessible to the earthbound by a rickety cable car and an even more rickety (and terrifying) ski lift.

But right there on the summit's where we're staging my succession announcement on live TV.

You know, for dramatic effect.

Tonight I'm sharing the airspace above Icarus Island with no fewer than circling three helicopters from the Witching News Network. Plus a literal swarm of WNN news drones.

I'm, uh, not used to this (to put it mildly).

I'm still learning to master the finer points of flight, despite those stolen hours sandwiched between our studies that my snake and my dragon and I have spent playing up here the past few days (when we haven't been taking our midterms, which I've miraculously managed to pass). Those flight drills in the clouds usually end with the three of us—and lately the four of us, since Ronin's figured out how horny the whole experience makes us—off fucking somewhere in a sweaty, cum-sticky pile.

Let's just say I've been getting plenty of dick (and definitely not complaining about it) while Max and the Goblin King figure out how to take all that sexual tension between them to the next level.

Long story short? The two of them *really* want to fuck. But they both want to be on top.

I know, right? Alphas.

Me, I'm gonna be more than good with either option.

Right now, I'm up here all alone. Vasili and Maxim are gonna enter stage left after a bit. My snake's still bipedal down there on the summit, hobnobbing with the news crew, choreographing the whole setup for tonight's performance.

And Max has agreed (reluctantly) to an exclusive pre-performance interview with those pseudo-journalists from that scandal rag *The Witching Inquisitor*.

My politically savvy Neo says we need to take control of the narrative, line up some positive press for once, and set the scene for the coming big reveal. Since Max is the Sagittarius prince and the last fully manifested male dragon (you know, that anyone knows about), it turns out Max is kinda, well, a celebrity. He's like the witching world equivalent of Prince Albert of Monaco—only a lot younger, a lot less stodgy, and a whole lot sexier.

Anyway, that's why I'm up here alone.

Just circling in the clouds, waiting to make my TV debut, and fighting a sudden attack of last-minute jitters. My six-chambered dragon heart is pumping adrenaline-laced ichor (that's dragon blood, and it's green) through my scaly body, the tail end of my mating heat's still burning like a low-grade fever between my legs, and the sweep of my wings through the moisture-laden clouds sparks flickers of lightning that dance along my scales.

I'm so amped up tonight I could power this whole island with my lightning.

Hopefully, it won't come to that.

You good up there, love? Ronin's telepathic touch slides along my senses in a welcome caress.

We've been experimenting, him and me, and he can link up with me as long as I stay over the island—and thus inside the wards—and don't rise too high above the clouds.

Little lonely up here without you and the other guys, I tell him. *You all ready for me yet?*

While I wait for the all-clear, I fold my wings and spin in a tight spiral that lets me see overhead—or *would* let me, if the cloud cover tonight wasn't so freaking thick. My mating flight showed me just how vulnerable I am to attacks from behind and above, so I'm clearing my six pretty regular these days.

Not that it does me any good tonight. Yeah, these clouds are helping me hide from the news cams till we're ready for prime time. But, given this same heavy cloud curtain, anything else could be hiding up here with me.

Dragon me gives a whickering snort of alarm.

Steady, showgirl, I think. *We're still behind the wards. Dean opened the door to let the news crew in, then closed everything right back up again.*

This is absolutely not the time to get paranoid.

Right, then. We're all ready for you. Ronin sounds cool and combat-ready, but his contained excitement crackles through our bond. *Max just wrapped up his interview and leaned pretty hard on the looming extinction of the dragon shifters, just like we planned. The news cams are rolling. Vasili says it's time for your grand entrance.*

Finally, the charged stillness of the heist settles over me. Once I'm in action, my nerves always evaporate with a *poof!*

I rumble out an eager puff into the damp air and angle my wings down.

I emerge from the clouds in a lazy spiral, mentally mapping a course to carry me safely through the circling choppers for maximum visual impact. That drone swarm better watch their mechanical asses, because one sweep of my wings can knock like six of them out of the sky.

In a wide slow sweep, I glide toward the circling aircraft. I find I'm resenting the noisy chatter of their blades after the clouds' bespelled silence. Lights flash and pop across the mountain's summit. Those are the still cams grabbing some shots, to supplement their film footage, of me in Lady Mothra mode as dragon me makes my TV debut.

Because dragon me is central to that whole narrative we're pushing.

I wing through a few last scraps of low-hanging cloud. I'm about to angle my body and plunge between the choppers when that niggling itch I've been fighting all night suddenly gets a whole lot worse.

Without stopping to question that tickle between my shoulder blades, I spin in another tight spiral to clear my six.

Which gives me about three seconds' warning as a dark shape spears through the clouds like an ICBM and hurtles straight at me.

My heart explodes with adrenaline and alarm.

A few days ago, I'd have been too green and way too clumsy in the air to react in time. Now, thanks to all those flight drills Max is putting Vasili and me through, lightning-fast instinct kicks in.

I spin out of my pivot and veer to one side. A massive reptilian form, crowned with wicked black horns and armored in scales of a sinister garnet red, streaks past like an inbound missile.

Somehow, it's yet *another* dragon. Lately, my life seems to be full of them.

What.

The.

Fuck.

Scattered over the summit and packed in the choppers, cameras pop and whirl. WNN's getting a show all right. It's just not the one we planned.

I backwing from the air traffic to give myself headspace.

And fighting room.

Which it looks like I'm gonna need.

Having totally failed in that whole Pearl Harbor sneak attack, Big Red down there trumpets in rage. And takes it out on the little guy. That horned head snakes to the side and vomits a torrent of fire from its scaly belly.

Fire engulfs the nearest chopper. It spins wildly out of control, wrapped in flame and billowing smoke. The tiny people in the glass bubble turn frantic. Their desperate screams fill the air.

And there isn't one fucking thing I can do about it.

The contraption's plummeting earthward when the whole damn bird explodes.

I bellow in total fucking outrage.

God damn it.

Those were innocent arcanes in there. And we don't have enough of those anymore to spare.

Pulsing with infrared heat in my enhanced eyesight, the red dragon soars around in a tight circle to challenge me and screams in triumph. Fire gouts from those wicked tyrannosaur jaws and curls straight toward me. I angle into one of the evasive maneuvers Max has been teaching me and tilt under the inferno. I wing hard to lead the fight away from the remaining choppers and the summit full of people, including my own mates, who are right in the line of danger.

I'm sure as shit not gonna let loose with my own gift until all those arcanes are out of harm's way.

Which makes one of us.

My need to keep everyone safe puts me at a major disadvantage. Since Big Red's only priority is apparently to sauté me.

Who the fuck is *this?* I shout wildly through the bond to Ronin.

Ronin says something, but I'm not hearing him. The red dragon screams in my six like a goddamn harpy. I dive barely in time to avoid another gout of fire, so close it singes my backside as it scorches past.

I twist my head around and bellow in the lightning voice. Electricity dances over my scaly skin and erupts from my mouth in a jagged fork of kilojoules that crackles through the air.

The red dragon cants aside, so my bolt of lightning only zaps the tip of that snaky tail.

She screams in hatred and I roar in response.

Because yeah, she's a girl dragon. There's no barbed tool jutting between those muscled hind legs.

By this point, I'm putting two and two together. I know Max has a sister dragon (that bitch Vasili was supposed to mate), but I've learned from my research that, among dragonkind, size means age.

Which means this big red monster isn't a young dragon. Nope. She's an old one.

She's Max's mother.

Anastasia.

The matriarch of the Sagittarius clan. The one who beats her own children till they're scarred to the bone and traumatized for life. The one who kills her own mates after she fucks them.

The one who kills for pleasure.

The one the AIB pays to kill for them.

And guess who's been walking around on a kill list, off and on, since I split from the Gemini clan's loving bosom years ago and never looked back?

Guess I'm back on somebody's list.

Bet she slipped in with the news crew (you know, in human form) when the Dean lowered the wards.

Sweet Jesus. My rump's already burning from that fireball I barely dodged that just blistered my booty. I'm not gonna have the same stamina or the same fighting skills in the air as this big behemoth.

But what I do have is the lightning.

And the speed to lead this bitch away from my warlocks and anyone else who could get hurt.

I pretty much pivot on my tail in midair and dive for the slope. Big Red hisses like a pot boiling over on a hot stove and plunges after me. A quick look back shows me her tail's smoking and blackened. Which means, if I'm reading this psycho right, she's not only gonna kill me if she catches me.

She's gonna make it hurt.

The belching cough of a flaming dragon hits my ears. The sulfurous reek of brimstone stings my muzzle.

I reach deep inside my already tiring body and twist aside.

As I evade, a familiar black shape hurtles past from below. Max roars like blazes and lets loose with his own fiery jet.

Big Red tilts to avoid his fire and screams like a nightmare. Son or no son, her head whips around and spews fire right at my mate.

Max twists aside, but they're both so close these flaming fusillades aren't totally missing their marks. The horrible charcoal scent of scorched dragon invades my lungs as I wing in a tight circle to come back around.

Straight ahead of me, Max and Big Red collide in midair in a thrashing, biting, clawing snarl. My guy's not quite that bitch's size, but as a guy dragon, he's way bigger than me. And he's wrathful as fuck. My dragon heart's wedged in my gullet, because these two are just one writhing knot of hatred.

I've got a straight line of fire, but I can't use the lightning when they're all locked together like that.

I bugle with rage and soar past, raking an exposed red flank with my talons and snapping at that burned red tail as I whiz by. Big Red howls and savages Max's exposed belly with her razor-sharp claws. He screams and buries his teeth in her throat.

Heart pounding in my ears like a war drum, I wing around for another pass. But I'm still out of range when that hideous red head with its demon horns swings around to gore poor Max's snarling face. She barely misses his eyes. Her saber-toothed jaws split wide and that awful rumbling cough rises from her chest.

She's gonna flame.

And she doesn't even care if she flames her own fucking body if she can incinerate *him*—this poor, lonely, isolated, unloved son she's abused and apparently hated, the same way she's hated and ultimately killed every male dragon she's ever encountered.

I roar lightning over her head to get her goddamn attention, because I'm the real business she's apparently being paid to conduct.

But I can't hurl lightning at her without hitting Max, and she doesn't even blink at my intimidation display. Her wicked eyes flame red with hatred and madness.

God damn it, I'm still too far away—

The air splits around a pure silver cry. A diamond glitter snares my gaze.

Vasili streaks past the twisting snarl of dragon vs. dragon in flying snake form and sprays that horrid red demon head with a flurry of snow and hail that encases her face with ice.

This fix is only temporary, but at least that bitch's jaws are glued shut till she can melt the ice.

Right away she starts clawing at her muzzle (because the ice is also blocking her airway). While she's distracted and vulnerable, Max fights his way free and wings unsteadily away. Horrific-looking gashes gouge his belly and flanks, his snout is slashed and bleeding, his steaming green ichor splatters the air in gobbets.

He's *injured*.

That bitch fucking *hurt* him.

The same way she's been fucking hurting him his whole life.

My whole body tingles and swells with the electric voltage of rage.

I'm about to go full cray when a brand-new visual explodes in my brain. That's Ronin, the strongest telepath at Icarus, literally shoving into my head what he wants me to do.

Okay, so *he's* the one going full cray while he watches the firefight from down there on the mountain. From his vantage, Ronin's helpless to act, and he's full-on losing his shit. After all, Max is his mate too. And so am I.

And Vasili's pretty close to losing his own shit, which never ends well for anyone.

My snake's telekinesis doesn't work in dragon form (we've learned) because he doesn't have access to his casting hand (or any hand). Now he's hovering close to Max, his iridescent wings an agitated blur of movement. I realize it's because he's worried our dragon's losing so much blood he'll pass out.

At which point, he'll fall.

Well, shit.

Looks like we're gonna do this Ronin's way.

I twist around to confront Big Red, who's just managed to claw and steam the ice off her muzzle. I bellow in the lightning voice. The mother of all lightning forks from my mouth and slams into that red bitch's chest like a fucking locomotive.

She's so big and such a goddamn monster that even my best shot in dragon form doesn't stop her. But my bolt blackens her chest, knocks the air she's desperately trying to replenish out of her dragon lungs, and throws her backward through the air.

Bet that got her attention.

I trumpet in derision, kinda the verbal equivalent of flipping her the bird, and plunge in a nosedive for the mountain. The big red bitch screams in rage and plunges after me.

Stay with Max, I send wildly to Vasili. *Get him down safe. I mean it, Goblin King. He needs you.*

I just hope he listens (though he isn't known for that). I hope both of them listen, and just leave the fight now to me.

And to Ronin.

The dark slope of the mountain looms right in front of me. My gaze locks on a rocky ledge that overlooks a steep plummet. Big Red's breathing down my neck, and I rely on all my speed and agility to twist and veer in case she gets a fix on me and bathes me in dragonfire.

I'm banking on the fact that she's pissed enough right now to want to rip me apart with her bare claws. It's definitely not the most efficient way to kill. But she's not into efficient.

Like a psycho, she kills for pleasure.

The ledge is right in front of me when Ronin winks into view.

He can't teleport, but Racetrack can. That's her Mogadon gift, and her witchcraft's strong as fuck. She's no telepath, but she can teleport herself, and anyone else she wants, as long as she's seen where she's porting. The light dancing glide of Dez's telepathic touch—one finger of awareness touching me, one brushing Ronin, the rest of her locked onto RT who's physically with her—Dez links us all together.

It's Dez who's looking through my eyes and showing Racetrack where to teleport.

It goes against every shred of protective instinct that I have, but I tilt and veer to expose my mate to the dragon. Glowing with infrared heat, a curtain of inky hair billowing behind him, his face snarling and suffused with rage, Ronin's arms sweep up. Golden fire sprays from his outspread hands.

The red dragon screams in anguish and dives straight for him. Flame boils up her throat.

My laboring heart erupts in rage and terror.

Racetrack! I bellow through the fragile link Dez has cobbled together between us.

A breath before death, Ronin winks out of view. That's RT whisking him away. Big Red flames the empty ledge and barely veers off in time to avoid colliding with the cliff.

I soar along the slope, scanning the rugged surface. The enraged dragon knifes after me. I barely catch sight of a rocky spur, Dez seeing what I see through the link, before Ronin blinks into view. I cant wildly to the side and his arms sweep up. He howls in raw fury. A literal storm of psi fire scorches past me.

The red dragon screams.

Even furious, Ronin's a precision instrument. Unlike me, especially in this form, he's been honing his gifts for years.

I'm still terrified as fuck for him.

He vanishes from sight an eyeblink before dragonfire engulfs the rocky spur.

We manage to keep this up for a while, this precarious tag-team of flamethrower-teleporter-dragon bait, all daisy-chained together by Dez's Valyrian gift. Buying time for Vasili to get Max down (I hope, because I can't see them, and I don't have time to look) before my dragon king bleeds out.

But I'm tiring, like, *really* fast.

And that monster who's hunting me seems to be tireless.

Dez picks this up and whispers where she wants me. Where Lucius wants me. I don't like this plan either—not one bit—but even I have to admit I'm not gonna last much longer up here.

I dig deep to dredge up a final spurt of speed and dash for the summit.

There's an ancient stone circle up there where the students study astronomy and practice the greater magics for senior seminar. That's where Vasili has the news cams staged for my big succession announcement. It's supposed to be this whole sacred vow-slash-ritual. I'm supposed to swear the oath of succession at the ancient altar on live TV.

But there's no safety to be had in the stone circle (because it's not, like, *Outlander*. This isn't that kind of circle.)

There's a World War II-era bunker carved into the mountain just beyond. That bunker was a last-stand kinda shelter when witches fought witches during the Arcane War.

That's where Dez is telling me Lucius wants me to go.

I soar over the madhouse mob of news crews and looky-loos, all glowing in my infrared sight, who've come to eyeball my succession announcement. (Looks like me being a dragon is definitely out of the bag now. And it looks like Vasili being one is out in the open too.) Those cameras are definitely rolling and getting a massive eyeful, so I guess that much of what we choreographed is still working out okay.

By this point I'm so exhausted I barely clear the stone circle and avoid the crowd, now scattering in all directions and screaming in mass hysterics, because they see what's roaring up behind me, blistered and smoking and full-on berserk.

I pretty much crash-land on the summit.

It's all I can manage to land with my legs under me and keep them under me when my dragon form falls away. I stagger naked on my human legs across the last feet of open ground (good thing I'm not shy, because that footage of my bare booty's gonna be, like, *everywhere*). The reinforced steel bunker door's swinging open, because Vasili was using it as a staging area for the show.

The earth trembles under my bare feet as Big Red comes crashing down behind me.

I wring a last burst of speed from my trembling legs and race into the bunker.

It's dark in there, someone's switched off the electric bulb. Or maybe I blew out the substation or knocked a line down again with all that lightning I've been hurling. But I know from my preshow visit there's a big storeroom in front and then a tunnel. I'm tearing across the storeroom when a shadow blots out the moonlight streaming through the door behind me and a distorted, rage-filled, Russian-accented female voice lashes after me like a whip.

"There is nowhere for you to run, usurper queen. Nowhere I cannot find you. Nowhere I will not kill you! Stop scurrying like the pathetic cockroach you are and face your fate."

"Come and get me, you child-molesting bitch!" I can't see much at this point, but I'm running on fumes and faith.

"With pleasure." Her hate-thick voice echoes off the walls as she dives into the bunker after me. "You are too great a coward to come to me in Mongolia, so now I come to you. I will crush you under my boot!"

She's not wearing a boot, she's naked like me, but whatever. There's no emergency exit in this place, so she's just cut off my one escape. But my bond with my fated mate flared to life the second I set foot in here. The steadying warmth of Neo's presence pulls me forward into the darkness like a guiding hand.

Even though I really, truly *don't* want this bitch anywhere near him.

Or any of my mates.

Not when she's doing her damnedest to kill them.

Inside the tunnel it really is pitch black, and I only have night-vision and infrared in dragon form. I pick out a little weak starlight that trickles through the grated ventilation shafts set at intervals in the ceiling. I stick out a hand to find the rough wall and use it to guide me as I hurry down the slanting tunnel. My ass stings and smarts like hell from that dragonfire that grazed me.

But I'll heal.

I don't even want to think about all the damage Max absorbed from that bitch's claws and teeth. Or, God, how much blood he must be losing—

"I can smell your fear, little cockroach," Anastasia whispers. I can tell by the echo that she's standing in the tunnel mouth. I've had to slow down in the dark, which means she's pretty close behind me. Definitely closer than I'd like.

A cold trickle of fear slides down my spine.

The monster's heavy breathing fills the air as she oozes in after me.

I force out a laugh, even though I can barely quiet my gasping breath, and nothing about any of this is funny. I laugh with derision to enrage her and draw her in.

"I can smell your filthy cunt!" she hisses with her thick accent. A claim that's really gross and hopefully not true. "That cunt you used to lure away my faithful son! He was supposed to be *my* mate. *My* king. The one I killed all others to protect."

Whoa. Jesus. We're in crazy town.

"Those little beasts from your rival college, without me to lead them, against you they could achieve nothing," she sneers. Which pretty much tells me who paid those Tiberius brats to hurl that Molotov cocktail. "All such things, it seems, I must do myself. Even then, to defend you, my son turns on me—his own mother! For this offense, I will more than kill you. I will make you suffer!"

She's right behind me. I can almost feel the brush of her hot breath on the back of my sweating neck. She's full shifter, so she can probably see better than I can in the dark.

Behind us, the door to the tunnel clangs shut. Neo's standing behind it, and sealing us all in here together, that's his job.

Now, babe, Neo whispers through our bond, shoving what Lucius needs me to do in my head. *Do your thing.*

"Smell this, you sick fucking excuse for a mother." I obey Lucius on blind faith, do my thing, and drop flat to the stone ground.

Meaning now I'm totally within touching distance of a psycho killer with professional assassin skills, but never mind.

I've fought with my bare hands before.

Over near the door, locked with us inside this horror show dungeon, Neo hits the light switch. The bare fluorescent bulbs that stud the tunnel ceiling light up in a blue-white blaze that makes Anastasia—who isn't expecting it like I am—spit out a Russian curse.

In the harsh spill of light, I catch a split-second glimpse of an apparition that'll be branded on my brain forever.

A freakishly tall, naked amazon of a woman with Max's golden hair and slitted eyes, her corded arms blackened with burns from Ronin's psi fire, her saber-teeth bared in a hateful snarl, her taloned hands curled and reaching to gouge my eyes out and rip my face off.

Then, from the tunnel depths, a blur of chestnut fur springs over me with a vicious snarl that raises every hair on my body straight up.

Lucius' wolf launches through the air over my prone body, buries his teeth deep in my enemy's skin and flesh, drives her sprawling and screaming with rage to the ground, and rips out the bitch's throat.

Chapter Thirty-Three
Vasili

Dear God, I look like an absolute fright.

There I am making my Hollywood debut, framed in the geriatric screen of the ancient TV in Max's guest studio at the *domus*, the vintage VCR player whirring away as it spools through the bootleg tape of Zara's rather dramatic succession announcement.

The image is mercifully blurred (since no twenty-first century tech, including digital photography, functions properly behind the wards). Still, I can clearly see that my shift from warlock to dragon to warlock last Wednesday utterly ruined my smoky eye and obliterated my lip gloss.

As for my wind-whipped hair, darling, you should simply pretend not to notice (if you can).

I look like a fucking haystack.

I drag my appalled gaze away from my disastrous film debut and slice my gorgon stare across the apartment, just to ensure none of my mates are here to observe this televised horror show. If they are, I'll turn them to stone with my glare.

Fortunately for them, I'm alone.

Mostly.

It's end-of-quarter recess, so no one's in class. Mercury's been spending hours on nursing duty with Maxim while our dragon recovers from his injuries (both physical and emotional) and works his way through everything that's happened with his hideous mother, although he really doesn't say much about it, and we're all quite careful not to press.

He'll speak about her when he's ready.

Meanwhile, Mercury fusses over that injured dragon so sweetly it's as though our First Boy is the witching world's Florence Nightingale. Which isn't to imply I'm jealous that Maxim gets *all* the attention these days.

But Mercury seems to be (uncharacteristically) sleeping late this morning, snuggled up with Zara and Lucius upstairs under a mound of eiderdown blankets in our queen's big curtained bed.

Fortunately, they're all still asleep.

As for Ronin, he's flooded with feel-good endorphins and humming with energy since he's finally come out of heat. My boyfriend slipped out early from the studio bed he shared with Max and me last night. Now he's downstairs training in the gym.

And Maxim is still asleep here in the guest studio in his bed.

Our bed, if you want to call it that, given the amount of time he and Zara and Ronin and I spend fucking in it. Miraculously unhindered by the chintzy 1980s ambience of aqua walls, chunky furniture, and framed Pop Art posters that was apparently trending when Lucius' predecessor last *renovated* (and I use the term loosely) this studio.

It's like fucking in a time warp.

Anyway. In the days since the fiasco-slash-triumph of Zara's succession announcement, no one's heard a peep from any so-called rival. It seems likely that piece in *The Witching Inquisitor* truly was no more than an elaborate lure, crafted by Anastasia to tempt our infamously rash and reckless Zara out from behind the island wards, where she'd be alone and vulnerable. When Zara refused to take the bait, she left Anastasia—out of her scaly mind with jealousy and hatred for her son's new mate—no choice but to slip behind the wards with the news crew in pursuit of Zara.

If Lucius' wolf hadn't torn out the bitch's throat, I would have taken unparalleled delight in killing her myself.

Lucius is still investigating, of course.

Those vile little rodents from Villa Tiberius have been quiet as church mice, since the entire cohort was interrogated by the Dean, the instigators of the Molotov cocktail attack identified and expelled, and the remaining miscreants placed on suspension.

Messalina was both a no-show at Zara's succession announcement *and* a no-comment on the question of a rumored Aquarius bastard. But the Senate (which proclaimed Zara the next queen in the first place), herded along by Mercury Senior, is standing squarely behind our girl.

Which means Zara's succession stands unchallenged.

At least, that's what the news is reporting.

Meanwhile, our dragon's been resting and healing (helped along nicely by his fast-repairing shifter DNA).

Still, he nearly died.

He too has needed more sleep than usual.

Relieved to be unobserved, I settle into the pastel cushions of the sofa, smooth a few creases from my silky sleep pants and the pretty black lace camisole Zara gave me for Valentine's Day, and return my attention to the TV screen.

There's my little queen now, standing at the altar in the stone circle with the news cams whirring away, her turquoise eyes blazing with witchcraft and her gorgeous face burning with resolve after that dreadful dust-up with Maxim's horrid and now mercifully dead parent. My queen looks like a teal-haired Scarlett Johannsen with her lush curves and suntanned skin encased in the sparkly purple couture frock I arranged for her announcement, since wearing purple *is* a royal tradition.

We're ranged behind her, all five of her kings, with a barely ambulatory but defiant Maxim bookended between Ronin and me (because the poor wounded dragon needed both of us to brace him, but he refused to be left behind).

I lean forward to adjust the volume dial a smidge so I can hear.

"…giving you my promise that I'm done running." Zara's firm voice trickles from the set. "I'm here at Icarus to learn to be the best queen I can be when it's my turn to ascend. I *will* take my throne. I'll be the first Gemini queen. And when I do, all five of these warlocks are gonna be my kings. The Gemini kings."

In the name of God, why didn't I at least swipe on a coat of mascara before the cameras started rolling? Why in Heaven didn't anyone tell me? I look horribly washed out in the blaze of electric light. I look positively *ill*.

And it's true, the camera really does add kilos to anyone's look, even my normally slim and trim physique.

"…we're gonna figure out together what we need to do to save the witching world." Zara's televised voice swells with certainty until it's edged in lightning. "I'm here to tell you we're *already* figuring it out. And here's the first thing. All you shifters out there need to be mating a lot more and, like, biting a lot more—anyone who wants that, especially anyone who's got a chromosome of shifter DNA. Forget about the inbreeding and crossbreeding. Stop trying to keep the bloodline pure. There aren't enough of you, um, *us* anymore to be ideological about this. We gotta, like, spread the love around."

Zara marches up to get right in the camera's face (as it were). Her eyes pulse with psi fire and determination. Her mane lifts and swirls around her shoulders.

"You saw what happened with me and Vasili?" she demands. "Both of us fully manifested shifters, even though neither one of us started out that way. Because we were both bitten by shifters, and those biochemicals switched on our shifter recessives. So that's the second thing. We gotta do a lot more of that—all of us—across the whole witching world. We gotta do a lot more, uh, group sex."

This is the part where Zara explains about the singular effect she and Max and Ronin inflicted on the entire student body the night of the orgy (which I'm really rather sorry I missed). Coupled with her rather scandalous theory that it should be the entire witching world, not merely our queen and her harem, who are permitted—even encouraged—to be polyamorous.

Now, darling, don't laugh. Truly, you should at least try it.

I've heard this all before, of course, live and in person.

I dial down the volume and saunter into the neon pink-and-black powder room that's attached to Max's suite. There I dab a little of Max's yummy cologne behind my ears (which makes me smell like a green apple. Hopefully a certain someone will want to take a bite.)

Alas, my pale early morning image in the fluorescent light leaves a great deal to be desired. Under my mop of frosted hair, my lips purse in a discontented pout.

In the mirror, my eyes narrow in displeasure.

My, my. Zara's simply going to have to cut my hair again. Shifter hair grows *so* quickly. Since she herself has started shifting, hers nearly grazes the small of her back.

Of course, none of us wants anyone cutting hers.

Well, I have no intention of going to that extreme. A style that grazes my chin is far more flattering to the shape of my pretty face.

I take a little *me* time to preen and fuss over my shoulder-length mane, then saunter out of the powder room. I'm simply craving a *caffe americano*, and I imagine Zara and the others will soon be up and about. But I sneer at the pedestrian Mr. Coffee unit in Max's vintage kitchenette.

I'll just nip out to the great room kitchen to whip up a double shot of espresso—

"Where do you suppose you are going, Romanov?" Safely asleep no longer, Maxim is leaning casually against the closed door that leads from his studio to the great room.

Well, well. He's wearing a pair of Ronin's black sweats, slung low on his narrow hips, and literally nothing else. His delicious golden hair frames the tawny a.m. stubble glittering on his angular jaw and spills around his shoulders in a tumbled mess that makes me simultaneously long to tidy him up and dishevel him far worse.

My gaze skates over his sleek chest and pierced nipples to his tight abdomen. He discarded the last of his bandages yesterday, so the healing scars slashed across his skin are very much on display.

My own tummy tightens with an echo of the wrathful rage that consumed me in the sky that night.

I might as well confess they make me rather savage, those scars of his.

They're a constant reminder of how close we all came to losing him. If I hadn't practically carried him down from the sky to the summit, protecting him the way my queen commanded, he would have fainted from blood loss and fallen to his death.

Not to mention, this dragon of mine carries enough scars.

"Now, *malchik*, there's no need to get overly dramatic at this hour," I say lightly, careful to betray none of what I'm feeling (since that's the cardinal rule I live by. I *am* the Scorpio scion, after all.) "I'm simply going to the kitchen to brew a proper *americano*. I'll even bring you one, if you ask me nicely."

Truly, I don't mean to provoke him.

Typically, these days, I only provoke him with Zara or Ronin (or both) tucked safely between us. Because I know perfectly well what he wants from me, which is the same thing I want from him, and he's not getting it.

To use that horrid American baseball analogy, I'm purely a pitcher. I *never* catch. Well, except for that one little time with Ronin in the shower, which (admittedly) I enjoyed, but which no one else except Zara even knows about.

Still, I can't seem to resist playing with (dragon) fire.

The dragon in question slits his fiery eyes. His deliciously smoldering gaze roams over me, all tousled and barefooted in my camisole and jammies.

"Do you wear this clothing to provoke me?" he growls.

Secretly, I'm delighted by the question. I do so love to be… provocative.

"Hmmm, I don't know." Hips swaying, I swank in close, very close, close enough to inhale a delicious whiff of the leathery scent of aroused dragon, and perch my hands light as butterflies on his barely clad hips. "If I do, is it working?"

His gaze drops to my smirking mouth. His nostrils flare wide. "You smell like me."

"That's because I'm wearing your cologne, darling. I smell like forbidden fruit."

I keep my tone light and teasing, even as I subtly maneuver him to one side so I can slip past him out the door. Don't imagine for one moment that I don't want to be alone with him, because I very much *do*.

But he and I, we're dangerous together when we're alone. Two alphas, designed by nature either to fight or to fuck.

We're not supposed to fall in love.

God knows I'm more than vulnerable enough these days, loving Zara and Ronin and now Lucius to indecent and extremely public excess. They're my weakness, and now all my enemies know it. Even the maddeningly elusive Mr. Mercury lingers far more in my mind than he should—

"Vasili." Maxim scowls at my attempted evasion. His hot hands lock around my waist, burning through my lace cami. Suddenly *I'm* the one whose back is pressed against the door. "Do not be obtuse. The reason you smell like me is because you are drenched in my mating scent. It is because you sleep in my bed. It is because I have scented you and claimed you and held you while you slept. When I have also fucked you, there will be no part of you I have not claimed."

Goosebumps race over my skin and every nerve in my body tingles with danger. I feel pursued and stalked and menaced—oh, deliciously so!

But one mustn't get carried away.

Even if he is pumping out mating scent by the pint and the morning air reeks of musk and brimstone.

I'm taller than he is, and I use every centimeter to my advantage. I glare down the length of my imperious nose, tighten my grip on his sexy hips, and arch my signature eyebrow. "*I* do the claiming and the fucking in this bed. That's the way it's going to be. Know your place, *malchik*."

His face hardens with delicious intent. He leans in close until our mouths nearly touch. "My place is here with you, snake. My place is buried inside you so deep you no longer know where you end and I begin. My place is locked tight inside you and filling you with my seed until you beg me for mercy."

Well, darling, what's a boy supposed to do with a declaration like *that*? My villainous heart is simply racing with the sexual thrill of danger.

And even though I want nothing at all to do with what he's threatening, my own traitorous cock takes a perverse interest in the entire dreadful notion.

"Not going to happen," I inform him haughtily (well, as haughtily as anyone can who's simultaneously flirting and willing an erection to subside). "It's really too bad for you, Maximka. You and that barbed dragon cock of yours had best resign yourself to disappointm—"

He snarls and smothers my rejection in a kiss.

I suppose I *did* ask for it, calling him that pet boyhood nickname that I know perfectly well he despises.

Perhaps I truly am being provocative.

His mouth slants over mine in ruthless demand, taking what he wants from me without asking, his hot tongue licking fearlessly over my horrible fangs and sweeping inside to ravage me. He tastes like hellfire and dragon and a bit like Zara, who flooded his mouth with mating scent when he buried his head between her thighs last night.

I moan and drag his hips against me, grinding his pelvis with mine. His cock juts electrically under Ronin's sweats, sending delicious jolts of friction through mine with every thrust. I sink my nails into his bare back. He fists my hair to subdue me until my scalp tingles.

"You cannot lie to me, *dushenka*," he mutters in Russian against my mouth. I swoon (in secret, of course) because now he's calling me *sweetheart*. "Admit it. My kisses make you weak."

Of course, if I'm being honest, this is precisely what I fear.

Above all else, I fear being seen as weak.

And that's the very last thing I intend to admit.

"Your kisses make me nauseous." I sneer horribly like the villain I am and push him off me.

Except that he doesn't actually let me go, but instead pulls me with him through his kitschy apartment toward the bed. Together we reel blindly across the floor, our kisses a savage war for domination I have no intention of losing, our bodies locked in a writhing tangle, bumping into walls and furniture, knocking over a standing lamp with a crash, him peeling my cami over my head, me pushing his sweats down his hips so I can then wrap my hand around his complicated and dangerous cock and jack him the way we're all learning to do, stimulating all his sensitive spots (because he *is* so deliciously sensitive) without impaling myself on his barbs.

He groans and shoves my PJs down my legs, nearly tripping me when I get tangled up in the fabric, then holding me up when I stumble. Of course, the real reason I stumble is because he's pumping my shaft in his naughty fist.

A pulsing pleasure makes me gasp and writhe.

My hand snakes down to return the favor, but he bats me aside and fists both of us together, our cocks aligned, the fork of his dick scraping mine in a way that teases out of me a desperate whimper.

It's the kind of noise that makes me tender and savage when Lucius makes it for me.

And it has exactly the same effect on Maxim, because of course he's reacting to me as my alpha, even though I've by no means conceded to any such arrangement. His pumping fingers tease me to a throbbing fullness that makes me buck in his grip, even as he drenches us both with an absolute deluge of precum. My eyes fall closed and my head falls back, letting him mouth a scorching trail down my neck. He finds a sensitive spot above my collarbone and his lips seal tight in a sucking kiss.

He's going to leave a mark.

His mark.

This entire assault is a power play.

And my fiendish little brain is so fevered I simply can't make up my mind whether that's an intimacy I should permit or a presumption I should punish (even if, very secretly, I like it) with one of my vicious backhands.

The scrape of his fangs against my skin dredges up a few particles of (belated) caution.

"No biting," I hiss.

He won't let me touch our cocks. He seems to have laid exclusive claim to that particular terrain for both of us, a usurpation which is both maddening and unfair. Instead, my fists knot in his hair.

"I will not give you my mating bite," he says thickly, "until you are certain. Until you beg me to bite you."

His mouth finds mine again before I can tell him I never beg, period, and in particular I will never beg for that. Being bitten once by Lucius was more than enough, believe me. My wolf hasn't tried to claim me in that way, not as my alpha, but all Lucius needs to do is kiss the healing punctures on my inner thigh to make me climax.

I'm still the top dog on our bed, damn it.

That goes for all six of us.

The backs of Max's legs collide against the bed and he sits down hard, which gives me a momentary respite (assuming I wanted one) from his punishing kisses.

His hands glide down my naked thighs and he spreads his legs to pull me between them. This choreography places my cock nicely within sucking distance. My hand sneaks out in front to position myself for him.

Again he brushes my hand firmly aside before I can touch myself.

I never tolerate this sort of defiance. Yet for some reason, in this case, I'm permitting it. It's actually making me hotter than running the show myself. I'm simply pulsing and throbbing and jerking with need. My cock is literally drooling for him. I angle my pelvis to get my point across, but his stern grip on my thighs holds me in place.

Frustrated and impatient and thwarted, I scowl down at him.

Whatever he sees in my face turns him positively smoky with purpose. His lids drop over his slitted gaze and his voice goes gravelly.

"Still you will not bend for me?" he rasps.

When I shake my head (coherent speech being rather beyond me at the moment, but my position on this topic certainly hasn't changed), his pupils dilate. "Then, *dushenka*, will you kneel for me?"

It's the *sweetheart* that does it for me. Besides, I can give a man head and surrender nothing of my power.

"Hmmmm." I let my own gaze wander over his deliciously naked chest and drum-tight abs to that forked cock jutting between his thighs. "Well, since you ask so nicely…"

I fold to my knees between his legs and spread him wider, my hands gliding up the hot skin of his inner thighs, my mouth already watering. I've watched Ronin and Zara play with his cock, watched them both fuck him, but everyone's been far too wary of braving his barbs to administer a proper full-throated blow job.

This poor dragon's been *deprived*.

Well, having made up my mind to oblige, I'm just the man for the mission.

I breathe in the delectable aroma of dragon and Ronin and Zara's mating scent. Between my hands and my mouth, I intend to make this man beg for me. My eyes close and my lips part—

"Hands behind your back," he growls.

My eyes snap open.

I freeze in place.

A cold trickle of resistance and rage cools some of my pulsing heat.

His voice turns coaxing. "Just to try. Just this once. You do it to please me. To please yourself. If you do not like, then we will stop. No one else needs to know."

Clearly he's still learning the way things work in a relationship with telepaths. We have no secrets from each other… for the most part.

Still, I've never been opposed to a little role play.

Slowly I sit back on my heels, bow my head for him just a little, and clasp my hands behind my back.

He rumbles with pleasure. "You are so beautiful like that. I swear to you, I will love you until the world ends."

Well, he certainly knows what to say to persuade me.

Somehow, every day, he manages to work into some conversation or other between us those three precious little words. The same way Zara and Ronin have started to do. For someone like me who never heard them once growing up, I'm horribly susceptible.

It seems love truly is my greatest weakness.

Which is why I'm so very careful never to say those words to the dragon myself.

I hum with approval and lean forward to swipe my tongue across his slit. I know his taste of leather and brimstone, I have tasted him in Zara's mouth and Ronin's, I have lapped up his seed spilling from Zara's pussy and dripping from Ronin's sweet pucker. Just as he has tasted me in all these ways, both of us burning to explore each other's passion through the two mates we share.

Now it's just the two of us.

He and I.

I certainly intend to make the most of it. I might be the one who's kneeling, but I intend to bring this king to his knees.

I intend to make him beg.

I lick along his length, circling that forked tip of his and the twin barbs that are so sensitive and so dangerous to touch, nudging him wider with my head so I can tongue the tight sac of his balls. His breathing turns harsh and ragged. When I nudge him even wider to taste his perineum, he bites down on a moan.

Oh, yes, he's determined to play the alpha to the hilt.

But he's never known an alpha like me.

I lick and suck and nibble my way up his shaft, pausing to deposit teasing little sucks around each sensitive barb, until he's panting and twitching under my mouth. Next it's his crown I'm teasing, nuzzling and licking his slit and circling his tip while he whispers curses in our mother tongue, and evading his increasingly urgent attempts to sheathe his length fully in my naughty mouth.

Truly, this is all too delicious.

"Vasili." His hands fist in my hair and his tone turns harsh with demand. "Stop playing the cock-teasing bitch and suck me off."

"My oh my," I purr against his tip, slick with precum. "We really *are* worked up, aren't we? Aren't you going to say please?"

"Vasili…" His hips twitch and his cock bucks against my elusive lips. "When I am finally buried deep inside you, I swear to Christ I will fuck you harder than you have ever been fucked in your entire spoiled and overindulgent life."

"Never going to happen," I whisper.

Just before I engulf his swollen crown with my mouth.

His cock nudges against my palate and I lick underneath and hum around his shaft, but I still won't take his barbs.

"More." His voice is silk stretched over gravel, laced with short desperate pumps as he grips my head and begs to go deeper.

My eyes lift to find his. He's riveted on the sight of me with my lips wrapped around his cock. Those eyes of his set me alight, fueling the heat that's pulsing between my legs, filling my balls and swelling my dick, a burning column of need he won't let me touch.

He's mastering me the way an alpha masters his mate, and I absolutely loathe him for it.

Except that, truly, I'm the one in control.

My gaze never leaving his, I sink just a centimeter deeper, my lips on the edge of engulfing his barbs.

"Saint Sergius grant me patience," he grits through his teeth. "Vasili. *Dushenka. More.*"

I sigh and envelop him to the hilt. His girth fills my mouth. All that sound he's been fighting to contain rips out of him in a hoarse shout. His barbs shoot out and lock into place, lodging his cock in my mouth, hooking me around his shaft like a gaffed fish.

Well, I know just what to do with all this.

I suck him off like a vacuum hose, my cheeks hollowing around his length, my tongue massaging his underside, my lips stretched tight around his width. All his resistance dissolves in urgent cries of pleasure and words of praise and desperate entreaty… *finally*, all those nice little phrases like *please* and *yes* and *oh Christ Vasili* that I've been waiting for.

Within seconds he's spilling over my tongue, hot jets of spunk hitting the back of my throat, his hands locked around my head and his pelvis flexing into my mouth, the first hard peak of his typically quite extended orgasm.

I ride him out and gulp him down.

It's important to keep up, unless I want him asphyxiating me with his spend or, what would be far more unaesthetic, unless I want his seed dripping out of my nose.

My own starved cock is simply *screaming* for attention. I shift about and try to slide a hand around in front of me to attend to things.

But he's paying very close attention to me indeed, just like a proper alpha (damn him) should. The moment I start to deviate from his diabolical plan, he growls, "Behave yourself. Or else I will bind you."

Oh, indeed?

As if!

But, for some reason that utterly escapes me, this annoying little threat is nearly enough to make me climax on the spot.

I hiss with frustration and clasp my hands behind my back.

I really can't imagine why I'm tolerating this imp who's at least three years my junior bossing me about. Why I'm kneeling obediently at his feet with my cock aching and my hands behind my back and my mouth earnestly servicing his dick, more or less helpless to do anything but devote myself to satisfying him completely until I can coax his barbs to retract.

We've gotten through his first peak, but those barbs are still securely engaged. The only thing to do is bob my head diligently up and down his length, suck him like he's a popsicle and I'm being timed on how quickly I consume him, and find the precise rhythm and pressure he likes most so I can coax him to spill in my mouth again.

All without using my hands.

It's truly perplexing how intensely wild this entire setup is driving me. My dick is throbbing and jerking and I'm really starting to think he's going to lure me into a hands-free orgasm just from blowing him—

No, he growls without speech. *You do not climax without my consent. Do you understand?*

I groan deep in my throat, a sound of violent protest.

The vibration triggers his next climax.

Or else it's the mate bond snapping into place between us that triggers him, because neither one of us are natural telepaths, and we could never hear each other like this before.

Now there's nowhere I can hide from him, not even in my thoughts.

He groans out my name and grips my head to hold me still and fucks my mouth and floods my tongue with gout after gout of dragon spunk. This climax is stronger than the last one and it goes on for ages. Again I swallow frantically, but this time I don't quite manage everything he's giving me. Trickles of his come leak past my lips and drip down my chin—

"Cheese on toast," Zara whispers at my side. "Jesus, that's hot."

My eyes flash open. An unfamiliar heat climbs in my cheeks. I don't have a modest bone in my entire body and I'm not normally one to blush, but I've certainly just been found in a *very* compromising position.

It must appear to her as though Maxim is calling the shots in this naughty tableau.

Zara's slipped in so quietly neither one of us has noticed, which was very likely her intent. She stands beside us now, clearly pulled from sleep by the bond we share, wearing nothing but a tiny pair of hot pink lace panties and one of Lucius' shirts half-unbuttoned so her gorgeous breasts threaten to spill out, her mermaid hair falling in a wild tangle nearly to her hips.

Neo looms behind her, shirtless and disheveled, his brawny arms wrapped around her waist, his wide eyes behind his spectacles riveted on the sight of me sucking Max's dick. His mouth is open and his cheeks are flushed.

I experience a sudden violent urge to fuck the elusive Mr. Mercury until he screams.

"Good Lord, V," he breathes. "That's just so… wow."

Zara reaches up to wind an arm around his neck and pulls his head down to hers. He bends to kiss her, his big hands fumbling to unbutton her.

Between a shower of hot kisses and plenty of Zara's sexy sounds, Mercury gets her shirt unbuttoned in record time. Her lush breasts spill fully into view. Her curves are no longer swollen and engorged with mating heat, but she's simply perfect, and her gentle fated mate has learned to be ruthless with her nipples and piercings.

Precisely the way she likes it.

Max's hands tighten around my head so that I don't forget about him. Admittedly, I've rather lost the edge of my enthusiasm for this little display of faux submission now that we have an audience, but my sudden lack of enthusiasm fails to signify. His thumbs swipe through the jizz that's dripping down my chin and tenderly, thoroughly, push every drop of the overflow back into my sulky mouth.

I snarl with outraged protest.

Be good for me a little longer, he coaxes through our bond. *You are doing so well. Let us show our queen how perfect we are together. Show her how well you can please me. How well you can take my cock.*

"Oh fuck, Goblin King," she whimpers, because of course she's hearing all this. "You're so hard for him."

Yes, because he won't let me come, I think with a vicious flash of spite that makes all three of them moan.

He's still lodged inside me, and I redouble my efforts in a furious frenzy, working all his barbs and inches with lips and tongue and throat, absolutely wrathful that this upstart dragon has seized the upper hand. I give that dragon the blow job of his miserable life, until he's reduced to writhing and shouting my name and pumping into my mouth in a blind frenzy. My cock is kicking out a steady stream of precum and I'm fighting to cling to my own looming climax with my teeth.

I'm enraged and maddened to be as blatantly aroused as I am by this entire humiliating predicament.

Dear God, it must be glaringly obvious to all of them how much this forced submission… well… excites me.

Still, despite my discomfort, it's worth keeping my eyes open to watch Zara bend to kiss the dragon, their mouths meeting in a tangle of tongues and heat.

Zara stays bent over the bed like that, her mouth clinging to Max's, while Neo shucks his pajama pants and works her delightful panties down her legs. It's worth watching our First Boy fist his monster cock while he watches me giving head as though he's fantasizing about being on the receiving end himself.

I lower one lid in a wink that makes him blush.

Still, he doesn't look away.

He holds my gaze while he widens Zara's stance and rubs his shaft against her pussy until she moans and arches her back and raises her pretty derrière to encourage him.

In fact, while he works his cock inside her and grips her hips and pistons into her with his brow furrowed and his glasses sliding down his nose, he stares fiercely into my eyes the whole time.

There's quite the fire burning in our Mr. Mercury today.

Well, color me intrigued.

The combined onslaught of Zara's ravenous kisses and my own ferocious ministrations wrings another explosive and quite lavish climax from the dragon. I swallow his spend again and again and pray that I won't drown.

Finally, mercifully, his barbs retract.

I disengage from his cock with a swipe that wrings a final shudder and a few last drops of seed from this impossibly blissed-out and self-satisfied creature whom, I can now see quite clearly, fancies himself to be thoroughly established as my alpha.

I drag a hand across my messy mouth, uncoil to my feet, and push that dragon flat on his back. Limp, boneless, mindless, he subsides with a tremulous sigh and a look of dazed contentment.

That makes precisely *one* of us, dragon, who is currently content.

But that's about to change.

At last, the poor darling is sex-drunk and entirely at my mercy.

I rearrange us all a bit, straddle the dragon's waist with my hips so that I'm facing Zara, and claim my own kiss from my darling queen. Her fated mate is pleasing her, and her naughty mouth is breathless against mine, tasting nicely of cinnamon toothpaste and a lingering hint of Lucius. Our tongues thrust and parry as Neo pumps into her from behind in a building rhythm, his hips slapping audibly against her bottom, her breasts swaying and her hair spilling around Max, who's half smothered beneath all of us and dreamily enjoying the experience.

Now it's time for that dragon's comeuppance.

I clamp a ruthless hand around his throat to pin him to the bed and wrap the other fist around my aching cock. Three rough pumps bring me right to the edge, while his dragon eyes struggle to focus. I choke him with murderous intent.

Brimming with tender menace, I glare straight into his eyes, whisper, "I warned you. And I only warn once. Know your place, *malchik*," and erupt with spurt after spurt of my own seed to paint his startled face.

No one's ever done anything like that to him before, because we've all been overly concerned about triggering any buried landmines from his homophobic past.

But I'm through coddling this arrogant dragon.

All ruddy-faced and dripping with spunk, he sputters and glares up at me.

He's simply speechless with indignation.

(And also with choking.)

Zara, for one, likes what she sees. She flings her head back, eyes pulsing with purple fire, and cries out in the lightning voice.

Neo whimpers, "Holy crap, V" and shudders with an orgasm that makes the curtains sway.

I release Maxim's throat, plaster my body over the dragon's, and give him a messy open-mouthed kiss that's coated with our mingled essence. He kisses me back like he's punishing me, his arms locking around me, one hand clamping around my head to hold me in place. His stiffening cock nudges against my belly.

My oh *my*. Looks like *someone* in this bed doesn't mind being rather dominated himself.

"You know you deserved that," I whisper, licking into his mouth and making us both messy. "And you'll never be my alpha. No, it's quite the other way around, isn't it, darling? I want to hear you admit it before I stretch your lovely hole and come fathoms deep inside your tight virgin ass."

He snarls with rage and rolls both of us over so he's on top again, which topples Zara and then Neo into the vacant spot.

"Oh, bloody hell," Ronin says from somewhere near the door. "No wonder the power's out again."

Lucius fills the doorway behind him, belted neatly into his lord of the manor smoking jacket, with his chestnut curls tied in a knot and his eyes already flaming red with need. He takes one look at the scene unfolding in Max's bed, shoves into the apartment, drags the door shut behind him, then scoops Ronin into his arms and strides to the bed.

Ronin's still wearing the tunic and trousers of the *gi* we use to practice our fighting forms. As Lucius lowers him to the floor, my boyfriend grins down at me, the tussling dragon, and our enticingly naked Zara wrapped up in an intriguingly still priapic Neo.

Ronin's tiger eyes ignite with interest. "Don't need me between the two of you then, loves?"

"This one has accepted me as alpha," Maxim asserts, discreetly mopping the remnants of my messy climax out of his eyes.

"And *that one* is hallucinating from his pain meds. Darling, you're horribly overdressed," I tell Ronin, rolling again to pin Max beneath me. Then my gaze shifts to Lucius. "As are you, pet. Help each other out, why don't you."

Lucius is already peeling Ronin out of his *gi* while Ronin unbelts Lucius' jacket with gratifying haste.

Although truly, I've just climaxed, I'm already contemplating an encore performance.

For some reason, Mercury is sexed up and frisky as fuck this morning. He currently has Zara spooned up against him, both of them lying on their sides to watch Maxim and me.

Our queen looks utterly smug and practically purring with contentment. And truly, why shouldn't she? We've all enjoyably fucked her within an inch of all our lives to bring her through her superheat.

Now that this dragon is finally settling into the polycule, perhaps we'll all finally have a quiet term between now and finals.

Nicely naked, Ronin crawls into bed like a panther, muscle rippling and flexing under his tawny skin and flaming dragon tattoo, eyes feral with intent. Looking equally feral, Lucius crawls in behind him and tugs loose the bun that holds Ronin's hair out of the way for fighting. It pours down around them, and Zara uncurls to her knees to reach for both of them, our mates.

Ronin pulls her into his arms and swoops to claim her with a savage kiss that bends her back, her blue curls spilling across Max's chest. Lucius looms behind Ronin, his fangs descending, one hand already rummaging around the nightstand for the big tube of lubricant Max has taken to storing there.

"Can't today, love," Ronin stops kissing Zara long enough to tell Lucius. "I've had dragon inside me half the night. Not that I'm complaining, but any bloke needs a bit of a breather after a shagging like that. Possibly Neo might do the honors—"

"Actually," Neo announces, sitting up with a purposeful expression, "I'd normally be all over that. But I'd like to be on the other end of things this time."

We all turn to stare.

If I'm the resident top of all the cocks in this bed, then Neo's the resident bottom. Ronin's temporarily out of commission, Max is still skittish, and Lucius only bottoms for me, so…

Neo clears his throat. "With Zara. If, uh, you don't mind, babe?"

"Oh Neo." Her voice goes all husky, because there's nothing our girl adores more than a well-executed back door rogering. "Pretty safe to say I definitely don't mind. You gonna get me all ready, baby?"

Now this is one performance I truly must see.

Chapter Thirty-Four
Neo

It's really hot in here.

I've actually been feeling warm since I woke upstairs smothered in blankets and spooning with Lucius and Zara. Whatever Maxim and Vasili have been doing down here is enough to make the whole house—and maybe the whole island—horny.

Boinking my cherished one to a rubber-legged climax and filling her divine pussy with my come like that would normally take the edge off. But seeing V like that, actually *submitting*, even briefly, to anyone in bed (whether he wants to admit it or not, and it's pretty clear he *doesn't* want to)…?

Wow.

Just wow.

He's still my enemy. But if he wasn't so busy being such a jerk all the time, maybe he could be, like, an enemy with benefits?

Even the way he's looking at me now after my big reveal, his eyes all sly and narrow, while he and Max tussle like a couple of kids trying to figure out who's on top (like that isn't already totally obvious)?

Oh, gosh, I know this is all messed up.

But he… just… does things to me.

I wrestle my attention away from V's dangerous stare to give Lucius an apologetic look. Because I did just sort of say no to something my teacher might've wanted, and I don't want him to feel like I'm rejecting him. He's looming over all of us with the lube in hand, all flame-eyed and fangy, with the morning sun streaming through the window to etch all those rangy muscles of his shoulders and abs and turning the chestnut curls on his chest and between his legs to gold.

He's also, like, really hard, his thick cock jutting in my direction like a weathervane pointing the way.

I guess I'm not the only one who's getting carried away by all the sexual energy in this bed.

I always want him, I love him, the same way I love all my mates, but also in a way that's just for him. I open my mouth to explain all this, but Zara gets there before me.

"Hey, Teach," she says softly from where she's kneeling in front of Ronin, one arm draped around his sexy neck and the other already wrapped around his cock and stroking. "Give that lube to Neo and get yourself and those yummy fangs of yours over here."

His fangs punch lower and his wolf gives a guttural growl, all low in his chest. Lucius hands me the lube without even looking at me and leaps at Zara and Ronin in full beast mode (except he hasn't actually shifted).

The two of them welcome him with slow hot kisses. His wolfish mating scent fills the air, adding to the overload of Mogadon pheromones and dragon-in-heat aromas that V and Max are already pumping out.

Maybe that's why I'm feeling so hot myself this morning.

Because this whole house literally reeks of sex.

Zara takes command of the situation, pushing Lucius flat on his back while he snarls and mouths and nips his way over both their naked bodies. My fated mate straddles his hips, gives him a few hard pumps to make sure he's ready (which is totally not an issue), then sinks down on his thick shaft and engulfs all those inches in her wet pussy.

Lucius' eyes flame redder and his lips peel back from his teeth and the cords in his neck stand out with effort. He grips her hips and snaps his pelvis into her amazing body and works her up and down his dick with a ferocity that's sexy as hell.

My precious one arches back in his strong arms, her hair streaming over both their bodies. They're both sweating, her hair's sticking to them in ribbons.

Gosh, I'm sweating pretty freely myself just watching them.

"Want me to help you with that lube, Red?" Ronin whispers in my ear.

"Uh-huh," I agree, because there is literally no time I will ever say no to the concept of Ronin rubbing lube on my body. I've finally forgiven him for ghosting me in Vegas. I kinda think of him as my boyfriend these days, even though I know that's what V calls him too, and I don't know if Ronin would actually even agree to that, but—

"Don't be mental." He gives me one of his lazy grins and leans in to suck my lower lip into his mouth in a teasing nip. "I'll be your boyfriend if that's what you fancy. Vasili doesn't mind. You're on his mind too these days. Quite a lot."

The always-alarming prospect of being on Vasili Romanov's mind is worrying until the exact moment Ronin Pendragon wraps his lubed-up fingers around my dick.

Then my body is transported to another dimension, one where Ronin's consuming my mouth with deep lingering kisses and I'm stroking his back and cupping the tight flex of his ass while his hands stroke up and down my dick, finding a rhythm that makes me pump into his grip and adding a twist on the upstroke that makes me groan.

My hole starts to pulse and flutter with wanting him inside me. But I've already announced to the whole group that I'm going to be the one on top this time (for the first time ever).

Right now, I gotta focus on that.

Not that I don't totally love being filled by Ronin (and, lately, Lucius, which is OMG so incredible). But I'm just so horny this morning, with this urgent edge of need that's way stronger and feels so much more out-of-control than usual, that I feel like I need something different.

"Mmmm, think you're all lubed up then," Ronin says, all thick and husky, tugging my pierced ear between his teeth and sucking on the lobe, which always makes me moan for him. "You want me to help you get Zara all nice and prepped, or d'you fancy doing that bit yourself?"

"I… by myself, I think. Just to start." I rock my dick against his. "I love you, Ronin."

"I swear to Christ, you're so fucking sweet, Red," he breathes in my ear, which makes me shiver all over. "We all love the shit out of you. You're half the reason this polycule even works. You know that, don't you?"

A warm wonderful feeling of belonging sweeps through me. Because, honestly, he doesn't have to say that to me.

"And Zara's the other half," I tell him happily.

Over his shoulder, my gaze meets V's. He's on top of the dragon right now (briefly) and rubbing his mating scent all over Max's not-overly-resistant body while he watches me through narrowed eyes like I'm something he's trying to figure out. He looks sharp and dangerous, like the Goblin King he is, even with his shaggy layers all tousled from being fisted in dragon hands and his delicate mouth all puffy and tender from being smothered in dragon cock.

Honestly, why does he always have to look so predatory? With him, you can never tell whether he wants to fuck you or set you on fire.

It's, like, the same look for him either way.

"Ronin," Zara moans, flexing her hips into Lucius' cock while he grunts with every brutal thrust. "You've got… about five seconds… to fill my mouth… with that sexy pierced dick."

"Bloody hell." Ronin nuzzles the side of my neck and gives me another of his smoldering grins. "Guess I'd better step lively."

He slips out of my arms and crawls over the bed to straddle Lucius' face (which is a view I strongly suspect our headmaster doesn't mind) with Ronin facing Zara. My precious one's still getting reamed by Lucius, but she's a multi-tasker. She bends to engulf Ronin's dick with her lips, flicking the heavy ring of his Prince Albert in a way that makes him curse and gasp before she takes him in deep.

This whole maneuver leaves her back arched and her ass tilted up at the perfect angle for me.

Which is obviously the way she's planned it.

I guess my fated mate's in a triple penetration kind of mood.

I line up behind her and drizzle a generous squirt of lube over her pretty pucker. I've helped Ronin and Lucius prep her and each other a few times, so I know how to handle this part. While I get started, I lean in to nuzzle the silky skin of her gorgeous ass, all golden with suntan except for a narrow creamy wedge over her crack.

She really likes anal, and she makes it really easy for me, gentling the pump of her hips into Lucius and basically working my own slick finger into her hole. I love the way she gasps and sighs and swivels her hips to widen the angle, and she's really good at whispering encouraging things like *oh Neo* and *more* and *feels so good baby*. She makes it easy and exciting and fun for me, even if I'm a tiny bit nervous about what comes next.

But what really makes me nervous is Vasili.

He's playing with the barbell studs in Max's nipples, nuzzling and biting them in a way that's making the dragon gasp and swear but still not push him off.

And only the Goblin King could literally make love to a dragon and menace a totally innocent bystander like me with his broody stare the whole time.

"C'mon, V," I mutter under my breath at last, when I'm all three fingers deep in Zara and she's moaning and fucking herself onto them and onto Lucius and whispering feverishly around Ronin's cock that she's ready for my dick. "Dude, you're, like, staring."

"I like to watch…" Around poor Max's tortured nipple, V's cruel mouth curls in a grin "…you."

Oh fuck, he's flirting with me again.

He does this sometimes, you know, to amuse himself.

"Now is not a good time," I grumble, because right now I'm kinda feeling some performance anxiety and getting all up in my head.

But I'm so darn hot for her, this, them—all of it, all of them—even him (my nemesis) watching, that I have zero plans to stop.

I slide my fingers out of Zara's slippery hole, wrap my fist around my goopy cock, and line myself up behind her.

Suddenly V's out of bed, on his feet behind me. His infernal breath brushes my newly pierced ear.

"Do you require assistance from the faculty, Mr. Mercury?" he whispers.

Which pretty much breaks my brain.

"Um," I tell him.

"Yes, I thought so," he purrs. "Allow me to assist you, First Boy, *do*."

His hand snakes around me from behind and wraps around my lubed dick. And it's like my entire body jackknifes with a spasm of craving.

"Ohmygod, V," I whimper. "I—I don't—"

"Darling, you very much *do*." His sinful hand tightens and strokes. "I know when a man wants me. You've evaded me quite long enough."

I'm still trying to wrap my head around what I can even say to stop him when he pushes me forward with a firm nudge of his thigh that bends me over and spreads my legs. His pumping hand presses my cock to Zara's hole. Then he works me into her rear passage, inch by inch, ringing the narrowing span of my available inches with two pumping fingers.

Between her hole and his hand, I'm about to lose my mind.

And it's definitely working for Zara, who now has cock filling every available orifice.

Ronin and I have her spit-roasted between our two dicks, and her head's bobbing along his length in a building rhythm that infuses Ronin's face with savage pleasure and makes fire spill from his amber eyes. Lucius is fucking into her with an intensity that makes the bed shake and all of us sway and his brutal grip on her waist is probably going to leave bruises. I'm clutching her hips and carefully easing my way into the tightest, hottest fit my junk has ever experienced.

Maxim wraps a hand around his own devil's tail dick and starts lazily flexing into his own fist, while he watches the five of us all linked together.

And Vasili, oh Lord, the Goblin King's cool hands are gliding over my whole body, tickling my ribs and teasing my nipples and stroking my thighs and cupping my balls in his wicked fingers in a way that makes me give a breathless yelp.

"H-hold on a sec…" I whimper. "V?"

"Yes?" he breathes on a long exhale. One cold finger traces up my crack and over my pucker. "You've teased and tormented and eluded me for the last time, Mercury."

"We… we're, like, not even friends," I wheeze pitiably between pumps into the tight literal heaven of Zara's hole. I mean to say *we're enemies*, but somehow that doesn't feel right anymore. It hasn't felt right since the day he and I kissed, and definitely not since the night he pierced my ear and jacked me off and made me all filthy and made me love it.

And made me love him a tiny bit too.

A slick of lube trickles down my crack.

My whole train of thought just derails.

"Hmmmm." He mouths the mostly healed bite Zara left in my shoulder and circles my slick pucker with an exploratory finger that pretty much melts my brain. "I do believe… I may owe you… a certain apology."

"Wh-what?"

Of course, this is exactly what I told Lucius I needed to hear. But V's such a snake I've always known he'll never apologize to anyone, even if Lucius has told him he should.

"For being, what was it, a total and complete shit until the literal moment I fell for Zara?" His fangs graze my bite. And all I can do is whimper.

So, clearly, Lucius did tell him. But, still, this viper *never* apologizes…

V's working me open, it would actually not be a total stretch to say he's finger-fucking me, and Ronin and Max are both watching him do it, and watching me let him, and I'm fiery blushing and my heart is hammering so hard I can barely breathe and—

"Fuck, Red," Ronin groans, cradling Zara's bobbing head in his hands and kneading her hair. "The look right now on your face."

Somehow I scrape a few words together. "I still haven't heard, like, an actual apology."

"Neo Theodophilus Mercury," Vasili hisses, with his voice all threaded with strain, because now he's teasing his cock against my hole and we both pretty much know where this is going. "For fuck's sake. I've been obsessed with your soft curls and your innocent face and your incessant blushes and your steel trap of a brain and your surprisingly sweet disposition and your ridiculously buff body for weeks. Months. Years! And I'm trying to tell you I'm *sorry*. I'm sorry for being such a horrible snake."

This isn't exactly going to go down in history as the world's most penitent apology.

But, coming from him, it's way more than I ever thought I'd get.

"If you're only apologizing to me so I'll finally let you fuck me," I mutter through gritted teeth, because he's already working his dick inside me and wasting no time (since he's probably afraid I'll change my mind), and he's nudging right up against that tight ring of muscle that I really have to relax and trust him if he's going to get past, "it's, uh, totally working. And if we're really gonna do this, like you and me together for real, and it's not just a one-time thing you're doing to prove a point?"

"It isn't. This couldn't be any more real." He presses his cock deeper and bites into the side of my neck with a moan, which only makes me more turned on, and also more determined.

I suck in a big breath. "Then I don't care about the risk. I want you to bite me."

Against my skin, his breath spills out in a trembling rush.

"What's that?" This is Lucius tuning in, sounding suddenly startled, but also muffled because he's just been tonguing Ronin's balls. "Blood of Christ—"

"Hush, pet," V mutters with tender violence. "No one's asking you. He knows the risk. This is his choice."

Then my enemy's lips part and his fangs sink deep into my shoulder over Zara's healing marks.

At the exact same moment, his cock pushes past my tight resistance and sinks *so* deep inside me, like all the way in.

I hang onto Zara for dear life and shout with shocked pleasure and a sudden spike of pain. My own hot blood spills down my shoulder before the snake's ruthless mouth clamps over my wound to seal it.

He kept telling me if I wanted his bite, all I needed to do was ask him for it honestly.

So I finally did.

And I guess he meant what he promised.

My orgasm takes me totally off guard and roars through me like an avalanche. My climax makes the walls groan around us and the earth shift under my feet and rocks all six of our locked and straining bodies.

But I've been so sexed up all morning, and really for days, that it also feels inevitable.

Ronin's arching into Zara's sucking mouth and exploding with his own big O and he's linked telepathically with me and with all of us—our Gemini queen and all five of her Gemini kings.

Max is pumping his complicated but fascinating cock into his own fist with a shout and painting his tight belly with gouts of dragon seed that someone's definitely gonna be licking off him in a sec.

Lucius is bellowing and writhing with the force of his own sudden climax under all of us, he's the physical and actual foundation for this intricate scaffold of bodies and psyches and powers that makes up our polycule.

Zara is coming because *we* are, all three of us mates who are filling her, and her lightning screams make thunder crash and lightning arc in the blue winter sky beyond our window.

Vasili's hips are snapping into my weak and swaying body in a quickening tempo, and he's holding me upright in his possessive grip, and his own sharp cries are spiraling through the racket. He's my alpha now too I guess, he's sharing me with Zara, and yet he's also Max's… something… he's whatever the two of them manage to work out between them.

And I'm *still,* amazingly, pumping what feels like quarts of come into Zara, who's definitely not complaining, but still, the volume seems, like, excessive…

Vasili's ragged laugh skids across my skin. Between short, desperate, punishing thrusts that ream my burning ass in the most incredible way you can possibly imagine, he plasters his slim body against my back and pants in my ear, "There's nothing at all excessive about it. Use that formidable brain of yours, First Boy. Haven't you seen enough of this in the rest of us to know?"

"Know what?" Because I'm definitely feeling a little slow.

Yeah, I might be first on the Dean's List and all, but fucking Zara's incredible ass for the first time ever and getting fucked by Vasili and apparently also now bonding with him at the exact same time does seem to have that effect.

"Oh Neo." His gasp is a sob of pleasure. His entire body shudders and jerks, and his cock spasms and spurts deep inside me and makes me his forever.

Not his enemy.

Not his rival.

Just his.

Theirs.

I'm all of theirs.

My eyes flutter closed in a reeling, swoony, brainless kind of bliss.

Through the swirling haze of pleasure that fills me, his silken lips find my cheek in a burning kiss. "Neo, darling, haven't you realized? You're going into heat."

THE END

Liked Zara & her sexy sword-crossing warlock harem?

Discover where it all started in Gemini Queen! Available free on Kindle Unlimited, in print, and soon in audiobook here:
https://www.amazon.com/dp/B09V1PQRPB

Want to read more intense and sexy out-of-this-world true poly, MM-infused why-choose romance starring the four witching world races, the same sweet found family vibe, and a whole new harem? Check out my MMMF Astral Heat Romance Series! Complete on Kindle Unlimited and in print.

Read more steamy psychic RH by Laura at
https://www.amazon.com/dp/B0918T7BGL

For exclusive access to more of my scorching paranormal why choose romance, plus monthly freebies, giveaways, sneak peeks from future releases, and updates from my nomadic travels, sign up for my newsletter at www.LauraNavarreSciFi.com.

THANK YOU!

Hello, lovely! Thank you so very much for reading *Gemini Kings*! What did you think of the story? I write to bring joy to readers like you—you're my whole "why" for this crazy romance author life!—so I'm dying to hear from you. If you loved reading about Zara and her sexy sword-crossing warlocks, not to mention this sudden influx of dragon shifters at the Icarus Academy, please consider dropping a quick review on Amazon, Goodreads, BookBub or your favorite review site! You don't have to write a lot! Your review is so

important to me. Your feedback helps readers like you give writers like me a chance. **Here's the link to post a review for *Gemini Kings* on Amazon:**
https://www.amazon.com/dp/B0BF952NCH/

Here's the Goodreads link:
https://www.goodreads.com/book/show/62839224-gemini-kings

Here's BookBub, if that's your thing!
https://www.bookbub.com/books/gemini-kings-a-dark-witch-academy-
paranormal-romance-by-laura-navarre

If you've been with me since *Gemini Queen*, you know my whole idea was originally to write Zara and her warlocks as a great big fat steamy standalone. Then so many readers like you asked (and asked!) for more that I wrote a bonus book, so Zara's story turned into a duet. In addition to the opportunity to explore more of the dynamic among these characters (especially the Vasili/Neo dynamic which literally *everyone* wanted more of… actually, you pretty much wanted more of all things Vasili… plus the edgy alpha/alpha dynamic between Vasili and Lucius, and the unexplored Lucius/Neo relationship that just barely started in *Gemini Queen*), lots of you wanted to see Zara master her dragon shifter powers… which also brought Maxim into the mix.

As I wrote, I found I wanted to explore the whole idea of trust, because for so many of us, it's so hard to give and so easy to lose, and just about everyone in this story has their own hang-ups in the trust department. I really love bi awakening stories, I think they're just magical, so Maxim gave me a chance to do more of that in *Gemini Kings* too. As a bi author myself, positive LGBTQ+ representation is always a goal for my stories, so I hope I delivered on that for you!

Now I've got the same question for you I had last time: What do you think I should write next? Are you happy with how things turned out for Zara and her warlocks? Or do you still want more of their story? Are there relationships or characters you'd like to see more of? Please drop me a line and let me know what you think. Your opinion really matters to me! In fact, your opinion will be pretty central to what I write next. You can **contact me through my website here: https://lauranavarrescifi.com/contact/**

Acknowledgments

I would never have written Zara's story if not for you—my readers! *Gemini Queen* was supposed to be a standalone, but you were having none of it! I was so delightfully overwhelmed by your absolute deluge of supporting emails, your pleas for more Zara, more warlocks, more polycule, and especially more Vasili! Your extraordinary kindness and generosity in recommending *Gemini Queen* on Facebook, liking and sharing and participating when I post in the groups, your absolutely wonderful reviews on Amazon, Goodreads, and BookBub, your interactions with me on TikTok and all the places, and your encouragement, enthusiasm, and support are the reason *Gemini Kings* exists! I also remain grateful to my fellow dark paranormal academy why choose authors Traci Lovelot, Yve Vale, Cara Bryant, A.J. Moran, and all the gals who released dark paranormal academy RH reads back-to-back with me in summer 2022. You all taught me so much about publishing and marketing in what's still a newish genre for me after a career writing traditional romance for mainstream publishers.

I couldn't have launched, sustained, or grown my indie author career without the wisdom, support, encouragement, and experience of my career coach and mentor Angela James, who was also my former editor at Harlequin. Her insights and feedback on this story were invaluable, and her author community From Written To Recommended (FW2R) has been an essential support and lodestar for my indie journey. Her Book Boss Success Alliance has been particularly central to coaching, advising, and steering every stage of my publishing journey. I heartily recommend to any aspiring or published author the incredible Angela, the FW2R community, the Book Boss Success Alliance, the Before You Hit Send (BYHS) self-editing course, all Angela's courses, and all the outgrowths and pockets of her supportive, diverse, and inclusive author community.

I am so lucky to have added to my team the world's greatest personal assistant—the incomparable Clare Harrison—whose gorgeous graphics, remarkable serenity, and impeccable organizational skills kept me sane during this release. Thank you, Biscuit, for all that you do so brilliantly! I remain deeply grateful to my unparalleled, enthusiastic, generous, and intrepid beta readers Taylor Ross and Kara Donovan, whose wise, candid, and tactful insights are critical to refining my rough early drafts. None of my stories would achieve their pristine appearance without my formatter, uploader, and hand-holder Judi Fennell at Formatting4U. Kim Killion designs my gorgeous covers, and Rochelle Parry of Megabite Design is the IT goddess who makes my website sing and keeps my email functional. And I could never pull off a book launch without my awesome ARC review team, the Astral Angels. Your incredible encouragement and help spreading the word make a massive difference!

Finally, neither my writing journey nor my life journey would be possible without the generosity, thoughtfulness, insight, encouragement, support, wisdom, understanding, and love of my alpha reader, proofreader, business partner and CEO of Ascendant Press, best friend, and happily-ever-after karmic mate Steven. He's the first reader and the last for everything I write before it goes to print. I'm so lucky and so blessed to be sharing my life with this phenomenal man.

***Keep scrolling down for a sexy sneak peek at my true poly, MM-infused, Hunger Games** in space paranormal why-choose romance **RENEGADE ANGEL**, available for free in Kindle Unlimited and now in print, along with the complete MMMF Astral Heat Romance Series!*

RENEGADE ANGEL:
An Astral Heat Romance #2
By Laura Navarre

Chapter One
The Duel

As a notorious scourge-of-the-galaxy space pirate, Zorin had survived a lifetime of guys trying to kill him. He'd even survived having interstellar war declared on his ass by Dex Draven, First Indomitable of the Mogadon Empire.

The guy who was Zorin's ultimate nemesis, his mouthwatering obsession, and the galaxy's premier military power.

But after four-plus decades of nick-of-time near misses, it turned out what was gonna kill him was the girl. The girl he'd fallen for harder than an asteroid collision. The girl whose bed he'd laid his life on the line to compete for, against five hundred ambitious, aggressive, testosterone-fueled yahoos, in the galactic mating contest called the Tombola.

To be real specific, what would kill him—or at least paralyze him, pretty much permanently—was the nerve gun his opponent in the fighting pit was pointing at Zorin's chest.

And Dex Draven, in his role as referee and master emcee, was gonna see it happen. Maybe once he did, he'd finally find his way past that whole butchering-Dex's-psychopath-dad-in-cold-blood incident that had gotten Zorin exiled from Mogadon, back in his prior-to-being-a-pirate days. Back when Zorin was First Indomitable himself.

Maybe.

But Zorin didn't plan to stand here, dead in space like a stalled starship, and let it all go down. Not when his girl was counting on him to survive.

And counting on him to win.

Ten cubits away in the blood-spattered clay of the fighting pit, ringed by tiers of screaming spectators, his opponent grinned at him. The guy was half his size—hard-faced, sorrel-skinned, lean and wiry under the colorful robes and battle-scarf of a Kryllian bloodletter. Which was how the bastard had smuggled an illegal weapon into the pit for what was supposed to be strictly an unarmed throwdown.

A stricture that should've ruled out the microfiber steel net the Kryll had just flung over Zorin's sorry carcass to pin him down.

That net was complicating the heck out of Zorin's survival odds.

Well, shoot.

Kaia of Kryll had been crystal clear from the get-go. Being tamely auctioned off to any joe in the show by her tyrannical dad was never part of her game plan. The fact that Zorin, out of all five hundred wannabe consorts in this galactic shindig, ended up being the guy who turned her crank?

He was one lucky sonofabitch.

And he wasn't gonna let his girl down. His rebel princess, his prize, his Prime Class cyber samurai.

Too bad all his struggles only tightened the net.

A guy could escape an unbreakable steel net in one of two ways. He could pick his way free with time. Or he could cut his way free with a blowtorch.

Zorin, right then and there, didn't even have a match.

"Come on, you big galoot," he muttered to himself. "Think it through."

Meanwhile, the Kryll was taking his sweet time lining up the kill shot with his contraband nerve gun. A gun that was outlawed across the galaxy due to that whole permanent paralysis issue.

Above him in the viewing box, Kaia was leaping to her booted feet—a breath away from drawing her cyber saber and flinging her furious body into the fray in his defense. In his periphery, Dex was charging into the pit, shouting rules and prohibitions despite the fact no one in this madhouse gave a single flaming shit. Because it turned out this hootenanny wasn't a ritual contest. Not anymore.

It was a hit job.

And the *only* reason that Kryll would be aiming a disqualifying nerve gun at Zorin's ugly hide was because someone had paid the guy to do it.

All around him in the arena's humid heat, his competitors were on their feet howling for his blood. Zorin's Syndax pirates—his best boys, brought aboard Dex's battleship to cover his six as they shot through space—were drawing their blasters and converging on the pit. Too bad for Zorin they were all moving way too slow.

The gamy scent of Mogadon pheromones flooded the air. That head-spinning hit of his own aggression gave him a biochemical kick in the pants, just the way Mogadon genetics intended. Adrenaline spiked his pulse and roughened his breath.

Danger streaking through his senses like a meteor shower, rage spurting through his veins like liquid nitrogen, he watched the Kryll's finger tighten on the trigger.

Way too close to miss.

Trapped in that goddamn net like a Solarian sardine, Zorin did pretty much the only thing he could.

He dove.

Directly into the Kryll with the nerve gun.

#

The nerve gun discharged—a shrill *bzzzzt* that pierced her eardrum like a drill. The combatants crashed to the dirt in a single thrashing knot.

"Let *go* of me, damn you!" Twenty cubits above the fighting pit in the viewing box, Kaia raged and writhed in her lifemate's grip like a harpooned eel. "I'll flipping kill you for this!"

"Not on your life," Ben Nero ground in her ear. "You're not going anywhere near that nerve gun. Let Dex deal with it."

"But he hates Zorin!"

"Give Dex some credit, Kaia. He'll handle it."

Chains and dreadlocks streaming, Syndax pirates were hurtling into the pit. But they couldn't fire without risking Zorin, their leader. Responding with precision to his steely orders, Dex's elite praetorian guard wheeled into motion, training stun rifles on the seething mob—barely holding off a full-scale riot. Only Dex's incandescent glare kept the agitated Syndax at bay. Someone was shouting for a blowtorch.

Over the chaos, the struggling knot of limbs and net erupted in a scream. A scream that cut short with jarring sharpness.

The entangled figures went fatally still.

Kaia, too, went slack, heaving for air in Nero's arms. He held her tight against his lean length, eyes glued on the scene in the fighting pit.

None of it remotely appropriate according to the Tombola ritual's sacred dictates. Not the nerve gun, not her ex-boyfriend's hands all over her, not her obvious favor for the Syndax pirate.

And she cared not a nanoparticle. Her entire being was riveted on the deadly drama like a rocket. Sure, she'd only just met Zorin when the contest launched. But she'd known from the start he was the only one of those five hundred candidates she wanted in her bed.

Because Dex and Nero, the only other guys she'd ever wanted, couldn't even bid. Dex Draven was her Tombola master, bound by a treaty with her father that Dex couldn't break, committed to deliver her fiercely resistant body to the winning candidate. And Ben Nero, her psychic lifemate and the galaxy's most powerful telepath, was oathsworn to guarantee it all went down the way her godlike father demanded.

Formidable and stern in his black uniform, Dex closed in on the combatants with a blowtorch, blue flame spitting from the nozzle. Swiftly he peeled back the steel net.

"I think…" Nero whispered. Clearly relying on his telepathic Valyrian senses to tell him what his eyes couldn't.

"You think *what*?"

Because Kaia, a half-Valyrian hybrid and unreliable telepath herself, was way too agitated to think or feel anything but sheer screaming panic.

"I'd say 'Nobody panic,'" Zorin announced dryly, untangling himself from the net. His Kryll opponent lay poleaxed at his feet. "But somehow I got a feeling it's a little late."

The bristling Syndax were first to react, jubilant fists shooting skyward, shouts of triumph ripping from a dozen throats. Dex was already in motion, seizing the contraband weapon and flipping back the Kryll's battle-scarf.

The would-be assassin lay sprawled at a nauseating angle, head violently wrenched to one side.

"Snapped like a wishbone," Kaia whispered, shaking with a violent surge of satisfaction. "He won't be saying a word. We'll have to interrogate his brothers to sniff out who hired them. They're Kryllian bloodletters, trained assassins—so they won't be easy informants. Promise me you'll do it yourself."

Because no one breathing can lie to you.

"If his brothers aren't long gone by now." Gently Nero released her and stepped back. "Those two probably had a getaway shuttle in the hangar bay on standby. Looks like Dex is battening down the hatches."

Dex was muttering into his wrist unit, nerve gun secure in his belt. His grim cobalt gaze sliced from the raucous Syndax and the agitated mob to Zorin's monumental frame looming over the dead Kryll. Jaw clenched with steely necessity, light flashing on platinum epaulets, Dex strode to his side and raised Zorin's mailed arm briefly overhead.

"The Syndax will advance," Dex clipped out. "The Kryllian brothers are disqualified."

The pirates roared in rowdy acclaim, echoed this time by the rest of the hoi polloi. Around Kaia, the rattle and flash of creds changed hands. Zorin had won himself more than a few allies with that impressive maneuver. Huddled in anxious pockets around the viewing stand, an array of less murderous candidates for her bed muttered and shifted in unease.

Fervently she wished Dex could disqualify them all.

From the pit, one fist raised high in victory, Zorin lifted his head and looked straight at Kaia—the rugged lines of his face etched with anticipation and triumph. Despite the physical distance that yawned between them, the smoking heat in his aquamarine eyes seared through her like an electrical charge. Beneath the bronze silk of her cybersuit, her breasts felt swollen and her knees felt weak.

Damn it to the moon and back. He'd just nearly *died*.

And in that raw moment of naked knowledge, when fragile life had never felt more vital, she knew on a visceral level exactly what he needed.

"Ready room," she whispered, shaping the thought with her lips. Somehow knowing he'd hear her, even though non-telepaths often couldn't. "I'll find you."

Zorin held her gaze while heat pooled and pulsed between her legs, making her slick and wet.

Even while Dex dropped his arm like Zorin was garbage and pivoted to confront his volatile viewers.

"The names of the two hundred finalists will be broadcast over interstellar news at midnight." Dex pitched his voice to carry above the ripple of anticipation. "The contest resumes for the finalists tomorrow. Transport from this battleship for the rest of you departs for the nearest spaceport at oh-one-hundred. I'd firmly advise each of you *not* to be late."

"In a rush to get rid of them, isn't he?" Nero turned to find Kaia halfway to the stairs. "Gods of Solaris, Kaia, wait!"

"Try to keep up—if you must." Without slowing, she swung energetically over the rail and scrambled down the stairs. "Because I definitely don't need a babysitter."

"Why the hells are you always running away?" he muttered, glowering at avid suitors to keep them at bay as Kaia powered past. "Drives me insane to be always chasing you."

"Feel free to stop anytime." She edged sideways to slip between the scrum of Syndax bunched outside the ready room with knives and blasters bristling. "I meant what I said last night."

"I assure you, so did I."

The harum-scarum horde eased readily aside for Kaia, appre-ciation gleaming in their wolfish eyes. But they closed ranks tight before Nero.

"Not you, pretty boy," one tattooed titan said with a sneer. "Zorin only wants *her*."

As tall as the Syndax but far less wide, Nero smoothed back a sleek curtain of raven hair from his sculpted face. And eyed the obstruction with interest. "I'm the Valyrian Precursor. The galaxy's ranking telepath. Which means I can pull your brains through your ears with a passing thought. Out of curiosity, how precisely do you propose to stop me?"

"Good gods, Ben! Don't you think we've seen enough slaughter for one day?" Impatience simmered in Kaia's blood, laced with an agitation she seemed helpless to control. "Do you honestly think Zorin would let anything happen to me?"

"Comets! You know you're not supposed to be alone with the candidates. Dex has been more than clear—"

"Dex isn't my father. And neither are you, Ben Nero."

"Let me put it this way." Over the pirate's chrome-studded shoulder, Nero's violet eyes smoldered hot with promise. "If you're about to give that Syndax a congratulatory kiss, I definitely want to watch. Maybe he'll even appreciate a private demonstration from the galaxy's leading expert on how to blow your circuits."

An alchemical sizzle of heat seared through her. An instinctive response to the arrogant accolade she reluctantly acknowledged he'd more than earned after the way he scorched her synapses when they'd finally come together last night—all without violating her no-penetration edict.

The problem was, after abandoning her and letting her believe he was dead in the biowar for eight flipping *years*, she'd rather swallow her own tongue than admit the way Ben Nero still made her feel.

"Blast it, Ben! I assure you I have zero intent—" She eyed the titillated pirates soaking up every syllable and finished coolly, "Why don't you make yourself useful and interrogate those Kryll for me. Because I can't stand the sight of them."

Spinning away before he could lob another sexually incendiary innuendo, she shrugged the curtain aside and escaped into the ready room.

Zorin stood in solitude, etched against the battleship's viewport, towering frame and shoulders blotting out the stars. His craggy profile snapped toward her with an alacrity that told her she wasn't the only one with fight-or-flight adrenaline still sparking through her circuits.

Not to mention sexual stimulation bubbling in her blood.

Shyness was an impulse she'd outgrown years ago. Because shyness wasn't any help at all for a circus acrobat or a runaway samurai with a vengeful god on her tail.

Now a powerfully inconvenient surge of shyness reared up and hammered her feet to the floor. Tongue-tied, hot-faced, she could only stand and stare. Knowing if she said a word, she'd stammer like a Prime Class simpleton.

Confronted with her dumbstruck silence, Zorin's scarred brow hitched. He even nodded like she'd said something he understood.

"It's real now, isn't it?" His deep voice rumbled through the starlit shadows.

Her tight throat unlocked to release a careful breath. "What's real?"

"You and me." One corner of his mouth lifted in a wry smile. "This is new to me too. It's okay to be afraid."

"I'm not afraid," she shot back by instinct.

But that was a lie, wasn't it? She'd barricaded herself from every man she'd ever met behind an unbreachable battlement. That vow of abstinence she'd made before she was old enough to know what it meant, soldered in place by the crisis of Ben Nero's betrayal, had become the armor she hid behind to keep anyone from getting too close.

Ever.

Now she was going to venture out of that protective shell for him. The guy standing before her. The guy who'd just killed a man to clear his path to her bed.

The guy she still barely knew.

"I'm not afraid," she repeated, to make herself believe it. "You're the one. The one I'll fly away with on the *Relentless* five days from now. Together we'll end this whole monstrous farce."

"Cuz I'm the only guy with a snowball's chance in a sun storm of taking on Dex." His tone was easy, but his eyes were wary. "Dex with his fleet and his nukes and his badass arsenal. You figure I'm your best bet to stop that galactic germ war he's threatening."

"Yeah." She leaped headlong for that face-saving logic. "That's pretty much why. I'm half Valyrian. One biowar was more than enough."

Enough to eradicate eighty-eight percent of the Valyrian race.

Even if the last war was his dad's fault, Maximus Draven's been dead for years. So the next one's all on Dex.

Carefully she cleared her throat. "That's why I wanted you… at first. To stop Dex and prevent the war. But… it's not the only reason."

His eyes never left her face.

Like he was waiting for something he didn't want to miss.

Her tongue traced her dry lips. "Do you even realize you're the only candidate in this Tombola who's offered me *freedom*? As in—the only one. I've read five hundred bids over the past two days. And yours is the only one that doesn't turn my stomach."

"Well, it's an honest offer. I want you willing and eager or not at all." A subtle tension threaded his voice. "But I'm not the only choice you got, am I. You don't think Dex would hand you the Mogadon moons or anything else in the universe you ever wanted? Just to keep you with him?"

"Dex?" Her bubbling agitation erupted. An eruption far too long suppressed. "Why are you asking me about Dex? He's my Tombola master. You know he's not an option!"

"It's a fair ask, Kaia. The kid and me—we go way back. I was Dex's mentor back on Mogadon. I'm the one who taught him to fight. The one who taught him to kill." His steely eyes hardened. "And I can smell his mating scent on you all the way over here. Long story short? He doesn't act like a guy who's planning to let you go."

"It's not up to him. He can't bid!" Her volume spiraled until she was all but shouting. "And that's a choice he made all on his own."

"A choice he made before he met you."

"A choice he can't revoke." She planted hands on hips and scowled. "Even if he wanted to—" *even if I wanted him to* "—he can't! He signed a binding treaty with my father. An ironclad pact for Kryll's merchant fleet to supply his battlefront. In exchange for Dex's service as arbiter and enforcer of this whole farking contest. If Dex voids the contest now by claiming me himself, he'll lose his war, his command, and probably his life."

Because my flipping father will declare a kill edict on his Indomitable head. And Kryll's faithful fanatics—men like those bloodletters—will carry it out.

"That might be a risk Dex is willing to take." Before her obstinate stance, Zorin's hard face softened. "Look. I might not know you the way I'd like. But he's a compelling guy, sweetheart, and I think he's caught your eye."

An uncomfortable heat climbed in her face. A heat she knew in her heart there was no point denying. Because the scourge of the galaxy was nobody's fool. And every word he said was true.

Shifting on her feet, she glanced aside. "I don't get it. Why are you arguing against your own interests?"

"Cuz I'm not so sure it's in my interest taking a consort who wants me solely for my military prowess and because I won't make her wear chains in my bed. Not to mention a consort who's already half in love with somebody else. Like a lotta folks, I've had consorts before. Everyone wants it to last forever, but it hardly ever does. This time's the real deal. Trust me to know what it takes to make this work."

Unable to meet his level gaze, she paced the shadowy confines of the ready room. "You make a fair point. You really do. Even though I'm not in love with him." *Why is this so farking hard to say?* "Anyway, um, I haven't been totally straight with you. Those aren't the only reasons I—I wanted you."

"No?" As solid and settled as she was jittery and jumpy, he leaned one armored hip against the wall and crossed his bulging arms. Starlight brought out the silver in his sandy hair.

"You know it's not," she whispered. She couldn't look at him. *Angels and asteroids, is he really going to make me say it?* "I want you because… I just… want you."

In the history of confessions, this wasn't much of one. But the heat of making it scorched through her until she thought her cybersuit would burst into flames. Slowly her gaze lifted to find him.

An outlaw. A space pirate. A wolf in blast armor.

Too smart to trick. Too strong to overpower. And probably too old for her to boot.

But the thought of climbing out of her armor and stripping him out of his and giving him everything he wanted from her—access she'd never given another man, had in fact been saving all her life just for him—made her weak with wanting.

"It's true," she said, throaty with the fever burning in her blood. "You say you want a woman who's eager for your bed? Trust me when I tell you that's not going to be a problem."

He hooked his big hands in his utility belt and lowered his head to eye her. "You got Dex's smell all over you. But Ben Nero says you spend your nights in *his* bed. The way I see it, you maybe got a thing for all three of us. That's a pretty big chance for an old guy like me to take, Kaia."

"I know. It's mixed up. It's just—I'm trying to figure things out." Her eyes pleaded for understanding. "I feel the way I feel. That's why I'm choosing you. What more do you want me to tell you?"

"Tell me?" His rough rasp sent shivers shooting down her spine. "Not a goddamn thing. Why don't you shimmy on over here and show me?"

Kaia's heart thundered like a war drum and every synapse in her body thrummed in a symphony of nerves. Tingling with tension, she prowled across the expanse of ready room floor that was all that stood between her and this Syndax pirate she'd chosen to mate.

Steady on, samurai. This isn't your mating night. There's zero reason to be nervous.

Even if he is watching you like he's finally letting himself imagine what you're going to look like naked.

He'd kept himself so carefully in check since the moment they'd met. When she didn't know who he was, when he let her do all the talking, when she fell toes over tailpipe for this interstellar menace until nothing else mattered except finding some way to be his.

He was always letting her take the lead.

Just so she wouldn't run away.

He'd kept whatever he felt himself so thoroughly under wraps that the raw hunger animating his war-hardened face right now felt as intimate as the slide of a hand down her naked spine.

Tonight was different. Because tonight he'd almost died. He'd snapped a man's neck with his bare hands to clear his path to her bed. And those genetic Mogadon instincts that still drove him even in exile were driving him now to claim her.

The prize he'd killed for.

The woman his most primitive self now saw as his exclusive property to protect and possess.

That image alone, that bare whisper from her erratic psychic senses of the primal imperatives that drove him, made her breath hitch and her pulse pitch. Beneath her cybersuit, she was slick with her own passion, her clit a swollen nub that chafed against her cybersilk with every step.

He was done waiting.

He wanted her.

And her entire body ached to give him everything he wanted.

Her eyes slid slowly up his frame, all size and strength and raw physical power encased in the starmetal mesh of his armor. Battle-scarred space boots and thickly muscled thighs spread to claim the space around him, biceps bulging in the arms folded across his chest, broad shoulders blotting out the stars.

She wanted to drop to her knees and wrap her mouth around his cock. She wanted to climb him like a tree and wrap her legs around him and let him sink deep inside her the way no other man had ever done. She wanted him to ride her until she forgot her own name.

She wanted to feel him come inside her.

She wanted him to sire the son the prophecy said she had in her.

"Mars," he breathed, raw and ragged with wanting. "A guy could get used to the way you look at me. Better warn you I'm about six ticks away from tossing you over my shoulder and taking you back with me to the *Relentless*. And to hell with the auction. You're mine."

She added an extra sway to her hips and watched his eyes darken to navy. "That doesn't sound very civilized."

"I'm a space pirate, sweetheart. I don't do civilized all that well. Never have." One tawny brow hitched. "Neither do you, by the way."

"To everyone's dismay." She laughed, but it held a bitter edge.

"Not mine," he fired back, gruff with anticipation. "I know what I'm getting. And I wouldn't change a goddamn thing."

"Right back at you," she whispered, low in her throat.

Two cubits away, she tilted her head and looked up at him. He was way too tall for what she had in mind.

She put her back to the viewport and hopped lithely to the ledge, using her acrobat's strength to swing her bottom up to sit. He was still taller than she wanted.

But not by much.

Booted legs dangling, gaze never leaving his, she spread her knees wide in invitation and hooked a hand in his belt to pull him close.

A growl rose from his cavernous chest. He planted one big hand on either side of her hips and moved into her space. She ducked her head to study his hands, her slim fingers sliding over scarred knuckles and calloused skin, and heard the harsh husk of his breath.

Plenty of women would find him brutal. Even terrifying. All that size and unapologetic violence.

But not her.

She wanted it—wanted *him*—wanted the threat and the promise of everything he wanted with an intensity that made her entire body throb.

Leaving her hands over his—a silent plea for restraint she didn't know if he'd heed—she let her eyes rise over his mighty chest and muscled neck and the strong line of his jaw. The golden glitter of day's-end stubble tempted her to touch. And his eyes, locked on hers like heat-seeking missiles, were so intense she couldn't sustain his stare.

Keeping her hands where they were, she leaned in carefully and touched her lips to the rough bristle of his cheek. His sharp exhale rushed out. He'd been holding his breath. The sudden scent of steel and predator rose dark and hot from his skin.

The intoxicating essence of mating scent.

"I know I barely know you," she whispered in his ear. "But I really, really like you."

"Show me how much—" His voice broke as her tongue traced his ear. His hands tensed beneath her palms and a groan rumbled from his throat.

"You like this, don't you?" She licked the hot salty skin under his ear and felt his pulse jump. "And this?"

"Your mouth on me anywhere, answer's gonna be yes." He sounded strangled with the effort of restraint.

Tingling with the energy that leaped between them, she backed away just a little and leaned in to kiss his other cheek, stubble abrading her tender skin.

"I like your strength," she breathed in his ear, just to feel him shiver. "I like your restraint and I like your patience. I like when you're brutal and savage like you were in the pit. I like the way you feel safe and the way you feel dangerous—all at the same time."

She pulled back and leaned close, his lips a breath away. "But most of all, Zorin the pirate, I like the way you make me feel. Like there's no part of me you aren't going to own."

With a harsh sound, he leaned in and kissed her. Fusing them together with his mouth on hers, tongue meeting tongue, hot and fierce with need. Demanding the response she'd been born to give. He tasted like sex and violence held barely in check. And just the feel of his mouth on hers ignited the dormant volcano of craving deep inside and made her burn with an aching caldera of need.

Gods, I need you. Need you inside me. You're going to be the one.
And I don't think I can wait.

She moaned and leaned into him, arms wrapping around his neck, hands threading through the short rough spikes of his hair. His hands closed over her thighs and dragged her hard against his bulk. Her legs wound around his hips and his armored cock nudged her clit.

"Please," she panted, rocking into his heat, hardly knowing what she was begging for. Just knowing she needed more than she was getting. "Please—I need—*more*. I need more of you."

"I'll conquer worlds and lay them at your feet. Every star system my army claims is another realm for you to rule." He leaned his brow against hers while they both fought for breath and her body begged him to ride her. "Just let me look at you. Let me at least do that much. I've been imagining you in my bed since the moment we met. I'm gonna lose my mind if I can't see the real you. *All* of you."

She closed her eyes against the molten metal of his stare and whispered, "Yes."

At that point, she would've said yes to anything if he was the one asking.

And she trusted him not to abuse the privilege.

His hands spanned her waist and eased up to find the tender fullness of her breasts. She arched her back to push into his touch, head falling back, stars swimming in her eyes. She heard the buzz of a zipper, felt her bodice release, shivered when the frigid cold of space through the viewport licked along her naked spine.

He muttered something rough and reverent in a language she didn't know.

Then his palms chafed her naked nipples. Twin jets of tingling pleasure shot through her. Straight to the pounding need between her thighs. The sudden musk of her own juices, hot and slick and pumping, mingled with the wolfish whiff of his mating scent.

He breathed her in deep and growled like the apex predator he was. His hands slid her cybersuit to her waist. Her wrists tangled in her sleeves' tight fabric, snared in her Valyrian torques. That paralyzing pleasure immobilized her—exposed and helpless as a harem slave. Hard fingers cradled her breasts and tweaked her nipples. He was different from Ben, his touch less polished and a lot more rough. His pace less thoroughbred and a lot more draft horse.

Her hips thrust against him with panting need. Desperate for the starmetal friction of his cock.

"Jumpin' Jupiter," he said hoarsely, "you like that, don't you? Being tied up while I work you."

"Seems so," she gasped, head falling back to give him more access. *Who'd have thought?* "Gods, Zorin. I never even… knew I wanted…"

"To be restrained? Sometimes what turns us on is what scares us. And you like it a little rough too, don'tcha?" His growl sent a shiver skidding down her spine that answered him without her having to say a word. "We can do this any way you want. You can't hurt me. And it makes me crazy that you smell like Dex. You're *mine*."

One solid arm slid around her back to close off her escape, but she only pressed harder into his heat. One deft pull of his hand, hard enough to sting, released the knot that held her hair. It slid down her back like a silk curtain. His mouth seared her breast, hard lips closing over one tingling nipple—the scrape of teeth over sensitized skin, the pulse of pleasure between her legs. She cried out and clamped her legs around him, booted heels digging urgently into the hard bulge of his ass.

That dark savage scent poured from his skin and made her head reel.

With an oath he lifted her, mouth finding hers in a scorching kiss—more certain, less restrained, more dominant now he knew how much she liked it—and staggered to the couch. Beneath her back, the sleek leather sank under their weight.

Gasping for oxygen, she forced her eyes open. "We can't, um, do everything. Not until the mating ritual…"

"Kaia." He straddled her hips without crushing her, one hand fisting in her hair, the other finding her breast. "Gimme some credit, will ya? I've been waiting for you my whole life. You're gonna be my consort and the mother of my sons. You'll rule the Syndax horde at my side. I'm not about to do this in the ready room of a fighting pit with a dozen of my boys listening in."

His voice deepened. "But damn if I'm not tempted."

The hard pinch of his fingers on her nipple rolled her hips and made her writhe. He caught her aching cry with a kiss that claimed her like a brand and made her even hotter.

One big hand freed her arms from her sleeves, then engulfed her wrists and pinned them overhead. Her eyes flew open to find his rough-hewn face looming over her, starlight gleaming silver in the spikes of his hair, eyes burning platinum with arousal, full mouth ruthless with intent. She tugged against his confining hand and his grip tightened.

And the hot rush of pleasure that rolled through her nearly made her climax on the spot.

"Angels of Anaxos," she panted, legs twining around his hips to pull him closer. "Zorin… I need…"

"Maybe this is what you need?"

Trapping her wide-eyed gaze with his, he eased a hand down her bare tummy under her open cybersuit to find the slick folds of her pussy.

And Kaia, who could count on one hand with fingers left over the number of guys she'd ever trusted enough to permit the privilege, let her thighs drift open and her body arch into his touch.

Feeling her arousal drench his fingers, his jaw clenched and his eyes darkened to lapis. Heat surged into her face. Suddenly way too conscious of just how much she wanted him—how close to the ragged edge of total surrender she was riding—she turned her hot cheek into the cool leather cushion.

"I'm right here, sweetheart," he said, thick with passion. "Look at me so I can see if you like this."

If he so much as grazed her clit, he was going to ring her bell. When he eased one careful finger into her slick heat instead, she clenched and pulsed around him.

A low savage cry rolled through her. Blind with need, her eyes found his and let him look straight into her soul.

"Gods, you're so wet for me, aren't you?" He eased back and her hips rose to meet him. With a groan, he slid deeper, hand cupping her soaked flesh, and she moaned in unison. "So wet and so tight and so darn perfect, I'm about a whisker away from losing my mother-loving mind. Guess the rumors were right. You're a virgin, ain't ya?"

"Story of my life. Does that… turn you off?" *Please, gods, don't let it turn him off.*

"Pretty much the opposite. I'm dying here, Kaia." He gasped out a laugh. Which sent a vibration through the careful rhythm of his thick finger inside her.

A vibration that pushed her hard over the edge.

With the force of a star imploding, a sonic wave of orgasm shot down her thighs and curled her toes. Her head fell back and comets streaked against her closed lids. Her mouth opened on a scream that he caught with a savage openmouthed kiss.

She cried out her climax into his mouth, barely caring if he managed to muffle the sound.

When her head cleared, her entire body was still rippling with gentle pulses of bliss. And he was still braced above her, sparing her his formidable weight, with the cataclysmic strain of sexual restraint engraved in his granite features and the galaxy's most monumental erection jutting between her thighs.

A flood of contrition scorched through her. "Ohmygods, I'm so sorry! I, um, wasn't actually planning on having that happen."

"Don't you dare apologize. I loved every bit of what just went down. Good to know I can rock your world, sweetheart. We're gonna need that."

With meticulous care, he disengaged and rolled off her replete and satiated body to sprawl on the floor beside her with a labored groan. "Shindig or no shindig, I'd take you to bed right now if I could. But scuttlebutt says you sleep in Draven's quarters."

His gaze swerved toward her. "It's true, ain't it?"

"He's very… protective," she managed to mumble, knowing the admission only validated every dark suspicion he was already harboring about Dex.

And Dex's fixation on me isn't exactly unrequited. Which I'm pretty sure you've also figured out.

This Syndax she'd chosen wasn't a telepath and couldn't transmit, but he seemed to have no trouble at all receiving. At least from her.

His measured curse rang heavy with frustration.

"You and Dex, huh?" He scrubbed a big hand against the back of his neck. "What in tarnation am I gonna do about you and Dex?"

Without a flicker of warning, one electrifying option sizzled through her. A visual of what would happen if he took her to her quarters and Dex found him in her bed. A sudden searing image of Zorin's big hand in Dex's burnished hair, the rough consuming hunger of mouth on mouth, a flash of tongue meeting tongue as these two fiercely dominant men came together above her. In her runaway imagination, while the two of them went at it, her hand slid under her soaked panties to finger her swollen clit.

Asteroids. She could come just watching the two of them kiss.

"Neptune's knickers," Zorin said from the heart. "What a visual. Is *that* what you want?"

"I, uh, think I might… want both of you," she admitted in a whisper. "Both of you together."

Breathless not only because the mere thought had her perched again on the naked edge of climax—but because she was reeling under the sudden, searing, completely unexpected impact the image was having on Zorin.

"Gods of my father, Zorin. You want him too… don't you? You've wanted him forever. You can barely even remember a time when you didn't want him."

Grappling to get her head around that revelation, she suffered through his complicated silence.

"I can see having a telepath for a consort's gonna take some getting used to," he said wryly, bowing his head against her bare shoulder. "This is a lotta excitement for an old guy like me. Gimme a tick to catch my breath, will ya?"

That's not a denial, she thought, skin tingling. *You don't need to catch your breath. And you're not old.*

But she knew better than to press. The first rule of courtesy any telepath learned was never to intrude without an invite.

Even when she was suddenly tingling under the rush of a shining, unlikely, utterly novel notion. The notion of becoming the bridge that finally brought these two galactic rivals together.

The way they were meant to be.

Against her skin, Zorin pulled in a long inhale. When he raised his head, his face blazed with masculine satisfaction. "Now you smell like *me*. And I damn well intend to keep it that way. No matter what it does to Dex. If he doesn't intend to claim you himself, he needs to stay outta my way."

"I smell like both of you." The deep ripple of sexual pleasure that rolled through her nearly derailed her train of thought—but not quite. "I'm into both of you. And I think both of you need to talk."

"And I think that particular parley's gonna have to wait," he said lightly, letting her read nothing in his face. "Cuz if Dex ever found me making love to you in his bed, you better believe joining in would be the last thing on his mind. He'd probably declare interstellar war on the spot. Oh, wait, he's already done that."

"Or it might be just what the two of you need," she murmured, wiggling regretfully back into her cybersuit. Because as much fun as she was having with Zorin on that couch, he wasn't her consort yet and she knew they needed to stop.

He lounged on the floor beside her and watched her with aqua eyes whose lidded heat made her shiver.

"Meaning?" he rumbled.

"Meaning I heard what you told him about his father—and I believe you." She pushed up to sit. "You killed Max Draven all those years ago because someone had to. You went into exile so you wouldn't have to kill Dex. He was your student. You were his mentor. And I don't think the two of you should be enemies."

"I happen to agree. But Dex isn't exactly on the same page, is he? And even if someday we buried the hatchet, it doesn't follow like two plus two that we'd end up in the sack. Anyway, I gave up that sorta thing years ago."

She made a neutral noise.

But Dex still turns you on. She gave him her back and swept up her hair so he could join her on the couch and zip her up. *Even if you've just spent years convincing yourself he doesn't. The bare fantasy of you kissing him, and him kissing you back, was just about enough to spank your monkey.*

And the thought of him alone in his space-cold quarters on that rusting hulk with his hand wrapped around his cock and Dex's name on his lips was just about enough to make *her* come.

Again.

Suddenly, with the certainty she associated with her inherited and unpredictable dash of Valyrian foresight, she wanted to see the two of them together. Wanted it so bad she could taste it. And the thought of both of them looming over her, pushing her flat, one bucking into her mouth to hit the back of her throat with every thrust, while the other spread her wide and rode her hard and fast—

"Kaia, I'm begging for mercy here." Half laughing, Zorin eased up her zipper. "Dex and I are not about to fall swooning in each other's arms, believe me. We're at war, in case you haven't noticed. And the one and only time he and I got a little too cozy—at my initiative, by the way—the bastard up and shot me."

She absorbed the inflammatory memory playing through his mind of Zorin's legendary escape from Mogadon. Which certainly gave her oodles to think about. Including the fact that Dex might've shot his former mentor for kissing him—but that didn't mean Dex hadn't liked it.

In fact, maybe it meant the opposite.

Clearly reading the speculation scrolling across her face, Zorin chuffed out a wry chuckle. "Aw, come on. If he walked in here right now and I laid one on him the way you want, I guarantee he'd haul off and sock me in the face. And that's if I'm lucky."

Would he?

She wondered.

His hands squeezed her shoulders, then firmly put distance between them. "Now pay attention, sweetheart. I gotta mosey on back to the *Relentless* for some shut-eye. Before I do that, I got something for you."

"A Tombola gift?" A happy sense of anticipation bubbled through her. She scooted around on the couch to face him and bundled her wine-red hair in a twist. "Because you haven't given me anything yet."

"Just my heart on a plate with a carving knife." He eyed her efforts to tidy up. "Leave it down. It suits you. And right now I want every guy on this ship to know I've been all over you."

"If they did, there'd be a riot." Apparently Dex wasn't the only Mogadon male who got possessive with his woman. She pressed her thighs together to suppress another wicked pulse of need. "What did you bring me?"

"Like presents, do ya?" Grinning at her enthusiasm, he dug from his utility belt a flat steel box the size of an antique postage stamp. "Gotta remember that. So I can spoil you, sweetheart. You'll find I'm a pretty indulgent lover."

"I like the sound of that." With a delighted little bounce that made him grin, she accepted the box and snicked it open. Eagerly she leaned in to check out the flat glittering object, no bigger than her pinkie nail, on its bed of velvet.

"A cyber chip!" Her astonished eyes flew up in surprise.

"Figured it was a fitting gift for a cyber samurai." He leaned forward and tapped the cyberport at her temple. "Was I right?"

"It's perfect." She lifted the chip to study it with a professional eye. "This is gorgeous work. How's it programmed?"

He looked pleased by her appreciation. "Well, it's really just a prototype. Ginned up by a cyber wiz who followed me from Mogadon into exile. It's a transcription chip."

Her mouth fell open. "A *transcription* chip? I thought they were an urban myth."

"They were." His big shoulders lifted in a self-deprecating shrug. "Jules—my man Julius—managed to make it work. I'm no samurai, but I've used it myself. Believe me, if it wasn't safe, I wouldn't be letting you anywhere near it."

"Never mind if it's safe. It works!" Excitement sharpened her voice and spiked her pulse. "Where did you go with it?"

"Ever wonder how I powered from the Omega Sector the night Dex declared war—the night I ambushed his patrol in deep space—onto the *Relentless* six clicks later to coast into Mogadon airspace for your auction?"

"I didn't think you commanded that ambush yourself. It takes weeks at hyperspeed to fly that distance."

"Yep." He grinned. "With that transcription chip, I plugged into a full-body cyberport and ported from the Omega Sector to the *Relentless* in less than a click. You need a working port at each end, dead accurate coordinates programmed into the chip, a decent level of skill to navigate the cyberverse—and titanium balls. I'm not gonna lie about that. Cuz once you commit, you can't back out. The only way out is through."

"No kidding!" She stared at the chip in fascination. Totally jonesing to try it. "Everyone who's ever tried to transport their physical body through cyberspace from one geospatial location to another has flipping *died*. Or else disappeared permanently trying it."

"Except Jules and me. And pretty soon you, if you're game to give it a whirl. That chip's programmed to navigate to the cyberport on the *Relentless*—where I'm at. With your chops in the cyberverse, you can program it to go anywhere in the galaxy, long as you have working coordinates to a full-body cyberport at the other end."

Her brain raced to juggle the implications. "If you can mass-produce these chips—and if the tech holds up—it's a game changer. Whoever holds the galactic patent will earn billions!"

"Spoken like a true Kryll," he murmured. "Fact is, that patent's the main act in my Tombola bid for your Pops."

"Who'll definitely appreciate the value. He may be a god, but he's also a merchant. Just don't call him 'Pops' when you bid. He strongly prefers 'Your Holiness.'" For the first time since she'd landed in this whole mess, she dared to feel hopeful. "All we need to do now is make sure you make the final ten."

Then hope like hell my father chooses you.

"And you'll leave that to me," he said firmly, unfolding to tower over her with his colossal height. "This entire gig's a bomb rigged to blow. You're supposed to be neutral, sweetheart. And after what just went down in the pit, you better believe every joe in the show knows I'm your guy. That's despite watching gorgeous Ben Nero with his hands all over you. By now, every poor schmuck on this ship either wants to fight him or fuck him."

"That's Ben for you," she murmured, studying the chip cradled in her hands. "He specializes in inspiring that effect. I keep telling him we're done. To go back to his telepath breeding program and his pedigreed stable."

"With the way he looks at you? And the way you look at him every boot-scootin' time he touches you? Doesn't look like you're done to me—not even close. And I guarantee you he's not buying it."

He held up a patient hand to fend off her flustered protests. "Not to mention whatever the heck's going down between him and Dex. Then there's the First Indomitable himself going hardcore Mogadon and threatening to rip the head off anyone who touches you with his bare hands. Long story short? Your shindig has this entire ship on edge. And two thousand Mogadon with twitchy trigger fingers packed on this nuclear-armed battle bus… well, it's enough to make a Syndax war dog like me a little twitchy myself."

Infected by the warning that threaded through his words, Kaia pushed to her feet and started to pace. "I know this Tombola isn't going the way it should. Dex took a knife for me today, and you almost died yourself. Obviously, I know it's dangerous. What do you think we should do?"

Zorin checked the blaster at his hip. "Play the game, samurai. Play it out like a champion to the last blasted move. That's what Dex is doing—shipping these wannabes off his ship by the boatload before they spark a mutiny. And preferably before he gets spaced by some political rival who's even more ruthless than he is."

Violently she shivered and chafed her arms to ward off the deep-space chill that tiptoed down her spine. She didn't like thinking about just how much danger Dex was putting himself in.

And she liked even less hearing Zorin treat the same danger so casually.

Once he cared about Dex so much he fled into exile to protect him. Maybe I'd even say he loved him. Surely all that emotion doesn't just disappear?

Feeling Zorin's thoughtful gaze, she shot him a pensive look. "What happens then?"

"Easy-peasy. When we're down to the last ten yahoos, that's when you tell Pops I'm your guy." One side of his mouth tipped up in a rueful smile. "Then we let the strength of my bid and my natural charm do the rest."

His plan was simple and solid. It made eminent tactical sense. Except for the lurking sense of dread she couldn't seem to shake that his easy-peasy plan wouldn't go down the way they both wanted.

Wanna read the rest of this steamy MMMF true poly adventure?
Renegade Angel is available free in KU and now in print!
Read RENEGADE ANGEL now!

Other Laura Navarre Adventures Now Available from Ascendant Press:
Anticipated Angel: An Astral Heat MM New Adult Novella Prequel
Interstellar Angel: An Astral Heat Romance #1
Renegade Angel: An Astral Heat Romance #2
Atomic Angel: An Astral Heat Romance #3

Or binge the complete series with The Astral Heat Romance Box Set

About The Author

Amazon category bestselling author Laura Navarre (she/her) is the wild and witchy why-choose romance author for smart and fearless readers like you! She offers intense and steamy out-of-this world adventure with powerful heroines who never have to choose, passionate prose that packs a punch, and enough male/male heat to set your Academy uniform on fire.

A long time ago in a galaxy far away, Laura wrote dark fantasy romance for Harlequin, while her sinister twin Nikki Navarre wrote sexy spy romance. Now, with fifteen sexy stories released worldwide, this Washington, DC-based nomad writes erotic paranormal adult academy why-choose romance featuring bi heroes, badass heroines, and sweet poly love with extreme poly steam.

Laura is a cat lover, globetrotter, wine addict, PhD student, and president of Ascendant Press. When she isn't conjuring witchy worlds, she's a diplomat with a professional background in weapons of mass destruction and an MFA in writing popular fiction. She's a 2009 Golden Heart finalist, two-time winner of the Golden Pen, winner of the Pacific Northwest Writers Association romance award, and many RWA awards. She's also relentlessly obsessive, alarmingly efficient, and a recovering perfectionist. She's deeply suspicious of the Oxford comma, but she's never met an em dash she doesn't love.

Stalk Laura across the galaxy like the queen killer stalks Zara at the Icarus Academy! Her adventures across the witching world are trackable by witches, warlocks, humans, and aliens alike at:

http://www.LauraNavarreSciFi.com
     (go here to sign up for Laura's newsletter & free reads!)
https://www.facebook.com/LauraNavarreAuthor
https://www.tiktok.com/@LauraNavarreAuthor
https://amzn.to/3FrX5t7
https://www.bookbub.com/authors/laura-navarre
http://www.goodreads.com/LauraNavarre
http://www.instagram.com/LauraNavarreAuthor

www.ingramcontent.com/pod-product-compliance
Lightning Source LLC
Chambersburg PA
CBHW061618210726
48287CB00001B/192